T0146475

SECOND CHANCES

When Colin got off the phone he said, "I've got to go, Harlee."

"Is everything all right?"

"Sophie and Mariah took some of their dinner guests over to the new house to show them the progress. It turns out the roof is leaking. Snow's getting inside. I've gotta see what I can do to cover it until Monday. I'll come back afterward to help you clean up."

"Don't worry about it." Harlee waved her hand dismissively. "Darla is planning to come over. She'll help. I'll keep Max for you."

"I hate to leave this way. That was the best meal I've ever had."

"I'm glad you liked it. I'll have the leftovers packed up for you when you pick up Max." She ran to get his jacket and watched as he put it on. "Thanks for the flowers, the wine, and cider."

"You're welcome." He took off out the door, but came back a few minutes later. She'd already begun doing dishes, but could hear him in the foyer.

"Harlee," Colin called. "Come here."

She returned, thinking that maybe he couldn't start his truck. That's when he pulled her hard against him and kissed her. A heart-melting kiss, raw and sensual, that went on forever and ever. She could feel his need pressing against her and his low growl of pleasure made her cradle his neck to drive him deeper. His tongue, tangling with hers, made her hot as molten lava. If not for the strong arms that held her, Harlee would've wound up on the floor, in a puddle. Colin pulled her even closer and she could feel his heart pounding. In that single, solitary moment, Harlee had never felt more desired—or more wonderful . . .

Books by Stacy Finz

GOING HOME

FINDING HOPE

SECOND CHANCES

STARTING OVER

Published by Kensington Publishing Corporation

SECOND
CHANCES

STACY FINZ

LYRICAL PRESS
Kensington Publishing Corp.
www.kensingtonbooks.com

LYRICAL PRESS BOOKS are published by

Kensington Publishing Corp.
119 West 40th Street
New York, NY 10018

All Kensington titles, imprints, and distributed lines are available at special quantity discounts for bulk purchases for sales promotion, premiums, fund-raising, educational, or institutional use.

Special book excerpts or customized printings can also be created to fit specific needs. For details, write or phone the office of the Kensington Special Sales Manager: Kensington Publishing Corp., 119 West 40th Street, New York, NY 10018. Attn. Special Sales Department. Phone: 1-800-221-2647.

First Electronic Edition: April 2015
eISBN-13: 978-1-60183-342-6
eISBN-10: 1-60183-342-3

First Print Edition: April 2015
ISBN-13: 978-1-60183-343-3
ISBN-10: 1-60183-343-1

Printed in the United States of America

To my mom, Iris Finz, for always being a cheerleader.

Acknowledgments

Thanks to Dr. Rick Morgan for his invaluable medical expertise and Daniel Jaujou for all things hair and salon related. Any mistakes, technical or otherwise, are mine.

A special thanks to my beta readers: Jaxon Van Derbeken, Amanda Gold, Wendy Miller, and, as always, my family.

To everyone who made this book happen: agent Melissa Jeglinski of the Knight Agency, my editor John Scognamiglio, production editor Rebecca Cremonese, and all the other folks at Kensington Publishing who worked tirelessly on the entire series. Thank you.

Chapter 1

Colin Burke pulled over to the shoulder, watched a car he didn't recognize struggle to make it up the steep grade, and shook his head. What kind of moron uses a Mini Cooper to tow a twelve-hundred-pound U-Haul trailer on a narrow, rutted dirt road?

The road was definitely too tight for the both of them. So he sat waiting, observing in dismay as the driver took the hairpin turn too wide, causing the trailer to plunge over the side of the embankment, dragging half the car with it. For a split second Colin sat paralyzed while the tail of the Mini Cooper hung suspended in midair.

Then he jumped out of his truck, shouting, "Don't get out!"

But it was too late. The motorist had already left the driver's seat and was now crouched down at the top of the embankment assessing the damage. Colin couldn't believe that the shift in weight hadn't resulted in the car tumbling completely over the side. Given that the embankment was slippery from the last rain, it could still happen.

"You okay?" he asked, making his way to the car.

"Yeah. But my trailer may be stuck."

You think?

The words were just about to leave his lips, when Colin was struck dumb. The driver might be incompetent behind the wheel, but she was extremely pretty. He wasn't used to seeing attractive women on Grizzly Peak. Hell, he wasn't used to seeing anyone up here. That's why he'd chosen the remote spot.

"Where were you headed with the trailer?" he asked, assuming that she had gotten lost and had been trying to turn around when she'd lurched over the side.

"My cabin." The woman dusted some dirt off her black pants, which Colin couldn't help noticing hugged a pair of truly awesome legs. She wore a fluffy sweater that looked expensive and a pair of leather boots—more fashionable than practical. Not exactly dressed for the back country, he noted as he quickly averted his eyes to keep from ogling her.

"Where's that?" he asked, presuming that most likely she'd been headed for town.

Surprisingly, she pointed down the driveway to an A-frame. Other than his, it was the only other house on the desolate road. For the three years that Colin had lived here, the cabin had been vacant.

"You think I should try to gun it?" she asked, turning her attention back to the Mini Cooper. "Maybe if I hit the gas hard enough I can pull the trailer back up."

He shook his head. "Nah. That little car doesn't have the horse-power. I think we should unhitch it and I can try to pull the trailer out with my truck."

"Okay." She was already scrambling down the hill, preparing to disconnect the receiver from the tow package.

"Hang on a sec. I want to think about this for a minute." He walked back and forth alongside the car, studying its precarious position. "This is the deal: We unlatch it and run the risk of the car taking a free fall."

"I can get back in and hit the gas the minute you unfasten the trailer," she suggested.

It seemed like a shaky idea to him. But Colin didn't think his truck had the juice to lug both the car and trailer out of the mud at the same time. So he supposed it was worth a shot.

"Yeah, okay." Before she could respond, Colin got inside the Mini, gingerly adjusting the driver's seat to give him leg room. The car had been made for Lilliputians—his head practically hit the roof.

"What are you doing?" the woman shouted up to him.

"I'll punch it, while you unhook the trailer. I'm pretty sure my weight will hold the car. But get out of there fast . . . just in case."

"You sure you don't want me to do it?"

"I got it." He found the keys in the ignition and started the engine.

Colin watched her through the rearview as she undid the safety chains and pulled up on the coupler latch with one hand while turning the handwheel counterclockwise about ten times with the other. He figured she either moved around a lot or had gotten really good instructions at the U-Haul store. When she lifted the bar, effectively releasing the trailer from the Mini Cooper, Colin pressed the pedal to the metal until he felt all four wheels find purchase on firm ground. He nosed the car forward and turned it back onto the driveway so that it faced the cabin. When he looked back, she was still standing next to the trailer.

He used the opportunity to surreptitiously check her out. She was about five-five, curvy, with pale skin, hair so dark it was almost black, and the bluest eyes he'd ever seen. An Irishman's dream.

She climbed back up the hill and waved to him. "You did it." Her bright smile pierced him like a bullet. *Damn.*

He got out of the car, trying to cover up how flustered he felt. It wasn't just her. People in general made him uncomfortable. Usually, if he stayed focused on a task, no one noticed his awkwardness. At least he hoped that was the case.

"We're only half done," he said, looking up at the sky. The days were getting shorter. "We'll have to move if we want to pull the trailer out while there's still daylight."

"Okay. What should I do?"

"Why don't you drive your car down to the house and park it out of the way. I'll hook up my truck to the trailer."

"Sure." She got into the Mini Cooper and slowly navigated it down the uneven driveway.

He backed his truck as close as he could get it to the trailer without going over the embankment, hoping the tow bar would reach. By the time his new neighbor had hiked back up the hill, he had the U-Haul hitched to his rig. "Here goes," he called, as he climbed into the cab and revved the engine.

But the trailer wouldn't budge, just spun its wheels deeper into the mud. Colin got out, jumped into the bed of his truck, found two four-by-four scraps of wood, and wedged them under the front tires of the trailer.

This time when he hit the gas, the trailer came with it. He pulled it over the embankment onto the road and slowly towed it down the driveway, swinging his truck around so he could back the trailer in as close to the house as possible. When he looked up, she was jogging down the hill.

"Thank you." She beamed, and this time his face flushed.

He considered unhooking the hitch and driving away—his good deed done for the day. But it seemed unchivalrous. As far as he could tell she was alone, and the trailer had felt heavy, like it was jammed full of stuff. She could probably use a hand unloading, especially the big items.

"I'm Harlee Roberts, by the way." She stuck out her hand. When he just stood there, his hands stuffed inside his jacket, she peered up at him. "And you are?"

"Your parents named you after a motorcycle?" he blurted. "I mean, it's a really nice name. I actually have one. Uh . . . a Harley, that is."

She laughed. "I get that a lot. Different spelling. My dad's name is Harvey. My mom's name is Leigh. H-A-R-L-E-E."

A little out there, but he liked it. "Cool," he said, and immediately busied himself with opening the back of the trailer, pulling out the loading ramp and reaching for a heavy wardrobe box.

"You don't have to help me with that." She stopped him before he carried anything into the house.

Now that the crisis had been averted, she seemed much more cautious. Here in the mountains everyone helped each other out, but Colin understood why she might be leery of a stranger. Once or twice he'd caught her looking at his license plate and sizing him up. He imagined he looked a little grungy, but that's the way guys looked up here.

"I'm safe. I swear," he said, holding up his hands. "I'm your neighbor—just live over the hill."

She gave him a contrite smile. "At least tell me your name."

"Colin Burke," he said, hoisting the unwieldy carton into his arms. "Where do you want this?"

She unlocked the front door and pointed down a long foyer off the entryway. "The master bedroom, I guess."

He faltered for a second, eyeing the large picture windows. As long as the house felt open, he'd be okay. Colin carried the load into the bedroom and returned for a second. There were five more wardrobe boxes in the trailer.

"I've got a lot of clothes," she said apologetically. "It's sort of an addiction of mine. That and footwear."

She wouldn't need much in Nugget. Just a sturdy pair of jeans, a few sweaters, snow boots, and a good down jacket. And if she'd come for the shopping, she'd be sorely disappointed. There weren't a lot of retail options, unless you counted the farm supply store. But she didn't look the Western-wear type.

He continued to carry carton after carton into the cabin. She tried to keep pace by lugging as much as she could lift.

"So where's your house?"

Harlee followed him up into the loft, where she'd asked him to set her computer. The ceilings were lower up here, but plenty of glass let in the outdoors. As long as he could see the sky.

"Just up the road," he said, and gave her the address.

"Really? There didn't used to be a house up there."

"How long has it been since you were here last?" He pointed at her computer. "You want me to hook that up for you?"

"Sure. If you don't mind."

"I don't mind."

"I guess it's been five, six years . . . Maybe even more," she said. "My family used to come all the time. Now, it's mostly my brother. He comes with his buddies to fish or to vacation with his wife and my niece."

"Your parents don't use it anymore?" He'd always been curious about why the place sat empty.

"They bought the cabin back when we were kids so we could spend weekends and vacations here. Now we're grown, with our own lives. It's just not the same for them. You know how it is?"

Actually, he didn't. But he nodded his head anyway. "I bought my property about three years ago. It took me more than two years to build."

"Wow. You live here full-time?" She sat on the floor next to him while he tried to untangle the cords of her monitor and printer.

"Yeah. You? I mean are you moving in full-time?"

"I am," she said.

He stopped what he was doing and looked at her. "Really?"

"Yep. I'm ready for some mountain living." She kept nodding her head as if trying to convince herself.

Dusty sheets covered the furniture, but the cabin seemed cozy enough. He couldn't tell whether it was winterized. For her sake, he hoped it was, because she sure didn't seem like the roughing-it type. In fact, she seemed altogether too glamorous for Nugget.

"You might want to order a couple cords of wood before it starts snowing," he said.

"That's a good idea. You have a contact for that?"

"Yeah, I'll bring by some numbers for you."

"So what do you do around here, Colin Burke?"

His name rolled off her tongue sort of singsongy. It sounded nice—the nicest he'd ever heard anyone say it before. "I make furniture and pick up a little carpentry and construction work on the side."

"Furniture, huh?" She unpacked several framed photographs from a box and arranged them on an end table near the desk with her computer. "You married? Kids?"

"No."

"Me neither," she volunteered. He got the impression she was just making idle conversation. She was good at it, because he'd talked more than he usually did.

Colin wanted to ask about her deal—why she'd come to Nugget. The town, being small and isolated, wasn't exactly a mecca for young, single people. The only jobs to speak of were on the railroad or as ranch hands. Most of the other businesses were small, employing just the folks who owned them. But where he'd come from, you didn't ask a lot of personal questions.

After hooking up her computer, he tested it to make sure it was working. She must've called ahead to get her cable turned on. "Looks like you're set," he said. "If you don't need any more help, I should probably get going."

She jumped up. "Okay. You want to exchange numbers? You know, in case of an emergency."

"All right."

Harlee raced down the stairs, grabbed her purse from the kitchen counter, and rifled through it until she found her phone. "Shoot." She programmed in his numbers and he did the same.

"Thanks for all your help, Colin."

"No problem." He started for the door and suddenly remembered that her trailer was still hitched to his truck. "What are you planning to do with the U-Haul?"

"I have to return it in Reno." Reno was the closest city to Nugget, about fifty minutes away. "But I have until tomorrow."

He didn't like the idea of her hauling that thing down Grizzly Peak. "I'll take it," he offered.

"That's incredibly nice of you, but I couldn't let you go to all that trouble."

"It's already hooked up and I have to hit Home Depot in the morning anyway."

"Really? You're sure?"

"Yep," he said, and got her U-Haul paperwork before he left.

When he got in his truck he looked at the contract. She'd rented the trailer in San Francisco. Must be where she was moving from. It explained the city clothes.

Instead of going to the grocery store, where he'd originally been headed, Colin decided to settle for canned soup for dinner and went home.

It was cold inside. He turned up the thermostat and got to work building a fire. Even though the temperature hovered around the low forties, the weather had been unseasonably mild for early November. Usually this time of year in the Sierra Nevada they got snow. And lots of it. But Colin wasn't complaining. He and the crew had almost finished framing Sophie and Mariah's new house and hoped to get walls up and a roof on before the weather turned bad. The couple owned the Ponderosa, a combination bowling alley, saloon, and restaurant on the town's commercial square, and were due to have a baby in December. Currently they lived above their business, but were anxious to move into the large home they'd designed.

After the fire blazed, he went inside the office to check his website. He had another order for a rocking chair. The business wasn't making him rich, but it got him by. Good thing, because the money he'd inherited from the sale of his mother's house was almost gone.

He'd used much of it to buy his property, twenty acres of forest and rolling hills, in a foreclosure sale. He'd stumbled upon it and the old railroad town by accident while delivering his brother-in-law's custom furniture to a ski resort not far away, and fell in love. The former owner, a Bay Area businessman, had planned to build his dream vacation home on the plot. But when the economy went south, he'd lost his job and couldn't afford to make the payments. A pad had already been cleared and architectural plans for a rambling rancher came with the property.

But Colin thought the landscape and logging history of the area called for something more dramatic and appropriate for the rugged winters. And the truth was he needed a house with tall ceilings and wide-open spaces—nothing that would ever make him feel hemmed in again.

So he'd ordered one of those chalet-style log-cabin kits and had modified it to include covered porches, stone fireplaces, and a curved staircase. It took more than two years to build, his hope being that by the time he finished, the place would bear no resemblance to the original mail-order, cookie-cutter plan.

His stepsister Fiona worried that he was drawn to the remote area—four hours from San Francisco—so he could live like a hermit.

The fact that Nugget was an excellent place to hide from society definitely had its advantages for the town, Colin admitted. But that wasn't the reason he'd settled here.

It was the feeling he got when he stepped outside and the smell of sweet pine sap stung his nose. It was the way the snow-capped mountains guarded the town like solemn sentries and how the distant wail of a train whistle lulled him to sleep at night.

But mostly it was the only place where he felt truly free. With its gold rush history, Nugget held the promise of a second chance.

And God knew he needed one.

Chapter 2

At six in the morning Harlee's internal alarm clock went off. She started to roll out of bed to hit the gym and suddenly realized: *This is not my Marina District apartment. And that's not my view of the Golden Gate Bridge.*

And then it hit her in the gut, like a wallop from a 250-pound linebacker. She'd been fired from her dream job, stripped of her building-access pass, marched out of the newsroom like a common criminal, and forced to live in her parents' cabin in the woods.

Away from her friends, away from Nordstrom, away from everything she loved.

There had been twelve of them laid off in total. HR had called it a "work force reduction."

As they'd been escorted out the door, the other newspaper reporters had stood at their desks, stomping their feet in a rhythmic tattoo of solidarity.

Unfortunately, they'd probably be canned in the next round of downsizing. The *San Francisco Call*, like most papers across the United States, was losing money faster than the presses churned out pages. Apparently only the terminally old cared about real news. The rest watched TMZ.

Six years earlier, straight out of SF State, she'd snagged a coveted internship at the paper. The other candidates had pedigrees from the country's top J-schools and impressive freelance clips from big magazines and newspapers. She'd had only a few articles printed in the *Golden Gate Xpress*, her student newspaper. So instead of trying to dazzle the *Call*'s upper management with her portfolio, she'd memorized the bios of every senior editor on staff and spent her entire interview interviewing them. Naturally she'd landed the job.

After a year of working night cops, covering homicides, fires, and protests, she began lobbying for a permanent position.

"Look, kid, you can't write worth a shit," the managing editor, Jerry Strean, told her after she'd cornered him by the coffee machine. "You get lost on your way to press conferences, and when I asked you to do that Libya piece you didn't have the first goddamn clue who Moammar Gadhafi was. Give me one good reason I should hire you."

"Because I can squeeze information out of a rutabaga." She raised her chin as if daring him to contradict her. Harlee knew her shortcomings, but her one true gift was getting people to talk. For some reason, sources thought of her as priest, therapist, and the sympathetic girl next-door, all rolled into one, and spilled their deepest and darkest secrets. And when that didn't work, she could find the key to the kingdom by searching Internet databases that most reporters didn't even know existed.

"Didn't I get the interview with Duckett after the legislative aide he was doing went missing?" Most editors had attention spans of two-year-olds, so she had to boil her twelve months' worth of scoops into pithy sound bites. "Wasn't I the only one able to track down the best friend of the kid who got mauled to death at the zoo by Tabatha the tiger? Oh, and who got the exclu with Tami Moore when her boat capsized and she survived six days on the open sea? Uh . . . That would be me."

Jerry rolled his eyes. "Is this where I'm supposed to say, 'Roberts, you've got spunk'?" He handed her his empty coffee mug. "Make a fresh pot, would ya?"

As she watched him stroll back into his glass office, she stood there, bewildered. Then she carefully measured out enough Yuban for twelve strong cups.

She waited a full forty-eight hours before approaching him again. This time she'd carefully cataloged a list of her accomplishments at the paper, barged into his office, and shoved the three pages of typewritten notes under his nose.

"Take your time looking it over," she told him. "And feel free to ask around the newsroom about how I'm doing."

She turned to leave, when Jerry called out, "Hey, Roberts, you misspelled Berkeley. Three E's."

Harlee could hear him laughing halfway down the hall. Four days later, after she'd unearthed a scandal at the police department—feral cats had taken over the storage room, peeing on crucial evidence—Jerry called her into his office. He told her to take a seat and then made her wait ten minutes while he creased the bill of his Giants cap until he got the perfect fold.

"You do have a knack for reporting, I'll give you that." He sailed the hat Frisbee-style across the room so that it landed smack dab on a hook, then leaned back in his chair and put his feet up on the desk. "So this is what I'm gonna do. I'm giving you six months to prove you can bring up the quality of your writing. If you can do that, I'll make you a full-fledged reporter. In the meantime, learn how to use the goddamn spell check."

She ran around the desk and threw her arms around him. "You won't regret this, Jerry. I swear."

"Yeah, yeah. Get outta here. And, Roberts, you screw this up, you're out on your ass."

From then on, any time a big story broke, Jerry would come out of his office, point at Harlee, and yell, "Legs, you're on it."

The first time it happened, Harlee turned to her editor, appalled. "Uh . . . Hello? It's the new millennium. He can't talk to me like that."

Her editor, a youngish guy with a master's degree in journalism from Columbia, who had the smarts to know calling a female subordinate "Legs" held all kinds of legal implications—none of them good—stifled a laugh.

"Don't take this the wrong way, Harlee. All Jerry means is he wants you to go out and do the legwork so I can rewrite your copy into some semblance of English."

"Oh . . . okay. Then we're all good."

After her six-month probation period was up, Jerry gave her the job. On her last day of work, as the two doofus security guards paraded her past his office, Jerry popped out, gave her an awkward hug, and whispered in her ear, "You'll do fine, Legs."

Yesterday a peacock, today a feather duster, she reflected as she considered getting out of bed. Losing a career she'd loved, moving into a log cabin miles away from civilization, and leaving her friends behind, it was overwhelming. At least her parents had been supportive, lending her the cabin for as long as she needed to regroup and get her business off the ground.

It was only temporary, she kept telling herself. Just a free place to stay while she got DataDate up to speed. She'd started the small business while she was still at the *Call*, to bring in extra money to help pay credit card bills. Now she needed the income more than ever. She was broke—her checking account down to a thousand dollars. And cold, she mused as she stuck one foot outside the covers. She better order that firewood soon, or her minuscule severance package would go to paying heating bills.

She got out of bed and looked around the room, deciding she'd made the right choice by taking the master suite instead of her old bedroom. The cabin for the most part was pretty rustic, furnished with hand-me-down plaid couches and leather club chairs from her parents' Piedmont house. But her mother hadn't skimped in the master. A king-size sleigh bed, flanked by two nightstands, anchored the room. Mom had chosen Ralph Lauren bedding done in a hunting-toile pattern and a companion striped fabric for the window treatments. It was French Provençal meets mountain chic.

Her mother had always wanted to be a decorator, but had settled for owning a small bric-a-brac shop in a trendy part of Oakland not far from home. She sold everything from throw blankets to funky chandeliers. Harlee's entire San Francisco apartment—a studio the size of a carport—had been furnished with items from her mother's store. Before coming to Nugget, she'd packed up her belongings, stored the larger pieces in her parents' garage, and broke her lease. Since her landlord could get twice the rent due to the city's tech boom, there'd been no problem.

That's how she wound up here.

Harlee stuck her feet into a pair of slippers and padded into the bathroom, got into the shower, and turned the faucet to hot. Instead, she got ice. That's what the water felt like as it sluiced down her back. No matter how much she twisted the knob, the water stayed cold, making her suck in her breath and shudder. Before hypothermia set in, she turned off the faucet and stood there covered in soap suds, shampoo dripping into her eyes. Shivering, she slowly turned the water back on and ducked under the rain showerhead for as long as she could stand it. She did it over and over until she was convinced she'd been thoroughly rinsed. Each time, she gasped from the shock of the frigid temperature and let out a shriek.

She got out of the shower, wrapped herself in a thick terry cloth towel, and rubbed vigorously until she got feeling back in her arms and legs. Then she thought about who she'd kill first. Her brother for shutting off the propane or her dad for not reminding her to turn it back on.

She pulled on her clothes, including a turtleneck, cashmere sweater, and thermal socks. But Harlee could still see her breath, so she crawled back under the covers. Punching in the numbers of her parents' house, she let the phone ring until the answering machine came on. Then she hung up and tried her brother Brad.

"Hey, how's it going up there?" He sounded so goddamned chipper she wanted to reach through her cell phone and grab him by the throat.

"Just hunky-dory." When she told him about her shower experience, he laughed so loud she promised to disown him. "How do I turn the gas back on and relight the pilot light?"

He walked her through the process, but no matter how many times she tried, the darned thing wouldn't light.

"You'll probably have to call the Nugget Propane Company," Brad told her. "They'll get it going for you."

She hung up, called information for the propane company's number, and dialed. When no one picked up, Harlee decided to hop in her car and drive there. When she arrived at the propane company there was a sign on the door: "Gone fishin'. Back on Nov. 12." That was four days from now—too long to go without heat or a shower.

She banged her head against the door and considered getting in her Mini Cooper and driving down the mountain all the way back to San Francisco. *Harlee Roberts, you are no quitter*, she told herself, and headed to the Bun Boy for breakfast instead. Her stomach growled from not having had any dinner—she'd spent the time cleaning and unpacking. The downtown frosty, with its weathered picnic tables and drive-through window, had been a regular attraction when her family came to visit. And if those fried egg sandwiches were as good as she remembered, they'd be worth one last splurge.

From here on in she planned to conserve her money, using every dime she made from DataDate to pay expenses and her outstanding bills. But the small business might never generate enough money. So until she got another newspaper job she'd have to put her old lifestyle on hold. No eating at good restaurants. No shopping in nice stores.

While she waited for her food, Harlee took a good look around the square. Someone had fixed up the old Lumber Baron. Last time she'd seen it, the Victorian had been boarded up. Now, the stunning inn blew away all the other shops in the commercial district. Maybe it was her imagination, but the Ponderosa also looked like it had gotten a facelift. Downtown Nugget had never been what you would call chichi, but to her it had always had a certain je ne sais quoi. Perhaps because she'd had such good memories here as a kid.

Out of the corner of her eye she caught a young woman staring at her. She obviously wanted to strike up a conversation. Harlee smiled, but kept her distance. It's not that she was unfriendly; she just didn't feel up to socializing. Not while she was still mourning her lost life. Ever since she'd gotten laid off, she'd hidden out, avoiding calls and emails.

"Would it be too personal to ask you where you get your hair done?"

"Uh . . . no . . . not at all," Harlee said. "Daniel Salon in San Francisco."

"It's a really nice cut." The woman stepped closer and started running her fingers through Harlee's shoulder-length layers.

Uh, forward much?

"They use a straightening treatment?" she asked Harlee.

"Why? Is it that obvious?" Harlee tried to back away, but the woman had a large hunk of Harlee's hair in her hands.

For years she'd been a slave to styling products, flatirons, and more recently, Brazilian blowouts. Big brother Brad had gotten the good hair in their family, while Harlee's looked like Howard Stern's. She'd also been bestowed with the dreaded unibrow. In high school, her mother had finally taken her to a place where for two hours a woman shaped, waxed, and tweezed Harlee's brows into perfect arches. Now she paid regularly to keep them that way.

"Only to a professional," the woman replied.

The stylist was stuffed into a leopard-print dress, wore plastic earrings the size of hula hoops, and had penciled a beauty mark above her lip. And if Harlee wasn't mistaken, that teased thing on top of her head was a hairpiece. Either she was channeling Dolly Parton or she was getting ready to audition for *What Not to Wear*.

"You're a stylist?" Harlee asked dubiously.

"Yep. I just moved here from Sacramento. I'm taking over my father's barbershop." She pointed across the square at an old-timey red, white, and blue pole and a sign that read, "Owen's."

Harlee looked at the barbershop then back at the woman. *Note to self: Continue to go to San Francisco for haircuts.*

"Well, congratulations. Nice meeting you." She hoped that would end the conversation. Like pronto. The woman was odd and Harlee didn't have the patience.

"Tell you the truth, it's been a little slow," Weird Dolly said, clearly unable to take a hint. "But I'm building a rep and hoping to attract clients from Sierraville and Quincy."

"Good luck with that." Thankfully, Harlee's food order was up.

There was no indoor seating at the Bun Boy and even though it was a tad too cold to eat outside, she didn't want to smell up her car with fried food. She walked over to one of the picnic tables and sat on a bench, hoping that the woman wouldn't follow. No such luck. Dolly carried her own tray over and camped out on the seat next to Harlee.

Fine, she'd just have to eat with company. Harlee bit into her egg sandwich and hash browns and chased it with a swig of coffee. The combination of grease and caffeine made her moan with pleasure.

"So good, right?" the woman said, taking a sip of the Bun Boy's famous hot chocolate. "At least you can afford the calories. Me, not so much."

"You look great," Harlee lied. Although the woman did have one of those to-die-for curvy bodies. If she just wore clothes that fit her and ditched the hairpiece, Harlee thought she'd be quite attractive.

"I'm Darla." Harlee nearly choked. Dolly. Darla. Close enough.

"Harlee." She went to shake her hand, thought better of it, and pulled a wad of napkins from the dispenser in the center of the table to clean up first.

"You just passing through?" Darla asked.

"No. My folks own a cabin up on Grizzly Peak. I'm moving in for the winter."

"No kidding? Are you rich or something?"

Harlee laughed because the absurdity of it was hilarious. She couldn't even afford to pay her own rent. "No. I own a home business."

"What kind?"

For some inexplicable reason Darla was starting to grow on Harlee. Maybe because she reminded her a little bit of herself, sans the hairpiece of course. The woman was fantastically nosy.

"I'm a cyber-sleuth," Harlee said. "I investigate the prospective mates people meet on dating sites."

The idea for the business had been born out of a how-to piece she'd written for the *Call* on navigating the complications of online dating services and vetting potential life partners. Instead of following tips in the article, readers had sent Harlee money, begging her to run background checks on their supposed dream matches.

Given her work at the paper it was easy to run the inquiries during her downtime. She used the same battery of databases she relied on for her stories, including the obvious ones—county records, court filings, and the registry of voters—to find out everything from a prospect's true date of birth to his or her political party. If something came up that wasn't traceable in the public domain, she sicced Brad on it in exchange for free babysitting. Brad was a cop with a stay-at-home wife, a two-year-old, and a mortgage. He'd do just about anything for free babysitting.

Darla's brown eyes grew wide. "Seriously? That's an actual business?"

"Yeah, it's an actual business." Harlee pulled her coat tighter to ward off the cold. "You'd be surprised how much people lie. Especially men. I'm not just talking posting ten-year-old pictures of themselves." They lied about their weights, about their ages, their careers, their sexual orientations, and sometimes they even lied about where they lived—like the man who failed to mention that his Folsom residence was actually a state prison.

"Do you have a special license to do it, like a private investigator's license?" Darla wanted to know.

"Nope. Not necessary." To shield herself from lawsuits, Harlee required that her clients sign a waiver that a lawyer friend had drafted, releasing her from liability.

"How do people find out about you?"

"Word of mouth." Harlee finished her sandwich and tossed the wrapper in a nearby wastebasket. "I also have a website."

"Wow." Darla acted like Harlee was doing something groundbreaking, which, for the first time since she'd been "downsized," gave her a nice burst of confidence.

"What about you?" Harlee asked. "Why'd you decide to cut hair in Nugget, besides the fact that your dad owns the barbershop?"

"To tell you the truth, I wanted to stay in Sacramento," Darla said. "I'd finished a two-year internship at one of the most prestigious salons in town. But renting a chair there would've been astronomical. I haven't built up much of a client list yet. Plus, my dad wants to go part-time so he can start easing into retirement. I thought I'd fill in on his days off."

"You must've grown up around here then?"

"No," Darla said. "My parents divorced when I was young and my mother and I moved to Sacramento. I used to come for visits, but other than . . . well, you're my first friend."

It didn't take a crack reporter to figure out that there was something Darla wasn't saying. But Harlee didn't know her well enough to press. Harlee had to confess that despite her initial impression, Darla was turning out to be good company. So good that Harlee spent an hour telling Darla her life story. Before parting ways, Harlee promised to visit Darla at the barbershop the next time she came into town.

On her way home, she swung by the grocery store to pick up provisions. Unfortunately, the Nugget Market was no Whole Foods. Fortunately, unlike at Whole Foods, she could actually afford to buy food in the no-frills grocery store. Harlee filled her shopping cart with enough staples to get her through the week, including ingredients for chocolate-chip cookies. She was going to thank that nice neighbor of hers and bribe him to fix her pilot light.

"Looks like you're planning to do some baking," the checkout clerk, a plump woman who reminded Harlee of her grandmother, said. "You new around here? I don't believe we've met."

"Sort of. My family's had a cabin here for ages. We used to come up for vacations and weekends. Now I'm moving in full-time." At least until Harlee landed a reporter job.

"Welcome back." The woman introduced herself as Ethel, the market's owner. "You prepared? The weather here gets pretty nasty."

"I think so." Why tell her about the pilot light? It would only make Harlee look like a clueless city slicker and she'd bet anything Colin could fix it. The scruffy mountain man seemed extremely capable and willing to help out. Hopefully she could at some point return the favor.

At home, she got started on the baking project. At least her electric stove worked and had warmed up the kitchen, because the rest of the cabin felt like an icebox. Two hours later, Harlee trekked up the hill, found Colin's driveway, and hiked down, carrying a neatly tied package of two dozen cookies.

"Holy moly," Harlee said aloud when Colin's house came into view. "Grizzly Adams is living large."

His log home reminded her of a ski resort with its enormous porch, massive picture windows, and a two-story stone chimney. She knocked on his door. When no one answered, she peeked inside the windows. The interior was just as lovely as the exterior—lots of cozy rugs and muted paint colors. Not what she would've expected from a man who drove a beat-up pickup and looked like he'd been hibernating in a cave for the winter.

He even had a porch swing. How sweet was that? She figured it was as good a place as any to leave the cookies and the thank-you note she'd written. Hopefully bears wouldn't be enticed by the smell. One summer, when she and Brad were still in their teens, a bear had turned over their barbecue to lick out remaining food bits. They'd thought it was the coolest thing ever and had hung out the window to take pictures. Looking back on it, not such a safe idea.

While here, Harlee decided to scope the place out a little more. Everything from the flagstone walkways to the hand-forged iron fixtures was stunning. Not at all what she expected from her rugged neighbor. A bachelor like him she figured more for a simple one-room cabin.

She could see through the window that the garage was spotless. Half the space had been dedicated to the Harley-Davidson he'd said he owned. Gleaming and safely stowed away for winter. Now that she thought about it, Colin did have a bit of a biker look, especially the long brown hair and bushy beard.

She strolled around back to check out the yard and found an outbuilding similar in structure to the main house, including a soaring roofline. Smoke from the chimney and the buzz of machinery drew her closer to investigate.

Between the power tool and loud music, Colin didn't hear Harlee knock. Finally, she let herself in and nearly stumbled over a farm table. Colin stood next to it in a pair of goggles, cutting wood on a band saw. When he saw her, he stopped, flipped up his goggles, and turned off the music. The Lumineers.

Gorgeous pine rockers and gliding benches lined one wall. A potbelly stove sat in the corner, a fire burning.

"Wow," she said, turning in place, not knowing where to look first. There were finished pieces and works in progress stacked everywhere. She ran her hand over the smooth logs of a four-poster bed frame. "You made all of this?"

"Uh-huh," he said stiffly, stuffing his hands in his pockets while she examined the log bed closer. "That was an experiment."

"It looks perfect to me." To which he shrugged.

"It's beautiful. Your house . . . this shop . . . Amazing." She continued turning in circles trying to take it all in. Nightstands, coffee tables, and porch swings like the one on Colin's deck.

He merely nodded, removed the goggles from around his neck, and set them down on a workbench. She couldn't tell whether he was peeved about her intruding into his private world or bashful about her seeing his work.

But why hide it? The man was an artist.

"Where do you sell it all?" she asked.

"Mostly on the Internet. In the summertime, I set up at the weekly farmers' market on the square." He swiped at the sawdust on his sweatshirt. "I returned the U-Haul. You come for the firewood contacts?"

"I brought you cookies," she said. "I didn't know you were home, so I left them on your swing."

"The crew on my construction site had to leave early." He cocked his head to the side. "Cookies?"

"To thank you," she said. "And to bribe you for another favor."

"What's that?"

"You think you could look at my pilot light? It's off and I couldn't get it going. The heat's not working and the water's ice-cold. I nearly froze to death in the shower this morning."

The corner of his lip lifted in a half grin and for the first time she noticed that he was handsome. Not Brad Pitt handsome, but nice looking with a chiseled nose, straight white teeth, and eyes the color of caramel. All the facial hair made it difficult to know what the rest of his face looked like. Or his age. But he was in good shape—tall, broad, and muscular—leading Harlee to believe he couldn't be too old.

"Yeah, okay," he said.

He opened the door on the cast-iron stove, snuffed out the fire, and they walked back to her cabin. She led him inside the garage, where the hot-water heater was strapped to the wall in a corner. He crouched down to get closer to the switch and pulled his sleeves up. That's when she noticed his tattoo. Five black dots arranged in a quincunx on his forearm. Harlee had seen plenty of body art, but the geometric pattern was so stark and simple that it piqued her curiosity.

She was just about to ask him the significance of the tattoo, when he caught her looking at it and abruptly pulled his sleeve down.

"Could you hand me the flashlight and the matches, please?" She'd found both in the garage earlier when she'd tried to light the pilot herself, and handed them to him.

Colin continued to fiddle at the base of the hot-water heater. "Hmm. It's not working," he said, and stood up. "You said the heat's giving you trouble? Where's the furnace?"

She showed him, and he fidgeted with the heater for a while. "Brad didn't say that I had to light both," Harlee said.

"Yep," he grunted. "Where's your propane tank?"

She took him outside to the front of the house, where the tank sat in a small enclosure, hidden on three sides by lattice fencing.

"You got a bucket I can fill with water?"

She didn't bother to ask why. "I'll find one."

Harlee came back shortly, hefting a mop pail full of water.

He grabbed it from her and poured it over the tank. "You're out of propane."

"How can you tell?" she asked.

"See that frost line?" He pointed to the lower part of the tank. "It's less than a quarter full."

"Crap! The Nugget Propane Company is closed for the next four days. The sign says the owner went fishing. Maybe I can find him and get him to open for just one tank."

Colin lifted his brows. "How do you plan to do that?"

"I don't know. But I'm a reporter. I'm good at finding people."

"A reporter?" he asked, slanting her a glance. "Like on television?" Clearly he was trying to remember if he'd ever seen her on CNN.

"No. Newspaper. The *San Francisco Call*. But not anymore." Man, it hurt to say that. She waited for him to ask the obvious question, but he didn't. Thank God. "Is there any other place around here I can get propane?"

"Reno," Colin said. "But they won't deliver to California on a day's notice."

"I'll go there and haul it myself."

"In that?" He nudged his head at her Mini Cooper in the driveway and choked on a laugh. "No one lugs around a five-hundred-gallon tank of propane. You have to get it delivered. And that may take a few days. In the meantime, you can use my shower. I've got lots of hot water."

"Seriously? Isn't that kind of weird?" She didn't even know the guy.

"Probably," he admitted. "But you can come over when I'm not there."

"Where will you be?" she asked.

"Construction site—I'm building a house. You'll have the whole place to yourself."

"Wow. That's so amazingly nice of you. I might take you up on it."

But more than likely she'd take sponge baths instead. Or hit up Darla. Even though she didn't know her any better than Colin, it seemed more kosher to shower at another woman's house. Although she was dying to see more of the inside of that fancy abode of his. Just not naked. "In the meantime, can I borrow some firewood?"

"Yup," he said, and she could tell that he thought she was a dope for not being better prepared. "I'll hook you up."

"Thank you. And, Colin, I want to take you to dinner for helping me out like this." She couldn't afford it, but the guy was a total saint.

"No dinner," he muttered.

"I insist. Pick a nice restaurant. Maybe something at one of the casinos in Reno."

That seemed to startle him. "I can't do that."

"Of course you can." Was the guy some kind of throwback that he wouldn't let a woman pay for his meal?

"No, I can't. So just drop it, please."

He said it so adamantly that for the life of her, Harlee wondered what she'd done wrong.

Chapter 3

Colin felt like the world's biggest prick for turning down her invitation in the way he had. She'd only been trying to show her appreciation and he'd all but bitten her head off.

But he had a good reason for saying no. For him to go to a restaurant was simply impossible.

Crowds and small closed-in spaces scared the hell out of him to the point where Colin couldn't breathe and felt like he was dying. Clinically, the diagnosis was social anxiety disorder, also known as demophobia, and claustrophobia. The former affliction made any kind of large gathering unbearable. The panic attacks came on so fast and furious—like a vise squeezing all the air out of his chest—that he avoided public places the way most people avoided gang-infested neighborhoods.

Outdoor functions, like the farmers' market, were about the only kind of large group gatherings he could tolerate. Something about being in the open, where he could see the sky, eased his anxiety. Inside, he could manage a half dozen people, but more than that sent him into a tailspin—sweats, nausea, and heart palpitations.

If he had to go into the Nugget Market or the Ponderosa for food or business, he waited until there were only a few customers. Sometimes it meant stalking the places for an hour. On job sites, he found ways to work alone, where no one would discover his dysfunction.

The phobias weren't anything he advertised—Colin firmly believed you kept your crazy in the closet where it belonged. For that reason, he spent a lot of time at home or in his workshop.

At least the claustrophobia he'd gotten a firmer grip on. If he did his breathing exercises and concentrated really hard, Colin could usually endure a tight space for a short time, despite feeling like the walls were closing in on him. Good thing, because in construction he found himself in a lot of cramped quarters. Basements. Attics. Closets. You name it.

He hadn't always been this screwed up, but like the shrinks said, he had extenuating circumstances. And until he could conquer his fears—so far, Colin hadn't had much luck in that department—he wasn't going to any restaurants.

Hopefully, he'd make amends by building Harlee a toasty fire and lending her a space heater. There was probably one in his garage somewhere. That pretty woman was so ill equipped for mountain life it made Colin scratch his head and wonder why she'd come here in the first place. Especially in winter, when the weather could be deadly. Her ridiculous car wouldn't make it one day in the snow.

Clearly, she'd run away from home because she was having some sort of crisis. Job related? Boyfriend related? Who knew? His policy was to never ask too many questions. Besides, she asked enough for both of them. Nosy little thing.

"Reporter," he huffed.

He'd set her up with heat, let her use his shower, but that was it. He didn't have time to be her mountain guide, and he had plenty of reasons to keep his distance.

One of those reasons sat at the bottom of his driveway when he got home.

Al Ferguson got out of a gray Crown Vic, the outline of his shoulder holster plainly visible through the cheap fabric of his suit jacket. "Long time no see."

"No offense, but I haven't missed you."

"None taken." Al shielded his eyes as he watched Colin come toward him. "Were you on a hike?" That was Al code for: Why aren't you working?

"What's going on, Al?"

"Just routine. You know the drill." Yes, Colin knew the drill.

He opened his front door and waved Al across the threshold. Al went straight for the coat closet, turned on the light, and methodically ran his hands between Colin's coats and jackets, checking the pockets, tapping the walls, and examining the floorboards. Satisfied, he followed Colin into the great room and stared out the mammoth picture window, letting out a low whistle.

"I still can't get over this view." He pivoted around the room. "You've always been a neat freak. You sure you're not OCD?"

Colin ignored the gibe—Al's lame attempt at humor.

Next, he let himself into Colin's office, rifled through his desk drawers, and turned on his computer. "You've got mail," he said, perusing Colin's in-box. "Looks like you've sold a couple of rockers today."

Colin stood over Al's shoulder reading the orders. Good. He needed the money to buy a new wood shaper.

"You get that seller's permit I told you about?"

"Yep." Colin rolled his eyes. "And I pay my taxes too."

"Good." Al got up. He was a big dude with an inch on Colin, who was six-two. Colin put him somewhere in his forties. Though his face looked lived-in, he took fine care of himself—hadn't let his muscle go to fat.

Colin got the impression no one messed with big Al.

After finding the master bedroom, Al searched the walk-in closet, then pulled up Colin's mattress, running his hands over the box spring. In the bathroom, he took his time going through the medicine chest.

He made quick work of the other rooms, peering under the guest bed, scouring storage spaces, checking the linen cabinets, and prying open the vents. Then he headed to the kitchen, sticking his head inside the refrigerator, moving around various containers of leftovers, and sorting through the produce drawers.

"I see you're eating healthy." He gave Colin a full appraisal.

Under the sink, he crouched down to pull out a number of cleaning supplies, lay on his back, and felt around the drainpipe. Finished, he sat up and put everything back in place.

"Is this going to take much longer?" Colin wanted to know.

"Why? You have an appointment?"

No way was Colin telling him about Harlee. Al would find her and ask a lot of unnecessary questions. "I've got work to do."

"Who's stopping you? In fact, I'll follow you out to your shed."

Follow? Al led the way, doing a thorough search of the wood shop's small bathroom, nosing around in Colin's toolboxes and generally making himself right at home. "Where you working these days?"

"I'm building a house on the other side of town for the two women who own the Ponderosa."

"How is that place? I keep meaning to eat there."

"It's good." Colin said it out of loyalty to Sophie and Mariah, but he'd prefer Al not eat there. In fact, he'd rather Al get the hell out of Dodge and go back to Quincy, where he came from, before he stirred up a whole lot of crap Colin didn't need stirring.

"How come you're not working today?" Al asked, continuing to snoop through Colin's workspace.

"I did. But we let out early on account of the crew having to finish another job."

"It's a good job?" More Al code for: Is the work legitimate? Are there permits? No under-the-table pay? No illegal substances on site?

"It's all good, Al." God, he resented these questions.

Al gazed up at the cathedral ceiling. "How you doing with the phobias?"

"Great," Colin lied.

"You seeing that therapist?"

"I did. But I don't like her."

"Why not?" Al asked.

"Because she judges me."

Al shook his head. "You do know that's part of your demophobia, right? Feelings of inferiority. Make another appointment."

He sat in one of Colin's rockers and tested the feel of it. "How much does something like this go for?"

"Two hundred fifty. But for you, five hundred."

Al laughed. "How's everything else going?"

"Fine and dandy." *Now get the hell out.*

"What about your social life? How's that going?"

What social life? He couldn't even accept a dinner offer from a neighbor. A smoking hot neighbor. "Terrific."

Al wasn't fooled. "Work on it, Colin." He stood up and paced the workshop, stopping every once in a while to admire a piece of furniture. Colin was surprised he didn't take every piece apart. "It's important to be part of the community. To have friends—upstanding friends."

Yup, he'd get right on that as soon as Al left.

But unfortunately Al wasn't leaving. He was still talking. "You seeing anyone?" he asked.

"Oh, for Christ's sake, Al. Of course I'm not seeing anyone. I can't step foot in a goddamn movie theater. How am I supposed to date?" Not to mention that the kind of woman he'd want to date, wouldn't want anything to do with him.

Al let out a sigh. "Look what you've accomplished here. Give yourself a little credit, Colin." This from the man who just moments ago had had his head down Colin's toilet tank, looking for contraband.

"On another note, how's that new police chief working out?" Al asked, and Colin froze.

The last thing Colin needed was Al making waves for him in this town. In the three years he'd lived here, he'd gotten along with the people just fine. He'd even made a few nice acquaintances. The police chief's wife being one of them. "Why?"

"Just curious. I remember last year he shot that meth dealer in his wife's inn. Weren't you the guy who found the lab in the basement?"

"Yeah." Colin had been helping to restore the Lumber Baron, which at the time had been so neglected that it should've been condemned, when he found a cache of chemicals and cooking equipment. Given his history, he'd seriously considered walking away and not telling anyone, knowing that it could come back to him. But he blew the whistle anyway, worried that someone might get hurt. Or worse: blown to bits. Rhys Shepard, the police chief, wound up killing the dealer during a hostage situation.

"So you get along with him okay?" Al asked, watching Colin closely.

"We're fine. Why the third degree, Al? I've been behaving."

"Just want to make sure you're staying out of trouble and maintaining good relations with the local law. It's my job to babysit your ass."

"The chief's father just died," Colin blurted, not knowing why he'd felt the need to throw that into the mix. It wasn't like it had anything to do with Al.

But the old man's death had hit Colin hard. Shep Shepard used to drop by the house sometimes, mostly because his Alzheimer's made him loopy and he'd get lost. On those occasions, he'd confuse Colin for Rhys. Colin supposed that watching a guy lose his mind had helped him put his own issues in perspective. Because of the demophobia, he hadn't been able to attend the old man's funeral.

"I'm sorry to hear that." Al reached into his jacket pocket, pulled out a small urine container, and nudged his head in the direction of the john. "Before I go, I'll need a sample. And, Colin, leave the door open, please."

Harlee suspected that Desmond Hopper IV was too good to be true. And he was.

In his online dating profile, he boasted of being rich, successful, and single. Unfortunately, he'd failed to mention that his business was in Chapter 11, there were two liens against his Pacific Heights Edwardian, and the bank was foreclosing on his wine country pied-à-terre. For all intents and purposes, Desmond was broke.

And while Harlee's client might be able to fall in love with a poor man, she sure as hell wasn't looking for a married one.

The jerk also had a wife.

Apparently Mrs. Hopper was home—probably avoiding calls from collection agencies—while her douche-bag husband was trolling online dating sites.

Desmond was definitely a no-go, Harlee told herself as she quickly finished filling out a background report and emailed it to Frances Guthrie. The woman had become DataDate's best client.

Frances would surely be disappointed, having had high hopes for this one. But Frances paid Harlee to leave no stone unturned, and that's exactly what she'd done.

She turned off the computer and went downstairs. Luckily, her propane was getting delivered today. It had only taken three days of badgering for the Reno company to finally get off its butt. And good old Brad had offered to pay for it, since he'd been the last to use the cabin and hadn't gotten the tank refilled.

In the meantime, she'd made do with Colin's space heater, the fireplace, sponge baths, and a free shampoo from Darla. She'd also ordered two cords of firewood, which were coming tomorrow—just in time for her mother's weekend visit.

Things were shaping up at DataDate central. She'd spent the morning cleaning the cabin until it shined and had even gotten two new clients. To celebrate, she and Darla were having lunch at the

Ponderosa. On her way out, she grabbed a coat, hat, and gloves. The temperature had dropped enough that Harlee wouldn't be surprised to see snow.

Fifteen minutes later she pulled into the square, found a place to park, and made her way inside the Western-style saloon and restaurant. The place had been completely made over since the last time she'd been there. Lots of red pleather banquettes, dark paneled walls, and Victorian light sconces. Kitschy, but fun.

Darla sat in a booth in the back of the dining room and waved her over. "Hey."

"Hi." Harlee air-kissed her, hung her coat and hat on the wall rack, and grabbed the other bench. "It is so cold."

"Yet look how cute you look."

Okay, maybe the Kate Spade dress and the four-hundred-dollar boots were a little overkill for Nugget, not to mention that the weather called for down and fleece. But she didn't want to look like the Stay Puft Marshmallow Man at her first ladies' lunch.

"You too," she told Darla, who had ditched the hairpiece in exchange for clip-on hair extensions. Magenta.

"See that guy over there, sitting at the bar?" Harlee whispered in Darla's ear. "He keeps staring at you."

"I see three guys sitting at the bar," Darla said.

Harlee thought two of them were gorgeous. But it was the third—a cop with big ears—who was doing all the goggling. She nudged her chin at the uniform. "Him. What do you think?"

"Why?" Darla asked.

"He seems interested."

"Well, he's not."

"How do you know? Do you know him?" Harlee asked, because it was obvious that she did.

"His name's Wyatt and he's an asswipe. Although I'm pretty sure he's a single asswipe, just in case you're interested for yourself."

"Why would I be interested in a guy who's clearly interested in you?"

"Because I don't want him," Darla said adamantly—too adamantly, if you asked Harlee—then opened her menu, feigning indifference.

Harlee arched a brow, knowing that there was definitely something going on here. "Okay." She held up her hands in surrender.

"So you're interested?" Darla asked, trying to sneak a peek at Big Ears, who was looking right back.

"No." Harlee would've laughed if Darla hadn't look so relieved. "I don't know how long I'll be here, so a man's the last thing I need. All my energy has to go into finding another newspaper job."

She leaned over the table to confide in Darla that she'd left San Francisco with a bit of a debt problem.

"How bad?" Darla asked, turning her gaze from Wyatt to eye Harlee's clothes. "Like collection agency bad?"

Harlee nodded her head. "It's a sickness. Just like some people are addicted to crack, I'm addicted to department stores."

Then there'd been the swanky Marina studio she hadn't been able to afford, all those pricey restaurant meals, and a hefty car payment. San Francisco was an expensive city and her friends—software designers, venture capitalists, and lawyers—had deep pockets. On her pathetic reporter's salary it hadn't been easy keeping up with the Joneses. And she'd gotten into a lot of trouble trying. Now it was time to pay the piper—part of the reason she'd been forced to move to Nugget.

"My cards are maxed out and I only have a thousand dollars in my checking account," she continued, deciding on the French dip with a side salad.

"What about DataDate?" Darla asked. "You just got two new clients."

"Business is picking up. But it's still not enough. Thank God for free rent, or I'd be living with my parents." As much as she loved them, moving back into her childhood bedroom would've been the cherry on top of her failure sundae.

A woman with a cloud of dark hair and soulful eyes came to take their orders. "Hey, Darla. How's business at the barbershop?"

"Good. Really good. You should come in sometime for a service. Mariah, this is Harlee Roberts. She's new in town, lives in her family's cabin up on Grizzly Peak. Harlee, Mariah and her partner, Sophie, own the Ponderosa."

"Nice to meet you, Mariah."

"You live next door to Colin," Mariah said, refilling their water glasses. "We love Colin."

"He's great," Harlee said, and changed her mind about the French dip, getting a Cobb salad instead.

When Mariah left, Harlee whispered, "Liar." Darla had confided during Harlee's shampoo that business was deader than road kill. The men still came to get trims and shaves from Owen, but most of the women in town already had stylists in either Reno or Quincy.

"What am I supposed to say? 'No one wants me to cut their hair'?"

"It's not that, Darla. You just need more time to get established. You'll see."

"Whatever," Darla said, and Harlee understood that she was just frustrated. "I didn't know you lived near Colin."

"You know Colin?" For some reason that surprised Harlee, who'd pegged Colin for the town hermit, although she knew he had a lot of construction jobs in addition to making furniture.

"It's a small town. Everyone knows everyone."

"Do you think he's weird?" Harlee asked, lowering her voice.

Darla vacillated. "Mm, maybe a little. More like quiet. And at least he doesn't stare at my chest, like that one." She pointed at Wyatt, who had turned around in his stool and was sure enough blatantly watching Darla.

"The one you're so hot for me to like?"

"Hey, pickings are slim around here."

"What's the deal with the other two?" Harlee motioned toward the bar, her inner reporter kicking in.

"The one in the hat is Clay McCreedy. He's the heartthrob of Nugget, owns a huge cattle ranch up the road, has two sons, and is engaged to a famous cookbook author. The other one is Nugget Police Chief Rhys Shepard. He's absolutely dreamy, sweet as can be, and is married to Maddy Shepard, owner of the Lumber Baron Inn. Together, they're like the cutest couple in town. It would make you sick, if she wasn't so sweet. And pregnant too. My dad's always bitching about her inn and how it's turning the place into Lake Tahoe, but secretly I think he's madly in love with her."

Someone other than Mariah brought their food, and Harlee dug in, starved. Darla took a big bite of her tri-tip sandwich.

"I have to say, the inn rocks," Harlee said between bites. "I haven't seen the inside, but the outside makes the square."

"They're doing high teas on the weekends. It was Emily Mathews's idea. She's the cookbook author engaged to Clay. You should take your mom. The inside is like seriously killer. Colin did the carpentry."

"Really?" Now Harlee was even more curious to see the inn's interior. "That's a great idea. You want to join us?"

"Sure. Why not?" Darla shrugged. "It's not like anyone's busting down my door for a cut and color."

"They will," Harlee assured her, wondering if perhaps Darla's unconventional getup might be scaring people off. Admittedly, she'd been thrown by it at first, but Darla was a good person.

"Hey," Darla said, "you want to take yoga with me? Pam, across the square at the dance studio, holds classes."

"Is it expensive?"

"I don't know. But how expensive can it be?" Darla pushed her plate of fries closer to Harlee so they could share. "After lunch we could go over and check."

And here Harlee thought that she'd be bored living in Nugget. It would be a lie to say that she'd stopped fantasizing that the phone would ring with Jerry on the line. *"Legs, the paper made a big mistake. We need you back. Stat!"* Or better yet, the *New York Times*. *"What were those idiots thinking? Come work for us in our San Francisco bureau. We'll pay you twice what you were making at the Call."*

Then she'd get her old apartment back—the one she couldn't afford. And life would return to the way it used to be.

"Shit," Darla cried.

"What?" Harlee nearly jumped out of her seat.

"Wyatt's coming over here. Do something, quick."

Chapter 4

On his way down Grizzly Peak, Colin passed a truck filled with firewood. He figured it must be for Harlee. The delivery couldn't come any sooner, because the weather service was predicting snow next week and it would be damned cold over the weekend.

At least she seemed to be getting into the swing of living in Nugget. He'd noticed her propane had been delivered the day before. Not that he was spying. And she hadn't called him for help—or for the use of his shower—since he lent her the wood and space heater. That was five days ago. Not that he was counting.

During the week, he and the crew had gotten Sophie and Mariah's new house pretty well buttoned up for the pending storm. After the rough framing had been completed, they'd applied plywood sheathing to the exterior walls and roof, which would hopefully keep out the snow. Today he planned to start installing windows and doors before knocking off for the weekend.

It would be a light crew, so he'd be able to breathe. When he pulled up to the site, he spied Sophie and Mariah's Volvo parked off to the side. Sophie, who was due in December and getting bigger by the day, waved as he hopped out of his truck.

"It's looking good." She walked over to join him.

Unlike the log homes and Victorians that were popular in the area, Sophie and Mariah had decided to go with a single-level contemporary plan that boasted vaulted ceilings, angular windows, and courtyards that took advantage of the Sierra and Feather River views. Colin really liked the way it was shaping up.

"Yep. We've made good headway thanks to the weather," he said.

Mariah strolled over, shielding her eyes to block the sun. "Nice day. Still doesn't feel like snow."

"It does to me," Colin said, zipping his down jacket. "You decide on your appliances yet?"

Pat Donnelly, the contractor on the project, liked fixtures and appliances to be ordered well in advance. Being the top contractor in this part of the Sierra, he was spread thin and got ornery when he had to wait on late shipments.

"We're pretty set on the Wolf range. But we're at an impasse on the fridge and dishwasher," Sophie said, flicking her head at Mariah and rolling her eyes.

"Don't look at me," Colin said. "I'm not getting in the middle."

The women laughed and Mariah said, "Hey, I met your new neighbor yesterday at the Ponderosa. Harlee, right?"

"Yeah," Colin said. They waited for him to say more, but what more was there to say other than she was gorgeous, had a screaming body, and was so far out of his league he had a better chance pitching for the Giants than getting the attention of someone like Harlee Roberts.

"Well, what's she like?" Sophie prodded.

"Nice."

"What does she do for a living?" Sophie pressed, clearly frustrated at Colin's reticence.

But he didn't want to dish. So he shrugged one shoulder and threw her a crumb. "I think she said she used to be a reporter for the *San Francisco Call.*"

Sophie looked impressed. "What's she doing now?"

"I honestly don't know. Maybe she's writing a book." Why else would she move here? Although he got the impression that her coming to Nugget was pretty last minute.

"How old is she?"

Geez, enough with the inquisition. Colin had stuff to do.

"I don't know," he said. "In her twenties, maybe. I'm not good at that."

"And that's why we love you," Mariah teased. "Well, is she single?"

Besides being a bunch of matchmakers, everyone in Nugget liked knowing everyone else's business. It was a town hobby. He knew people wondered about him. Luckily, no one thought he was interesting enough to dig deep. It helped that he kept a low profile.

"I better get to work." He started for the house.

Members of the crew had spread out to staple Tyvek to the exterior walls. Colin planned to come in behind them to install windows and doors. Some of the special-order glass hadn't come in yet. Those openings he'd cover with plastic.

"We're taking off," Sophie said. "If we don't see you around, have a good weekend, Col."

They were good people, Sophie and Mariah. They'd all moved to Nugget about the same time—he from LA and Soph and Mariah from the Bay Area. Sophie had worked for a big-time marketing firm and Mariah had founded her own software start-up. Neither wanted those lives when they turned forty.

They bought the Ponderosa, moved into the apartment above it, and hired Colin to bring the place back to life. They took one look at his house in progress and decide he was the man for the job. He and a consultant who knew everything about modern bowling alleys. He restored the original hardwood floors, did all the carpentry in the dining room, and refurbished the bar, which according to town legend had survived the gold rush.

The couple persuaded their friends Maddy and her brother, Nate Breyer, to buy the run-down Lumber Baron and recommended Colin for that job too. He'd been working ever since.

Colin strapped on his tool belt and started on the south side of the house, where the exterior had already been wrapped. He taped a window-and-door schedule to the wall and got to work. By the time he finished that side, the men had stopped for lunch, eating sandwiches on the tailgates of their pickups.

It was this time of day, while the workers took their breaks, that Colin got the most done. One blissful hour of solitude. When they finished, Colin would find a quiet spot to eat his own lunch.

He tugged the schedule down and readied to start at the back of the house. That's when he heard a whining sound come from underneath the deck.

At first he thought he'd imagined it and continued to tack the list to the back wall. But he heard it again. This time the noise, a painful whimper, was louder. Colin got down on the deck and listened through the floorboards and heard scratching.

Someone or something was down there. Colin grabbed a flashlight from his toolbox, hiked down the embankment, and swept the light over the crawl space.

"Anyone in there?" he called.

Another whimper. This one more pitiful than the last.

Shit! The last thing Colin wanted to do was crawl around in a hole twenty-four inches tall. He could get one of the guys. But then he'd have to hand in his man card and leave his balls at the door.

"Hey," he called back under the deck. "Do you really need me to come in and get you? Or can you come out on your own?"

He got his answer in the form of a yelp. Then a wounded cry. Colin did another sweep with the flashlight and saw nothing, which meant whatever he was dealing with was jammed way back there, farther than Colin wanted to go. Hell, he didn't want to go in at all. Every time he looked at the crevice, it got smaller and smaller. Darker and darker. Even with the flashlight.

He took off his jacket because it had suddenly gotten so hot that Colin couldn't breathe. "How you doing in there?"

"*Errrrr*," came a weak cry.

"Okay. I'm coming in."

He crawled in halfway, but quickly came back out, his heart pumping so hard that he thought it would explode out of his chest. "Breathe," he told himself, and for the next few seconds concentrated on the exercises the therapist had taught him.

"*Errrrr*."

"Okay, chill. I'll be there in a few seconds."

He got on his hands and knees and inched his way back in, using the light to guide him. The joists and beams felt like they were closing in, smothering him, as if someone were holding a pillow over his face.

Inhale.

Exhale.

Inhale.

Exhale.

Focus.

Task.

Straight ahead.

"Where you at?" Colin called into the darkness.

"*Errrrr.*"

A few feet away, huddled next to a deck post, was a black-and-white fur ball. "You okay?"

The dog, which looked like some kind of shepherd, let out a long whimper and thumped its tail like it sensed Colin was a friend, not a foe.

"There better be a good reason that you made me crawl through hell."

The dog made another high-pitched, "*Errrrr,*" then cocked its head to the side.

The mutt was a mangy thing. Scrawny and disheveled. And if Colin wasn't mistaken, the animal's belly was matted in blood.

To keep from spooking the dog, Colin slowly reached out his hands, getting a wet-nosed sniff and a few tentative licks for his trouble. Sticking the flashlight in the waistband of his jeans, Colin gingerly lifted the animal, crawled back out, and didn't stop until he saw blue skies.

"We made it." Colin gasped for breath and tried to regulate his breathing as the dog licked his face. "Knock it off. That's gross."

Once his pulse returned to normal, Colin used the sunlight to closely examine the animal—a male—and found a nasty cut. Maybe from barbed wire; he couldn't tell. But the raised incision was oozing blood and looked infected. Colin put his jacket back on, hefted the dog into his arms, and carried him to his truck.

"Whaddya got there?" Jack, one of the workers, finished a soda, crushed the can, and chucked it into the Dumpster.

"An injured dog. I found him under the house. You know where there's a vet around here?"

"Nearest one's in Graeagle. Right there on Main Street," Jack said, coming over to pet the patient. "He's bleeding, poor dog. Here, let me put some Tyvek sheeting on the seat of your truck."

"Thanks," Colin said. "You guys okay with me taking off? I'll come back later and close up the openings before the snow hits."

"Sure." Jack checked his watch and smiled. "It's practically the weekend anyway. You want me to call the vet, let him know you're coming with an emergency?"

"Yeah, that would be great." He didn't think the bleeding was life threatening, but the infection could be serious.

Two hours and three hundred dollars later, Colin drove up Mc-Creedy Road. "This place look familiar, boy?" The dog, whose nose rested on his two front legs, looked up at Colin with doleful eyes— one blue and one brown. "You buzzed on doggy tranqs?"

When Colin knocked on Clay McCreedy's door, his fiancé, Emily, answered and looked a little surprised to see him. "Hey, Colin."

"You by any chance missing an Australian shepherd mix, about two years old?"

"No. I don't think so." Emily invited him in and called to Clay, "We're not missing a dog, are we?"

Clay came into the foyer and nodded a greeting at Colin. "Nope, at least not that I know of. One of the barn dogs might've gone for a stroll. You got her with you?"

"It's a he, and he's in my truck."

Emily and Clay grabbed their jackets off a hall tree and followed him outside. Colin opened the passenger side of his truck. The dog thumped his tail a few times, stood up, did a couple of turns, and dropped back down, looking up at Colin like *What now?*

Clay scratched the dog under his chin. "Not one of mine."

"He's so sweet," Emily said. "Where did you find him?"

"Under Sophie and Mariah's new deck. He was filthy and cut up on barbed wire. The vet cleaned him, gave him a shot of antibiotics and stitched him up. He didn't have a collar or one of those tracking chips. Dr. Weil thought I should check with some of the local cattle ranchers, since he's a herd dog."

"Sophie and Mariah's property is a good five miles from any cattle ranches," Clay said. "While it's possible that the dog might've gotten hurt and run off to lick his wounds, it's more probable someone dumped him off. Unfortunately, it happens all the time. You could put a notice in the paper, but I doubt anyone will claim him."

The dog had cuddled up next to Emily's leg as she stood inside the truck door, stroking his head.

"You want me to take him off your hands?" Clay asked. "I got room in the barn for one more."

Colin scrubbed his hand through his hair. The dog would probably like a place like this. Plenty of animals to keep him company, young kids to play with, and a nice roof over his head.

"Nah," Colin said. He and the dog had kind of bonded—maybe because they were both a little lost. "I'll keep him unless someone comes forward to claim him."

"Man's best friend," Clay said, wrapping his arm around Emily's shoulder.

Colin could use a friend. Once they got back on the road, he reached over to scratch the dog behind his ears. He seemed to like that. "You got a name, boy?"

The pooch just gave him another one of his doleful stares and licked his hand.

"You look like a Max to me," Colin said, sliding the dog a sideways glance. "What do say? Max work for you?"

The dog let out a bark, and Colin grinned the rest of the way home.

"Oh my God," Darla mouthed to Harlee, her mile-long fake eyelashes fluttering at the array of miniature pastries, finger sandwiches, and salmon pinwheels decoratively arranged on tiered silver servers.

"Wow." Harlee waited until their host was well out of earshot. "This is not what I expected. It's so sophisticated."

"It's absolutely lovely, girls." Harlee's mom poured each of them a cup of tea.

At sixty-one, Leigh Roberts had the kind of grace and beauty that still turned heads. She wore her hair, now completely silver, in a stylish chin-length bob. Unlike Harlee, who'd become a slave to designer labels, Leigh chose clothes that were arty, one-of-kind pieces that she liked to accent with exotic scarves or interesting jewelry.

"Thank you so much for thinking of this," Leigh said to Harlee.

"It was Darla's idea," Harlee told her mother, taking in the ornate dining room with its decorative cornices and antique sideboard. "This part of Nugget is not at all like when we used to come here, is it, Mom?"

"No, but I always thought that this old building had tremendous potential. And someone with a fine eye for detail must've seen it too, because the place is gorgeous."

"Why, thank you." Maddy Shepard, owner of the Lumber Baron, introduced herself. "I was eavesdropping," she admitted, and scoped out their group. "I know Darla, of course, and you must be Harlee, and you . . ."

"This is my mom, Leigh Roberts."

"So nice to meet you," Maddy said. "Thanks for coming to the inn's first English high tea."

"Honestly, we thought it would be a big flop," said another woman, who had joined Maddy at the table. "I'm Donna Thurston, owner of the Bun Boy. I love that necklace you're wearing." She pointed at the strand of chunky amber stones Leigh wore around her neck, pulled up a chair, and plopped down. "Was it terribly expensive?"

She didn't wait for an answer, just swept her arms around the room and said, "The tea was actually Emily's idea." Harlee only knew who Emily was because Darla had told her. "I myself thought maybe two people would show up. But color me wrong. The place is packed."

Harlee looked up at Maddy, expecting to see her aghast. But the innkeeper was smiling.

"She's an acquired taste, but we love her." Maddy kissed the top of Donna's head.

"Don't you need to mingle?" Donna shooed Maddy away.

"How long have you lived here?" Leigh asked Donna.

"My whole life. But in the last few years it's started to get interesting. Lesbians bought the Ponderosa." She nudged her head in the direction of the square. "They're having a baby. The baby's father is Maddy's brother, Nate." She leaned across the table and with a conspiratorial gleam in her eye said, "I helped set the whole thing up. Let's see, what else? A hot bazillionaire just moved into town— bought the Nugget Gas and Go and the fancy bankrupt planned community down the road. And Emily ghostwrote Della James, the famous country music star's cookbook." Donna put her finger to her lips. "That's supposed to be classified. But the little strumpet—Della, not Emily—came to Nugget to do the photo shoot."

"You're kidding!" Harlee said. "I love her."

"Not if you'd met her in person." Donna took a quick glance around the room and whispered, "She's a biotch."

"Really?" Della's songs about cheating men and crappy jobs made her seem like one of the girls, Harlee thought, disappointed.

"With a capital B."

Maddy returned to the table to introduce everyone to Emily, who Harlee immediately recognized but couldn't quite pinpoint from where.

While Harlee tried to figure out where she'd seen her before, Emily said a quick hello and rushed back into the kitchen.

Maddy tried to pull Donna away, but the Bun Boy owner wasn't having it. Apparently she liked a captive audience. Harlee actually found Donna to be quite entertaining. Leigh seemed to be enjoying her as well. And of course, Darla had known her since childhood.

Donna hooked another chair with her foot, dragged it to the table, and told Maddy to sit. "Take a load off, sister."

"So, Harlee," Maddy said, "I hear you're Colin's new neighbor."

"I am," she said, and reached for one of the mini éclairs, trying to take a dainty bite. "My God, these are good."

"That's our Emily," Maddy said. "She's an amazing cook."

That's when it hit Harlee who Emily was. It was the cooking that triggered her memory. Emily Mathews, once a well-known Bay Area food writer, had been huge news. Several years ago, her daughter, Hope, had gone missing from the family's Palo Alto backyard and was never found. Harlee had been on another story at the time, but remembered the details quite well. She also recalled that over the summer there had been a new wrinkle in the cold case, something about a serial killer falsely confessing to Hope's abduction. Apparently, Emily now lived in Nugget. Interesting.

When Harlee got home, she planned to do a little research on the matter. But now wasn't the time to bring it up.

"Colin," Maddy continued, "did all the Lumber Baron's carpentry. I absolutely adore him."

"Mmm." Harlee, who'd lost track of the conversation, nodded. "I'm taking my mom over later to see his furniture."

Maddy turned to Leigh. "You'll love his shop. He built all the rocking chairs on the Lumber Baron's veranda. Take a look on your way out. Are you staying in Nugget long?"

"Just the weekend, I'm afraid. I own a shop in the Bay Area and need to get back."

"Too bad you all missed our annual Halloween festival on the square. Hopefully you'll come next year, especially since Harlee's a full-time resident now. Someone said you're a journalist?"

"Yes," Harlee said. Well, it was true, even if she was between newspaper jobs. "But I'm taking some time to build my start-up company."

Harlee knew that buzzwords like "start-up" made people take you more seriously. Otherwise, they thought you sold Mary Kay or Amway, instead of inventing something that would save the world, like, say, Pinterest.

"What is it?" Maddy and Donna said in unison.

"Tell them," Darla said, nudging Harlee's arm with excitement.

"It's called DataDate. I do background checks on members of online dating sites."

Leigh poured another round of tea, while Maddy pulled her chair closer to the table.

"Does the service hire you to do the checks? Like to make sure the members are legit?" Maddy asked.

"Nope," Harlee explained. "Individual members hire me to make sure they're not being duped before taking their relationship to the next level. Some people fabricate entire stories about themselves."

"She's like a private investigator," Darla bragged.

"So say a guy's a serial killer," Donna posed. "You can find that out?"

"Only if he has a criminal record," Harlee said. "All my research is done using public databases. I can find out a person's real age, marital history, divorce information, real estate worth, military record, and sometimes even employment past—stuff like that."

"Hell, girl, if I were single, I'd pay you to do it. Thank God I have Trevor." Spying the rock on Donna's wedding finger, Harlee assumed Trevor was her husband.

"You really are like a private investigator," Maddy said.

"Right?" Darla reached for a cucumber sandwich. "These are so good."

"Feel free to put the word out. I'm always looking for clients." Harlee wanted to mention that Darla was also looking for clients, but she didn't want to embarrass her friend. Darla had revealed that her dad had been forced to pick up some of her hours. Business was that bad.

After they finished gorging themselves on finger food, Darla went back to the barbershop and Harlee and her mom headed for Grizzly Peak. On their way, Harlee tried to ring Colin, but no answer.

"Maybe he's in his shop and can't hear the phone," she said, directing her mother to go past the Roberts' log cabin to Colin's house. Leigh's SUV took the jagged road a heck of lot better than Harlee's Mini.

As they dipped down Colin's driveway, Leigh hummed her appreciation. "This is lovely."

"He built it. Can you believe it?" Harlee hopped out of the passenger seat and knocked on the door. "Let's go around back."

Sure enough, she could see Colin in the workshop through the window. This time, Neko Case's twangy voice boomed through the speakers while Colin sanded the top of a table.

She opened the door just enough to pop her head inside. "Hi. I brought my mom. Is it okay if we come in?"

A dog started barking and Colin yelled, "Quiet, Max."

He turned off the iPod and tried to finger comb his thick, shaggy hair. "Come on in. He's friendly."

"I didn't know you had a dog," Harlee said, crouching down to pet Max, who sat at her feet, swinging his tail.

"Uh . . . He's new. I found him at a job site. So far, no one's come forward to claim him." He tugged the dog by his collar to a spot near the cast-iron stove. "Lie down, boy." Max did a few turns and plopped down on a corduroy doggy bed that looked brand-new.

With the fire going, the room felt thirty degrees warmer than it did outside. Colin had clearly shed some layers. A ski jacket dangled from a hook and a thick sweater hung over a chair, leaving him to work in a pair of cargo pants and a snug, long-sleeved waffle-weave T-shirt that stretched across his broad chest. Harlee had always known Colin was fit. But until now, she'd never realized just how ripped Grizzly Adams was. Besides truly impressive shoulders and washboard abs, his arms bulged with muscles.

He caught her gaping and self-consciously brushed away specks of sawdust. She introduced her mom, who'd been too busy browsing through the furniture to notice that her daughter was having a moment. An OMG-my-neighbor-is-hot moment.

Colin turned his attention to Leigh. "Nice to meet you."

She glided over to where he was standing and gave him a big hug. Harlee would've liked to have caught Colin's stunned expression on camera.

"Thank you for being such a wonderful neighbor to my daughter. Harlee told me how helpful you've been. Harvey and I wanted her to move home when she lost her job. But she insisted on coming here to the mountains."

Thanks, Mom.

Besides Darla, Harlee didn't need the whole town knowing that she'd gotten canned from the paper. News in these parts traveled faster than an avalanche. By tomorrow, all of Nugget would know she was a loser.

Colin seemed to sense that Leigh had given away more than she should have, because he looked at Harlee with those caramel brown eyes as if to say, *"Hey, it happens to the best of us. Don't sweat it. Your secret is safe with me."*

"Your furniture is absolutely exquisite," Leigh continued, examining a row of rocking chairs. "And your house ... Harlee says you built it yourself."

"Would you like to see the inside?" Colin asked, and you could've knocked Harlee over with a feather. Other than the generous—yet slightly bizarre—shower offer, he'd never invited her in.

"I would love to," Leigh gushed.

They followed him through the back door into the mudroom, a generous space off the kitchen with built-it cubbies and racks that held snow boots, cross-country skis, and fishing equipment. The kitchen was equally impressive with inset cabinets and stone countertops.

As he guided them into the dining room, Leigh oohed and aahed over a pine sideboard and a massive trestle table Colin had built.

"Do you entertain a lot?" Leigh asked.

"Nah." He let his gaze fall to the floor.

"With such an amazing place like this, you should show it off."

"Mom"—Harlee nudged—"let's see the rest of the house."

Colin flashed her a faint smile, which she took for gratitude, and led them into the great room. The homey scent of wood smoke filled the air. The stone fireplace was so big that Harlee could stand up in it. She noticed there was another dog bed in front of the hearth and earlier had spied stoneware crocks in the kitchen for food and water. Lucky Max had found a good home.

Harlee ran her hand over the interior walls—massive hand-hewn logs, dovetailed at the corners. When they walked into the entryway, she stared agog at the winding staircase. "You did this?"

"I had some help from my stepsister's husband. He's a master carpenter."

"And the beautiful paint colors. Did you pick those, Colin?" Leigh asked.

"That was Fiona . . . my stepsister," he said, and Harlee heard affection in his voice. She had a feeling that Fiona was important to him. "She's a sculptor with a good sense for color. Me, I would've painted everything white."

Leigh laughed. "It's a very special home, Colin. Just spectacular."

"Thank you."

"Did Harlee tell you about my store?"

He looked at Harlee for guidance.

"No, Mom. I didn't tell him."

"It's just a small home interiors shop where I sell everything from soaps to linens. And I'd love to carry a couple of your pieces—maybe one of the rockers and one of the smaller farm tables. You do have a seller's permit, don't you?" She waved her hand through the air. "If not, we can figure a way to get around it."

"I do," he blurted.

"Excellent. Then let's step back into your shop and make a deal."

Chapter 5

Darla sat at a makeshift desk at the back of her father's barbershop applying her press-on nails, embellishing each one with a smiley face. Why? She didn't know. It wasn't like she had a whole lot to smile about. Other than a couple of kid haircuts and a wash and blowout, business was in the toilet.

She stuck the last nail to her pinky and just for the hell of it painted it with a frownie. She should've done them all that way. The bell over the door chimed and about the best-looking man she'd ever seen came strutting in.

"Owen around?"

"No. He's fishing. But I'm his daughter, Darla, and I do hair."

"Yeah? He won't think I'm cheating on him if I let you trim me up?" He turned his face from left to right in the mirror, stroking his scruff.

"Nope." Darla smiled. "My dad's trying to retire."

"Owen?" The man blew a raspberry. "What'll the Nugget Mafia do without him?"

Darla knew that was the nickname of the band of old farts who hung out in the barbershop. One of them was her dad's best friend and Nugget's mayor, Dink Caruthers. "They'll probably hang out at the bowling alley."

"Nah. They'll hang out at my gas station, haranguing me night and day."

She laughed. "So you're the rich guy who bought the Nugget Gas and Go and designs custom motorcycles?" Owen had told her all about him. Her dad constantly bragged that he'd taken "the boy" under his wing and showed him how to run a business.

"That would be me." He stuck out his hand. "Griffin Parks at your service."

"So you want me to crisp up your lines?" It would screw up her nails, but finally a real client.

"Sure." He climbed into the leather barber chair that Owen had been doing haircuts in since before Darla was born. "Just clean me up."

"Come over to the shampoo bowl."

"Owen never shampoos me."

"Well, today you're getting the works." She was a stylist, not a barber. No way was she giving him a dry cut.

Griffin followed her to the sink and let her wash his hair. "That feels great," he said as Darla massaged his scalp.

She'd stocked the barbershop with premium salon shampoos and had plans to sell all kinds of styling products. There wasn't any place in Nugget to buy quality hair-care items and she figured she could make bank selling them out of the barbershop. But so far that had been as much of a bust as her career as a stylist.

Darla pumped a dollop of conditioner into the palm of her hand and rubbed it through Griffin's sandy blond hair. "You bought Sierra Heights too, didn't you?"

Nugget had fought the luxury planned community tooth and nail, fearing that it would turn the town, which was filled mostly with ranchers and railroad workers, into Lake Tahoe. The developers had won, only to wind up bankrupt. Word had it that Griffin purchased the development for half its value.

"You know anyone who wants to buy a house?"

Yeah, me.

Living with her dad at twenty-seven wasn't exactly what she'd had in mind when she'd moved here. But until business picked up at the barbershop, she was thankful to have the free rent.

"No one I know could afford one of those gargantuan homes," she said.

"I know what you mean. I'm doing a big open house next week-end. Come on by and bring your friends. At least the place'll look crowded. We might even convince the city folk that the homes are selling like hotcakes."

"Are sales that bad?" Darla turned on the sprayer, waited until the water turned warm, and rinsed Griffin's hair.

"Too soon to tell. We just got the models spiffed up and the sales office up and running. I've got high hopes."

Darla wrapped a towel around his head and directed him to get back in the barber's chair. He had a great head of hair and she was looking forward to giving it a little more shape. As skilled a barber as Owen was, he hadn't kept up on modern styles. Darla swished a cape around him and clipped away.

"Owen always wants to shave off my whiskers," Griffin said. "But I like my whiskers."

She put her hand on his shoulder to reassure him. "Don't worry. I'll just even them out."

"You think he'll really retire?" Griffin started to turn around in the chair, but Darla held him still.

"He'll probably stay on a few days a week. But he's sixty-three and deserves a break. Part of the reason I came here is because I thought he'd work himself into the grave without help."

"So," Griffin asked, "how's it working out so far?"

"The truth, not so good. People seem reluctant to give me a chance."

Griffin watched her through the mirror. "Give it time. This town has issues with change. But they eventually come around. When I first got here, your dad accused me of being a drug dealer."

"Get out." She laughed, and then asked, "Are you?"

"Actually, I'm a high-end hooker."

Darla laughed again, enjoying his personality as much as his looks. "Do you have a girlfriend, Griffin Parks?"

He was quiet for a few minutes, and Darla wondered if he thought she was trying to pick up on him, because she wasn't. That would be completely unprofessional.

"Yes and no," Griffin finally said. "We're supposed to be taking space and seeing people if we want to. She doesn't even live here anymore."

"But?" Darla continued snipping Griffin's hair.

"I don't really want to see anyone but her."

"So why don't you tell her that?" Darla thought men for the most part were idiots.

"I have to stick to the bargain—at least for a year," he said, and she wanted to ask why they'd made such a ridiculous bargain, but figured she didn't know him well enough yet.

"How 'bout you? You seeing anyone?"

"Nope," she said.

Griffin chuckled. "Not a lot to choose from here in Nugget—at least not in our age bracket."

"Maybe we should get a singles group together to go bowling," Darla suggested. "I'll bring my friend Harlee."

"With a name like Harlee, I like her already." According to Owen, Griffin was a motorcycle fanatic.

Darla took out the clippers to clean up Griffin's whiskers when Wyatt walked in the door. He must've been on duty because he wore his police uniform. As soon as he noticed Griffin in the chair, Wyatt scowled.

"I see you're busy," he said in a clipped tone. "I'll come back another time."

"I'm almost done, Wyatt, if you want to wait."

But he'd already sailed through the door. Darla shook her head.

"I guess he was in a hurry," Griffin said. "When do you want to do this bowling thing? Because I've got to tell you, I love your old man and the rest of the mafia. I love playing pinochle with them. But I need to get with some people my own age before I start driving an Oldsmobile and watching *Gunsmoke* reruns."

"Let me talk to Harlee and we'll come up with a night."

If circumstances were different, Wyatt would be invited into their group since he fit their demographic. But if circumstances were different, Darla would be married to the jerk.

"This cannot be happening," Harlee yelled into the darkness.

She'd just gotten cozy in her flannel pj's, turned on the computer to do some cyber-sleuthing for a client, and run a little background check on her eccentric neighbor just for the fun of it. Because who knew? Maybe Colin Burke was a high-profile business titan who'd given up fame and fortune to make furniture and couldn't go to dinner with her for fear someone might recognize him.

Yeah, right.

That's when the lights started to flicker off and the rest of the power went dead. Which meant no heat.

Now she'd have to go outside in the snow to check the circuit box. Her mom had left on Sunday afternoon, missing the storm by less than twenty-four hours. Harlee wished she was still here. Being alone in the pitch-black woods gave her the creeps. She came down the steep loft stairs on her butt, afraid she'd fall down and break her neck. In the front hall, she found her boots, struggled to put them on in the dark, grabbed her jacket, and felt her way into the garage, where she'd left the flashlight. After fumbling around, she found the Maglite next to the hot-water heater, clicked it on, and went in search of the breaker panel.

Although she'd seen her father come out here many times, she hadn't exactly paid attention to what he did with the switches. As an experiment she slid one breaker off and on again. Nothing happened. She tried a few others to no avail, warming her hands inside her pockets to keep them from turning to ice. Once they no longer felt numb, she flicked all the switches at once. Still nothing.

Crap. It was a real outage. She went back inside the house, shaking the snow from her jacket, planning to build a fire, when the phone rang.

"You okay?" Colin's voice came reassuringly across the line.

"Did you lose your power too?" she asked.

"Yeah, but I have a backup generator. How 'bout you?"

"Uh . . . not that I know of," Harlee said. "I'm surprised the phone's still working."

"It probably won't for long. What are you doing for heat?"

"I was just about to—" *Damn.*

"Harlee, what's wrong?"

"My flashlight just went out." She opened up the Maglite and wacked the batteries, but it still didn't work.

"I'll come over and get you." He hung up before she could tell him to stay home, where it was safe and warm.

She could've made do, even lit a fire in the dark, but she'd be happy for the company. With the wind howling and the tall pines swaying like they could snap in half, the storm was a little scary. On the couch, she wrapped herself in a throw blanket and waited for his truck lights to stream through her front window.

When she heard the rumble of an engine come down the hill, Harlee opened the door. With the plow attached to Colin's truck he cleared the driveway, parked in front, and jumped out of the cab as Max came bounding into the house.

"Hey, boy." Harlee grabbed the dog around the neck and gave him a kiss on the head.

"You ready to go?" Colin asked, flashing his big-beam flashlight and eyeing her pajamas. She still had on her snow boots.

"We're going to your place?" She'd assumed he would come build her fire, sit for a while, and go home.

"I have power. You don't."

"Okay." It made sense. "Let me borrow your light to pack a few things."

He and Max made themselves at home on her couch while she went into the bedroom. She emerged fifteen minutes later with a satchel and cosmetics case.

He cocked his brows.

"What?" she said defensively. "I have a nighttime regimen."

"Does that include a coat?" He continued to goggle at her pajamas. She checked to make sure a button hadn't come undone.

"I'll get it," she said, leaving her bags in the entryway while she grabbed the jacket she'd hung in the mudroom after jiggering with the circuit box, and locked the back door.

When she came back, he'd already loaded her luggage into the truck along with Max. He helped her into the passenger seat and they slowly drove to his house, clearing snow as they went.

"This is quite a storm," she said.

"This is nothing. Just a little autumn snow." He looked over at her and squinted. "I've been wondering this whole time, are those pink flamingos?"

She looked down at her flannel bottoms. "Yeah. So? What's wrong with them?"

"Nothing." But even in the dim light of the truck she could tell he was smirking.

"What do you sleep in that's so great?"

"Not pink flamingos," he said, pressing the remote stuck to his visor to open the garage door.

Max shot out of the truck, did his business and came trotting back in. Colin closed the garage and carried Harlee's bags inside the house, switching on the light. Nice. It was toasty, too.

He led her down a hallway into a spacious guest room with a rag rug, a big log bed, and a down comforter that looked so soft and comfy it would be a pleasure to crawl into.

"This is beautiful," she said. "Better than a hotel."

"You warm enough?"

"Mm-hmm. Are you going to bed now?"

He shrugged. "I might watch some TV."

"You mind if I join you?" It seemed too early to go sleep.

"No," he said, and Harlee couldn't tell whether he was just being polite or if he wanted her company. The guy was such a damned enigma and possibly the most socially inept person she'd ever met. She still didn't know why he wouldn't go to dinner with her. What did he think? She'd jump him on the way to the restaurant?

At least she didn't have to worry about him making a pass at her.

"I'll be right out." She wanted to clean up a bit. "The bathroom?"

"Right in there." He pointed to a door that she had assumed was a closet. Wow, an en suite setup. It really was like a hotel.

"Great."

After Colin left her alone in the room, she sat on the edge of the bed, removed her snow boots, and rifled through her suitcase for her slippers. Good thing she'd left the matching pink flamingo ones at home and brought her Uggs. She'd never hear the end of it.

In the bathroom, she unpacked her cosmetic bag, washed her face, brushed her teeth, combed her hair, and spritzed on a drop of perfume. Why? She had no idea. She looked in the mirror to see if it was obvious that she didn't have a bra on. Because who wears a bra under their pajamas? She decided to hell with it; she'd leave it off.

Harlee found him in the living room building a roaring fire. He'd taken off his flannel and was wearing a green henley over his jeans. The man really did have about the best body she'd ever seen.

"You turned off the lights." She smiled to herself, noting all the lit candles. Maybe Colin wasn't such a dud after all.

"I don't want to use up the generator. Who knows how long this power outage will last."

"Oh," she said, a little embarrassed for imagining that he might've wanted to be romantic. "Want me to make hot chocolate?"

"Uh, I don't have chocolate."

"Okay. How 'bout tea?"

"Don't have that either."

Thinking three's the charm, Harlee asked, "You have wine?"

"I don't drink," he said, and scooted Max down the couch so he could have the arm. Harlee watched him stretch out his long legs. "There's milk if you're thirsty."

She went into the kitchen and checked the cupboards. Lots of canned soups, chili, and stews. In fact he had more treats for the dog than he did for himself. The refrigerator had a lot of leftovers, milk, and apple juice. "Hey, I can make hot apple cider," she said.

"Whatever you want."

She grabbed a pot off the rack hanging over the center island, poured in the juice, and put it on the stove top to boil. From the pantry she actually found allspice, cloves, and cinnamon sticks—odd, since Grizzly Adams didn't seem like the baking type. And tossed that in, too. She grabbed an orange from a well-stocked fruit basket—at least he wouldn't die of scurvy—and tossed a bit of the peel into the pot.

As soon as the mixture came to a boil, she turned down the heat and let the liquid simmer for a few minutes before pouring it into two mugs.

"Here you go." She put down a napkin on the coffee table and set the cup in front of Colin, who was channel surfing.

"What do you want to watch?" he asked.

"I don't care. What do you usually watch this time of night?" Most of the guys she knew would've said porn.

"Nothing. I'm usually asleep."

"Well, why didn't you say you wanted to go to bed?"

"Because you seemed like you wanted to hang out."

She smiled because for all his weirdness, he really was very sweet. "Drink your cider before it gets cold."

He dutifully took a sip. "It's good."

"You really like it? Or are you just saying that because you think that's what I want to hear?"

"I really like it." He took a few more sips. "So you lost your job, huh?"

"Yes." She frowned. "Please don't spread it around. Other than Darla, you're the only person in Nugget who knows."

"What happened?"

She put her mug down. "I didn't do anything wrong. I was . . . I am . . . a great reporter. But the paper is losing money and they had to reduce staff. It's a union shop. Last ones hired are the first ones fired, according to the rules."

"Did you like the job?"

"I loved it. It was who I am." She heard her voice tremble. "I'm looking around. But it's tough right now. Just about every paper in the country is downsizing."

"Why didn't you move in with your parents while you're looking?"

She blew out a breath. "Honestly, it would've made me feel more like a loser."

"You're not a loser, Harlee. You lost your job through no fault of your own. These things happen."

She sniffled and swatted at her eyes. "Thank you for saying that. This whole thing has taken a toll on my confidence. You'll probably find this hard to believe, but I used to be really outgoing."

She could see him smothering a smile. "You don't say. What . . . uh . . . How are you getting by in the meantime?" Harlee could tell that he didn't like prying, but she didn't mind.

"I have a business I'm trying to get off the ground. So far it's going okay. But I sort of lived high on the hog in San Francisco and it's caught up with me." A skosh of an understatement, but it was better than saying she was swimming in debt.

His brown eyes warmed and he smiled at her. Something about that smile melted her insides. She'd never been around someone who was so nonjudgmental.

"I get the feeling that you're the type of person who makes things happen. As far as the layoff," he said, "just a minor setback."

"What about you?" She leaned her head against the back of the couch, feeling sleepy. But she didn't want their conversation to end. "How'd you get into furniture making?"

He looked away, gazing into the fire. "It's just something I like to do. And people seem to think my stuff is nice enough to buy."

"Are you kidding? Colin, you should be taking your work to trade shows and furniture conventions all over the country. I'm serious. You could make a lot of money."

"I'm not all that ambitious," he said, and she could've sworn she saw a flicker of sadness. "I did sell a piece to Della James's manager."

"Get out! I heard she was here for some cookbook photo shoot. Oh my God, Colin."

He chuckled. "Emily Mathews, Clay McCreedy's fiancée, was the editor and she used some of my pieces as props. She said I'll be listed in the book on some sort of a resource page."

"That's awesome." He tried to look like no-big-deal, but she could tell he was really proud. "When's the book coming out?"

"Christmastime," he said.

"Colin, you better be ready. That book's likely to be a *New York Times* best seller. You're going to get orders up the wazoo."

"I doubt that," he said sheepishly. "You tired?"

"No." She stifled a yawn. "You?"

"Nah," he said, but she could tell he could barely keep his eyes open.

"Hey, Colin, you want to go bowling with us this week? Darla called and she and some guy named Griffin Parks want to get a group together. Do you know Griffin?"

"I know who he is." Harlee got the sense that Colin didn't like him. "I don't bowl."

"Uh, it's not like I bowl either," she said. "It's just something to do. Get out with people. Have fun. It's sort of the only thing to do in town and it's relatively cheap."

He started to get up. "I can't, Harlee. I think I'm gonna hit the hay."

"Why can't you?" She tugged at his arm to pull him back down. "It's just bowling with a group of people. It's not like it's a date or anything. Jeez, Colin, you're starting to give me a complex."

"It has nothing to do with you, Harlee." He deliberated, then said, "I have demophobia."

"What's that?" But she figured it must be some sort of fear disorder, which explained a lot.

"I'm afraid of crowds," he said matter-of-factly, but his face told a different story. Shame. "And while the Ponderosa's bowling alley isn't exactly Mardi Gras, there's enough people to give me a panic attack."

"That's why you wouldn't let me take you to dinner?"

"I can't do restaurants," he said, his eyes downcast. "Occasionally, I'll have to meet someone at the Ponderosa for business. It takes me an hour just to work up the courage to go in. Once I'm there, I pretty much feel like I'm going to die from lack of oxygen."

"That's awful," she said, unable to imagine what it must be like for him. "But there must be a treatment for . . . What did you call it?"

"Demophobia. There are breathing exercises and therapy. I've done both."

"It doesn't work?" she asked.

He shrugged and she reached out to touch his arm. He just seemed so mortified and disgusted with himself.

"Colin, people have all kinds of phobias. You have nothing to be embarrassed about. Maybe, together, we could work on it. I could be your wingman."

He leaned into her until he was barely a whisper away. "You're a nice woman, Harlee. Too nice for me."

She thought Colin might kiss her, but he suddenly pulled away. "Time to go to bed," he said, and for a crazy second she imagined he might have meant together.

"I'm too tired to move," she said, sprawling out on the couch.

And just like that two strong hands slipped under her, and the next thing Harlee knew, Colin was carrying her to the guest room.

She snuggled her head against his rock-solid chest and let out a self-conscious giggle. "I can walk."

"Almost there," he said, and gently dropped her on the bed. He took off her slippers and pulled the comforter back. "Get under."

Harlee crawled under the blankets and patted the side of the bed for him to sit. "Thank you for letting me stay here tonight. And thank you for telling me about the demophobia. I'm sorry, Colin. I know it must be awful."

Tomorrow she planned to research the disorder on the Internet. It certainly didn't sound like something impossible to overcome. He just needed a friend to help him.

He brushed a few strands of hair away from her face and again Harlee got the distinct impression he wanted to kiss her. "I have to leave early for work," he said.

She could tell he was warring with himself, so she tilted her head back in clear invitation. "Me too," she whispered.

"For your business?"

Shut up, Colin, and just kiss me. "Mm-hmm."

"What is your business, exactly?" He stretched out on the bed and moved an inch closer.

She let out a sigh. "I run background checks on people's girlfriends and boyfriends."

"Why?" He propped up on one elbow.

She rolled into him, hoping to stop all this talking nonsense. "To make sure they're not already married, wanted by the FBI, or have a criminal record. Boring stuff like that."

Okay, she told herself, no more chitchatting. She reached for him, hoping to take matters into her own hands, but he'd gone stiff. And not in the good way.

Just like that, the man had turned cold. An iceberg would more aptly describe him.

"Goodnight, Harlee." He got to his feet and walked out the door.

Chapter 6

Colin lay in his bed, staring up at the open-beamed ceiling, hoping that the answers to his messed-up life would magically appear. Specifically, the answer to why he'd been playing kissy face with a woman like Harlee Roberts, when nothing good could come of it?

He rolled over on his side and reached down to pat Max. "She sure is pretty, though. Isn't she, boy?"

She was pretty without knowing it. Well, maybe she knew it a little, Colin admitted. The woman had too much confidence otherwise. And why shouldn't she? She was classy and educated—a big-time reporter, and come to find out, some kind of investigator, no less.

Just what he needed.

Her family was obviously the wholesome sort, like the kind you saw on television sitcoms. Hell, her mother looked like she'd just stepped out of a lifestyle magazine.

Whereas, his mother had been a drunk. Not always. She'd once been a struggling actress who'd had limited success, but never hit the big time. The antidote to her disappointment became the bottom of a Tanqueray bottle. Then she'd met Sam. Together, they drank themselves into sheer oblivion.

Sam and his daughter, Fiona, had come into his life when he was ten. Fiona, six years his senior, used to come to stay with them on alternate weekends. But when the couple's drinking got too bad, his stepsister would load him into her Corolla and drive them to her mom

Janis's cottage in Topanga Canyon. He spent more time there than he did in his own home.

When he was fourteen, Fiona went away to art school in Rhode Island. He'd thought her moving across the country was the end of the world. Little did he know the worst was yet to come.

When Colin had first gotten out of Donovan Correction Facility, he'd moved in with Fiona and Steve, her husband. He'd done woodworking in prison as part of his vocational training, but it was Steve who'd taught him everything he knew. While hauling Steve's cabinets and furniture halfway across the state, there'd been plenty of women. One-night stands he'd met in dive bars and at truck stops. Before the demophobia had set in. They hadn't been interested in his life story. And the only thing he'd been interested in was making up for lost time.

When he'd moved to Nugget and built the house, Fiona had tried to convince him to date. She wanted him to find a nice woman, settle down and have a family.

"*Col, everyone has a past,*" she'd insisted.

But his past made other peoples' skeletons look like dollar-store Halloween decorations. That's why someone like Harlee Roberts was out of the question. He fell asleep by telling himself that, over and over again, like counting sheep.

The next morning, the power was back on. Colin shut down the generator, ran ten miles on the treadmill, jumped in the shower, and made himself a green smoothie. He didn't want to disturb Harlee, so he wrote her a note that he'd cleared a path with the snowplow for her to get home and could she please keep an eye on Max. Ordinarily, he took the dog with him. But the temperature had dipped below freezing again and the ground remained blanketed in snow. Not the best conditions for a dog on a construction site.

Halfway down Grizzly Peak, his cell phone rang. It was Pat, calling to say that the crew was taking a snow day, but could Colin check the site to make sure everything held up in the storm. It made sense, since Pat lived in Sierraville.

"You want me to meet with Sophie and Mariah—go over the change orders?" Colin asked.

"Yeah," Pat said. "That would save me a trip and at least the whole day won't be a loss. Thanks, Colin."

"No problem." He clicked off, and continued scraping the snow off the road.

On his way to the site, he called Sophie to set up the meeting. He managed to convince her that they should get together at the Lumber Baron instead of the Ponderosa. Fewer distractions, he told her. Colin knew that the Ponderosa would be packed for breakfast on a weekday, whereas the Lumber Baron would be practically empty. Probably just a few business travelers who'd gotten stuck in the storm.

After checking the project, which, other than requiring the reapplication of a few sheets of loose Tyvek, had withstood the weather, Colin headed to the inn. He parked in the square and climbed up the stairs to the veranda, where he paced back and forth, peeking inside the windows.

Rhys Shepard, the police chief, came out the door and gave Colin a funny look. "You want to come inside? It's like thirty degrees out here."

"Uh . . . I've got my work clothes on. Might not be a good idea if there are guests eating in the dining room."

"No guests. Last one left a half hour ago. My wife just put on a second pot of coffee. I suggest you get yourself some." He walked across the square to the police station, shaking his head.

Colin went inside and not for the first time marveled at the rich beauty of the Victorian. The elaborately carved staircase alone filled him with pride. He himself had stripped the wood down to its natural grain after someone had painted it putrid pink. A year ago, the place had been an absolute wreck.

"Colin!" Maddy rushed down the hall and enveloped him in a hug. "What brings you here today?"

"I'm meeting with Sophie and Mariah on the house. We decided it would be quieter to talk at the inn."

"Is everything okay?" She looked worried.

"Yeah, everything's great. In fact, we're ahead of schedule. This is just routine status stuff, like getting them to quit dragging their feet on ordering kitchen appliances and to go over their change orders."

"Good." She sounded relieved. "With Sophie and Mariah's baby coming, I know they're anxious to get into the house."

Colin smiled. "Speaking of, how are you doing?"

"I'm doing fine." She mechanically touched her protruding belly. "All the first-trimester sickness is gone. I can actually look at food without throwing up. Colin, you want some coffee and some of Emily's banana bread?"

"I wouldn't turn it down." All he'd had was the smoothie.

Maddy tugged him into the kitchen, another room he'd restored from top to bottom, and told him to sit at one of the island stools while she poured him a cup.

"Cream? Sugar?"

"Black's fine," he said.

"How about that storm?" she asked. "Did you lose power?"

"Yep. But I have a generator."

"That's good. We've got one here, and at home. Before Shep died we figured it was a necessity."

Toward the end, the old man had been pretty messed up and needed all kinds of medical devices to keep him comfortable. Rhys and Maddy had hired full-time caretakers for him so he could live at home.

"I was worried about your new neighbor, Harlee," Maddy went on. "I had Rhys send Wyatt up Grizzly Peak last night to do a welfare check, but he said she wasn't there. Do you think she might've gone home with her mom?"

"No," he said, and cleared his throat. "She stayed with me."

"Oh?" He didn't think Maddy's smile could get any bigger. "Something going on there?"

"Yeah," he said. "I have a generator and she doesn't."

"That's all? Because she's really pretty and obviously very smart. Do you know she's a newspaper reporter and has her own business?"

"Yep," was all Colin said.

"So? You're not interested?"

"We're friends, Maddy. I don't think her stay here is too permanent."

She gave him a you're-so-full-of-bull look, but let the topic of his romantic life drop. But not the topic of Harlee Roberts.

"What do you think of DataDate, her business? I told Rhys about it and he wasn't too keen on it. Then again, he's a cop. They think they're the only ones qualified to investigate people. Although, I have to say, what if she gives someone her stamp of approval and he turns out to be a murderer?"

The conversation had veered into intensely uncomfortable territory, so Colin just shrugged. "I think I hear Sophie and Mariah."

Sure enough, the two women entered the kitchen, putting a merciful end to the discussion.

Ninety minutes later he drove back up Grizzly Peak, passing Harlee's cabin. Smoke rose from her chimney and he wondered if she had his dog. When he got home, a big basket sat on his kitchen counter. Before looking inside, he read the card.

Thanks for rescuing me last night and letting me stay in your ab-fab guest room. A little something to return the favor, because, dude, you live like a freakin' monk.
XOXO
Harlee
P.S. Max is at my house.

He pawed through the basket, finding powdered cocoa for hot chocolate, marshmallows, a box of assorted tea bags, a jug of organic apple cider, mulling spices, microwave popcorn, and a tin of shortbread cookies. Colin put everything away, jumped in his truck, and went down the hill to Harlee's.

She answered the door wearing a pair of tan skinny pants, a long, clingy sweater, and furry boots that came up to her knees. Her hair was fixed and she had glossy stuff on her lips. Max was sacked out in front of the fire. At the sound of Colin, the dog lifted his head, cocked it to one side, and came loping toward him.

"How you doing, fellow?" Colin gave the dog a good rubbing.

"Hi," Harlee said. "I guess you want Max back."

He nodded. "Thanks for the care package. Totally unnecessary, but very nice."

"It was my pleasure. You off early?"

"The crew didn't want to work in the snow. How 'bout you?" He wondered why she was all dressed up and what was with the pile of paperwork on her dining room table. It hadn't been there the night before.

She followed the direction of his gaze and blew out a puff of air. "Those are bills I'm trying to sort out. You want a drink or something to eat?"

"Water's good."

It was unusual for him to ever make himself at home at someone else's house, but for whatever reason, Colin felt comfortable here. He grabbed a seat at the dining room table while Harlee poured him a glass of water, and furtively glanced at the bills.

Apparently not that slyly, because she said, "I'm trying to decide which ones I should pay now and which ones can wait."

"I would suspect phone, electric, and propane can't wait," he said.

"Yep." She sighed. "I'm thinking more in terms of Nordstrom versus Macy's."

"You mind if I take a look?"

"Go ahead, knock yourself out," Harlee said. That's what he liked about her; she was an open book. Nothing like him.

He examined the bills, which she'd put into some semblance of order, based on due dates. "Whoa."

"I know, right?"

He looked up at her sympathetically and went back to the mound of late notices. "Harlee, you're paying five hundred bucks a month on your car." *Which, by the way, is a piece of crap.*

"Yeah, that's how much cars cost," she said defensively. "And San Francisco has a parking shortage. The Mini fits into teeny, tiny spaces where no other car can."

"Okay, but you're in Nugget now. Plenty of parking. And the Mini doesn't have all-wheel drive." He pointedly looked out the window where a layer of frost still blanketed the forest. "Sell it—hell, return it—and buy a used vehicle for cash that will get you around in the snow. One less payment."

"But I love that car. It's so cute."

He held up the bill. "Not cute. Sucks."

To that she let out a laugh. Colin liked the girly sound of it. He pretty much liked everything about her.

He held up one of the department-store bills. "Pay this one first. They're charging you eighteen percent interest. The other one is twelve. But, honestly, you should try to get a debt-consolidation loan. One payment for everything, with a lower interest rate."

"Without a job? How am I going to get that?" She handed him the glass of water and stood there with her hands on her hips. Colin noticed she had nice hips. Nice legs. Nice butt. Nice breasts. Nice everything.

"What about your business?" he asked.

"I've sort of been doing everything under the table." She sat across from him.

"Maybe your parents would cosign for you," he said.

"Uh-uh. I don't even want them to know. I'll figure it out." She looked at the clock in the kitchen. "Shoot, I have to go. I told Darla I'd hang with her at the barbershop. We're going to plan that bowling outing I told you about."

"Okay." He got up and took his glass to the sink. "You want to take my truck? I really don't recommend you drive the Mini Cooper in the snow."

"Isn't most of it plowed?"

"Yes. But the roads are slick and icy."

"It's just to town. I'll go slow. Oh, and Colin, I read up on demophobia. You need cognitive behavioral therapy. It's a special kind of—"

"I know," he said.

She frowned. "You've done it and it didn't work?"

"Yeah." Nothing had worked.

"What about acupuncture?" She came into the kitchen and locked on him with those big baby blues. God, a man could drown in those eyes.

He gently maneuvered her out of the way so he could get by. "I don't think so, Harlee."

"Are you afraid of needles?"

"No." He dragged a hand through his hair. "I just know it won't work."

"You can't know until you've tried it. I read on the Internet that they've had really good results. We could find a reputable acupuncturist in Reno."

"Harlee, why is this so important to you?" he asked.

"Because you're my friend and I want to help you."

That left him with a lump in his throat. In his entire lifetime the only people who'd ever helped him had been Fiona, Janis, and Steve. Not even his own mother.

"I could go with you," she said. "Hold your hand."

He might do it for that reason alone. "We'll see," he said, knowing that he could handle the needles.

The problem was handling the woman and not letting her make him wish for things that he couldn't have.

Chapter 7

"Jeez, how much longer do we have to do this?" Darla whispered to Harlee as she tried to hold her downward dog position.

"Suck it up, girlfriend. You're the one who thought it was a good idea to sign up."

"I need exercise," Darla said. "I'm like a total gut queen. All I've done since I've gotten here is eat." Because every day was snack day in Nugget. She hadn't had one client since Griffin. Not unless you counted the blue-hair who'd wanted Darla to shampoo and comb out her shih tzu. So she ate out of boredom. Out of frustration.

Pam, the too-perky yoga instructor, had the class move into a downward-dog split. "Not you, Maddy." Apparently, pregnant women weren't supposed to do downward dogs of any kind. Darla suddenly wished she were pregnant.

"For the rest of you, I want to see that leg straight up in the air." Pam demonstrated like she was a freakin' contortionist.

"I swear I'll kill her," Darla said, and Harlee began to laugh.

"You girls okay back there?" Pam asked, and told everyone to assume the dolphin pose.

Darla nodded as she brought her forearms to the ground and stuck her ass up in the air.

"I'm going back there with them." Donna Thurston picked up her mat and lined it up next to Harlee's and Darla's. "What's so funny?"

Harlee started to laugh again, this time so hard Darla thought she might choke.

"You're going to get us kicked out of the class," Darla muttered.

There were a few titters at the front of the studio from Maddy and Emily. Soon everyone in the class, except for the instructor, was laughing like hyenas. It reminded Darla of when she'd been in grade school and had to leave class for getting the giggles.

"For God's sake," Pam said. "Should we call it a day?"

"Hell yes," Donna said.

"Fine."

"I'm sorry," Harlee said. "I don't know what came over me. I really didn't mean to interrupt the class."

Pam brushed her apology off with a wave. "Don't worry, it happens sometimes."

Maddy and Emily were wiping tears off their faces, trying to control themselves. The rest of the women sat cross-legged on their mats while Pam did a few quick stretches. Darla was a little awestruck by how limber the woman was. She had to be in her forties, though you'd never know it from her body. Or from her stamina. Darla had seen Pam many times running herd over half a dozen little girls in tutus. It probably beat running herd over five obnoxious adults who couldn't keep from getting the giggles.

"You and Clay pick a date yet?" Donna broke the silence.

"June," Emily said, and her whole face lit up. "We're doing it at the ranch, under a big white tent with lots of good food."

"And an open bar, right?" Donna scooted closer to Emily.

"Yep," Emily said, and Darla had never seen anyone look so happy. "Maddy and Sophie will have had their babies by then. Lots of babes at this shindig."

"Let's do something at the inn," Maddy said. "A shower or a bachelorette party, where we can take all the rooms and have a sleepover. My gift to the bride."

"Ooh, I like it," Pam said.

"I'll burger us, compliments of the Bun Boy," Donna chimed in. "Gracie and Ethel will want in, too."

"Of course," Emily said. "We can't have a party without the entire Baker's Dozen."

Darla knew that the Baker's Dozen was a local cooking club.

Maybe she and Harlee should join. God knew she could use some cooking lessons. She and her dad pretty much lived on frozen fish he'd caught. It was the only thing Owen seemed to know how to make and she was getting serious steelhead and salmon fatigue.

"I could do all of your hair," she exclaimed, wanting so badly to fit in. But her offer was met with silence.

And more silence.

Harlee came to the rescue. "Darla is an amazing stylist. Did you guys see the fabulous cut she gave Griffin Parks?"

Harlee hadn't even met Griffin yet. She only knew about his haircut because Darla had told her. Of course she'd meet him when they attended his open house at Sierra Heights on Saturday. Darla had volunteered her and Harlee to help show the models. Afterward they planned to go bowling.

"You cut Griff's hair?" Maddy asked, obviously sensing the awkwardness in the air.

"Mm-hmm," Darla said, wanting to change the subject before she felt completely humiliated.

"Have you seen all the great hair products she carries now?" Harlee asked, pimping Darla like she was Paul Mitchell. She loved Harlee for her loyalty, but her gushing rang a little desperate. For Darla.

"What brands do you carry?" Donna seemed genuinely interested.

Darla ticked off lines Donna had never heard of. Most of her products were new on the market. Only very contemporary metropolitan salons carried them. The companies were pretty snotty about whose shelves their items went on. Luckily, she'd become friendly with quite a few reps during her internship and they'd been willing to let her sell their merchandise in the barbershop.

Darla couldn't help but run her hands through Donna's hair. "You could use a little moisture. Your ends are brittle from color treatments." The color was good, but she needed a protein treatment, and fast.

She could feel Donna bristle and wished she'd kept her mouth shut.

"How does mine feel?" Emily asked, leaning her head toward Darla.

Better than Donna's. "Fine. But make sure you're only applying your conditioner from the ears down. Not on the scalp. That makes your hair dull."

"Really?" Emily said, and the other women gathered closer.

"I switch my shampoo brand every six to eight months," Pam said, clearly wanting validation.

"That's important," Darla said. "Also try to use milder shampoos—something with a lot of fatty acids and protein."

"Darla knows everything about this stuff," Harlee bragged.

"The thing is," Donna said, "we all get our hair done in Reno at a place I've been going to for fifteen years."

"I totally understand." It was starting to look to Darla like if she wanted to make inroads in this town it would have to be with the male population. Her dad's old clients. Basically, all that time she'd spent studying at a fancy salon would be wasted on giving ranchers and railroad workers buzz cuts.

After they left the yoga studio, Harlee said, "Don't get discouraged, Darla. There are other women in Nugget. Not everyone wants to travel forty-five minutes for a great stylist."

Darla let out a sigh. "I know. It's just that they're the popular girls."

"The popular girls?" Harlee laughed. "Where are we, in high school?"

"You know what I mean. I'm starting to think it was a mistake coming here." For far bigger reasons than her lack of business.

Every day she saw Wyatt coming and going from the police station. The sight of him, so manly in his uniform, was torturous. Not to mention that she thought about him every day—of what might've been, but would never happen now.

"Maybe I should've gotten a chair in a low-rent Sacramento salon until I built up a good clientele. Then I could've moved to a nicer one."

Harlee stopped in the middle of the square's greenbelt and put her hands on her hips. It was colder than the North freakin' Pole, so they both burrowed deeper into their down jackets. "You are so not giving this a chance. Businesses take time to get off the ground, Darla."

"Okay. Okay," she said, knowing that it would be easier to agree with Harlee than tell her the real reason she was having second thoughts about having moved to Nugget.

They walked the few remaining yards to the barbershop and

Harlee pulled her car keys out of her purse. "You want to drive to-gether to the open-house deal on Saturday?"

"Sure," Darla said. "I can't wait to see the development. My dad says the homes are like mansions. Last time I saw the place, they were just being built and the whole town had their panties in a bunch over it."

"Why?" Harlee asked.

"They were afraid Nugget was getting too built up. That it would lose its down-home charm." Darla made a noise of exasperation. "Anyway, you'll love Griffin, the king of hotness."

"I'm looking forward to it. Even the bowling." Harlee laughed. "I haven't been *out* out since I left San Francisco. I might even wear my Jimmy Choos."

"Well, come early and I'll straighten your hair for you."

"Darla, I can't afford you. Otherwise, I'd come in for the works. Colin is even trying to talk me into selling my Mini Cooper."

"The straightening is on the house, hon. And Colin is right. The car is precious, but totally impractical for the Sierra. So you and Colin hanging out a lot?" Hopefully one of them was getting some.

"Just friends," Harlee said, and Darla didn't press further. She had her own man trouble to figure out.

When she got inside the barbershop, the Nugget Mafia was there, lounging around the waiting room, drinking coffee and discussing the big topic of the day: Griffin's open house.

"I tell you, that boy is up to his ass in alligators," Owen said, "be-tween the gas station, his custom bike business, and that Sierra Heights fiasco he wasted his money on. Who's gonna buy one of those fancy-pants houses in this economy?" Apparently her dad hadn't got-ten the memo that the economy had shifted—people were spending money again. Just not on her services.

Dink, the mayor, piped up, "You been by the Gas and Go lately? He's ripped the place to shreds. He's even going through with that id-iotic car wash."

Owen kissed Darla on the top of her head. "Can you hold down the fort, missy? We're grabbing some lunch at the Ponderosa."

"Sure, Dad." She kissed him back.

After he left, she tidied up, swept the floor, and rearranged the magazines. The place sure could use a facelift. The checkerboard floor had been dulled by the sun. The walls were a drab off-white.

And the art consisted of a Josey Wales poster featuring Clint Eastwood, and a row of plaques and letters thanking Owen for buying local 4-H kids' prize-winning livestock at the county fair.

No wonder women never stepped foot in the place.

Darla had gone to the back of the shop to find a new bulb to replace one of the recessed lights that had burned out, when she heard the door chime. Wyatt stood just past the threshold, his hands jammed into his police jacket, red faced from the cold.

"Can I help you?" she asked, committed to her promise to always stay professional.

"Darla"—he let out a breath—"are we ever going to talk about it?"

Nine years had passed and not one word from him. Not one goddamn word about what they had lost. Just a lousy note that said he'd joined the army. Then she'd never heard from him again. Even after he came back and she'd occasionally visit, he never uttered a peep. She'd been living in Nugget for more than a month now and the most she'd gotten out of him was lingering looks. At the Ponderosa the other day she thought he'd finally worked up the nerve to approach her. But no. He'd walked across the room toward her and Harlee's table, only to change direction to the men's room.

It was a little late for talking.

"I have nothing to say to you."

She did have a question, though. The same burning one she'd carried for nearly a decade.

Why did you leave me when I needed you the most?

Saturday morning Harlee put on skintight jeans, a cashmere sweater, and her favorite boots. Despite Darla's offer, Harlee flatironed her own hair until it hung stick-straight to her shoulders. After applying a little makeup and putting on a heavy coat and hat, she walked up the hill and down Colin's driveway, straight to his shop.

It wasn't difficult to know his routine. He worked and slept without much in between. Sure enough, he was sawing away, while Max lazed in front of the iron stove, soaking up the heat. This time, Colin jammed AC/DC on his iPod. A little jolting first thing in the morning. At least to Harlee. Colin seemed to be enjoying it though, bouncing his head and moving his hips to the pounding beat of "You Shook Me All Night Long." He had absolutely no rhythm whatsoever, but

Harlee found the dance irresistible. Completely un-self-conscious—until he caught Harlee watching.

"Ha, ha. Caught you." She laughed.

He took off his plastic goggles, turned off the music, and bobbed his chin at her—the universal man gesture for *What's up?*

"My mom sold your rocking chair and table."

"Really?" He appeared both pleased and surprised.

"Yeah, really." Harlee smiled up at him. "She wants more. Can you ship?"

"Yup. Should I send the same?"

"Why don't you send another rocker and table and try something new?" She pointed. "Like one of those swings."

"I can do that," he said, and took her in from head to toe. He did it every time he saw her. Not in a creepy way, but like he thought she was the most ravishing woman in the world. It would be a lie to say she didn't get off on it a little. Okay, a lot. "You hanging out with Darla again today?"

"We're going to the open house at Sierra Heights. You want to come and gape at the big homes?"

"I've seen them before," he said, but Harlee knew he wouldn't go in case there were crowds. What a way to live.

"Have you given more thought to acupuncture?" she pushed, stepping closer so that they were nearly toe-to-toe.

"What are you doing, Harlee?" He tilted his head so that they were almost eye level.

"Trying to get you to conquer your demophobia." *And kiss me.* She thought it might loosen him up and help him fight his demons.

He gently clasped his hands around her waist and effortlessly lifted her to the side. "I'm still thinking about it." Which in Harlee's mind meant no.

"I could make an appointment for next week," she said.

"Harlee, leave it alone, please."

"So I guess you're definitely out for bowling?"

"Definitely out." He put his goggles back on and began sanding what looked like the arm of a bench. "Text me your mom's address for the furniture."

"All right." Harlee started to leave, but his phone rang. So she stayed, because, hello, she was nosy.

"Hey, Fiona." His whole face lit up as he talked to his stepsister and Harlee realized that she'd been wrong. He was definitely as handsome as Brad Pitt.

When she got back to her house, Darla was waiting. She had an ancient Jeep Cherokee that had more dents than an empty tin can. But it was all-wheel drive.

"You ready to go?" Darla called, hanging out of the driver's window. She'd tinted her blond hair purple.

"Yep." Harlee jumped into the passenger seat. "Thanks for driving."

"You look great," Darla said.

"You too. Love the color."

Darla shrugged. "It washes out."

"Is your dad holding down the barbershop?"

"For a little while, then he's coming to the open house too."

From what Harlee could tell, the whole town was attending, to lend Griffin support. She suspected that they were also a little curious and were using the event as an excuse to get a gander at the homes. Griffin had supposedly advertised the grand opening in Nevada and Northern California, hoping to hook buyers in the market for vacation houses.

"Griffin wants us to each take a model, in case anyone has any questions and to make sure no one steals anything," Darla said. "He'll brief us when we get there."

"Sounds good," Harlee said as they drove through an elaborate gate and stopped at a guard station, where a security person waved them through. "Wow, this is nice."

The place was a winter wonderland. Although most of the snow from the storm had melted, some of the giant log homes were still frosted in a thin layer of white. They parked near the Sierra Heights clubhouse and went inside to be greeted warmly by Griffin. He was everything Darla had described and more. Incredibly good-looking, but equally laid-back. He was also attached at the hip to an impossibly gorgeous brunette. Harlee got the sense she and Darla had interrupted something between the two of them. But this is when he'd told them to show up.

Griffin had just enough time to give them a quick tour before kickoff. There was an eighteen-hole golf course, a swimming pool and spa, outdoor kitchen with pizza oven, and tennis courts. The development certainly seemed like a mismatch for the working-class vibe of Nugget. But Harlee had to admit that it was awesome.

"You shouldn't have any trouble selling these homes," she told him optimistically.

"We'll see," he said, his eyes drifting off in the direction of the brunette, who he'd introduced as Lina. She returned a wan smile.

It didn't take a psychic to see that something was going on there.

During the next hour, all the so-called Baker's Dozen ladies arrived. Donna and Emily had gotten there shortly after Harlee and Darla to set up the food, mostly trays of finger stuff and cookies that wouldn't make a mess. There was also coffee and hot apple cider, which made the clubhouse smell heavenly.

Harlee and Darla grabbed a few nibbles and drinks before heading off to their assigned models—Darla the "Pine Cone" and Harlee the "Sierra."

"Text me if anything interesting happens," Darla said.

"Likewise."

Harlee'd just gotten inside her model when Maddy, her police chief husband, and a spectacularly hot guy Harlee had never seen before popped in. "Hi. Welcome to the Sierra."

Maddy gave her a hug. "This is so nice of you to do for Griffin."

The hot guy gave her a once-over and introduced himself as Nate Breyer, Maddy's brother. "So you're the private investigator?"

"I'm not a licensed private investigator. I'm more like an investigative reporter."

"You're on hiatus from the *Call*?"

"Something like that," she said, because it was a hiatus. A forever hiatus.

"I call it the *Crawl*," he said. "You know why?" When she shook her head, he proceeded, "Because every Sunday it's nowhere to be found, even though I pay for a full subscription."

She laughed. "You should call circulation about that."

He leaned in a little closer. "Why can't I just tell you?"

"A, because I'm not working there. And B, because I'm a reporter and have nothing to do with home delivery."

From the way Nate was looking at her she got the impression that he'd like her to deliver his paper. Naked. She also figured that he was about ten years older than her. Not necessarily a problem.

"Nate, come look at this kitchen," Maddy called.

He let out a sigh of resignation. "She wants me out of her guest house."

"You live here?" For some reason he didn't strike her as the mountain type, not to mention that the *Call* didn't deliver this far north.

"Nah. I live in San Francisco, but Maddy and I own the Lumber Baron. So I'm up here a lot."

"Are you thinking of buying a place?"

"Maybe, depending on what kind of deal I can get. I better catch up with the sister," he said, and winked.

As soon as he walked away Donna came up behind her. "Foxy, isn't he?" Who said foxy anymore? Harlee tried not to laugh. "That's Sophie and Mariah's baby daddy."

"Oh yeah, I remember you telling us something about that."

"He's single," Donna volunteered.

"Really?" Maybe she should invite him bowling. Although a small part of her still held out hope that Colin would come.

That day at least fifty families from outside the area traipsed through the models. Griffin sold two houses and took her, Darla, and Lina to dinner to celebrate. Afterward he treated them all to bowling, for helping. One of his new mechanics, a nice-looking guy named Rico, joined them. By the end of the night he'd proposed to Darla more times than Harlee could count. He kept telling her in Spanish, "*Me encanta tu pelo morado.*" I love your purple hair.

She and Darla had taken to calling him "Rico Suave."

By the time Harlee got dropped off at her cabin it was almost midnight. That's why she was surprised to find Colin and Max sitting on her porch in the freezing cold.

Chapter 8

Colin had waited all night for Harlee to get home and now that she was here he felt pathetic. Griffin Parks had dropped her off in his overpriced Range Rover. They'd looked hella cozy sitting in his leather-upholstered bucket seats.

"Hi." She waved to him as she jogged up the stairs, her face wreathed in alarm. "Is everything okay?"

The dog stood up, shook his coat, and wagged his tail, happy to see her. Colin searched for something to say. Even he knew that camping out on a woman's porch in the wee hours of the morning bordered on restraining-order behavior.

Yet, Harlee opened her door and ushered Max and him inside, like he'd dropped by to borrow a cup of sugar. "You guys look frozen."

She turned on the heat and went straight to the kitchen to put a kettle of water on the stove. He followed her, taking a seat at the dining room table.

"How long have you been here?"

"Just a few minutes," Colin said, studying the legs of the table so she wouldn't see that he was lying. "Max and I were on a walk and decided to stop by."

"At midnight?" Her brows shot up and then her lips quirked in a half smile. "You've totally been waiting for me, haven't you?"

He shrugged nonchalantly. "Just a little while. I've decided to do the acupuncture."

"Really?" She went from radiant to shamefaced in under forty seconds. "You felt left out tonight, didn't you?"

No. Maybe he'd bowled once or twice as a kid, but had no memory of it. It wasn't like he craved wearing smelly rental shoes. He certainly hadn't missed going to the real estate open house. That appealed to him about as much as getting smallpox. He'd just really wanted to be with Harlee.

Yeah, it was sixty kinds of stupid, given all his issues. Especially the ones she didn't know about. He'd once read that male bees died during midflight sex. If that wasn't tragic enough, their penises were ripped off during the mating ritual. That would be him, if he didn't watch it.

"Is there anyone good in Reno?" he asked. Knowing her, she'd research until she found the most acclaimed acupuncturists in the surrounding area.

"I'll research it. I'm really good at that. And I want to get the best."

Yep, he called that one right. She made his insides warm—she was such a good person. What the hell could she possibly see in him? But she saw something. *That* she'd made abundantly clear. He wasn't so arrested that he couldn't tell the signs. The way she checked him out when she thought he wasn't looking. The way she'd folded into him the night of the power outage when he'd carried her to bed.

"Okay," he said, and stood up to go.

"I'm making tea." She pouted, and he sat back down, his boots bumping Max under the table.

"Did Griffin sell any houses?" He'd been over to Sierra Heights a few times to do handiwork for Griffin and thought the guy was out of his mind. Although ruggedly beautiful, Nugget didn't strike Colin as the kind of place people bought million-dollar homes.

"He sold two," she said, pouring loose tea into some kind of strainer deal. "And I think Nate might buy one."

"Nate Breyer? He was there?"

Harlee stopped what she was doing. "You must know him from when you worked on the Lumber Baron."

"Yep."

"What? You don't like him?"

"I like him fine. He's Maddy's brother. He bought that inn when she was going through a tough time, to help her work her way out of it. Of course I like him. I just didn't expect him to be going to open houses. That's all."

She handed him a mug. "Let that steep for a while. Why was she going through a rough time?"

"You're a nosy little thing."

"Well, of course I am. I'm a reporter—and an investigator."

"Her husband left her for another woman," Colin said, not knowing why he was telling her this since it wasn't any of her goddamned business. But the whole town knew anyway.

She gasped. "The police chief? What a creep."

"Not him," Colin said. "Her first husband—some big hotel mogul."

"Oh. That's awful. Is that how she met the chief?"

"Yeah," he said, wanting to change the subject. He didn't like gossiping about people.

"For a guy who doesn't get out much, you seem to know a lot about this town." Harlee took the strainer out of his cup. "You can drink it now."

He took a sip and got a nice taste of peppermint.

"It's herbal," she said. "That way it won't keep you awake."

"It's good. Thanks."

She rested her chin in her hands with her elbows firmly on the table. "That was your sister on the phone earlier, wasn't it?"

"You don't miss anything, do you? Fiona, her husband, and kids want to come for Thanksgiving. We're watching the weather."

"Where do they live?" Harlee asked.

"Los Angeles."

"Is that where you're from?"

"Yeah," he said.

"You're killing me with all the long answers."

"I'm not much of a talker," he said.

"No. Really?" She smiled at him to make sure he knew she was teasing. "Why don't you just go to Los Angeles?"

Colin let out a breath. "Because I don't fly. And it's about ten hours by car each way. I don't have the time off."

"Is it because of the demophobia that you don't fly? Airports must be horrible for you."

They were the worst. The one time he'd gone inside Reno-Tahoe International to meet Fiona at the gate, Colin had thought he'd suffocate to death. "Yup. I also have claustrophobia, so even if the plane is empty I won't fly." He hadn't intended to tell her that, but maybe she'd see how screwed up he was.

And the phobias were only the beginning.

"Claustrophobia too?" Harlee gave him a sympathetic look, but didn't seem to be judging. "Did you always have them? Or did something happen?"

Oh, something happened all right. He'd been locked up like an animal with the worst people on earth. But he wasn't going there. "Hey, Harlee, you think we could talk about something else?"

"If you want to."

"Yeah, I want to," he said, and grinned at her, because when he did that it seemed to shut her up.

"Guess what?" She didn't wait for him to guess. "Griffin is going to help me find a used four-wheel drive so I can get rid of the Mini."

Griffin, huh? When he'd proposed the idea, she'd shot him down. "That's good."

"You want to sit on the couch? It's more comfortable."

He knew where this was going, but like that poor honey drone, he couldn't seem to stop himself. "Sure."

He passed the fireplace mantel on the way to the sofa and looked at the framed pictures. He recognized Harlee's mom, who posed with a man who must be her father. "Who's this?" He held up a photo of a younger Harlee with a guy maybe a few years older.

"That's my brother, Brad." She pointed to a side table with another picture of him, a woman, and a baby. "That's his wife and my niece."

"Nice," he said. "You two close?"

"Yup. When I was younger I used to be jealous of him. But now that he's my father's greatest disappointment, I love him like crazy."

"Why is he your father's greatest disappointment?"

"He's not." She laughed. "I just like to give him crap about not becoming a doctor. My dad is an internist and wanted his son to follow in his footsteps, so Brad went to law school instead."

"Well, a lawyer isn't bad," Colin said. Hell, her family was a freakin' Norman Rockwell painting compared to his.

"Except he's a cop," Harlee said.

Colin wasn't sure he heard right. "Like with the police department?"

"Oakland PD, to be exact. That's a badass department," she said.

And there was serious pride there. "After he got out of Stanford, he had this epiphany that he was meant to protect and serve. He helps me out with my business sometimes...I mean, it's all legal. He would never do anything unethical."

She patted the seat next to her. "Colin, come sit down."

She looked so pretty sitting there. Her sweater was blue and it matched her eyes and he could see the curves of her breasts through the material. And he really wanted to sit next to her. But her brother was a fucking cop.

He looked at his watch. "It's one in the morning, Harlee. I really should go. I've got a long day."

"Okay." She got to her feet and he could tell that she was disappointed. But everything about her life—her brother, her business, her perfect family—told him to back off.

"I'll call you Monday with what I come up with on acupuncturists," she told him.

"Sounds good." Colin whistled for Max and headed to the door, Harlee on his heels.

"Colin." She reached up on tiptoes and brushed his lips with hers. It was a friendly kiss, not a let's-go-to-bed-and-I'll-rock-your-world kiss.

But hell if it didn't rock his world anyway.

So far, the fireman had checked out. No wife waiting in the wings, pretty good credit history, and his chili had won first place at the Sonoma County fair five years in a row.

This could be The One for Alex, Harlee hoped as she filled out her report. Like Frances Guthrie, Alex Bean had become one of Harlee's regulars. Like them all, she was desperate to find love.

Harlee was starting to believe that love was as unattainable as a department store in Nugget and that there were no good men. At least most of the ones she'd investigated hadn't been good. In fact, they'd been bad to the bone. Her dad and brother seemed to be the exception. And Colin, who despite his quirkiness and reticence had an amazing spirit. Even though she hadn't known him long, she could feel it. The way he took care of Max. The way he helped people. And the fact that he was the carpenter of choice for everyone in town. People trusted him.

Unfortunately, he was either asexual or completely not into her.

Because she had literally thrown herself at him—shoved her body so tight up against his that a piece of paper wouldn't fit between them. Most guys she knew would've gotten the message by now. And she was pretty sure that Colin had. But nothing. He hadn't even tried to kiss her back when she'd pecked him on the lips last night.

It was weird, because she'd so gotten the impression that he liked her. Like really liked her. Like he thought she was a goddess.

Maybe she scared him. People had warned her before that she came off a little aggressive. Hey, that's how you got the big stories.

It's not like she scared everyone. Take Nate Breyer. He seemed perfectly at ease with her and had even asked for her number after the open house. On paper, Nate had more going for him than Colin. He was a big San Francisco hotelier, an excellent conversationalist, and dripped with sophistication. Like a numbnuts, she'd politely turned him away. She just wasn't looking to get involved right now, not even casually.

That's why this little torch she carried for Colin was crazy. She didn't understand it, but the man did something to her. Perhaps it was the vulnerability she sensed under his rough exterior. Or maybe she just wanted to fix him. Anyway, it didn't matter, because he'd made it abundantly clear that he just wanted to be friends. All for the best, she told herself, as she hit the button on her computer, sending the firefighter's CV to Alex.

Next, she took a quick peek at Journalismjobs.com, perusing the board for anything that looked interesting. The Bozeman paper wanted a political reporter. She supposed she could just as easily freeze her ass off in Montana as she could in Nugget. Then again she got free rent here. In Calgary, they were looking for an energy reporter. Getting a Canadian work visa would be a bitch. And she didn't know anything about energy, unless you included energy bars, Harlee's breakfast of champions. Her favorite was an ad wanting a "slick city reporter," in Temple, Texas.

That would definitely be her. She was so slick that she'd gotten herself culled from the herd.

Downsized.

Reduced.

Fired.

For the next hour she distracted herself by researching acupuncturists. She found two—one in Reno and one in Truckee—who were members of the American Academy of Medical Acupuncture, which required two hundred hours of training. Both were affiliated with the National Certification Commission for Acupuncture and Oriental Medicine. So definitely not quacks.

She printed their backgrounds and literature from their websites, then checked Yelp for the hell of it. Both acupuncturists got rave reviews, so she printed those too, wanting to give Colin plenty of information before he made his choice. She contemplated running Colin through a few of her databases just to see if anything stood out that could shed some light on his phobias. But Harlee shut down the computer instead, deciding she'd stalled long enough. It was time to go into town and make the dreaded trip to her post office box. She'd been avoiding her mail like a kale juice cleanse. Bills, bills, and more bills. In her closet, she found her parka, bought for half price at the outlet store, thank you very much, and shrugged into it. Today she opted for her fleece-lined rubber boots because it looked like snow. On her way out, she grabbed a scarf, hat, and gloves, before cranking the heat in the Mini.

Brrr!

Cold didn't even come close to describing the temperature. Nugget was only four hours away from San Francisco, yet it may as well have been the frozen tundra. Located in the Sierra Nevada, near the southern border of the Cascade Range, Nugget was one of the snowiest towns in America; a fact that people had trouble believing, given that this was California. But on a day like this, Harlee believed. And it wasn't even Thanksgiving yet.

She pulled up to the post office, which was a few blocks from the square, and got that leaden feeling in her stomach. In the lobby, she found her box, unlocked it, and pulled out piles of envelopes. It seemed like just yesterday she'd filled out the change-of-address card. Still, her creditors seemed to have found her.

She quickly sifted through the stack, throwing the junk mail into the recycle bin, and despite the folly of it, kept the Neiman Marcus and Bloomingdale's catalogs. She just wanted to look at the pictures and sniff the perfume ads. That's all. At the bottom of the pile was a large square envelope that didn't feel like a bill. She pulled it out, scanned the front, and smiled. The return address read: The Ninth Circle of Hell, San Francisco, CA.

Inside, was a "missing you" card signed with little messages from each remaining member of the staff. Even Jerry had written: "Legs, give 'em hell."

She'd pulled up stakes so fast that there hadn't been time for a party, or even drinks. And while Doofus One and Doofus Two were marching her out of the building there definitely hadn't been time for Costco cake—a newsroom tradition when someone left, because the *Call* spared no expense.

She felt her eyes well up and wiped them with the back of her hand. God, she missed it. The long days. Her snarky colleagues. The cluttered newsroom that always smelled like ass. It had been her life.

Well, she had her start-up now, and according to her P&L, the business was headed for profit in the next month or two. Given that she was the sole employee and had zero overhead, she didn't see how this could be such an impressive feat. But according to all the business books she'd read, it was huge. Like seriously epic. So yay for her, she silently celebrated, while blowing her nose in an old Starbucks napkin she'd found at the bottom of her purse.

In the meantime, her checking account continued to dwindle and the bills piled up, she thought as she weighed the stack of mail in her hand. It really would help not to have such a sizable car payment. With that in mind, she got back in her car and drove to Main Street, where she hoped to find Griffin at the Gas and Go.

He was there all right, along with Darla's dad and a few old men she didn't know, but figured they must be the legendary Nugget Mafia she'd heard so much about. They'd set up lawn chairs around a space heater inside one of the garage bays, drinking coffee and watching Griffin and Rico install smog-check equipment.

"I don't think you're doing it right," one of the men said, and Harlee saw Griffin's jaw clench.

Griffin caught sight of her out of the corner of his eye, grinned, and waved. "Hey, Harlee. You come to check out the place? It doesn't look like much now. But soon it'll be awesome."

He seemed way more enthusiastic about the gas station than he was about Sierra Heights. Supposedly, he was a wiz mechanic, so she guessed it made sense that this was where his passion would lie.

"I wanted to see the place, but also talk to you about trading in my car, if you're still interested in helping me do that."

"Absolutely." He winked at her and came over. "You have the Mini with you?"

She pointed to the street, where she'd parked in front of the station. "Colin doesn't think it's a good snow car." Nor could she afford it, but she didn't need to tell him that.

"Actually, they're front-wheel drive and with studded tires they do okay. But he's right that you could probably do better with something more durable."

The old guys had come out and were walking around her car. One of them shouted for her to pop the hood. She looked at Griffin.

"Just ignore them." He turned to the men. "There's nothing wrong with Harlee's car. She's thinking about getting something more heavy-duty."

They nodded their heads in approval and went back inside the garage to warm themselves at the space heater. Griffin scrubbed his hand over his face. "They are such a pain in my ass." But Harlee noticed that he said it with affection.

"You think I should trade it in?" she asked.

"You'll get crap for it at a dealership. Let me try to sell it for you, and in the meantime I'll look around for something with all-wheel drive. How much you want to spend?"

She chewed on her bottom lip. "Honestly," she said, "not a lot. Like maybe three thousand dollars." She still had to pay what she owed on the Mini, but a used car would save her money in the long run.

"It's doable," he said. "It'll probably be a beater. But up here, that's all you need."

"Do you, uh, take a commission?" she asked, wondering if she'd be better off doing it herself. Selling it probably wouldn't be difficult. But she'd need a mechanic to check out the new car.

"Hell no." He looked up when an old SUV pulled in. Harlee recognized Lina behind the wheel and she didn't look too thrilled to see her and Griffin together. "I'm just helping you out, Harlee. That way you'll feel honor bound to have me service your vehicles in the future."

Lina didn't get out of the truck and Griffin told Harlee to hang on a second. He walked over and talked to Lina through the driver-side window. From the looks of it, their conversation wasn't going too well. Harlee pretended not to be trying to eavesdrop, though she couldn't hear much anyway. She did see Griffin try to kiss Lina, who jerked away, rolled up her window, and drove off.

Uh-oh.

When Griffin came back, Harlee said, "I hope I didn't make any problems for you."

"Nope," he said, looking miserable. "Lina is having problems keeping to a deal we made. It has nothing to do with you."

Luckily, the old guys were immersed in an argument over the exact size of a steelhead Dink had caught over the summer, and hadn't witnessed Griffin and Lina's quarrel.

"I'm sorry you're having issues," Harlee said. "She seems like a really nice girl." *Just way too young.* While bowling, Lina had told Harlee and Darla that she'd just started her first semester at USF and was up visiting for the weekend. Her brother was the police chief and she lived with him and Maddy when she wasn't going to school.

"I need to get home," Harlee told Griffin, who had gone sort of vacant, obviously upset over his disagreement with Lina.

"All right. I'll put some feelers out on selling your car and finding you another one. By next week I should have something to report."

"Thanks, Griff. I really appreciate this."

"No worries," he said, and returned to the garage to rejoin Rico on connecting the smog apparatus.

Harlee considered swinging by the barbershop to see Darla, but she decided that it would be prudent to get home before the weather turned bad. Just in the last hour, she'd felt the temperature drop and could feel snow coming. Hopefully this time the power wouldn't go. But Harlee had prepared by stocking up on flashlights, batteries, and candles at the Nugget Market.

Maybe she'd check on Colin to see if he needed any of her extras. Just being a good neighbor.

Chapter 9

Darla's cell phone was missing and her entire life with it. Every one of her contacts and pictures, not to mention important text messages, was on that phone.

"This can't be happening," she muttered, checking and rechecking the counter, hoping that maybe it had accidentally been pushed to the side of the barbershop and was now blending into the woodwork.

One minute it had been sitting next to the cash register and the next minute gone. Poof. Like it had vanished into thin air.

The more she searched, the more she realized that the only logical explanation was that someone had stolen it while Darla had gone to the back of the barbershop to retrieve her latest shipment of hair products. She'd spent the entire day stocking new shelves with shampoos, conditioners, and styling gels so the display would be the first thing people saw when they entered the shop.

She must've been too preoccupied to hear the bell chime over the door or to notice a person coming in. Apparently even Nugget wasn't safe from thieves, who by now were probably calling Finland on her tab. She grabbed Owen's old wall phone with the curly cord and called the Nugget Police Department.

After the third ring, Connie, the 911 dispatcher, answered. "Nugget PD. Is this an emergency?"

"Yes, it's an emergency," Darla said. "Someone stole my cell phone."

"Hey, Darla," Connie chirped into the phone. "I've been meaning to come over for a haircut, but haven't had the chance. I was thinking some layers might be nice."

As much as she wanted a customer, she wanted her phone back more. "Great. Come over anytime. Now, about my phone . . ."

"Where and when was it stolen?" Connie wanted to know.

"At the barbershop. As far as the time, maybe in the last few hours?"

"Okay. I'll send someone over." Connie hung up.

And Darla paced, consoling herself that at least the phone could only be activated by punching in her four-digit security code. Otherwise the thief would've had access to all her personal information, including her dad's home address.

Wyatt came in the door a short time later, dusting snowflakes from his police jacket. It was warm in the barbershop, so he took the jacket off and hung it on the coat rack. For the first time Darla noticed how broad his shoulders had gotten. Even his arms had become ropey with muscle and he'd gained a couple of inches in height. Or maybe he was just holding himself taller these days. Either way, his once rangy frame had filled out since the time they'd been engaged. Engaged. What a joke.

Why couldn't Connie have sent Jake, the older officer who looked like Clint Eastwood? Or even the chief?

"Connie says you had a burglary," Wyatt said, walking to the back of the room, opening and closing closet doors, peeking into the bathroom.

Clearly, he thought whoever stole her phone was still here, hiding out. Right. Like who would be stupid enough to do that?

"Not a burglary," she said. "Someone stole my phone. Just walked in and grabbed it off the counter. Right here," she pointed. "Next to the cash register. Maybe you should dust for prints."

"Did you get a look at the person?" He came over to the cash register, gave it a quick perusal and pulled out a notebook.

"No."

"Did you actually see anyone take it?"

"No. As if someone would snatch it right in front of me." She may as well have said, "Are you new?"

"Why's your hair purple?" His upper lip inched up into a half grin. She noticed that he had a five-o'clock shadow and his eyes were still as mossy green as ever.

"Because I like it purple," she said, a little heavy on the attitude even to her own ears.

He came closer and sniffed. "It smells good. Like apricots."

"Are you going to find my phone or stand around snorting my hair?" She backed up a good three, four inches. Hadn't the man ever heard of personal space?

"Did you leave the barbershop at any time today?"

She blew out a breath and thought about it for a few seconds. Sometimes she ran out to get a fountain drink or fries from the Bun Boy. "Nope. Not today. I was here the whole time."

"So the person who took your phone was a ghost?" He scraped the top of his lip with his bottom teeth, trying not to laugh.

"You don't need to be sarcastic, Wyatt. This is very traumatic for me. My whole life is on that phone."

"Didn't you back up all your data on the cloud?"

"Well, of course I did." Didn't her phone do it for her automatically? Uh-oh. No way in hell was she asking him.

"Why don't you walk me through your day?" he said, flipping his notebook open.

"Um . . ." She nodded at her display. "I spent most of the time stocking these shelves."

He whistled through his teeth, gazing at the rows of bottles and jars, picking up a few to read the labels. "So you're in the shampoo business now?"

"All salons sell product. Good profit margin."

"But this is a barbershop," he said.

"We're in a transitional phase." Except no one in this town seemed to accept that Owen planned to retire and she was his replacement. His only replacement. "Wyatt, do you think you could focus on the crime?"

He let his eyes roam down the top of her fitted wrap dress all the way to the toes of her boots. "You look good, Darla. I'm not really into the purple hair, but you grew up real pretty. You always were, but now—"

"You don't get to say that to me, Wyatt. You lost those privileges when you walked away nine years ago and left me with nothing but a Dear John letter. Just stick to my phone, please."

He at least had the decency to look contrite. "Go ahead and walk me through your day."

"Okay," she said, leading him to the back door, where her shipment had been delivered on a wooden pallet. "I was here a good amount of the time, unpacking and inventorying products."

The room was longer than it was wide, with Owen's chair and a waiting area at the front, two shampoo bowls that Darla had added in the middle, and a small desk, storage space, and the bathroom toward the back.

She bent over the pallet to show him how easy it would've been for someone to sneak in unseen. But Wyatt seemed more interested in her ass than he did in surveying the crime scene.

She stood up and huffed, "You're just humoring me, aren't you? You think by now my thief is long gone, don't you?"

He flashed a sardonic smile, fished his cell out of his pocket, and asked for her number. A few seconds later, "Sexy and I know It" played from the bathroom. He pushed open the door, followed the ringtone until he found her phone jammed under the latest edition of *Hair's How*, and handed it to her, eyebrows up.

"You must've forgotten coming in here with your phone for a little reading time," he said.

God, she wished the floor would swallow her up. And when the hell had Wyatt Lambert become so self-assured? Back in the day, he'd been a quiet, unassuming young man, not such a . . . know-it-all.

"I guess you think this is hilarious?" she said, refusing to look at him.

"No. I'm glad I got your phone back . . . and that we don't have a burglar on the loose."

"Whatever." She moved to the front of the barbershop like she had a million things to do and couldn't waste any more time with him.

"Darla?" He said it low, deep in his throat, making her knees go weak.

"What?" She kept her back to him because it was easier than having to look at the man he'd become. The man she didn't know anymore.

"Have dinner with me."

"I can't, Wyatt." Before moving here, she'd convinced herself that she'd written him off. That he no longer meant anything to her because what he'd done was unforgivable. But she was weak. Without distance, he'd wind up crushing her all over again.

"Okay." Wyatt let out a sigh, sounding resigned. "I'll go now."

She resisted saying, "You're good at that."

"It's a good truck," Colin said, slapping the driver's door.

"You sure? You don't think I made a mistake, right?"

Harlee had asked him for a second opinion on the old Nissan Pathfinder. It was a 2000 with a lot of mileage, but tough enough to handle Nugget's rough winters.

"Griff said it's in really good condition." Her breath froze in the cold.

Griffin this, Griffin that. Colin was really sick of hearing about Griffin. But he had to admit that Griffin had done well by Harlee, getting her a good price for her Mini Cooper and finding her an appropriate set of wheels.

"You have enough to pay off the Mini and the Nissan?" he asked, standing close enough to smell her perfume. Something flowery that drove him crazy.

"Can we go inside? It's freezing out here," she said.

He opened the door for Harlee and motioned for her to go first. "Do you like the way it drives?"

She immediately moved to the front room to stand next to the fire. Max lifted his head from his dog bed, licked her boots, and went back to sleep. "I've only driven it from Griffin's garage to your house. It's bigger than what I'm used to, but I'll adapt."

He was impressed that she'd given in on the Mini Cooper, although it chafed him that Griffin had been the impetus. Honest truth, he was jealous as hell. The guy was richer than gold, had serious moves, and didn't piss his pants at the thought of going inside an eff-ing bowling alley.

And the best one of all: Griffin didn't have a parole officer.

Colin had heard from Maddy that her sister-in-law, Lina, and Griffin had a thing going. But Lina was just eighteen and Griffin had to be in his late twenties. The age difference was kind of skeevy, if you asked Colin. He wondered if the relationship ended when Lina went off to college, and now Griffin was putting the make on Harlee. Even though Colin had no right to be bothered by it, he was. A lot.

"Hey, Col, you want to go over tomorrow?" Harlee called from the fire.

"What's there to go over? A guy's going to stick needles in me."

"You're not nervous, right?"

No, he wasn't nervous. Small spaces and large groups of people terrified him. But needles, knives, guns? Not so much. "I'm fine with it, Harlee. You hungry?"

"I could eat." She wandered over to the kitchen, where Colin scanned the pantry. "Chili or soup?"

She took the cans out of his hands and placed them back inside the cupboard. "What do you have that's quasi fresh? I'll cook."

Forty minutes later she served them up plates of pasta, a tossed green salad, and searched the fridge for something to drink. "Have you always stayed away from liquor?"

By now he knew when Harlee was fishing. "I'm not a recovering alcoholic, if that's what you're asking. My mother was a hardcore drunk. Her husband, Fiona's father, was a hardcore drunk. Watching them get hammered every night sort of killed my desire for booze."

That and the worst night of his life.

"Do you still talk to your mom?"

"She died five years ago." He'd been notified by the warden and allowed to attend her funeral in shackles with a couple of escorts from the state.

"I'm so sorry, Colin. Was it from the drinking?"

"Nope. I mean who's to say for sure, but she had breast cancer."

"That must've been awful," Harlee said.

"We weren't that close." That was the understatement of the year. In all those years the woman hadn't come to visit him once. "But when my stepfather sold her house, he gave me the proceeds." He suspected Fiona had pushed him into it. Not that Sam had been a bad guy, just an unreliable alcoholic.

"Is that how you paid for this?" Harlee stared up at the skyscraper ceilings, then out the big glass doors to sweeping views of the Sierra mountain range.

"Yep. My mom's house was pretty modest—a cottage, really. But it was in the Hollywood Hills. It's a desirable neighborhood."

"You didn't live there?"

"Not for a long time," he said, wrapping strands of spaghetti around his fork. "This is good, Harlee. Where'd you learn to cook?"

"My friends and I took a cooking class. It's kind of a thing in San Francisco. Everyone tries to outdo everyone else in the kitchen. You're really great if you can make meals with ingredients no one has ever heard of. And you have to know the farmer who grew it all, or people will run you out of town."

He laughed. "You miss it, don't you?"

"Uh, not San Francisco so much." She let out a breath. "I just really miss my job."

"What about your business?" That investigative stuff she did scared the crap out of him. It would take her approximately ten minutes to find out about him with the right search terms.

"I like it," she said. "But it's not the same as seeing your byline on the front page, above the fold. I'm looking, but there's not a whole lot out there. Especially at large-circulation papers."

"Does it have to be a big paper?" Dumb question. Harlee was a go-getter. Ambitious.

"If I want to pay my bills. Newspapers pay lousy to begin with. Starbucks probably pays better than a small-circ paper."

She took equal bites of her pasta and salad. Colin loved to watch her eat. She did it with the same enthusiasm she had for everything.

"Where did you live before you came to Nugget?" she asked.

"San Diego."

"I love San Diego. Were you in the military?"

"Nope." He picked up his empty plate and put it in the dishwasher. "Carpentry."

"Did you live near the beach?"

"Uh, closer to Mexico," he said. Donovan was actually on the border. "Tell me more about this appointment tomorrow."

"I think first he's going to diagnose you to figure out the root cause of the phobias and what points he should stick the needles in. The whole purpose is to stimulate a reaction in parts of your brain and release endorphins and strengthen the nervous system. It worked for my friend who was trying to get pregnant."

"Pregnant, huh?" Colin said, making a face that caused Harlee to laugh.

"I don't think you have anything to worry about, Colin."

"You sure?" He winked at her and reached for her plate. "You done?"

"Yes, but I'll help with the cleanup. What do you have for dessert?"

He pulled out the tin of shortbread cookies she'd given him and lifted the lid.

"You still have these?" she asked, surprised. "If they were in my house they'd be gone in a matter of hours. I'd think you were a health food nut, but too much of what you eat comes from a can."

"I don't eat a lot of sweets. But I like the cookies," he added, not wanting to sound ungrateful for the gift.

"Is your sister's family still coming for Thanksgiving?" It was a week away.

"We're playing it by ear, depending on the weather. They can't afford to get snowed in. The kids have school and Steve has a big job to finish on a deadline."

"My parents are having the same dilemma. They were planning on coming up, but if there's another storm . . ."

"Your brother too?" Colin tried to sound casual.

"No. They're going to Leslie's folks'," she said. "Hey, Col, if your people can't make it, you should come to my house. Even if my mom and dad come, we're only three. That won't bother you, right?"

"We'll see." Which was the universal code for no way in hell. But Harlee seemed to take it as a yes.

She got up from the table to help him with the dishes and they worked in companionable silence. A couple of times he brushed against her, feeling the soft curves of her body. He was finding it more and more difficult not to touch her. In every way a man could want a woman, Colin wanted Harlee. And for no reason he could understand, she wanted him too. He could see it in her body language and the way she looked at him.

In the three years he'd lived in Nugget, Colin hadn't gone without. He was a thirty-one-year-old man with a healthy libido. But his hookups had been limited to just sex. No dinner, no dancing, not even much talking. The women had all tacitly agreed to the setup. Everyone got what they wanted out of the deal and no one got hurt.

But with Harlee that kind of arrangement would never fly. The woman was all heart. She embraced everything she did with gusto. Her work. Her friendships. Her projects. Fixing him.

Especially fixing him.

For someone like Colin, whose life had become so solitary and private that it wasn't unusual for him to lock himself away in his wood shop for days without hearing another person speak, she should've been too much. Typhoid Harlee.

Instead, she made him question his limitations. She made him feel worthy, instead of an outcast living on the sidelines. She made him feel like a man. A desirable man.

But when she found out what he really was, he'd go back to feeling like himself again. A convicted criminal.

Chapter 10

Darla eyed Colin's hair in the mirror before dropping his chair down two or three feet. Her last customer must've been a child.

"Maybe I should wait for Owen," he said, already having second thoughts. Darla didn't look like she knew what she was doing. And if Colin was going through with this, he wanted it to look good. He'd grown pretty attached to his long hair and frankly didn't know what he'd look like without it.

"I told you already, my dad's on a fishing trip. If you want it done now, I'm it." She fluffed his hair with her hands, pulling strands this way and that, feeling the shape of his face like she thought she was a freakin' sculptor. "I'm thinking a little less *Duck Dynasty* and a little more Charlie Hunnam."

"I have no idea what you're talking about, Darla."

"*Sons of Anarchy*. Don't you watch it?"

"Nope." Colin fidgeted nervously in his seat. The ceiling in the barbershop hung low. It felt like the white acoustic tiles were closing in on him. He tried his breathing exercises, but it was difficult to be inconspicuous while inhaling and exhaling with his hand on his diaphragm.

His appointment with the acupuncturist had been a bust as far as Colin was concerned. But Harlee kept telling him he couldn't expect miracles from one visit. Thankfully, there wasn't a pack of people in here today. He'd made sure of that, circling the barbershop at least six times before coming in. The only reason he finally did was because Donna Thurston came out of the Bun Boy and gave him the evil eye. She probably thought he was casing the place.

"It's a television show about an outlaw motorcycle gang," Darla replied.

"I don't want to look like a member of an outlaw motorcycle gang. Just give me something clean-cut."

"Charlie Hunnam is hot and you look like him—same bone structure. High cheekbones. Strong jaw. Trust me on this. If you don't like it, I can always go Tom Cruise/*Top Gun*."

When Colin didn't say anything, Darla pressed, "Colin, I'm really good at this."

"Okay," he said. "But if I don't like it, you can change it, right?"

"Uh-huh. You'll look great. I promise." She grinned at him in the mirror and Colin could see that she was ecstatic at the chance to get her hooks into him. She got him up out of the chair and walked him over to the shampoo bowl. "So you're having Thanksgiving at Harlee's tomorrow?"

"Yeah." Why he'd finally relented was a total mystery. But Harlee had a way of wearing a person down. Colin thought she might have some kind of reporter voodoo.

Darla adjusted the temperature of the water before leaning his head back into the sink. With a dollop of girly-smelling shampoo, she lathered up his hair, scrubbing his scalp and massaging the back of his neck. "Relax, Colin. Jeez, you're over-the-top tense. This is supposed to be enjoyable."

She put more glop in his hair and made him sit with it on for ten minutes. "This is a conditioner. It'll work out all the tangles. I might come over after dinner, for dessert."

Great. More people. Just what Colin needed. But right now he was focusing on getting out of the barbershop without having a full-on anxiety attack.

"Is that why you're getting your hair cut, to look good for Harlee's folks?" Darla rinsed him and wrapped his head with a towel, making a turban.

"No." What did she think, that Harlee and he were an item? Well, they weren't. "It was getting too long and out of control."

She led him back to the chair. "When I'm done with you, you won't recognize yourself."

Yeah, that's what he was afraid of.

Swishing a cape around his neck, Darla turned the chair so his back was to the mirror and began clipping away. "You have great hair, Colin." His locks fell to the floor, making him cringe.

"Thanks, I guess. When is Owen coming back?" He figured if she screwed his hair up that bad, he could always have the barber fix it.

"Tonight, so he'll be back in time to help me cook. We're bringing the green-bean casserole to Ethel and Stu's." The couple owned the Nugget Market.

"Is he really serious about retiring?"

"He says he is." Darla turned the chair sideways so she could focus on the back of his hair without him seeing himself in the mirror.

"Who will run this place?" Colin looked around the barbershop.

"*Moi*. Who else? Now hold your head still." She grabbed his chin and straightened his shoulders. "Why do you think I moved back?"

Colin shrugged. "It just seems like a guys' place."

"Well, times have changed." She continued to clip away, lifting sections of his hair with her fingers. He couldn't see what he looked like, but already he felt lighter.

"Darla, why is Wyatt pacing in front of the barbershop?" The dude walked back and forth, back and forth until it made Colin dizzy. The Nugget police officer had always been courteous, more than likely oblivious to Colin's past. But he was starting to worry Colin.

"I don't know," she said, annoyance tingeing her voice. "He comes around whenever I have a man in my chair."

Colin started to turn his head, but she held him still. "Don't move."

He wondered if they were a couple. If so, he hadn't heard. Every drop of news or gossip was telegraphed in Nugget like a twenty-four-hour cable broadcast. Even a loner like him usually got looped in on the doings and rumors of the town.

"We have some history," she said. "But it's over and done."

Obviously not, if Wyatt kept coming around. But he didn't say anything. Not his business.

"He wants me to go to dinner with him." She let out a sigh, and Colin got the distinct impression Darla wanted him to weigh in. "Nine years ago, he left me at the lowest point of my life. Both of us should've been mourning. But he went off and joined the army. Didn't even have the decency to say goodbye. Now, all of a sudden, he's all over me. Weird, right?"

Why the hell was she telling him this? "Maybe he realizes he made a mistake, Darla. Maybe he wants to make amends."

"So you think I should give him a chance?"

"I think you should do whatever is right for you," he said, wondering how she was able to concentrate on his hair with all the chitchat. "Talk to Harlee about it. She's probably a better sounding board."

"Maybe," Darla said. "But DataDate has made her a hard-ass. You should see the lies she's caught people in. It's enough to make you become a cynic for life."

Colin could feel another wave of anxiety coming on. "You almost done?"

"Not quite." She started strategically trimming his beard. "You've got a lot of hair, Colin."

"Just shave it off, Darla." He needed to get out before the room closed in on him.

"Remember, you said I could have my wicked way with you. Now just sit back and get comfortable. Let me work my magic."

She wrapped a hot towel around his face, and he had to admit that the heat relaxed him somewhat. Not so good when she removed the towel, lathered him up, and started scraping at his facial hair with straight razor.

"Be careful with that thing, Darla."

"I've been doing this since I was ten. You've got nothing to worry about." She finished with the razor and took another thirty minutes, snipping and trimming. Then she wrapped his face in another hot towel and aimed a blow dryer at him.

"What are you doing with that?" Colin asked.

"I'll give you one guess." Before he could answer, a blast of warm air hit the back of his shoulders. "I just want to get you dry before I shape you a little more."

This might well rank as the longest haircut on record, Colin thought as Darla took another whack at his hair, doing weird crap with the sharp edge of the scissor.

"Colin, you're in for a big surprise," she said, finger-brushing his hair until she got it the way she wanted. After removing the hot towel from around his face, she continued to trim little wisps from his facial hair, moving his face from side to side.

When she finished, Darla just stood there, cocking her head from left to right, appraising him until he felt his face heat under her scrutiny.

Finally, she spun the chair around so he faced the mirror. Holy shit. He did a double take, not recognizing the person staring back at him. No longer did he look like a man who'd just come off the mountain. The difference was startling. Shocking, really.

"Well, what do you think?" Darla stood tapping her toe, waiting in anticipation.

Colin bent closer to the mirror, studying his profile and played with the sandy brown locks that barely hit his chin. "I think it's pretty good," he said.

She shot him a look. "How about, 'Darla, you're a flipping rock star.'"

After ringing him up at the register, Colin left a big tip and walked out onto the square, relieved to inhale a rush of cold air and embrace the wide open.

"Colin?" Maddy, who'd been leaving the police station, came walking toward him, wearing a quizzical expression on her face. "Is that you? Oh my God, you look amazing."

He felt his cheeks turn red and said, "I got a haircut."

"I'll say. Owen didn't do that, did he?"

"Owen's fishing," Colin said. "His daughter, Darla, did it."

"You're kidding." She stepped back to take it all in. "It's a beautiful cut. And I love how she did the goatee thing . . . It's so *GQ*. What prompted this sudden makeover?"

He shrugged, his ears turning hot from the praise. "I was starting to look like a bum."

"You look like a movie star now," Maddy said, moving in closer so she could brush at his hair with her fingers.

"Hey, don't get me on the wrong side of the law." As if on cue, the police chief walked out onto the square.

"Honey," Maddy called to her husband. "Come look at this gorgeous haircut Owen's daughter just gave Colin."

Rhys Shepard bobbed his chin at Colin in greeting.

"Doesn't it look wonderful?" she prodded.

"*Sexy*," Rhys said, and Colin had to stifle a grin. The chief turned to his wife. "You going back to the inn?"

"Just for an hour. I promise." Rhys clucked over his pregnant wife like a mother hen. Colin was glad to see them happy. Maddy was one of the few people he counted as a friend, and when he'd first met her she'd been going through a rough patch.

"Colin," she said, "I know that Sophie and Mariah already invited you, but I want to make sure you know how much we'd love to have you and your family for Thanksgiving. Emily is cooking. You don't want to miss out on that."

He smiled at her. "Thanks. I appreciate you including me. My family can't make it, so I'm going to Harlee's."

"They're not coming?" Maddy asked, surprised.

"No." He looked up at the dark clouds that filled the sky. "They're afraid that with the storm moving in, they won't be able to get out."

"Harlee, huh?" Maddy's expression grew smug.

"Don't read anything into it, Maddy. She's my neighbor. That's all."

Pretty soon, he knew, the news of him having dinner with Harlee would be spread all over town. That's the way it worked here. Even though he was only a bit player in Nugget, people were hard up for gossip. And Harlee, as pretty as she was, managed to draw a lot of attention.

"I'm not reading anything into it. Nor am I reading anything into the fact that you got that beautiful haircut." She continued to grin in that self-satisfied, knowing way that made Colin feel like the liar he was.

"Don't mind her." Rhys came to Colin's defense. "It's hormones."

"I better get going," Colin said, looking up at the sky again, trying to gauge how long he had before the next dump of snow.

He wanted to bring a bouquet of flowers to tomorrow's dinner and the pickings in Nugget were slim to none. There was a small market in Graeagle that sold nice arrangements, so he jumped on the highway and headed to the neighboring town. At least there, they had their own gossip. No one would care who he bought flowers for.

And if he decided to stock up on condoms for the long winter, no one would care about that either.

Harlee's parents had made it as far as Donner Pass before turning back to the Bay Area. They'd forgotten chains and the roads were too treacherous to drive without them. It looked like it would just be Colin and her for dinner. And she'd made enough for an army.

She took away two place settings from the table, and replaced the silly cornucopia she'd bought at the Nugget Market with candlesticks, and lit them. May as well have a little ambience, since it would just be the two of them. Outside, the snow came down in buckets. Harlee had never seen so many flurries.

The sound of Colin's truck engine pulled Harlee to the front door. Max bounded out of the passenger seat and covered her face with kisses as she bent down to hug him. Colin came bearing gifts too. A big bunch of mums, sunflowers, Gerber daisies, and roses. A bottle of Zinfandel and a jug of cider.

"Oh my goodness, Colin." He'd gone to so much trouble.

"I didn't know what to bring."

When he handed her the flowers, Harlee reeled back in surprise. "You cut your hair . . . and your beard." He still had scruff. A short, boxed beard, like Ryan Gosling. She'd thought he'd rocked the Grizzly Adams look, but now he was drop-dead gorgeous. And younger than she'd originally pegged him for, definitely closer to her age.

She walked around to check out the back of his hair. "Who did it?"

"Huh?" He turned around to face her. That's when she noticed the dimple in his right cheek.

"Your hair. Who cut it?"

"Darla," he said, definitely uncomfortable with the attention.

She moved in closer to brush back a stray lock. "You look amazing, Colin. And you smell good too." He had on a woodsy cologne. And he'd dressed up in a crisp button-down shirt and a pair of dark blue jeans.

"You look good too." They just stood there together, gawking at each other. Well, maybe it was just Harlee gawking. But God, was he delicious.

"I'm sorry your parents couldn't make it," he said. "And thanks for letting me bring Max."

"Of course. I love Max. I hope you brought your appetite." She moved into the kitchen, where she rummaged through a cupboard for a vase for the flowers and checked the oven. The turkey was just about done. She'd let it rest while making the gravy.

"What made you decide on this?" She pointed to his hair and beard.

He shrugged. "I wanted something lower maintenance."

"Darla did a great job." Harlee kept stealing peeks at him. "She's having a difficult time making a go of the barbershop. Besides you, Griffin, and a few kids, she hasn't had any clients to speak of. Hopefully you'll be a walking advertisement for her."

"I did notice the place was empty," Colin said, taking the oven mitts away from her and hefting the bird onto the counter. "I thought the shop would be buzzing the day before Thanksgiving."

"Colin, you think it has anything to do with . . . How do I say this?"

"The blue hair, the feathers, the dagger nails." He smirked.

"Yeah. That."

"No." Colin shook his head. "I think it has everything to do with Nugget's reluctance to accept change. When Maddy and Nate rehabbed the Lumber Baron, the town fought them tooth and nail. Now the townspeople have come to terms with the inn. I think most people really like it. The same will eventually happen with Darla. But in the meantime, Nugget is hanging on to Owen."

"It would be great if you could talk her up." Harlee whisked together a roux for the gravy and slowly added turkey drippings to the pan.

"I'm not much of a talker-upper. But I'll do what I can."

Once the gravy was done, Harlee checked the Brussels sprouts roasting in the oven. The potatoes had been kept warm on the stovetop. All she had to do was carve the turkey and they could sit down to eat.

This would be the smallest Thanksgiving in Harlee's history. Usually her whole family gathered, and often the Robertses invited friends. The kitchen always bustled with people and the football game played in the background, which reminded Harlee to turn on her iPod. She knew Colin liked music and had made a playlist.

"What do you want me to do?" Colin asked.

She took another look at his chiseled face and thought, *Me*. Fat chance of that happening, given his past standoffish behavior. "You want to pour us drinks?"

"Sure." He opened the bottle of wine and let it breathe and poured himself some of the cider.

She put serving bowls and platters on the dining table and told Colin to dig in. No sense standing on ceremony with just the two of them. She put a bowl out for Max with dog food and turkey drippings and she could hear the dog scarfing in the mudroom. Before Colin sat down, he stoked the fire.

"This looks great, Harlee."

"A lot of food for just the two of us." She surveyed the spread. "But I'll send you home with plenty of leftovers. Turkey sandwiches for the next week."

As he reached for the bread, his sleeve inched up and Harlee saw the quincunx tattoo again. He saw her looking at it and said, "Don't ask about it, Harlee."

She held up her hands in surrender. "Okay. I was just curious, because it's so different."

His face softened. "Is there anything you're not curious about?"

When it came to him, she was curious about everything. "How come you're single?"

He let out a breath. "Because I like being alone." Harlee noted the emphasis on "alone."

"Why are you single?" His gaze heated as his eyes moved over her sweater dress.

"San Francisco is a tough town for single women," she said. "All the really good men are gay. The others are either tech nerds or unctuous hipsters. And the one thing I've learned from DataDate is you can't trust any of them."

She served herself up more cranberry sauce. In her family she was the only one who ate it. "So you've never been married or in a long-term relationship?"

"Nope," he said, proceeding to inhale everything on his plate and going for seconds.

"What about . . . the uh . . . physical part?"

He tilted his head to the side. "Sex? Is that what you're asking me about? I have sex, Harlee."

Just not with her. "I'm sorry, it's not my business."

His mouth quirked. "Since when has that stopped you, Lois Lane? What about the reporter guys at your work?" She got the impression he didn't really want to know but was trying to put her on the spot, the way she had him.

"A few," she said. "Don't get me wrong; I dated."

For a minute she saw something flicker in his expression. Maybe sadness, but it was so fleeting she couldn't make it out. "Oh, I almost forgot. My mom sold all three of the pieces you sent her. She wants more, Colin, especially for Christmas. She's thinking about selling one of the log beds. That way she can do it up with handmade quilts and pillows."

"I could do that," he said. "Maybe I should deliver it, save her on shipping. I could also set it up for her."

"Ooh, if you do that I'd like to go with you. We could stay at my folks' house." She got the feeling he hadn't liked that idea. The man was so damn prickly.

When they finished dinner, Harlee insisted that they leave the dishes and relax in front of the fire with a slice of pie. They were halfway into it when he got a call on his cell phone. Harlee figured it must be his sister to wish him a happy Thanksgiving. But she could hear a man's voice on the other end and it didn't sound good.

When he got off the phone he said, "I've got to go, Harlee."

"Is everything all right?"

"Sophie and Mariah took some of their dinner guests over to the new house to show them the progress. It turns out the roof is leaking. Snow's getting inside. I've gotta see what I can do to cover it until Monday. I'll come back afterward to help you clean up."

"Don't worry about it." Harlee waved her hand dismissively. "Darla is planning to come over. She'll help. I'll keep Max for you."

"I hate to leave this way. That was the best meal I've ever had. I mean it, Harlee."

"I'm glad you liked it. I'll have the leftovers packed up for you when you pick up Max." She ran to get his jacket and watched as he put it on. "Thanks for the flowers, the wine, and cider."

"You're welcome." He took off out the door, but came back a few minutes later. She'd already begun doing dishes but could hear him in the foyer.

"Harlee," he called. "Come here."

She returned, thinking that maybe he couldn't start his truck. That's when he pulled her hard against him and kissed her. A heart-melting kiss, raw and sensual, that went on forever and ever. She could feel his need pressing against her and his low growl of pleasure made her cradle his neck to drive him deeper. His tongue, tangling with hers, made her hot as molten lava. If not for the strong arms that held her, Harlee would've wound up on the floor, in a puddle. Colin pulled her even closer and she could feel his heart pounding. In that single, solitary moment, Harlee had never felt more desired—or more wonderful.

Then, just like that, he stopped kissing her, let her go, and left.

Chapter 11

On Monday Sophie came into the barbershop. Even eight months' pregnant, Darla thought she looked stunning. Whoever did her hair was a true artist.

"Hi, Soph. What can I do for you?" she asked, figuring that she was passing out some Neighborhood Watch pamphlets. Sophie and Maddy had organized the merchants on the square ever since last winter when some dope dealer terrorized the town.

"Maddy said you were selling hair-care products." Sophie turned to the large set of display shelves and blinked. "And boy, are you ever. This is good stuff, Darla."

"Thanks." Word was finally spreading. "What are you looking for?" Darla came off the barber chair where she'd been clipping in an *I Dream of Jeannie* ponytail. She'd dyed it pink to match her latest hair color.

"Shampoo and conditioner. But nothing with parabens." Her hand went unconsciously to her belly and she looked at Darla skeptically, like she probably didn't know what parabens were.

Darla felt Sophie's hair. "Very healthy. But you're prone toward oily, aren't you?"

"You've got it."

Darla rummaged through the shelves until she came up with two red bottles. "These will regulate your extra sebum without damaging your hair. There are no preservatives in it, so you don't have to worry about hurting your baby's development."

"This is wonderful," Sophie said, obviously impressed. "It'll save me a trip to Reno. And Darla, I saw Colin today. What a fantastic job you did. The man has been talking you up like you're the Second Coming."

"He has?" It didn't seem like Colin's style, since the man barely spoke. Maybe her career was looking up after all.

Sophie paid for the shampoo and left. Woo-hoo! Her first sale. She was dancing around the shop when Griffin came in.

"What up, Pink?"

"I just made a sale. Sixty bucks in shampoo and conditioner. And my dad thought the products would be a big flop."

Griff smiled. "Your dad is driving me batshit. He and the mob won't let the bait thing go."

"What bait thing?"

"They want me to sell fish bait at the gas station. They think it's the best idea since the Snuggie."

She laughed. "Just humor them. Tell them there's a world shortage on night crawlers. What did you do for Thanksgiving?"

"I went to McCreedy Ranch. Emily killed it with her deep-fried turkey. There were a ton of people over there, including your boyfriend, Wyatt."

"He's not my boyfriend. Did Lina go?"

"Yeah."

"What's wrong?" she asked, sensing trouble in *Romper Room* paradise. Darla didn't think the girl was old enough to vote.

"Uh, she's dissatisfied with our arrangement." he said.

"And what's that?"

"Friends."

"With privileges?" Darla arched a brow.

"No. She's too young. I want her to get the full college experience, not have a boyfriend waiting in the wings. But I don't like making her unhappy. She's important to me."

Ah, Griffin was one of the good ones. "What are you planning to do?"

"Stand firm. Luckily, her brother will kill both of us if we start something. I hear he's a good shot."

Everyone knew the police chief was a good shot. Last winter,

Chief Shepard killed that meth dealer. Darla had lived in Sacramento then, but even she had heard the details. It had been the biggest news in Nugget since the eighteen hundreds, when the Donner Party got stranded in the Sierra and turned to cannibalism to keep from starving to death.

Griff changed the subject. "What did you do for Thanksgiving?"

"We had dinner with Ethel and Stu, Dink, and Grace and Earl from the Nugget feed store."

"So pretty much the entire Nugget Mafia?"

"Yep," Darla said, chuckling. "Afterward I went over to Harlee's. Colin left before I got there because of an emergency at Sophie and Mariah's construction site."

"Is everything all right?"

"I think so. Sophie was just here and didn't say anything."

Griffin straddled one of the chairs in the waiting room. "Let's do another bowling night. That last one was fun. This time we should invite Wyatt. What's the deal with you guys, anyway?"

Darla had decided she wasn't going to talk about him anymore. After unloading on Colin the other day, she'd felt pretty bad. Her and Wyatt's business should stay private. "We had a thing once. It's ancient history now."

"So you don't mind if I invite him?"

She did, but what could she say? "No."

"I was thinking that we should include Colin too, since he's been hanging out with Harlee a lot. But then we'll need more women to even up our numbers."

Darla didn't know that many women their age. When she used to come to stay with her dad it had always just been Wyatt. "I'll see what I can do. What about Lina?"

"She's not coming back until Christmas," he said. "Hey, I sold another Sierra Heights house. Nate Breyer bought one of the midsize ones. Right on the golf course. I guess with Sophie due, he wants to have a place here." Everyone knew that Nate was the biological father of Sophie and Mariah's baby.

"That's great." And here she was throwing a ticker-tape parade for a bottle of shampoo and conditioner.

Griffin checked his watch. "I've gotta bounce. A guy's delivering my car-wash equipment. Talk to Harlee about our bowling night. Pick a good date."

"I will," she said, and walked out with him for a breath of fresh air. It had stopped snowing and the sun had peeked out from behind the clouds.

Across the square, someone was blowing leaves off the Lumber Baron's expansive porch. A group of teenagers lined up in front of the takeout window at the Bun Boy. And Darla almost threw up in her mouth when she saw Wyatt Lambert come walking out of the Ponderosa with his arms draped around a woman's shoulders.

Colin drove back to Nugget from his second acupuncture appointment not feeling any less phobic than he had the day before. Of course he wasn't in a large crowd or even in a tight spot. So to be fair, who really knew? But wouldn't he at least notice the cells in his body coming alive with Qi, or whatever crap was supposed to happen to him after being stuck with needles?

Nope. All he had was a scratchy throat and throbbing headache. Colin hoped like hell he wasn't getting a cold. He'd been coughing and achy the last couple of days. But he didn't have time to get sick. Not with furniture to make for the Christmas rush and construction projects to finish.

At the last minute, Harlee hadn't been able to come with him to the appointment. One of her clients needed soothing after finding out that the "divorce lawyer" she'd been dating for the last six months had actually been disbarred two years earlier for having sex with his clients—men and women.

It was probably for the best that she hadn't been able to accompany Colin. Ever since the kiss, he'd been on shaky ground where she was concerned. Too much temptation. But he couldn't seem to give her up either. He was a masochistic bastard.

Before reaching Nugget, he pulled off on McCreedy Road. Emily Mathews had called earlier and wanted him to give her a bid on a kitchen. As far as work, this town had been good to him. He never went long without a job and his furniture had begun to take off. He wasn't what you would call wealthy, but he had enough to live comfortably. At least by his standards.

One of the reasons he liked Nugget so much was the people here were self-sufficient and humble. Lots of mom-and-pop businesses, artisans, farmers, and ranchers. Take Clay McCreedy. The man owned a fortune in land and cattle, yet he wore faded old Levi's, dusty boots, and the same brand work shirts as Colin.

As he pulled into the driveway, the two McCreedy boys waved to him. Colin didn't know them well. He'd heard through the Nugget grapevine that the older one had had some behavior issues, but was currently riding the straight and narrow. Colin sincerely hoped the kid's problems were behind him. Bad things happened when they got out of hand. He knew that from experience.

Clay greeted him at the door. "Thanks for coming over, Colin. I know you're busy with Sophie and Mariah's place, especially while the weather holds." He popped his head outside and gazed up at the clear sky. "Lord knows how long it'll last."

"You looking at a new kitchen, huh?"

"Emily is looking at a new kitchen. I just write the checks."

"Oh, be quiet, you." Emily came up alongside them and blinked up at Colin. "You look fantastic. Maddy told me Darla cut your hair."

"Yeah. It was getting out of control."

Clay grabbed his Stetson off a hook. "You two get started without me. I've got a few things to do in the barn."

When he left, Emily said, "He grew up in this house and is a little nostalgic about the kitchen. So I want to keep the general feel of it. But for my work it's a bit antiquated. You have a good eye, Colin. Hopefully, you'll know how to make it modern and old at the same time."

"What about the barn? Why don't you use that for working on your cookbooks?" Emily had moved here last summer and had rented a barn that Clay's late wife had converted into a beautiful apartment.

"For the most part it'll be my office, but I'm constantly testing recipes and I want to be here for the boys when they get home from school. I love what you did with the Lumber Baron kitchen and have actually used it a few times for photo shoots. Speaking of"—she broke off, disappeared for a few seconds, and returned with a book under her arm—"it's out."

She showed him the cover of Della James's new cookbook, quickly flipping to two facing pages showcasing pies and featuring his farm table and rocking chair. The photographs credited Colin as the craftsman. Emily turned to the back of the book to a resources page and showed him where Colin Burke Furniture and his website were listed. *Pretty cool*, he thought as he leafed through the book.

"That's yours to keep," Emily said. "Della signed it for you."

"No kidding." He was quite taken aback, knowing full well that Emily was behind the kind gesture. "Thank you."

"I hope it brings you business. You do such phenomenal work."

He brushed off the praise with a sheepish smile. "Thanks. Let's take a look at your kitchen."

Two hours later, Colin headed for home, his head throbbing worse than ever and his chest burning like a chemical fire. He still had to pick out a few pieces of furniture for Harlee's mother and hadn't decided whether to ship them or drive them himself. The trip was four hours each way, which would burn a day. And it sounded like Emily wanted the kitchen work done as quickly as possible, which meant Colin would have to fit it in between Sophie and Mariah's job. He needed to be flexible if he wanted to continue getting work.

When he pulled into his driveway, Harlee's Pathfinder was there. She stood off to the side, playing fetch with Max. Colin sat in his truck, watching her for a while. She didn't seem to mind that the ball Max returned was covered in slobber. Harlee just scooped it up while the dog stared up at her in expectation with those multicolored eyes, and pitched as far as she could. Colin thought she threw like a girl.

Eventually, she came up to his driver's door. "How was acupuncture?"

He tried to appear enthusiastic because she wanted it to work so badly. "Good, I think."

"Is it too soon to go somewhere? Maybe try a restaurant to see if it's working?"

"Yeah, too soon," he said, unable to keep his eyes from moving over her. Today she wore painted-on jeans and a short, fitted jacket that hugged her curves. Her hair was tied back in a ponytail with little wisps falling around her face. A face that could launch a thousand ships, he thought, because she was that beautiful.

He wanted to kiss her again, but instead shoved Della James's cookbook into her hands. "Check it out."

She let out a little squeal of delight. "This is the one you're in, right?"

"Not me," he corrected. "My furniture."

Flipping through the pages, she found the spread with Colin's table and chair. "Wow! This is huge. I'm calling my mom."

She followed him into the house with her phone pressed to her ear. Colin went into the kitchen and rummaged through a lower cabinet, looking for a bag of dog food, while Harlee talked to her mother. She spoke in a stream of exuberant non sequiturs and Colin found it difficult to track the conversation. Something about how Harlee's mother should buy Della's book and display the furniture pages in her shop.

"My mom wants to know when we're coming down."

He stopped what he was doing and stood up, the motion making him dizzy. God, he felt like hell. "I got another job today, remodeling a kitchen," he said. "It looks like I'll have to ship the furniture."

"That's great, Colin." She got back on the phone. "Mom, did you hear that? Okay, I'll call you later."

She reached down, grabbed the dog food, and put it up on the counter. "Whose kitchen?"

"Emily and Clay's," he said, and crossed to the other side of the room, needing air. "I've got to check my email."

"Okay." She got Max's bowl and replenished his food. "You want me to heat up leftovers?"

He should've told her to go home, that he needed to go to bed, but he liked having her around so much that he couldn't bring himself to do it. "Sure."

"Are you all right? You seem a little weird," she called to him in the office.

He rested his forehead against the window, letting the coolness from the glass revive his damp skin. "I'm good," he called back, but he wasn't. He felt weak, clammy, and like an eighteen-wheeler was speeding through his head. "Probably just a little tired."

She came into the office holding a dishtowel. "Any new orders?"

"Let's see," he said, and started to walk to his desk so he could turn on the computer. But he felt like his feet were nailed to the floor. And where had the strobe lights come from? All he knew is that they were flashing and whirling, making his eyes feel like they were going to burst.

"Colin?"

He could hear Harlee's voice, but it sounded so small and muffled, like she was far, far away.

"Colin?" She reached for him, but her hand singed him. He was so hot. "Colin, what's happening to you?"

He held on to the windowsill for stability, trying to keep upright.

"Acupuncturist," he said, but wasn't sure the words had made it past his lips. "Trying to kill me."

Then everything went black.

Harlee grabbed the phone and dialed 9-1-1. About twenty minutes later, Chief Shepard and an ambulance rolled down Colin's driveway.

"He's conscious," she told the chief as he came through the door, amazed at how calm she sounded, when she'd never been more worried in her life. "I've been applying cold compresses, but he's burning with fever."

Two paramedics pushed by her and the chief followed them to the office, where Colin lay prone on the hardwood floor.

"Hey, Colin," one of the medics called, while the other checked his vital signs and inserted an IV into his arm. "Heck, man, the last time I saw you, someone had tried to knock your head off."

Colin didn't reply, but Harlee flicked her head at the police chief. "What is he talking about?"

"It's a long story." The chief turned to the paramedics. "You taking him to Plumas General Hospital?"

"Yeah," one of the medics responded. "His temperature is close to a hundred and four degrees."

"Could acupuncture do this?" Harlee asked, and all three men stopped what they were doing to look at her.

"Come again?" one of them asked.

She didn't want to give away any of Colin's confidences, but if it had something to do with his fever, they needed to know. "He just got back from an acupuncture appointment."

"If the needles weren't sterilized, he could've gotten a bacterial or viral infection. But same day?" The guy looked dubious. "Seems unlikely."

"We've gotta go," the other one said, and they lifted Colin onto a gurney, strapped him down, and started to carry him out of the house.

Harlee jogged to keep up with them, and when they reached the back of the ambulance she said, "Wait a sec. He's got claustrophobia. Did you transport him in an ambulance last time, when he got hit in the head?" She had every intention of getting to the bottom of that story, but it could wait.

"He was unconscious," the police chief said, walking to the side of the stretcher. "Hey, Colin, you okay to ride back there?"

Colin groaned something unintelligible.

"I'm going with him," Harlee said, afraid that Colin was delirious from fever but would freak out as soon as he found himself in close quarters.

"Are you related to him?" one of the medics asked.

She knew the rules. "I'm his wife."

The chief rolled his eyes but didn't rat her out.

She waited for them to load the gurney into the ambulance, then got inside. "I'm here, Colin." Considering how high his temperature was, his hands were so very cold. She leaned over and kissed his forehead. "You're okay."

They made the forty-minute drive to Quincy without lights or sirens. And without incident. Colin was so out of it, he didn't seem to realize he was in the small hull of an ambulance. The two paramedics wheeled Colin into the emergency room when they got to the hospital. Harlee tried to go with him, but a nurse told her that someone would come for her in a little while.

She went to the waiting room and called her father. He was a doctor and would walk her through this, assure her that Colin would be okay and that she hadn't nearly killed him by sending him to an acupuncturist. When she couldn't reach him, she left a message on his voice mail.

A short time later, a scowling Chief Shepard and his wife walked through the door. Harlee waved to them and they joined her.

"How's it going, Mrs. Burke?" the chief asked.

"You can cut the sarcasm, Rhys," Maddy admonished, and directed herself at Harlee, whispering, "I'm glad you lied. Poor Colin. Rhys thinks he has the flu. Apparently there's a particularly virulent bug going around. Colin is the fourth person in the county who has had to be hospitalized."

"But everyone survived, right?" Harlee asked.

"Oh yeah," Maddy said. "Colin is a big, strong man. This is the kind of flu that's mostly dangerous to old people and young children."

"And pregnant women," Rhys piped in. Maddy stared daggers at him, and he stared right back.

"Have they come out yet to let you know what's going on?" she asked Harlee.

"Not yet."

"It's a good thing you were there with him. Otherwise no one might've realized that he was sick until he failed to show up for work."

Harlee nodded. She wondered if Rhys had told Maddy about the acupuncture and the claustrophobia. Colin would be upset if a lot of people knew. He guarded his privacy. And despite how unassuming he was, Colin was sort of a macho guy. That's something she'd learned very quickly about him. He had a wariness and toughness that made her think of a street fighter.

She wanted to tell Maddy that they didn't have to wait. But it seemed presumptuous, given that Maddy had known Colin longer than Harlee. Still, she could tell that her husband was concerned about her catching something.

"If you guys want to go, I could call you and give you updates. All three of us don't need to be here," she said.

"How you planning to get home, Mrs. Burke?"

She'd forgotten that she didn't have a car. Before she could reply, a man in scrubs with a stethoscope around his neck came out and quickly perused the waiting room. Besides them, there was only an African-American family seated.

"Are you Mrs. Burke?" He addressed her, and she caught Rhys doing the eye-roll thing again.

"Yes," she said, sending the police chief a death glare, silently warning him: *Sell me down the river and I will cut you. Screw HIPAA.* "Are you the doctor?"

He nodded and held out his hand. "Rick Morgan." Dr. Morgan joined them on one of the faux-leather beam seats that killed Harlee's back and made her butt sore. "Colin's got a severe case of the flu and a lower-respiratory-tract infection. We've given him amoxicillin, made him as comfortable as possible, and want to keep him at least overnight."

"But he'll recover, right?" Harlee knew that a lower-respiratory-tract infection was basically pneumonia. She wasn't a doctor's daughter for nothing.

"He's a healthy young man. As long as he responds to the antibiotics, he should be feeling much better in a few days."

"I'd like to see him," she said.

"Me too," Maddy said, adding, "I'm a friend of the family."

Rhys mumbled something that sounded a lot like an expletive. And Maddy shot him a murderous glare.

The doctor took one look at Maddy's rounded belly and gave Rhys a commiserating smile. "I think it would be best for just Mrs. Burke to visit with him." He turned to Harlee. "They're admitting him right now, but as soon as he's settled into a room, someone will come get you."

When the doctor left, Harlee told Rhys and Maddy, "You guys shouldn't wait. I'll stay the night here with Colin."

"That's nuts," Maddy said. "We'll wait until you've checked on him and then we'll take you home."

"I don't want him to be alone," she said, concerned that the hubbub of the busy hospital might trigger Colin's demophobia.

"That's very nice of you, Harlee," Rhys said. "But Colin will probably sleep through the night. He won't even know you're here. Go home, get a comfortable night's sleep, and come back first thing in the morning."

"I'll be fine," she argued. "They might even have a cot they can put in the room."

"You sure?" Maddy asked.

"Positive." They exchanged cell phone numbers and left with the promise that Harlee would keep them abreast of Colin's condition and would call when she needed a ride. They'd also take care of Max in the interim.

Subsequently, a hospital volunteer came to escort her to Colin's room. The short-stay unit was next to the intensive care unit, which was next to orthopedics. All on the second floor. It was a small country hospital to be sure. Harlee's father worked at Alta Bates in Oakland, which was ten times the size.

At least Colin had a single room. Although barely large enough for a hospital bed, table, and a narrow chair, which held his neatly folded clothes, she knew he would be glad for the privacy. Sound asleep, he took in shallow breaths as he struggled to draw in air. As big and strong as he was, he looked vulnerable lying there. She reached for him and then thought better of it. He needed to rest.

Instead, Harlee grabbed the small plastic pitcher from the table and went in search of ice.

By the time she got back, Colin had come awake, staring at the wall, bleary eyed, seemingly trying to get a fix on where he was.

"Hey." She returned the pitcher to the table and took his hand. "Welcome back. You're in the hospital."

"Yeah," he said, struggling to sit up. "I think they told me I have a lung infection. But maybe I dreamt that."

"Nope. You have a bad flu, complicated by pneumonia." She gently pushed him back down. "You want something to drink?"

"How come you're here?" He tried to elevate the top of the bed but couldn't find the remote, so she did it for him.

"I came with you in the ambulance. You don't remember?"

"I think so. It's a little hazy."

"Maddy and Rhys came too . . . in their car," she said, brushing hair away from his face. "They're worried about you. But Rhys was concerned about the baby. You're probably pretty contagious."

"Why didn't you go home with them?"

"I thought you should have company." She went into the closet-sized bathroom, where she filled the pitcher with water and poured him a glass, feeding it to him from a straw. "Thirsty?"

"Yeah," he said, draining the cup. "My mouth feels like someone jammed it with cotton."

"I'll get you some juice in a few minutes."

"You should've gone home, Harlee."

"You'll be happy I stayed. I used to be a candy striper."

"Really? You still have the uniform?" He lifted his brows suggestively.

She figured he must be delirious to flirt with her so overtly, because he'd never done it before. Just that one, mind-blowing kiss and a lot of heated gazes. He made room so she could scoot onto the edge of the bed.

"By the way, this"—she waved her hand over him in the hospital bed—"has nothing to do with acupuncture. You said the acupuncturist tried to kill you."

"I did?" He let out a scratchy chuckle.

"Right before you went down for the count," she said. "And what's this about you getting knocked over the head a while back? One of the paramedics told me about it."

He pulled the blanket tighter around him. She took the one folded at the bottom of the bed and tugged it up under his chin.

"When we first started rehabbing the Lumber Baron, I found a meth lab in the basement," Colin said. "The owner wanted his stash back. Unfortunately, he believed that I was standing in the way of that happening, so he bashed me over the head with a tree branch."

"Oh my God. You could've been killed. Was he ever caught?"

Colin's eyes fluttered closed. "Yeah. Rhys shot him."

Dead? she wondered. But Colin was dozing off and she wanted him to rest. She started to move away, but he grabbed her hand. Then he lifted the blanket and pulled her under.

"Sleep," he said, fitting against her like a spoon.

Chapter 12

It took Colin two weeks to recover and even still he wasn't 100 percent. But he'd only had to spend one night in the hospital. The next day, Rhys had picked him and Harlee up and he'd convalesced in his own bed.

Harlee had spent the entire time fussing over him, the nurturing so alien he didn't quite know how to respond. Even though Fiona had hovered when Colin had first gotten out of Donovan, the outside world was such a foreign place that he was constantly on guard, never letting anyone, even the people he loved, too close.

Ever since Della's book came out, furniture sales had gone crazy. Harlee had taken over the business, checking his email and website daily for orders and methodically keeping his books. The woman couldn't balance her own checkbook, but he noticed she was meticulous with his. Griffin came regularly to help her package up heavy pieces for FedEx and UPS, which trekked up and down Colin's driveway so many times, he'd lost track. He wasn't thrilled about having Griffin in his space, spending so much time with Harlee, not to mention making Colin feel like an invalid because he couldn't get out of bed.

But he reminded himself to be grateful. Like Griffin, some of the other townsfolk pitched in. Emily brought soups and her famous lasagna. Maddy kept him in books and magazines. Mariah made regular visits, commandeering his blender to make him the green smoothies he liked so much, while updating him on the house and Sophie's progress.

She was almost ready to pop. Darla showed up a couple times a week, to sit by his side, talk his ear off, and generally drive him crazy.

And one day it hit him like a two-ton bag of bricks. He had friends. By nature, Nugget was the kind of town that pulled together in times of crisis or need. The people here looked out for one another. Being this remote necessitated self-reliance. But as much as Colin had gone out of his way to avoid becoming part of the community, they'd taken him in anyway.

How betrayed would they feel when they found out the truth? They'd run him out of town with shotguns. That's what they'd do. As generous as this town could be, it could also be a judgmental bitch. Colin had seen it firsthand when Nugget residents had tried to take down Maddy and Nate's inn, fearful that it would turn the town into a tourist trap.

And Harlee? How would she feel? The answer was too screwed up to contemplate. So he tried not to. Instead, he dragged his ass out of bed, showered, dressed, and fired up the Vitamix. He took his smoothie with him into the office, where he emailed a few different designs for Emily and Clay's kitchen.

He had a lot of catching up to do. The phone rang, Colin checked caller ID, and answered.

"Hi, Fiona."

"Is it still snowing there?" she asked, and Colin looked outside the window.

"Not at the moment. Why?"

"I just want to make sure you're still coming. You're feeling better, right?"

"I'm feeling good and you know I'm coming," he said. Colin had made the trip every Christmas since moving to Nugget.

"I hope so. I don't like you driving on the slick roads."

"In a week it could be sunny and dry." Not likely, but if it eased Fiona's mind . . .

She cleared her throat and said, "I don't want you to go to the cemetery this year. You've paid your debt, Colin. Enough."

"It'll never be enough, Fiona. Never."

"You know how I feel about this," she said, and he did, because they'd been over it a million times. "What happened that night . . . It's time to move on, Colin."

"It doesn't work that way, Fi. Look, let's not do this. I'm looking forward to seeing you, Steve, and the kids. What should I get them, by the way?"

"Don't worry about that," she said. "Just get here in one piece."

"I'll call you before I leave."

"Col," she said, stopping him before he hung up. "I have a friend I want you to meet."

He rested his forehead against his computer monitor. "No friends, Fiona."

"She's great, beautiful, and you'll love her."

"Not interested."

"You're never interested, Colin. It all goes back to the fact that you're continuing to punish yourself. You deserve to have a good life, Col. To have companionship. Someone who'll love you."

"I'm seeing someone, all right? I've gotta go, Fiona." And with that he hung up. He shouldn't have told her that. First off, it wasn't true. He didn't know what Harlee and he were doing, but technically they weren't seeing each other. He was pretty sure that involved dates—and sex. They weren't having either. Secondly, Fiona would interrogate him until the cows came home.

"Come on, Max, let's take a walk," he called to the dog.

Max trotted out from underneath the desk, thumping his tail. Colin shrugged into his ski jacket, pulled a wool beanie over his head, and tugged on a pair of fingerless gloves. It was cold and he didn't want to have a relapse. Tomorrow he was due back at work on Sophie and Mariah's house.

Man and dog trudged up the driveway, then down the hill to Harlee's house. But she wasn't there. Probably went into town to hang out with Darla or to buy groceries, Colin decided, and headed home to his wood shop.

He was halfway up Grizzly Peak when he heard Harlee's Pathfinder. He started back down, Max at his heels, but when he got to the top of her drive, he saw Harlee wasn't alone. Griffin was helping her unload a Christmas tree from the top of the truck rack. While he pulled the tree down and stuck the base inside a stand, Harlee gathered up enough snow from the slushy remains, made a snowball, and threw it at Griffin. Griffin chased her, hurling his own snowball in retaliation. Too busy laughing, neither noticed Colin.

He stood there a few minutes, watching them carry the red fir pine through the front door. They looked good together. Too good. Colin turned around and went home.

Christmas passed in a blur of thunderstorms and white flurries. After suffering four days of cabin fever with her family, including a sniveling toddler, Harlee decided to make the pilgrimage to town and meet Darla at the barbershop. She took Max, her four-legged charge until Colin got home from LA, for a quick walk, hopped into her SUV, drove to town, and parked on the square.

Inside, Darla sat in Owen's chair in front of the mirror, removing red and green ribbons from her hair. It looked to Harlee like they'd been woven in, which seemed like a lot of work just for Christmas. But she supposed Darla had plenty of time on her hands.

"Hey," Darla said, standing up to buss Harlee on the cheek. "The fam finally gone?"

"Yes." Harlee said. "I love 'em, but thank God. How was your mom and Sacramento?"

"Looking better every day."

Harlee knew that business at the barbershop still hadn't picked up. "It's the holidays, Darla. People can't afford haircuts. They're tapped out from buying Christmas gifts."

Darla tipped her head and crossed her arms over her chest. "Harlee, it's the busiest time of year for a stylist, and you know it. I really thought the products would make the difference, get people in the door. Connie came in for layers a few days before Christmas. But since then, nada."

Harlee started to give her a pep talk, but Darla stopped her. "I so don't want to think about this right now."

That was a sentiment Harlee could identify with, given her own issues. Although DataDate trucked along, generating roughly a new assignment every week, she was still broke, in debt, and her search for a newspaper job had netted exactly nothing.

"You want me to play with your hair?" Darla took out the last ribbon and pulled her hair back into a loose ponytail. Today it was plain old natural blond, the way Harlee liked Darla's hair the best. "I could give you an updo or something."

"Sure." Harlee didn't really want an updo, but maybe passersby would see her in the chair and think Darla had a booming clientele.

Looking busy was everything when it came to marketing. Harlee had friends who wouldn't step foot in a restaurant unless they couldn't get a table.

Darla got out of the chair, cleaned it with a rag that smelled like alcohol, and motioned for Harlee to hop up. She scoured a pile of magazines in the waiting area and came back with a *People*. "What do you think of something like this?" She showed Harlee a picture of Zooey Deschanel in a modern-day chignon with bangs. "She looks like you."

Harlee had been told before that she resembled the actress. "Okay." The style really was quite nice, and conservative by Darla's standards.

Darla got to work back-combing Harlee's hair for volume. "When is Colin coming home?"

"I'm not sure," she said.

He'd sent her a text to ask about Max, but that had been their only communication. Before he'd left, Colin had hastily dropped off the dog and a gift—a gorgeous jewelry box he'd made—barely saying a word. She'd sensed that he was anxious about going home.

The man could be such a mystery, but no doubt about it, Harlee had a thing for him. She'd never considered herself as having a type, but if you would've asked her two months ago, it would not have been Colin Burke. He was too quiet, too solitary, and too . . . well, mountain-mannish. The men she dated in the city had polish. They went to the best restaurants, drove Teslas, and subscribed to *Wired* magazine. And they would've had her naked by now.

But unlike those men, Colin was steady, real, and a million times more complicated. He was also a million times more detached.

"I had hoped he'd be here by tomorrow. In time for our New Year's Eve bash," Darla said. They were having drinks and bowling at the Ponderosa.

Darla reached for a bristle brush, when the bells chimed over the door. A woman Harlee had never seen before came in looking frazzled but well dressed. Everything from her supple leather handbag to her cashmere camel coat spoke money.

"Can you fix this?" she asked, taking off an angora beret. It looked like someone had gone to town on her hair with a machete.

Darla lifted her brows and asked mildly, "What happened?"

She let out a breath. "I'm a cutter."

When Harlee quietly examined her for whatever knife or scissor marks she could find, the woman let out a wry laugh. "Just my hair."

Darla stepped closer to get a better look at the damage. "I could cut it real short, or try to layer. But it's pretty chopped." She grimaced, because chopped didn't begin to describe the woman's hair.

"I'd prefer to keep some length," she said, taking in her surroundings. "The lady over at the inn recommended you. I didn't realize it was a barbershop."

Apparently she'd missed the large red, white, and blue barber pole outside.

"We're unisex," Darla said.

The woman took off her coat and draped it over one of the waiting chairs. "Okay. Can you fit me in after her?" She nudged her chin at Harlee.

"Oh," Harlee said, "we're just playing. Let me check Darla's appointment book."

Darla glowered at her like she'd gone mad. But Harlee knew this kind of woman. Hell, in an earlier life, she'd been this kind of woman, and appearances meant everything. Camel Coat could be a regular if they played their cards right. So she ignored Darla's dagger stares, walked over to the cash register, grabbed the iPad sitting there, and pretended to scroll through it. "Um, you don't have anyone else coming in until two."

The woman glanced at her watch, which Harlee was pretty sure was a Patek Philippe. "Is that enough time?"

Darla slanted Harlee another WTF look and waved the lady into the chair. "I think so. I'm Darla, by the way, and this is my trusted assistant, Harlee." Again with the look.

"Samantha," she said.

Darla wrapped a cape around Samantha and played with her trashed hair in the mirror, sifting her fingers through the woman's auburn locks and weighing them in the palm of her hand. "This is what I'm thinking, Samantha."

"Sam. Everyone calls me Sam."

"Okay, Sam." Darla pulled Samantha's hair to above her chin. "I'd take it to about here." "I'm thinking choppy bob. You good with that?"

Sam pulled a face. "Do I have a choice?"

"No." Darla shook her head. "Not really."

"All right. Go for it."

Darla walked her to the shampoo bowl while Harlee tried to get a closer look at the designer name on Sam's purse. Prada. Harlee happened to know that her shoes were Christian Louboutin—the red soles gave them away—and retailed for nine hundred bucks at Barneys.

"How do you know Maddy at the Lumber Baron?" Harlee asked.

"I'm staying there," she said. "I got off the interstate to find a ladies' room and there it was. Such a charming place."

"Where you headed?" Harlee tried to look receptionist-like, straightening magazines and flitting around the room as if there were a million details to see to in Nugget's most prominent salon. *Look at us, so professional.*

"I don't know yet," she said as Darla twisted a towel around Sam's wet hair. "Any ideas?"

Harlee and Darla stopped to see if the woman was joking.

"Christmas Day I got in my car to go to a wedding and just kept driving."

"Where was the wedding?" Harlee asked.

"New York City." She said it so nonchalantly, her eyes slightly glazed, that Harlee thought she might be a little cuckoo. "It's actually a straight shot—2,786 miles. I clocked it. The roads got a little dicey in Illinois and Nebraska—black ice. But everything was so crisp. Fresh. And the people in Wyoming . . . salt of the earth."

"You didn't know where you were going?" Harlee asked.

"Nope."

Darla caught Harlee's eye as if to say *"Is this woman messing with our heads?"* because that's like a forty-hour drive to make on the spur of the moment with no destination in mind.

"But you stopped along the way, right?" Darla began cutting her hair.

"Of course. I needed clothes." The woman was wearing a Diane von Fürstenberg pantsuit.

Harlee and Darla looked at each other again. *Are you thinking what I'm thinking? Uh, bipolar.*

"Did you tell anyone back home that you were leaving?" Harlee asked, scanning Sam's left hand for a wedding ring. Maybe she was running from an abusive husband.

"No. No, I didn't. Maybe I will today."

Uh, good idea, since it had been five days since Christmas. By now Sam was probably on the back of a milk carton. Harlee wondered if the woman was having a mental breakdown.

"Are you okay, Sam?" Harlee asked, trying to seem casual and not like *Are you freaking insane?*

"You know," Sam said, and started to turn her head toward Harlee, but Darla stopped her. "I've never felt better in my life. Except for my hair, of course."

While Darla continued to snip away, focused on trying to save Sam's hair from the butcher job, Harlee went back to the cash register.

"Hey, Sam, I'm super anal about Darla's books, so I'm plugging you in." She casually held up the iPad. "What's your last name, hon?"

"Dunsbury," she said without hesitation.

Harlee jumped on Google faster than Danica Patrick could lap the Indianapolis Motor Speedway. Just as quickly popped up the headline: Missing Heiress Feared Kidnapped. She read the first few lines of the article, enough to learn that Samantha Dunsbury lived in Greenwich, Connecticut, and her father managed a multibillion-dollar hedge fund, then closed the page.

"Uh, I'm gonna grab a cup of coffee next door. Anyone want anything?"

"I'm good," Samantha said, watching intently as Darla razor-cut sections of her hair at an angle. Darla really did seem to know what she was doing.

"I'll take a latte," Darla the Clueless said.

"Okay." Harlee skipped out the door and right on over to the police station. Connie, Nugget's police dispatcher, sat at the reception desk. "Is the chief here?"

"Why are you whispering?" Connie asked. Harlee hadn't realized she was. "I'll get him."

Rhys popped out of his office and waved her back. "What's up?"

"Google Samantha Dunsbury," she said. He looked annoyed, but he returned to his desk and did it, pulling up the same article Harlee had read.

"What about her?"

"Read it," she said. "Because the woman is next door, getting her hair cut at the barbershop, and happens to be staying at your wife's inn."

That got his attention. He read through the article and clicked on a few more. "Is she alone?"

"She is right now. Her hair looks like someone set a lawnmower loose on it and Maddy told her that Darla could fix it. She said she drove here from New York—just got in her car and kept going, stopping along the way to buy designer clothes. She doesn't appear to be afraid or anything—just a little cray cray, if you know what I mean."

Rhys got to his feet.

"Where you going?" Harlee asked.

"I want to take a look at her, make sure she's the same woman in the picture." He motioned to the photograph in the New York *Daily News* article up on his monitor.

"Trust me, she's the same woman."

"Yeah, I forgot, you're a private investigator." He started for the door.

"Hey," she shouted after him. "I won a George Polk award for investigative reporting."

He returned a few minutes later and she flashed him a good dose of smug.

"I need you to wait outside," he said, and picked up the phone. When she didn't leave, he pointed to the hallway.

She loitered by his door and tried to listen in, but she couldn't make out what he was saying. The glass must've been double paned. Leaning against the wall, she watched as he paced his office, the phone pressed between his shoulder and ear. Finally, he hung up and let her back in.

"The FBI knows she wasn't kidnapped," he said.

"How?"

"She's been using her credit cards. The feds have been tracking her purchases. There's camera footage of her at the Four Seasons in Chicago. She checked in alone."

"Why would she just take off like that?" Harlee sniffed a good story here, but more important, she sensed Sam was in a bad way.

"Didn't you read all the stories?"

"Just the one," Harlee said. "As soon as I saw 'kidnapped,' I rushed over here."

"Christmas was her wedding day. But at the eleventh hour she called it off. The groom thought it was better to concoct a kidnapping story rather than tell the truth. I suppose he thought it was less embarrassing.

"She's an adult," Rhys continued. "Nothing against the law about leaving town without telling anyone. But, Harlee, if you have any sway with her, urge her to call her folks. They know she's safe, but just the same, they're worried about her."

"I'll see what I can do, but she doesn't know me from Adam." Harlee left the police station, stopped at the Bun Boy to get Darla her latte, and went back into the barbershop.

"Whoa! Wow . . . You fixed it." Harlee just about spilled Darla's coffee. Samantha's bad hair had been transformed into the cutest layered bob she'd ever seen. It was short and edgy—a style that could easily become the next "Rachel."

"So good, right?" Darla said, tweaking the ends with styling gel.

"Beyond good," Harlee marveled. The people of Nugget were morons, because Darla seriously had game.

"I love it," Sam said, turning her head this way and that.

"Hey, Sam, you need to call your parents," Harlee said, growing somber. "They're really worried about you."

Sam let out a sigh. "I guess you're right."

She found her phone in her handbag and took a selfie. Harlee watched over Sam's shoulder as she tapped out the message: Wish you were here, attached the photo, and hit the send button.

"You're a magician, Darla." Sam handed Darla a hundred dollar tip and they watched her saunter across the square to the inn, stopping every few feet to yank the heels of her Christian Louboutins out of the muddy grass.

Chapter 13

"Knock, knock." Colin opened the unlocked door to Harlee's cabin and popped his head inside. Her Pathfinder was parked in the driveway, and Max greeted him, barking up a blue streak.

Colin crouched down and scratched the dog behind his ears. "Hey, boy, you miss me?"

Max licked his face, his tail thumping so hard on the plank floor Colin thought it would leave a mark. "Where's Harlee, Max?"

Max, thinking it was a game, chased his tail in circles before bounding toward her bedroom, barking. She came out, wrapped in a towel, to check on the commotion.

"You're home," she squealed, throwing her arms around him, and for a second Colin thought she'd lose the towel.

"Hey"—he hugged her back—"you shouldn't leave the front door unlocked when you're in the shower."

"Why? This is Nugget."

"There's crime everywhere, Harlee." Like the meth asshole who'd hit him over the head.

She continued to cling to him, terry cloth molded to her slippery body like a second skin, so he let his hands roam down her back. Then he let them wander a little farther, until he was palming her perfect ass.

"When did you get in?" she asked, and her voice came out breathy.

"Late last night. But I didn't want to wake you." The whole time in Los Angeles he'd thought about her. Wondered what she was doing, whether she'd be spending the bulk of the holiday with her family—or with Griffin.

Yet here she was, beyond happy to see him. And man, was he happy too—the evidence of that now pressing hard against her.

"Colin?"

"Hmm?" But before she could speak, he kissed her.

Soft, because he didn't want to go too far. In good conscience, he couldn't take Harlee to bed without telling her the truth. And once she knew the truth that would be the end of them. Over before they started. So he went in just for a taste, feeling her cool skin, still slick from her bath, against his heated body. His mouth moved against hers like a whisper, her lips so sweet that he wanted to take more, like the first time, because he could already feel the earth move and he'd barely touched her.

Of course, it didn't help that she responded with fervor, rocking into him, making sexy noises low inside her throat, letting him know in every way that she wanted more.

"Harlee." He pulled away, resting his forehead against hers. "I've got to talk to you about something."

"Now?"

"Yeah," he said, pinching the bridge of his nose.

Her expression went from beatific to worried. "Is everything okay?"

No. "Yes." He eyed her towel, which she now held together, because the toga fold had come apart. It was distracting as hell. "It's important, but I'd rather you got dressed first."

"All right." She disappeared inside her bedroom, and through the closed door called, "The gang is going bowling tonight for New Year's Eve. I had hoped that maybe you would go with me as . . . you know . . . as sort of a test. And at any time if it becomes uncomfortable, we could leave. Come back here or go to your place."

Gang? He was not part of "the gang." And on New Year's Eve the Ponderosa would be mobbed. Especially given that it was the only game in town. But after he said what he needed to say, it wouldn't matter anyway.

Although a small part of him, a part that went dead after the judge announced his sentence then flared back to life the first time Harlee looked at him with those denim-blue eyes, hoped that she might give him a chance. Not for a minute did he think it would happen, but he sure the hell dreamed.

"Did you hear me?" Harlee asked.

"Yeah. I'm thinking about it."

"It'll be fun. Griffin is having problems with Lina. This is a good distraction for him."

I bet. "What's taking you so long?" He wanted to get this over with.

"I'll be right out. Jeez. You swear you're not dying?"

"I'm not dying. I'll meet you in the living room." This way she would stop talking and get dressed.

Colin rambled around the open room and checked out the Christmas tree. Decorated in colorful balls and tinsel, it looked pretty. Not too overdone. Maybe next year, he'd make wooden ornaments to sell. Miniature rocking chairs, tiny birdhouses, and cutout reindeers. Yep, he could get started early, because as soon as he told her about his past he'd have plenty of free time on his hands. Harlee wouldn't be coming around anymore. He'd stop with the stupid acupuncture, which was a total time suck.

The trees swayed outside as the wind picked up speed. He spent a little time gazing out the window at the distant snowcapped mountains. He couldn't see the Feather River from here, but knew it was just beyond the railroad tracks, rushing west through the Humbug Valley, past Long Valley, through gorges and mountains, until it met up with the Sacramento River, 220 miles away.

After spending what seemed like a lifetime staring at concrete, chain-link, and bars, these views never ceased to amaze him. He turned from the window. As usual, Harlee's dining room table was covered in paperwork.

On the top of the stack sat a letter from the *Boston Globe*. Even though it was private, he read it anyway.

> Dear Ms. Roberts,
> Thank you for your interest in the *Boston Globe*. Unfortunately, we have nothing that fits your qualifications at this time. This could change in the future, so we encourage you to stay in touch.
> Sincerely,
> Kelly Reed, Human Resources Specialist.

Boston. Wow, Colin thought as he continued to stare at the letter. She was willing to relocate clear across the country to hold on to her journalism dream. He didn't know why that struck him as surprising. Maybe he'd wanted to block the possibility from his head. It also told him how temporary her stay in Nugget was. How temporary she considered him, not that they were anything more than friends. Hell, they'd shared a mere few kisses. But to him, they'd been life-changing kisses.

She came into the room in tight stretchy pants tucked into boots, a long sweater, and a fringy scarf. He had trouble tearing his eyes off her, but managed to nudge his head in the direction of the letter.

"You applied to the *Boston Globe*?"

"Yes," she said. "And got rejected by the *Boston Globe*. And the *Washington Post*. And the *Wall Street Journal*."

He held up the note. "They said to try back."

"It's a form letter, Colin. They send it to everyone. I was delusional enough to think that at least their recruitment editor would contact me."

"You'll get something," he said. It killed him to see her dejected like this.

"What did you want to talk to me about? Let me guess: You think we should just be friends?"

He swallowed and looked away. "I think we're on different tracks, Harlee. You're on your way to some place bigger and I'm satisfied to stay here. You're social, the life of the party, and I'm a loner who has problems with crowds."

He turned to meet her gaze and wondered how soon until she left this little town. Because there was no way he was divulging his secret if she planned to just take off. Colin didn't need the agony.

She stood there, deflated. "Okay, this is a little awkward."

"Ah, Harlee." He let out a breath. "You're so out of my league that I don't even rate a seat in the nose-bleed section."

"Yet you're the one turning me down for sex."

"That's because I only have meaningless sex, and you're not meaningless." *You're everything.*

"Are we still gonna be friends?"

"Hell yeah." He kissed the back of her hand and prayed he had the fortitude to make it to the door without scooping her up and taking her to bed.

* * *

Darla had a problem on her hands. A big, fat problem named Wyatt Lambert. She didn't want him joining them tonight. She didn't want to ring in the New Year with the old guy. And she certainly didn't want to have to pretend that all was forgiven and forgotten.

Because it wasn't.

But Griff had invited him and it would look petty and pathetic to uninvite him. So she was stuck. At least Rico had decided to come. The guy was nuts for her, and she, quite fond of him. Who knew, maybe they'd get married and have five kids.

Before she could dwell on her new life with Rico, Donna Thurston came barreling through the barbershop door. "I just saw what you did to the whack job's hair."

"Who? Samantha?" That was the only person's hair she'd cut recently. Whack job or otherwise.

"Whatever her name is. I was in the Lumber Baron when she first booked a room and thought one word: wig. But you, brilliant girl, saved the day."

Darla puffed up like a rooster. "Looks so good, right?"

"It looks fantastic. I tell you, if I didn't have my gal in Reno, I might give you a whirl. So what's the deal with that woman? Word on the Internet is that she ditched her groom at the altar and that she's worth a small hedge-fund fortune."

"That's all I know," Darla said. "I feel sorry for her. She seems so lost. Like sad and relieved at the same time. And with what she did to her hair, she's a danger to herself."

"She's booked two weeks at the Lumber Baron."

"That's good." Darla started to sweep the floor so she could get home to shower and dress in time to meet everyone. "She could probably use some rest."

"If I had her kind of money I'd rest in Antigua."

Darla nodded. She didn't even know where Antigua was, but she got the sense that it would be warm—not in the low thirties.

Donna browsed the product shelves. "Which do you recommend for me? I want to try something new."

Darla picked out a moisturizing shampoo that would bring Donna's pH back to its natural level and a conditioner that would help replenish some of the oils she'd stripped away with whatever crap she'd been using. Her ends were so brittle they made Darla thirsty just looking at them.

"This should help rejuvenate your hair," Darla said.

Donna took one look at the price tag and blinked. "Jeez. This is a money mint right here."

"It's worth it." Darla rung her up, gave her a peck on the cheek, and wished her a happy New Year.

As soon as Donna left, Darla closed out the cash register. Not that there was much money in there. She cleaned and sanitized her dad's chair, scrubbed the shampoo bowl—not that she'd used it—and started to flip on the closed sign on the door when Wyatt came in.

He shoved his hands into his police jacket and rocked on his feet nervously. "I'm going tonight."

She tried for bland. "Did you want me to alert the media?"

"For your sake I planned to decline Griff's invitation. But this is my town too. It's not like we can avoid each other forever."

"For my sake? You've got quite an ego on you." She tossed a few extra combs into the jar of Barbicide solution just to look busy. "Look, Wyatt, I doubt I'll even notice you're there." *I'll be too wrapped up in Rico.*

"Good. Because I'm looking forward to this. It'll be the first holiday in ages when I'm not on call."

She figured Wyatt must be low man on the totem pole compared to Rhys, a former Houston narcotics detective, and Jake, who used to work homicide in LA. "Whatever will the town do without you?"

He responded with a shake of his head, making her feel silly for being bitchy. And immature. Darla wondered if he planned to bring the blonde he'd been with the other day at the Ponderosa, but wouldn't dare ask.

"I was thinking about inviting Connie," Wyatt said. "No one would mind, right?"

Connie? Was he seeing her too? "The more the merrier."

"She's fun, but I get the feeling she doesn't get out much."

"Then by all means, invite her," Darla said, because she liked Connie. She really did.

"Griffin said the male-to-female ratio needed work. So Connie will help even up things."

"Wyatt, you don't need an excuse to invite Connie. Everyone thinks Connie is great."

"You bringing anyone?" he asked.

"Besides Rico, you mean?"

"Who is Rico?" He asked it innocently enough, but Darla couldn't meet his eyes.

"He works with Griff at the Gas and Go." *And he worships me.*

"You seeing him?" That too, he asked casually. Like, *"Hey, no big deal, just curious."*

"I hardly see how that's your business," Darla said, knowing that she'd sounded a tad too defensive.

"Sorry, Darla. I was just trying to make conversation. Part of this"—he waggled his finger between them—"is so it won't be awkward tonight."

"It won't be," she promised, because she had every intention of ignoring him, even though he looked more handsome now than ever before. And he seemed to have his life together. Good job. Pillar of the community. Too mature to resort to snarky banter.

"Good." He stuffed his hands into his pockets. "I don't want the past to make us bitter."

She flinched. How could he say that so cavalierly? As if their past had been a frivolous summer romance. It might've started that way, but that's not how it ended. He'd promised to marry her, take care of her, love her until the end of time. And then, without so much as a backward glance, walked. *Ran* was more accurate. As if someone held a gun to the back of his head.

That whole summer had been a fairy tale for Darla. She'd been helping her dad in the barbershop, making appointments, working the cash register, and sweeping. Mostly grunt work. Wyatt had come in for a haircut, his eyes tracing her every move. When it came time to pay, he'd forgotten his wallet.

"You live around here, don't you?" she'd asked. He'd nodded, his ears turning bright red. "Then just go get it and come back. We trust you."

He'd run out of the shop, clearly mortified, only to return ten minutes later with the cash and a handful of snickerdoodles. "My mom baked them."

"Thanks," she'd said, wondering why he hadn't at least wrapped the cookies in a napkin. They still felt sweaty from his hand.

"Would you consider going out with me?" Again, his ears had turned a bright red.

She hadn't been that attracted to him, but she'd also never had a real date. For that reason alone she accepted. And two weeks later, knew she'd fallen head over heels in love with Wyatt Lambert. Her dad had warned that it was puppy love—that it wouldn't last.

"It probably won't even survive the summer," he'd warned.

But she'd known instinctively, the way animals that mate for life do, that he was the one. And she'd been right, because to this day, Darla had never gotten over him. She still yearned for his kisses, the ones that had started out wet and sloppy, but with much practice had progressed to the gold standard. The benchmark by which she measured all others.

No one had ever loved her the way Wyatt had. And Darla would never again let someone leave her in pieces the way he had.

"Bitter?" she said. "Our past was a child, Wyatt. We made a baby. We lost a baby. And then you left."

Chapter 14

Everyone was having a perfectly miserable time, except for Rico and Connie, who appeared to be oblivious to the sour vibe permeating lane two of the bowling alley.

Harlee couldn't help but notice that Darla and Wyatt were doing their best to avoid one another, occasionally stealing glances when he or she thought the other wasn't looking. Lina, home for winter break, was a no-show and Griffin silently sulked. And if Harlee suffered any more rejection, she'd have to go on Prozac.

Everything Colin had said, with the exception of her being out of his league—because please, he was the kindest, sexiest, and most honorable man she'd ever known—rang true. Nugget was just a stopping station until she could reconnoiter, pay off some bills, and find another big newspaper job. Whereas Colin had made a fine life here. He had a big, beautiful house to prove it and a business that was on the cusp of taking off. And here, where trees outnumbered people, he could skirt his phobias.

Despite the fact that he was trying to save them both a lot of heartache, Harlee still felt raw disappointment, like maybe she had found someone worth hanging on to.

"Who wants nachos?" Connie asked. She seemed so grateful to have been included that Harlee didn't want to ruin her night, and tried to snap out of her funk. Harlee got the distinct impression that the thirty-something police dispatcher didn't get out much.

"Nachos sound good," she said. "I'll go with you to the snack bar."

But a line spanned the length of the bowling alley. Half of Plumas County had jammed into the Ponderosa to ring in the New Year. Earlier, she'd seen Rhys, Maddy, Emily, and Clay in the restaurant having dinner. Clay's sons and Rhys's little brother were here somewhere, either bowling or playing arcade games. Darla's dad and his posse had commandeered a table for the night for their annual pinochle tournament. Pam—Harlee and Darla's yoga instructor—and her husband sat at the bar with the Thurstons.

Nate, filling in for Sophie and Mariah, who had just had a baby girl, served drinks. The festive atmosphere, which included a garish amount of streamers and enough party hats and blowers to go around, had even attracted a good number of tourists looking for party central.

Harlee wished she had stayed in bed with a gallon of ice cream.

"Maybe the line is shorter at the bar," she suggested to Connie. They headed for the restaurant side of the Ponderosa and pushed through the crowd waiting for seats, only to find that the bar also had a considerable queue.

"Can you believe this?" Harlee gave silent thanks that Colin hadn't come. For a demophobe this would be like Times Square before the ball dropped.

"See that table at four o'clock?" Connie nudged her head at a group of men in camouflage. "They're checking you out."

Great, Harlee thought, a bunch of rowdy hunters. "How do you know they're not checking you out?"

"Puhleeze. No one checks me out."

Harlee shot Connie a look. "Of course they do." Although it might help if she lost the thick, black-framed eyeglasses. They detracted from her pretty brown eyes. And her clothes—baggy cargo pants and a shapeless sweater—could use a little tarting up. Something for her and Darla to work on.

"We may as well get the nachos here," Harlee said. Although the line was just as long, it seemed to be moving faster.

"Roger that," Connie said, and they joined the cattle call, while someone played Cracker's rendition of Ray Wylie Hubbard's "Redneck Mother" on the jukebox.

"Don't look now," Connie said, "but one of those hunters is coming over here."

Harlee turned away, waving to Donna and Pam, acting distracted in hopes of avoiding the guy. No such luck.

"Hey, gorgeous, why don't you and your friend here join me and my buddies over at our table." The man had onion-and-beer breath.

"We're here with a group," Harlee said. "But thanks for the invite."

"Suit yourself, honey." He gave her a once-over, then lingered on her breasts long enough to memorize her cup size. "But we've got beer. With this wait, it'll be 2015 before you get a drink."

"Yeah, we'll take our chances," Harlee said. "And like I said, we've got people waiting for us."

He looked around the dining room as though he didn't believe her, then stuck his face an inch away from hers, like he was moving in for a kiss.

Connie wedged herself between them. "Back off, bub."

He looked down at Connie, who barely reached his chest. "You two lesbos?"

"As a matter of fact, we are," Harlee said, and pulled Connie by the hand back into the bowling alley. "What a colossal douche."

"I think we could've taken him," Connie said. "Should we tell Wyatt? Let Hunter Boy meet the long arm of the law?"

"Nah," Harlee said. "Let's just get our nachos and have a good time."

"I'm having a great time." Connie punched her in the shoulder.

Nate must've sent reinforcements to the snack bar in the bowling alley, because the line moved faster now. They got their nachos and a bucket of kettle corn. Harlee wanted to get a couple of pitchers of beer, but because the snack bar servers were underage, they would have to get alcohol back in the bar. Later, Harlee told herself. They'd already been gone too long.

When they returned to the gang, the mood had swung from glum to glummer. Griffin was off in a corner on his phone, having a heated discussion. Harlee assumed that Lina was on the other side of that conversation. Darla had paired off with Rico and they flirted outrageously. Harlee thought all of Darla's hair flipping and boisterous laughter rang a little false. Especially given that every few seconds Darla would dart a glance at Wyatt to see if he had noticed. As soon as Harlee could get Darla alone she planned to find out what that was all about. Since the beginning of the night, Wyatt had painted a permanent scowl on his face and was the only one bowling.

"Wow, you're pretty good at this," Harlee said, watching him roll his third consecutive strike. "Do you bowl a lot?"

"I'm in a league," he said.

Connie put the food down on a bench so everyone could share. But she and Harlee seemed to be the only ones interested. They stood there stuffing their faces.

"Let me try," Connie said, heading over to the ball return.

"At least clean your hands first," Wyatt said.

Harlee searched through her purse and came up with a Wet-Nap. It had probably been at the bottom of her bag, among the flotsam, for more than a year—since the last time she'd eaten Dungeness crab on Pier 29, back when she still had her job at the *Call*. She'd been celebrating that night with friends from the paper, after breaking a big story. It turned out that San Francisco was the only city in the state that had hydrants that wouldn't fit a standard fire hose. The city's firefighters, overly attached to their big hoses, had managed to get exempted from a law that required smaller hydrant fittings. Residents had been kept relatively in the dark on this, despite its having to do with public safety.

Bottom line: While the city went up in flames in a catastrophic earthquake—because they were known to happen in the Golden State—firefighters from other counties who had come to help wouldn't be able to hook up their equipment. San Francisco's brilliant solution was to run around the city handing out adapters while the place burnt to the ground, like it had in 1906.

Jerry had liked the article enough to reward her with his box seats for a Giants-Dodgers game. He did that occasionally with reporters he liked, causing much animosity in the ranks. God, Harlee missed it.

Connie tore open the square package, wiped her hands, then inserted her fingers in a speckled ball and tossed it down the lane. Wyatt squeezed his eyes shut and cringed as the ball made loud thumping noises while it bounced across the polished floor into the gutter.

Harlee howled with laughter as heads popped up from neighboring lanes to watch.

"Ah, crap," Connie muttered.

Griffin sauntered over. "What did I miss?"

"Connie's mad bowling skills," Wyatt said.

"Let me try again," she said.

"I think we should let the floor heal first." Wyatt handed a ball to Harlee. "You try."

She had only slightly better success than Connie. The ball actually rolled quite gracefully down the lane, only to veer into the gutter at the last minute. Rico went next and did some kind of fancy hip-shake boogie move that got him four pins. He got to go again and knocked down the remaining pins.

"Spare, baby." He turkey-walked back to the bench and Darla hugged him like he'd just won the Elias Cup. Acting much?

Harlee seriously wanted to grab Darla by her clip-in extensions, drag her to the back of the room, and ask her what the heck was going on. But they'd just started having fun, and she didn't want to break the momentum.

Wyatt gave Griffin some tips on form. "It's all about the geometry," he kept saying.

"Yeah, well, I flunked geometry," Griffin said, aiming and releasing the ball, only for it to zig to the left and wind up in the gutter. "Dude, I suck."

"Yes, you do," Rico said. Again, more over-the-top giggling from Darla.

"Come here, Connie. I'll coach you." Wyatt waved her over, showed her some moves, and stood behind her as she took a step toward the target and swung the ball onto the lane.

Holy cow, the woman got a strike.

"Woohoo!" Connie cheered.

"Beginner's luck," Rico said, and grabbed a ball from the return.

"Hey, I get to go again," Connie said.

"You got a strike," Wyatt said in exasperation. "Your frame is over."

"Oh," Connie said. "I knew that."

Harlee noticed an older couple in the lane next to them giving their group dirty looks. But since they were wearing ridiculous bear appliqué sweatshirts, Harlee didn't take them too seriously. Annoyed that they kept staring, she finally whispered to Darla, "Who are those people?"

"Those are the Addisons. They own the Beary Quaint motor inn outside of town."

"They're glaring at us," Harlee said.

"Yeah, they're kind of dicks. Just ignore them."

Harlee slid them a sideways glance to see if they were still staring, but the couple appeared to have gone back to their bowling game. "I've got to use the restroom," she told Darla.

"Want me to come? We can use the one in the dining room and grab a couple of pitchers of beer."

"Okay." It would give Harlee the opportunity to ask Darla what in the world was going on between her and Wyatt.

They told the others where they were going. Griffin and Wyatt shoved a wad of cash into their hands for the beer, while Rico and Connie fought over who got to bowl next. Of course there was a line at the ladies' room.

"What's the deal with you and Wyatt?" Harlee asked as they waited.

Darla hitched her shoulders. "Nothing. What do you mean?"

"Give me a break, Darla. You're so obviously trying to make him jealous with Rico. Why?" And then it suddenly dawned on her. "You guys used to have a thing. Didn't you?"

Darla let her gaze fall to her wedge boots. "A long time ago."

"Why didn't you tell me? That's why he was staring at you at the Ponderosa that first time we had lunch."

"You were going through your own stuff with your money situation and everything. Besides, it's ancient history now."

"Obviously it isn't," Harlee said. "If you want him back, stop with the game playing and go for it."

Wyatt at least had been an adult by making it clear that he was interested.

"He did something really bad to me," Darla said in a soft voice.

"What?" Harlee got her hackles up. No one messed with her friends.

"I can't talk about it here. Later," Darla said.

"He didn't hit you or anything?" Because with all the background checks she'd done for DataDate, nothing would surprise her anymore.

"Nothing like that. I'll tell you when we're not in a crowded restaurant." Someone came out of one of the stalls and it was Darla's turn. "I'll meet you over at the bar when you're done."

Harlee waited for the next stall to open. When she came out there was no more line. Wasn't that always the way? she mused. She started to head for the bar when she was approached again by the jerk-off hunter who'd bothered her and Connie earlier.

"Hey," he said, giving her another one of his perverted once-overs, making her skin crawl. "You looking for me?"

"Nope. I'm looking for my friends." *"One of them is a cop,"* she wanted to add, because for now they were alone in the corridor and he made her nervous. "See ya."

She quickened her pace, but he grabbed her arm. "What's your hurry?" He pulled her into an alcove where linens were stored and pressed her against the wall. From his breath and bloodshot eyes she could tell he was three sheets to the wind. "I thought we should get to know each other."

Stay calm, she told herself. Someone was bound to come soon. It was the bathrooms, for goodness' sake. But he had shoved his knee between her legs and she felt pinned. And particularly vulnerable since she was in a dress. At least she had on tights.

She pushed against him hard, but he weighed at least two hundred pounds. "Would you mind?"

"Actually, I would." He bent down and shoved his nose into the crook of her neck. "You smell good." Licking his way to her ear, he muttered something about it being close to midnight.

She turned her head away from him and tried to shove his concrete chest with her arms, but he held her so tight she could barely move. "Let me go!"

Harlee started to scream, but he covered her mouth with his. God, she was going to vomit. He tasted like booze, onions, and chewing tobacco. On top of that he was working his knee between her legs until she could feel him hard up against her. Pelvis to pelvis. His hands reached up her dress as she struggled to free herself, which only made him more aggressive. Like this was sport to him.

Then suddenly she felt him being lifted off of her. Colin stood there, holding the cretin by the collar of his camo jacket. If Harlee didn't know Colin, she'd have been more frightened of him than her attacker. A flat glint filled his eyes, which made him look a little savage and his body had gone taut and strained, like a tiger ready to pounce on its prey.

"You came," she croaked, wondering how he'd managed to materialize out of nowhere. And thank goodness he had.

He spared her a momentary glance to make sure she was okay, then slammed Hunter Boy's head into the wall. Hard. The man's nose spurted blood like the Old Faithful geyser. Colin pulled the hunter's head back until Harlee was afraid that his neck would snap in half.

"Colin, don't," she called.

So overcome by rage he must not have heard her, he was preparing to slam the man's head into the wall a second time. Fortunately, Chief Shepard heard the commotion, and the next thing Harlee knew he was pulling Colin off the man.

At first, Colin just stood there, breathing hard. But little by little he seemed to emerge from his fury-fueled adrenaline rush, take in the crowd that had begun to assemble around them, and stared down at his hands, now covered in blood.

"Shit," he said, and hightailed it out of the Ponderosa too fast for anyone to stop him.

Harlee started to run after him, but made a split-second decision. She turned around, found the hunter leaning against the wall trying to stanch his bloody nose, and kicked him in the balls. Then she went after Colin.

Colin drove as far and fast as he could go, but with his gas gauge almost on empty, he wound up at Sophie and Mariah's construction site. He parked, got out of his truck, and bent over, resting his palms on his knees, letting blood flow to his brain.

Brain? That was rich. If he had a brain, he wouldn't have lost it back at the Ponderosa. But seeing that dude with his hands all over Harlee, forcing himself on her, had set him off like a bottle rocket. Then his fight instincts had kicked in and he'd overreacted. Old habits die hard. In Donovan, if you didn't fight to kill, you died.

Going in so young, Colin had been particularly susceptible to the gangs and the lifers, who had nothing to lose. Luckily, he'd honed his skills at the California Youth Authority, where survival meant becoming the meanest scrapper in the yard. Together, he and Latwon, his one and only friend, had covered each other's backs.

Last he'd heard, Latwon was back in, doing a third strike on a drug rap. He was never getting out. And at this rate, Colin would be going back in.

He fished his cell phone out of his back pocket and hit automatic dial.

"Hello?" Al's voice came across groggy, like he'd been sleeping. Colin looked at his watch. It was one in the morning.

He'd wanted to kiss Harlee when the clock struck midnight. He knew it was crazy, given that he'd just kicked her to the curb. But he couldn't seem to make himself stay away from her.

For an hour he'd circled the Ponderosa, working up the nerve to go inside, doing his breathing exercises. When he'd finally mustered the courage, Darla had been standing by the bar and told him where to find Harlee. That's when he saw the dude pawing her and became too blinded by rage to even notice the crowds.

"That you, Colin?"

"Yeah," Colin said. "Sorry to wake you."

"You call to wish me a happy New Year, or what?" Al sounded more alert now, disguising his concern with flippancy. Colin knew the tone well.

"I'm in trouble, Al."

"Where you at?"

"Not far from home." Colin didn't want to tell Al that he'd run like a little pussy. He got back in his truck because it was cold as hell and cranked up the heater.

"What did you do?"

"I got into a bar fight—beat up someone."

"You went into a bar?" Al asked, sounding more surprised that Colin had worked up the nerve to go into a public place than the fact that he'd pummeled the hell out of a guy.

"The Ponderosa. The dude was pushing himself on a friend of mine."

"You hurt him?" Al asked.

Colin exhaled. "I don't know how badly. The police chief broke it up. Shit, Al."

"He didn't arrest you?"

"I left." Colin had walked away from a crime scene and ditched Harlee when she needed him. Hell, who was he kidding, he'd scared her to death. He'd seen the way she'd backed away from him, stared in horror, like he was a goddamned berserker.

"Go home," Al told Colin. "If they come for you, call me. But don't buy trouble. We'll pay the chief a visit together. And Colin?"

"What?"

"Why were you going inside the Ponderosa?"

Colin shoved his hand through his hair. "To go bowling."

Al chuckled. "Bowling? That's good, Colin. Bowling's good."

The next day, Al parked his cruiser on the square. "You sure the chief's working on New Year's Day?"

"No." But Colin didn't want to wait. The guy he'd beaten up could choose to file charges anytime. Fighting was a clear violation of his parole.

"All right," Al said. "Fix your tie."

Al said he should wear a tie, which was ridiculous because he never wore ties. No one in Nugget wore ties. But Colin had relented, just wanting to get this over with. Harlee had left six frantic messages on his machine. He hadn't called her back for fear that by now everyone knew he was an ex-con.

"Let me do the talking," Al said, getting out of the car.

Last night, there'd been so many vehicles crammed inside the square that Colin had had to park a block away. Today it looked like a ghost town. He supposed that everyone had stayed home either to sleep it off or to watch the game.

They went inside the Nugget Police Department to find Rhys standing in a tiny kitchenette, fidgeting with a fancy coffeemaker. He glanced up at the door.

"Chief Shepard?" Al said, and Rhys took in his suit, lizard cowboy boots, and the outline of his shoulder holster.

"That would be me. What can I do you for?" He nodded a greeting at Colin.

"You working on a holiday, huh?"

"It's a small department," Rhys responded. "Either one of you know how to get coffee out of this thing?"

Al walked over to the machine, checked to make sure there were beans in the grinder and water in the reservoir, did something to a dial, and flipped a switch. The coffeemaker made a loud whirring noise and all three of them stood there watching coffee drip into the pot.

"Y'all want a cup?" he asked, reminding Colin that Rhys had been a cop in Texas. As the story went, he'd fled Nugget at eighteen and wound up in Houston working as a narcotics detective. He'd come home last year to care for his ailing father and take over the town's beleaguered police department.

"I'll take one," Al said. Colin shook his head no. "I'm Al Ferguson, by the way. Department of Corrections."

"Yep," was all Rhys said.

No show of surprise. No questions like: Why does Colin have a parole officer? What did he do time for? Which in Colin's mind meant Rhys already knew. The chief had probably run Colin when he'd discovered the meth lab in the Lumber Baron's basement last year. The question was, did everyone else in Nugget know?

Rhys handed Al a mug and led them to his office. "I'm gonna keep the door open so I can hear anyone coming in."

Al nodded. "We're here because Colin's concerned over what happened last night at the Ponderosa."

Rhys didn't say anything at first, just sipped his coffee. "We got the guy to the hospital. Made sure he and his friends made it out of town this morning. The busted nose will heal. His sperm count . . . not so much. Nothing to be done for that now."

Sperm count? Colin had nearly split the jack-off's head open. No reproductive organs involved.

"Is Colin facing possible charges here?"

"Maybe a lawsuit, but I doubt it," Rhys said, taking another long drag of his coffee. "As far as charges: We don't arrest people in Nugget for rescuing citizens in distress. Although from where I was standing, this particular citizen has a hell of a kick." He grimaced and moved in his chair uncomfortably. "Right in the nut sack."

Colin tried not to crack a smile.

Rhys leaned across the scarred oak desk. "Look, Officer Ferguson, Colin's a law-abiding, productive member of our small community. Those flower boxes out on the square, he built 'em. The benches too. Besides being one of the most sought-after carpenters in these parts, Colin keeps his nose clean. So we've got no problems."

"Good," Al said, and got to his feet. "We know you're busy, so we'll get out of your hair."

Colin also stood and Rhys nodded at him. There was a world of meaning in that simple head bob. *I've got you covered, but don't screw up, because this is my town, these are my people, and I'm watching.*

Fair enough, Colin thought, because right now he felt so damned relieved that even the police chief knowing his sordid past paled in comparison to a parole violation that could put him back inside. Rhys was a thorough cop who looked after the townsfolk of Nugget like a ferocious mama bear. It should come as no surprise that he knew the backgrounds of each and every one of his residents. In fact, Colin respected the hell out of him for it.

That didn't mean he wanted his past to become public record, or grist for the gossip mill.

He followed Al to the car and got in. Al waited for him to buckle up before pulling out of the square and driving up Grizzly Peak. "I think that went pretty well. Good guy, that chief."

"Yeah," Colin said, staring out the window, wondering how to handle this with Harlee. So she'd kicked the guy in the balls, huh? His chest expanded with pride. Good for her.

"So who's this friend of yours?"

Al must've been reading his mind. He had a way of doing that sometimes. Spooky. "Just a neighbor. Her mother buys my furniture to sell in her shop."

Al slanted him a sideways glance. "This neighbor get you to go bowling?"

"It's a whole group, Al. Not a lot to do in this town."

"I've never known you to mind that. And I've never known you to join groups. The crowd didn't bother you?"

Colin had never gotten a chance to find out. Not with that dickhead molesting his girl—okay, Harlee was not his girl. But rushing to her rescue had distracted him from the throngs of partygoers, which under normal circumstance would've had him in full-blown panic mode. "I'm getting acupuncture for that."

"Acupuncture?" Al was a good old boy, born and raised in the San Joaquin Valley. Definitely not the type to embrace ancient Chinese medicine.

"What of it?" Colin spat.

"Nothing, if it's working."

The truth was Colin had only gone the two times. "It might be."

Al tried to hide a smile. "Or maybe it's that neighbor. What did you say her name was?"

"I didn't," Colin said. "Look, she's a newspaper reporter and she's only visiting. So please don't go talking to her."

They pulled up in front of Colin's house and Max came bounding toward them. He was getting the hang of the newly installed dog door. Occasionally, Max would wander down to Harlee's house, but he always came back.

"When did you get a dog?" Al got out of the car. Colin had hoped he'd just go home—salvage the rest of the holiday.

"He's a rescue. I found him on a job site."

Al crouched down to pet Max. "Good-looking fellow."

"Not when I first got him. Someone had dumped him and the poor guy was pretty mangled."

Lifting his head, Al gave Colin an assessing look. "Let's go inside for a few minutes."

It was cold outside, maybe in the high twenties. Colin wouldn't be surprised if it snowed again. There was a note taped to the door. Colin took the paper down and stuffed it in his jacket pocket before Al could remark on it.

"You want something to drink?" He led Al into the kitchen, not sure if he wanted to search the house first. Pretty stupid since Colin would've had all night to rid the house of any guns or drugs. But maybe Al just wanted to mark it off his books so he wouldn't have to get back to Nugget for another few months.

"No, but I'm hungry," Al said. "Never had breakfast."

Not for the first time Colin wondered if Al had a wife and kids. The guy had been pretty stingy with personal details. All Colin knew was that he lived in Quincy.

He hung up his jacket, got eggs and bacon out of the refrigerator, and popped an English muffin into the toaster. It was the least he could do, given that Al had dragged his ass out of bed to take his call in the wee hours of the morning, then drove more than forty minutes on a holiday to smooth things over for him with the chief.

"You keep this place so damn clean." Al sat on a bar stool, taking in Colin's kitchen.

Colin knew he was a neat freak. It was probably a control issue. In the joint you had no say over your environment. You shit and showered when they told you to. No privacy whatsoever. When he'd first gotten out, just using real eating utensils—metal forks and knives, instead of the standard-issue plastic prison spoon—took adjusting to.

"I want to talk to you about this whole thing," Al said, watching Colin flip an omelet. The room had filled with the scent of bacon.

Colin didn't have too many good memories of his childhood, but sizzling bacon was one of them. If he could smell it wafting through the cottage into his bedroom, it meant that his mother hadn't been too drunk to get out of bed. "You want coffee?"

"I'm fine. That stuff the chief had was good caffeine. You got any juice?" Colin pulled a jug out of the refrigerator and poured Al a glass.

"You did good calling me like that, Colin. A lot of guys get scared and wind up making it worse for themselves. You kept your head. Hell, boy, you've already beaten the odds."

Most ex-cons didn't make it past three years before screwing up and getting thrown back in. Colin had been on the outside for nearly four years.

"Then again, you never were like the rest of them," Al said, hovering over the plate Colin had pushed in front of him. "Always a fish out of water. But, son, you have to make a life for yourself. The furniture, the carpentry, this house—all good. All anchors. But I like that you're finally getting yourself a social life. This newspaper reporter, she good people?"

That was parole speak for, Does she have a sheet? A drug or alcohol problem? Basically, can this woman get you in trouble?

"Pure as the driven snow." Colin handed Al a couple of napkins. "Don't talk to her, Al. She's just a neighbor who occasionally invites me to things. She doesn't know about my past and I want to keep it that way."

Al nodded in acquiescence. It wasn't like him. He never skimped on the job. As much as he advocated for you, Al was a hard-ass. Part of his job was keeping an eye on Colin's friends and family and making sure they weren't bad influences. For whatever unfathomable reason, Al had decided to make a concession this time. For Colin.

"What makes you think she doesn't know?" he asked Colin.

Because if she did, Harlee wouldn't want anything to do with him. "I just know. She's from a nice family. Dad's a doctor and mom owns a store. Her brother is a cop." He looked at Al pointedly.

"The chief is a cop. He seems to like you." Al wiped up the rest of his omelet with his muffin and popped it into his mouth.

"His wife likes me," Colin said. "I helped restore her inn."

"Even more reason not to like you." Al let out a harsh laugh, and Colin got the impression that he might've had a bad experience in that area.

"This neighbor the one who told you about the acupuncture?" There went Al again with his spooky powers of deduction.

"Yeah," Colin said.

Al got off his stool, went to the sink, rinsed his plate, and put it in the dishwasher. "I've gotta go." He slapped Colin on the back. "Glad we could have this talk. Stay out of trouble."

Colin waited to hear the door click closed and Al's tires on the gravel road before going into the mudroom to get his jacket. Searching the pocket, he found the note, unfolded it, and read.

> *Where are you? I've been calling like crazy and even came by your house right after you left the Ponderosa last night. Came by this morning too. But you weren't there. Please let me know you are okay. I'm very worried.*
> *Harlee*

Colin noted this time there were no hugs and kisses. Colin banged his head against the pine log wall. What the hell was he supposed to tell her?

Chapter 15

If Harlee didn't hear from Colin by noon, she planned to put out an all-points bulletin. Or at least she'd get Wyatt to do it. Or maybe even the chief. He'd seen the whole thing go down. He knew how freaked out Colin had been.

Now that Harlee had had time to think about it, she'd come to the conclusion that a combination of his demophobia—the crowd had been elbow to elbow—and seeing Hunter Boy maul her had strained him to the limits. It was the only way to explain his feral behavior. Especially taking off like that at the end.

In the meantime, she kept herself occupied by running a background check for DataDate. Even on holidays, the Internet remained open. And so far, everything about Paula Duggan's boyfriend had checked out. Except one crucial problem.

According to his social security number, Eric Wong was dead.

She'd already had Paula double- and triple-check the number. Finally, out of frustration, she picked up the phone, called Brad, and explained the situation.

"Either it's a mistake," Brad said, "or the guy got himself a fake green card. It happens all the time. Let me guess: He works in Silicon Valley."

"Yep," Harlee said. "How much trouble can he get into if he's caught?"

"Look, I'm not ICE, but it's a pretty good guess that he'd be deported."

Eric might not be a bad person, but if he got deported, he'd be geographically undesirable. And that would seriously suck for Paula. "Thanks, Brad. And happy New Year."

"You too, Harveyleigh." He always called her that. It used to bug the bejesus out of her; now it just made her laugh.

She heard someone knocking on the door, quickly got off the phone, and ran down the stairs. *Colin!*

"I was getting ready to call search and rescue," she said, pulling him across the threshold and shutting the door. "Where's Max?"

"Home," he said.

"I'm so glad you're okay. Where've you been?"

"After I left the Ponderosa I went for a drive. Tried to cool off." He ran his thumb along her cheek. "Did he hurt you, Harlee?"

"Hardly. He was a drunken troll. Nothing I couldn't handle." Not exactly true. Until Colin had come along, she'd been in a bit of a fix.

He examined her from head to toe and she was glad that she'd actually dressed this morning, instead of lounging around in her pink flamingo pajamas. Ever so slightly he turned her face up so that she was looking directly into caramel brown eyes.

"Did I scare you?" he asked, and his voice held a barely traceable tremor.

"No." *Yes.* "You were just very intense. I don't think I've ever seen you like that."

He let out a breath and scrubbed his hand over his face. "When I saw you struggling against him, I lost it."

She pulled him into the living room and patted the couch for him to sit. "How did you find me?"

"I saw Darla at the bar. She said you were in the bathroom. I went to wait for you, heard noise coming out of that little closet area and . . . Ah, Jesus, Harlee."

"Why did you change your mind . . . about coming?"

His shoulders hitched and he suddenly became very distracted by something outside the window. "I wanted to be with you at midnight."

She couldn't tell if that meant *I didn't want to be alone* or *I changed my mind about us.* The man was all kinds of mixed signals. "Did the crowd bother you?"

"It took me about an hour to work up the nerve to go inside," he said. "Then I saw that man touching you and nothing else mattered. I know I overreacted, but . . ."

She brushed a stray strand of hair away from his eye. He looked tired and something else that Harlee couldn't quite read. Ashamed, maybe?

"Colin, I appreciate what you did more than you know. When you're a reporter, you have to stand up for yourself, or no one will respect you. Even when I was in sticky situations, going door to door in a bad neighborhood to get quotes or getting creepy email threats from someone who didn't like what I had written, I never asked for backup."

"I don't want to hear that," Colin said, closing his large warm hands around her smaller ones. "Ask for backup. Always ask for backup."

The concern she heard there made her breath stall. She felt it deep in her midsection and for a second she considered crawling into his lap and burying her face in his chest, absorbing all the goodness that was Colin. But he'd made it clear: They were strictly platonic. "Where did you go this morning? I knocked on your door until my knuckles turned red."

"To the police station. I wanted to make sure I hadn't killed the idiot. Chief Shepard says he'll live, although, according to Rhys, you may have turned him into a eunuch."

"Yeah, that," she said, mildly embarrassed. "I was so angry that he ruined your big night. Colin, I think the acupuncture might be working."

"Maybe," he said, but she sensed that he was just trying to placate her. "I should go." He started to edge up from the couch.

"My mom sold more of your stuff," she said, following him to the door. "She wants more."

"Then I better get to work." He stopped for a moment to look at her, his eyes wanting and mournful, like a boy with his face pressed against a shop window, surveying all that he couldn't have. Well, he'd been the one to put up barriers, not her.

"Don't go," she pleaded, then silently cursed herself for sounding pathetic, like a bottomless pit of need. Men did not find begging particularly sexy.

He closed his eyes and stepped into her. "Ah, Harlee. This isn't going to turn out well. Don't say I didn't warn you."

He should have told her right then and there. About everything—the conviction, prison, how he was on parole. But he wanted her so badly, more than anything he'd ever wanted in his life, that the words stayed choked up inside of him. When things went bad, because they would, they always did, he'd have Harlee. Or at least the memory of Harlee. Even though he knew she was only temporary, a fleeting instant of true happiness, Colin would feed off this moment forever. So he took what she offered and hoped that he would last long enough to savor it.

He kissed her against the hallway wall, rocking up against her until the hard ridge in his pants pressed against her belly. Harlee threaded her fingers around his neck and pulled his head down lower so she wouldn't have to go up on her tiptoes. They stayed like that for a while, just kissing. Her mouth was warm and sweet and he'd never known a woman to smell so good, like soap and baby powder. His hands inched up her sweater, where he felt the smooth, warm skin of her stomach. So soft and supple that he just rested his hands there, feeling her breathe in and out. She pressed her full breasts against his chest and his blood pounded.

"Harlee, baby, let's take this into the bedroom."

"Okay," she whispered, but didn't move.

"Change of heart?" he asked, afraid to hear the answer because he was burning for her.

"Are you sure you're into this? I just feel like I might've . . . you know . . . thrown myself at you. I don't want you to feel like you'll hurt my—"

He covered her mouth. "I've never been into anything more in my life. So if you don't get moving into the bedroom, I'm gonna take you right here, against the wall."

"You sure?"

"That I'll take you against the wall? Yeah, I'm sure." He covered her mouth again and murmured into her lips, "You talk too much. The only words I want to hear are 'Oh, Colin, don't stop.' "

She giggled. "Oh, Colin, don't stop."

"You think that's funny? Just wait and see." He tossed her over his shoulder in a fireman's hold, carried her into the bedroom, and tossed her onto the middle of the bed, falling down on top of her. Pushing up on his elbows so he wouldn't crush her with his weight, he stared down into her deep blue eyes. With the light seeping through the shades, hitting the red plaid bedspread, they looked almost violet.

"God, you're beautiful."

She reached up and drew a line down his face, staring into his eyes, not saying anything. She didn't have to, because it was as if those small hands, strumming his cheek, had wrapped around his heart. He lifted her sweater with his mouth, exposing an expanse of her tummy and kissed her there, licking into her navel.

"All the way off?" she asked.

He didn't answer, just peeled it over her head. She had on a black-and-white lacy bra that extended lower than her rib cage and pushed up her breasts. "What is this thing?" He kissed the vee of her cleavage.

"It's a cami bra. You like it?"

"Are you kidding? I effing love it. What do you have down here?" He dipped his fingers under the waistband of her jeans.

"Hopefully more good stuff." She pushed her hands up under his henley and he sucked in a breath. "But I can't remember. I may have opted for the granny panties this morning. You want me to check?"

"No, I don't want you to check. Whatever you have on I plan on getting off in about twenty seconds flat."

"Mmm." She laid her head back as he stroked her breasts, then reached around to unfasten the clasps of her bra, or whatever she'd called it.

"I thought you liked my lingerie."

"I do," he said, pulling the straps down, tossing the bra somewhere on the bed and weighing each one of her breasts in his hands, studying their shape and size. "But I like these better."

He sucked her nipples until they puckered into tight pink beads. "And these," he hummed.

She played with his chest hair, so he tugged off his shirt to give her better access. He liked her hands on him; it aroused him even more than just looking at her.

"Take these off." She started undoing his belt. Impatient to get out of his pants, which were growing tighter by the second, he took over.

He got off the bed and slid his Levi's and boxers down his legs, while she watched with darkened eyes.

"Your turn." With one flip of a button and the draw of a zipper, he had her pants and underwear pulled down and bunched around her ankles. Standing there, gazing down on her as the light filtered over her pale skin, he wondered how he'd ever gotten so lucky.

"Come back." Harlee sat halfway up and reached out to him, kicking off the remainder of her clothes.

Colin found his wallet and pulled out a couple of foil packets, checking the expiration date. It had been a while, but apparently not that long, because they were still good. He put them on the nightstand and rolled next to her on the bed. She twined herself around him like a cat and he could feel her purr. God, she drove him crazy.

He nuzzled her neck and went back to work on her breasts, laving them with attention. She moaned and whimpered, assuring him that he was doing everything right. He'd never wanted to please a woman more than he did Harlee. She rolled to her side and wiggled against him as if she couldn't get close enough. Colin slid his hands down her back and cupped her ass. Then he rolled her onto her back and she let him take the lead, stroking her between her legs. It surprised Colin. Harlee liked to run the show. But he liked being in charge in bed. To be truthful, he liked being in charge of everything, the residual results of a regimented decade behind bars.

Hopefully, later—if there was a later—they'd work that out and divvy up who got to be the boss of what. Anything she wanted. For now, though, he was going to rock her world. Make her see shooting stars and hear trumpets.

"Colin?"

"Hmm?"

"Please."

"You want me inside of you?" She kissed him hard in answer, making his body tremble. He suited up and slid in, giving her time to adjust to him. "This okay?"

"So good," she said, impatiently starting to move under him. Yup, that was his girl.

He spread tiny kisses across her forehead, nose and chin, building a rhythm that had her moaning with pleasure and shutting her eyes, heat sizzling between them.

"Open your eyes, honey." He liked looking into those pools of blue.

She opened them, her lips forming a sensuous O that was nearly Colin's undoing. He pumped harder and faster, urgently reaching under her bottom to pull her closer. She wrapped her legs around his waist, moved them higher so he could go deeper and deeper, giving her all she wanted. Everything he had, because she felt good. So right. So connected to him that he thought he would lose his mind.

She called his name over and over again, virtually sobbing, as her tempo became frantic. Her legs loosened from around his back and she put her feet flat on the bed. Colin pounded into her, feeling her heart rate quicken. She was almost there. He slid his hand between her damp thighs, worked her with his fingers until she shouted out, convulsing around him, coming again and again.

He thrust one . . . two . . . three times more inside her, threw his head back and let himself go.

They lay there plastered together on the bed, breathing hard and feeling sweaty. Colin got up to go to the bathroom. When he came back, he crawled back into bed with Harlee and ran his hand down her spine. She curled into him and they nodded off like that until they heard barking at the front door.

"Max," Colin said, wiping sleep from his eyes.

"Let him in and come back to bed."

"I should go home and feed him," he said, leaning over the bed, searching for his pants.

Harlee glanced at the clock on the nightstand. "It's only three. Go feed him. I'll shower and we'll have an early dinner. I'm starved."

He hitched his shorts and pants up and scrounged along the floor for his shirt. It was slung across a chair. Funny, he didn't remember tossing it there. He pulled it over his head, sat at the edge of the mattress, took Harlee's face in his hands, and kissed her.

"This was amazing and you're amazing. Please don't take this the wrong way, because the last thing I want to do is hurt you. But I need to go home, feed my dog, and think." Think about whether he should come clean and tell her everything at the risk of ruining whatever little time they had together, before she went off to Metropolis to be Lois Lane.

"I wasn't expecting something like you and me to happen," he continued. "But we're happening. And I'm great with it. The thing is, I've always been a solitary guy and just need a little space to reason it through. That's all. You okay with that?"

Harlee pulled the sheet up to her chin and Colin pinched his eyes shut, girding for the worst. Tears. A punch in the face. Or *"You're a real dick, Colin Burke."* Because it sounded like a brush-off even to his ears, when all he wanted was time to contemplate what to do. How to make this right between them.

But when she flashed a tight smile and said, "Do what you need to do," he knew exactly what he was going to do—not tell her a damn thing.

Chapter 16

Colin didn't come back that night and Harlee wound up reheating leftovers for New Year's dinner. Darla, Griffin, Connie, and Wyatt had all called to make sure she was okay. Honestly, she hadn't given the imbecile who'd attacked her a second thought. All her energy had been focused on Colin.

Colin. What was she getting herself into with him? The man was a claustrophobe, a demophobe, and obviously a commitment-phobe. But she didn't want a commitment. Certainly nothing beyond them enjoying each other's company until she left. Sure, if they were going to continue sleeping together she wanted exclusivity. Otherwise it would feel wrong. She wasn't the type to have multiple partners and she didn't want to have sex with someone who did. But Colin didn't strike her as a player. Although, sweet Moses, had the man been good in bed. Beyond good. Spectacular. And he had a way of making her feel like the most special woman on the planet.

That couldn't be an act. Colin didn't do slick or smarmy. The man rarely left his damn wood shop. As far as she could tell, he didn't even have any friends. Just Max.

Okay, the brawl at the Ponderosa had been scary. If Harlee didn't know better, she might think that Colin had anger management issues. But he'd been protecting her. She'd appreciated him having her back and a little part of her—all right, a big part—had gotten off on it. Big burly man rescues somewhat medium-sized woman from creepy asshole.

Sue me, Gloria Steinem.

But all this "I need space to think it through" drama was giving her hives. Not to mention that she was bored out of her skull. On New Year's in San Francisco, she'd be whooping it up. Okay, not exactly whooping it up, but going out with friends, maybe having a private dinner at a hot new restaurant where for a hundred bucks she could sample some "it" chef's tasting menu, then go home and stuff her face with Nutter Butters because she was still starved.

God, she missed it.

What she should do is tell Colin that the sex had been grand, but she was moving on. Except that she didn't want to move on, because she was totally into Grizzly Adams, who wasn't even Grizzly Adams anymore. He was a hot L.L. Bean guy now, and he made her lame heart go pitter-patter. The bastard.

She padded into the kitchen and grabbed a pint of Häagen-Dazs. God, she was a cliché. Maybe she should use the time to write a few more cover letters to newspapers because, hey, she hadn't been rejected enough. Or hop on the computer and do a background check on Jacob Silberman, her latest assignment. The guy's bio on the website Make-a-Date was so glowing that Harlee suspected that he was really the Zodiac Killer.

While she was at it, she should run Colin too. Not that she would find much. The man didn't drink, didn't go to public places, and worked for himself. His house was paid for and his business was completely transparent. She knew that from working on his books. So instead of playing cyber-sleuth, she finished the carton of Häagen-Dazs and went to bed.

The next morning, Harlee decided to go into town, get Darla to trim her hair, and do a little grocery shopping. First, she swung by the Gas and Go and got out to say hi to Griffin. He had bought a few old truck benches on eBay and created a little waiting room in the garage where Darla's dad and the rest of the old guys seemed to have made a permanent home for themselves.

In the shop, Griff ripped out a countertop with a crowbar as the radio blasted classic rock from a Reno station. He stopped when Harlee came in and turned down the music.

"Hey," he said, and kissed her on the cheek. "What's going on?"

"Not much. I was on my way to the square and thought I'd stop by. Check out your progress." She looked around at the mess. The floor was covered in debris from the demolition. "What are your plans for in here?"

"I'm thinking of going mini Seven-Eleven. Foodstuff, maps, sundries."

"Sounds good. Can't you get any of them to help you?" Harlee nudged her head at the garage and grinned.

"The Nugget Mafia?" he asked, and crossed his arms over his chest. "They just like to tell me what to do."

She laughed. "Where's Rico?"

"Getting lunch. You talk to Colin? Find out why he took off like that the other night?"

Harlee didn't want to tell him about the demophobia. Colin wouldn't appreciate it. "He said he needed to cool off."

"I can see that. He was probably pissed that Rhys broke it up. That guy messing with you deserved to leave the Ponderosa on a stretcher."

"He was just a drunken moron," Harlee said, trying to downplay the whole event. "Did you and Lina patch things up?"

"Not really. She's pretty adamant that we become a couple."

"Aren't you a couple?" Harlee asked, confused.

"Before she started at USF, we made a deal to wait a year. She's only eighteen and I wanted her to put all her energy into experiencing her first year of college—not be focused on a boyfriend back home."

"Wow, that seems pretty selfless of you." Harlee wondered if Griffin really just wanted to play the field. The guy was gorgeous, fabulously wealthy, and a sweetheart to boot. He could pretty much have any woman he wanted.

"Yeah. Maybe too selfless. But there is an eight-year age difference between us."

Normally, Harlee wouldn't think eight years was too much. But the difference between eighteen and twenty-six may as well be an eternity. "I hope you're able to work things out."

Griffin stared off into the distance, looking sad enough to make Harlee change her mind about his and Lina's age situation. She could see he cared about her.

"Me too," he said.

Rico came wandering in, laden with bags from the Bun Boy. "Hey, Harlee. What's up?"

"Not much," she said. "I was on my way over to Darla's and decided to stop by and say hello. The place is shaping up."

"Wanna share a burger?" Rico held up a greasy sack.

"No, thanks. I should get going."

"Hey, before you go," Griffin said, "what do you know about this Sam woman?"

"You mean Samantha Dunsbury?" *The runaway bride?* "She seems . . . uh . . . in transition. Why?"

"She wants to rent a house in Sierra Heights. I'm good with renting. Not a lot of buyers in the winter. But you think she can afford it? I'm not leasing them out cheap."

"She can afford your price," Harlee said. *The woman was an heiress after all.* "She's settling in Nugget? I got the impression she was just passing through."

Griff shrugged. "I don't know what her deal is, but Maddy told her to talk to me about renting a place."

"I'll see what I can find out," Harlee said.

"I thought you would." Griffin grinned. "How's the job search going?"

Sucky. "Holidays are a slow time in the newspaper business. Everyone is on vacation." Harlee glanced at her watch. "I better get going. I'll see you guys later."

"Say hi to Darla," Rico shouted after her as she got inside her truck.

At the square, Harlee pulled into a parking space in front of the barbershop. Inside, Darla sat at the cash register, reading a magazine. Still no business. Harlee thought for sure Darla's stunning work on Sam's hair would've netted some appointments.

"You've been quiet like this all day?" she asked Darla.

"Yep. I'm chalking it up to the fact that it's the Sunday after New Year's. Right?"

"Is that typically a slow day?"

"Most salons, at least in Sacramento, are closed on Sunday."

"Okay," Harlee said. "Then no worries."

Darla pulled a face. "Whatever."

"So tell me the deal with you and Wyatt. We never got to talk about that and I'm dying to know."

"It was a long time ago," Darla said. "We used to date when I was eighteen."

Harlee waited for her to say more; when Darla didn't, she asked, "Was it serious?"

"I thought it was. We got engaged."

"You did?" Harlee couldn't believe it. Darla acted like she barely knew the guy.

"I got pregnant and he wanted to do the right thing. When I lost the baby, he left."

"Whoa, whoa, whoa. Slow down," Harlee said. "You had a miscarriage?"

Darla nodded her head, her face grim, the memory clearly still painful. "The next day he joined the army. He didn't even talk to me about it, just left a note and headed off to Fort Benning."

"He knew you'd had the miscarriage?"

"Yes. He's the one who took me to the hospital. Held my hand. Told me he loved me. I didn't think about whether we would still get married. At the time I was too consumed with the loss of our child. I would've understood if he wanted to call it off, but we never even had a conversation about it. He just left me alone to pick up the pieces."

"Darla, I am so sorry. I had no idea. Why didn't you tell me?"

"It was a long time ago. And you have enough to deal with. Really, I've moved on."

Clearly not if New Year's Eve was anything to go on. "Did your parents know?" Harlee asked.

"My mom was planning the wedding. Given the circumstances it would've been just a small one, but both my parents were good with it. My dad had known Wyatt his whole life. I don't think he has ever forgiven him."

Harlee leaned forward in the barber's chair, which she had turned to face Darla. "So what was that all about the other night?"

"I don't know. He's been coming in a lot, like he's hoping to put it behind us. Sometimes I think he's interested in us starting up again. Then a couple of weeks ago I saw him with some blonde. What am I supposed to think about that?"

"Are you willing to forgive him?" Harlee asked.

"Jury is still out. You think I should?"

"I think what he did was pretty awful. But you guys were kids. He probably freaked out and didn't know how to handle the grief. You still have feelings for him, though, don't you?"

Darla lifted her shoulders. "He was my first love."

Just then Nate came in the door. He looked even more handsome than Harlee remembered. If a man could glow, Harlee would say he glimmered like a lightbulb. She wondered what the etiquette was on congratulating him on Sophie and Mariah's baby.

"Hey, Darla." He did a visual lap around the empty shop. "You have time for a trim?"

"Sure," Darla said, hopping out of her chair so fast she nearly gave Harlee whiplash.

Harlee moved out of the barber's chair to make way for Nate and flashed him a smile, hoping that it wouldn't be awkward after she'd turned him down for a date. "How's it going?"

"Good," he said, and beamed. "You see the baby yet?"

"No. I figure Sophie and Mariah could use a little time."

Darla had Nate suit up in a cape and walked him to the shampoo bowl. "Can we just go up to their apartment and knock on the door?"

"Sure. They love showing Lilly off."

"Ahh," Harlee cooed. "Lilly is such a pretty name."

When Darla finished washing Nate's hair, he whipped out his phone and showed them pictures of the baby. "Good-looking kid, huh?"

"Gorgeous," Harlee said. Truthfully she looked like every other newborn—squished and red faced. "Are you hanging around to help out?" She knew he spent most of his time in San Francisco, where he operated nine other hotels and came up on occasional weekends to check in on the Lumber Baron.

"Yep. And I'm closing escrow on the house in Sierra Heights tomorrow."

Harlee seized the opportunity. "I hear Samantha Dunsbury is planning to rent a place there. She's a guest at the Lumber Baron."

"I know who she is," Nate said sharply.

"You don't like her?"

"She's a nut job and she's managed to talk my sister into hiring her to work at the inn."

"You're kidding," Harlee said, because it wasn't like the woman needed to work. Not according to the newspaper clips and her designer clothes.

"I wish I was. She doesn't have a drop of hotel experience, not to mention that she's flighty as hell. I heard she left some poor guy standing at the altar. Didn't even bother to show up and call it off, face-to-face."

Harlee and Darla looked at each other. "Why do you think she wants to live in Nugget?" It was about as different from New England high society as you could get. Harlee knew, because she had a cousin who lived in Greenwich, Connecticut. Junior League and country clubs.

"Who knows," Nate said as Darla clipped away. "Have you ever talked to the woman? She's a complete ditz—can't even string a sentence together."

Harlee hadn't found her to be a ditz, just confused, like maybe she was depressed. "Then how come Maddy's willing to let her work there?"

"Rhys doesn't want her putting in so many hours at the inn with the baby coming. I'm trying to pick up the slack, but I'm spread pretty thin as it is."

"Sounds like it might be good to have Sam." *"Seriously,"* Harlee wanted to say, *"did a person need a PhD to take reservations?"*

"She wants to be the inn's event planner. Besides the fact that she has no qualifications, the woman couldn't even make it to her own wedding. As far as I can tell she's never had an actual job. So you heard she's moving to Sierra Heights, huh?"

"That's what Griffin said."

"Great! Now I'll be stuck with Crazy Town for a neighbor," Nate said, and Harlee had to wonder why the man was so hostile toward Samantha. Sam might be an odd duck, but she certainly seemed pleasant enough. Hell, she'd given Darla a hundred-dollar tip.

Darla finished his trim and used a fat brush to wipe hairs from the back of his neck. He really was a nice-looking man, Harlee noted. Thick brown hair like his sister's, mocha-colored eyes, and a square jaw with a cleft in the center of his chin. He wasn't as tall as Colin or as broad, but he reached at least six-feet tall and looked like he took care of himself. Definitely worked out or jogged. He had the loose-limbed body of a runner.

He checked out his hair in the mirror. "Looks good, Darla. Thanks."

"Feel free to spread the word," she told him.

"Business still slow?"

"A little," she said.

"This is a town that's slow to embrace change," Nate said. "We had a big fight on our hands when it came to the inn. Nugget didn't want it and the Addisons were dead set on seeing us run out of town. But everything turned out fine." He smiled, showing off a mouth of straight, gleaming white teeth. "Hang in there, Darla."

Nate paid his bill and walked across the square back to the Lumber Baron.

"Were the Addisons the ones giving us the evil eye at the bowling alley New Year's Eve?" Harlee asked.

"Yep. They're the ones who own the Beary Quaint."

It was a funny little town, Harlee thought. Despite everyone being up in everyone else's business, there was comfort in knowing your neighbors. She'd lived on top of people in San Francisco, could hear them showering and flushing their toilets through the thin walls, yet she couldn't pick out most of them in a photo lineup. Here, people took the time to get to know one another. Nugget might be isolated, but with its sense of community it wasn't lonely. Perhaps that's why Sam had decided to stay. Maybe she needed people who were different from the ones she'd run from.

Harlee thought that in a weird way Nugget had healing powers. Look at her. She'd come depressed and defeated, but the town wouldn't allow her to wallow. The beauty and strength of the mountains and trees, the power of the clean, fresh air, and her newfound clique of creative friends had lifted her up. When she finally moved on, found another newspaper job, this place would leave an indelible mark.

"Yoga starts up again next week," Darla said. Pam had given them a hiatus for the holidays. "I don't know about you, but I could use the exercise."

"Me too."

"There she is again," Darla said as she gazed out the window onto the square.

"Who?"

"Wyatt's blonde. See him walking with her?"

Harlee joined Darla at the window and watched them stroll together in the direction of the Ponderosa. They didn't touch but walked close to each other, their heads bowed in conversation. When they got to a Volvo station wagon, the woman searched her purse for a set of keys. Wyatt braced his hand against the car door and kissed her on the cheek, then the woman slid behind the wheel and drove away.

"What do you think that's about?" Darla asked.

"I don't know." But Harlee definitely thought they had the familiarity of a couple.

Colin bolted the last glider bracket to the bench leg, turned it right-side up and sat in it, testing the rocking motion with his foot, making it go back and forth and back and forth. Not bad for a Sunday afternoon. He'd finished the glider as well as a nice-looking nightstand, trying to bulk up his inventory, which had been reduced to a few odds and ends. With the amount of finish work that still needed to be done on Sophie and Mariah's house and the demolition on the McCreedy kitchen starting the following weekend, he wouldn't have a lot of time to build furniture.

Still, he was grateful to have as much construction work as he did, especially in the dead of winter. Colin looked at his watch, knowing full well that he'd buried himself in his shop partly to avoid Harlee. After he left her last night, he should've at least called. He'd basically screwed her brains out and gone running for the hills. Not because he'd wanted to ditch her, but because the fear of losing her had been as intense as the sex.

He needed to make good on taking off the way he had, and prayed she was still talking to him. First, he wanted to shower off the sawdust and wood oil before putting on fresh jeans and a sweatshirt.

Ready, he loaded Max into his truck and drove down the hill. Harlee's Pathfinder wasn't parked in the driveway. Colin assumed that she'd gone into town to hang out with Darla and decided to wait for her on the porch. It was one of those clear Sierra days, where if you could find a spot in the sun, the cold wasn't too bad.

He must've dozed off in the redwood chair, because he jerked awake at the sound of gravel crunching. Max stood up, stretched his legs until they shook, and barked his head off. Harlee got out of her truck, using the running board to get down in her high-heeled boots. Why she wore those in Nugget, Colin couldn't imagine, but they were sexy as hell. Her face held no expression. She didn't look happy to see him, but she didn't look angry either. Colin thought it best to presume the worst and tried to appear as repentant as possible. Although he didn't exactly know what that was supposed to look like. Maybe he should've brought flowers.

"Hey," he called down to her.

"Hey," she called back.

"Your hair looks great." It always looked great to him, but it was a bit shorter, like she'd gotten it trimmed, and had big, bouncy curls.

"Thanks. Darla."

He didn't need a lot of experience with women to know that the terse one-word responses were not a good sign. "How's her business doing?"

She made a so-so sign with her hand. "You need something? Like maybe some sex to go?"

Ah, hell, here it comes. "Don't be mad, Harlee. I told you I needed a little time to think."

"How's that working for you?" She scratched Max's head, brushed by him, and went inside the cabin.

"Apparently not too well." He followed her and watched as she took off her jacket and hung it on a hook in the hallway.

She had on a clingy top with a lacy thing layered underneath and a pair of snug, low-riding corduroys tucked into her boots. It was probably the wrong thing to do under the circumstance, but she looked so goddamn hot that he couldn't help himself. He hooked his hands around her waist and pulled her into him. The contact made him grow hard and her eyes went wide as she felt his erection pressed against her belly.

"Hey, buddy, this ain't In-N-Out Burger."

He nuzzled her neck—she smelled like that fantastic perfume she sometimes wore—and whispered into her ear. "Please. I won't leave this time."

"I don't know," she said against his lips. "I felt pretty ill-used, Colin."

He pulled apart from her. "I feel bad about that, Harlee. I never want you to feel ill-used. Never."

She kissed him, snaking her tongue into his mouth, making him groan with pleasure. Colin inched his fingers under her top, feeling the soft filigree of her undershirt.

"What is this thing?" The woman had a fondness for lingerie. Usually he only liked lacy bras and underwear when they lay in a heap on the floor, but on Harlee it reminded him of unwrapping a most excellent present. Something worth waiting for.

"Just a shell."

"Can I see it?"

She pulled the shirt over her head and stood there for his perusal in a skintight red lace long-sleeved top and matching bra. For a minute he didn't think he could breathe. Then he kissed her through the sheer fabric. On her belly, her breasts, her collarbone, anywhere he could feel warm skin inside the lacy pattern. Her fingers nimbly unbuttoned his denim shirt, pushed it off him, and tugged the thermal undershirt over his head. Then she wrestled with the buckle on his belt.

"We doing this here?" he asked. They were still in the hallway, just inches away from the front door.

"I want to. Do you?"

"I'm definitely game." Because he couldn't wait any longer, he pushed her hands away and finished with the belt and got his jeans around his ankles. She immediately took him in her soft hands.

"Slow down, Harlee."

He fought with the buttons on her pants, shimmied them down as far as the top of her boots, and slid his hand under her panties, working her with his fingers until she whimpered over and over again. Going down on his knees, he pulled the panties down, spread her thighs apart, and laved her with his tongue and mouth.

"Oh God," she moaned, and he felt her legs buckle.

"I've got you." He gripped her around the waist and Harlee clung to his shoulders until she cried out as her body shuddered.

He watched her rest the back of her head against the wall, her blue eyes hooded, as she tried to gain control. Prying off his boots, he kicked his jeans off, pulled his wallet out of his back pocket and rose to his feet, pulling her against him. She wrapped her legs around him and he carried her into the bedroom, across the gleaming wood floor to the sleigh bed where they'd first made love.

Without ceremony, he got rid of her boots, pants, and the underwear that matched her lacy top. She sat up, propped on her elbows, watching him undress her.

"What about my shirt and bra?"

"The bra comes off. The lace thing stays on."

"Okay." She stripped off the top, removed her bra and wriggled the shirt back on. It was completely see-through.

"Yeah, that's good." He kissed her, his hands racing over her, touching and molding, as she arched under him, offering and taking as much as she could.

The room dimmed in the fading sunlight, leaving shadows on the walls. They rolled together on the bed, fondling and groping. Kissing and licking. She got him onto his back and straddled him, her dark hair cascading over each side of his face. He flipped her under him, somehow managing to roll the condom on, and dove into her.

Joined, they rode the wave, higher and higher until they reached the crest and came tumbling down. Afterward, they lay in a heap of tangled limbs and wrinkled sheets. Colin got up to get rid of the rubber and she frowned.

"Leaving so soon?" She tried to sound light, but it was clear that she anticipated his pulling another disappearing act.

"Just going to the bathroom," he said, returning a few minutes later to join her under the covers. "I turned the heat on."

She let out a low laugh. "I thought it was already on."

"Yeah?" He kissed the back of her neck and wrapped himself around her. "What did you do today besides get your hair done?"

"Went over to the Gas and Go to say hello to Griffin. He told me that Samantha wants to rent one of the Sierra Heights homes."

"Who's Samantha?"

Harlee rolled over so she faced Colin. "You were in LA when she got here. She's sort of this tragic woman who ran away from home. She was supposed to get married on Christmas Day. But instead skipped the wedding, got in her car, and drove west from New York City."

"Oh yeah?" Colin ran his finger down the length of her nose. He'd never noticed the smattering of tiny freckles sprinkled across the bridge. "So how did you meet her?"

"She came into Darla's to get her hair fixed. She'd taken a scissor to it herself and did a real number. At the time she didn't mention anything about ditching her fiancé at the altar. But I read the newspaper clips online."

"You? Never." He chuckled. Colin didn't much care about this Samantha woman's personal life. People were entitled to their privacy and as far as he was concerned it was no one's business that she ran out on her wedding. Maybe she even had a good reason for doing so.

But he did enjoy the way Harlee told a story. She liked punctuating her anecdotes with colorful details and interesting bits of information. He imagined it was the same way she wrote her articles for the newspaper.

"So she's decided to settle here?"

Harlee nodded. "Maddy gave her a job working at the Lumber Baron and Nate is being incredibly pissy about it."

"Why's that?"

"He thinks she's a flake," Harlee said. "And he says she has no hotel experience. But there has to be more to it than that, because the woman really pushes his buttons. He just went on and on about how much she annoyed him and how he didn't want her for a neighbor at Sierra Heights."

"The hotel has innkeeper's quarters," Colin said. He knew because he'd built them for Maddy, who had wound up marrying and moving in with Rhys. "Why doesn't she just live there?"

Harlee shrugged. "I don't know. She's really rich, so she's probably used to living in high style. Maybe I should run a background check on her just in case she's a klepto deb with a record."

"Deb?"

"You know, a debutante," Harlee explained. "It would probably make Nate feel better about her working there if I checked her out first."

Colin stiffened. "Leave it alone, Harlee. Don't go sticking your nose in where it doesn't belong."

"What are you talking about? That's the work I do."

"Did Nate or Maddy hire you to check her out?" Colin didn't wait for an answer. "Of course not. Why would they when Maddy is married to the police chief?"

"I suppose," she said with reluctance. "But the woman is such a mystery."

"Not all mysteries have to be solved," he said brusquely, and kissed her, hoping it would put an end to any more conversation about background checks.

"I guess," she said. "You hungry?"

"I need to swing by Sophie and Mariah's to drop off a gift for the baby." Colin figured there wouldn't be a lot of visitors over at their place on a Sunday evening. If there were, he'd just leave the present at the door. "You want to come with me? We can get takeout at the Bun Boy afterward and bring it back home."

"I'd love to see the baby, but I don't have a gift," she said.

"I'll make mine from both of us." After the words left his mouth, Colin realized how very much it made them sound like a couple, which hadn't been his intention.

For both their sakes it would be best to keep whatever they had together as light as possible.

Chapter 17

On the second weekend in January, Colin started work on Emily and Clay's kitchen. Harlee had been champing at the bit to get a peek at McCreedy Ranch. According to Della James's cookbook, the cattle ranch had been in Clay's family since the gold rush and boasted thousands of acres of gorgeous land, a spectacular farmhouse, and a barn full of pretty horses. Harlee wanted to see it up close and personal.

So she packed a lunch for Colin and headed out to McCreedy Road. It wasn't exactly a ruse, since Colin needed to eat. But she figured he'd probably bristle at her tactics, knowing full well that her wicker picnic basket was partly an excuse for a tour.

Tough. Unless she got invited to Clay and Emily's wedding—and why would she? Other than sharing a yoga class with Emily, she barely knew the couple—this might be her only chance to see the place. She'd heard that even when the town had been besieged by reporters last year to cover the serial killer who'd falsely confessed to the kidnapping of Emily's missing daughter, no one had been allowed to step foot on the property.

The long driveway up to the McCreedy house did not disappoint. Harlee noted that unlike Grizzly Peak, mountainous and thick with pine trees, the terrain here was more rolling pastures, green with frothy patches of white. In the distance she saw three boys riding on horseback and assumed that at least two of them were Clay's sons. As she drove up the grade, the house came into view. It was white, with a wide porch larger than most San Franciscans' backyards.

A few dogs, including Max, greeted her as she pulled in behind Colin's truck. She tried to get out of the driver's seat, but the Mc-Creedy dogs stood at her door, barking. They looked a little blood-thirsty to Harlee. Clay called them away and she was able to hop out, collecting her basket from the backseat.

"Hi." She waved. Every time she'd seen the man he'd been sitting down. Standing, with his hat on, Clay was as tall, maybe even taller, than Colin. And handsome. "I'm Harlee. I don't think we've officially met."

"Clay." He extended his hand and flashed a set of pearly whites. "You come to hang out with Colin?"

"Bring him lunch." She held up the basket.

He eyed it for a second, started to say something, but stopped himself. "Come on in."

He led her up the porch steps, where she immediately recognized a couple of Colin's rockers, and smiled. They walked through a wide foyer with walls covered in family portraits, past an enormous living room with incredible views of the snow-capped mountains, and an expansive dining room with a giant stone fireplace, into a kitchen that looked like a bomb had gone off. Today was demo day, she remembered.

At a table pushed up against the wall sat Colin and Emily, eating what looked like short ribs and mashed potatoes. Colin looked surprised to see her.

"Hi," he said, and started to stand up.

"I brought you lunch." Harlee motioned for him to sit back down and looked at his heaping plate of food. "But that looks better than what I brought."

"Emily cooked," Colin said, and Harlee looked around the room at the gaping holes where she suspected appliances used to be.

Clearly anticipating the question on the tip of Harlee's tongue, Emily said, "I made lunch in the barn." She pulled a plate from a stack at the end of the table and made an extra place-setting. "Come join us. Clay, you too, honey."

"You have a kitchen in your barn?" Harlee asked as she found a tidy spot to put down the basket and took the chair next to Clay's.

"It's a barn that Clay's late wife converted into a beautiful apartment. I used to live in it, but now use it as an office and test kitchen."

"Well, that should certainly come in handy during the remodel," Harlee said, taking another look around the room.

The cabinets were still intact, but the dated tile countertops had been partially ripped out, floral-themed wallpaper peeled from the walls, and huge chunks of linoleum pulled up from the floor.

Clay served her enough short ribs and potatoes for a small army, then served himself twice as much. "Dig in. It's good stuff." He pushed a big wooden bowl of salad her way and handed her a small plate.

"That was so nice of you to bring Colin lunch," Emily said, and met Clay's eyes across the table, conveying a silent message.

Harlee knew what the message was. *Told you they were an item.* No secrets in Nugget.

Colin, on the other hand, was conveying an altogether different message with his eyes. *You're not fooling me for one second, Miss Nosy.*

"So I hear you're some kind of an investigator," Clay said.

"Actually I'm a journalist. But I'm taking a break to get my start-up off the ground before I go back to newspapers."

"That's this DataDate online deal you've got going?" Clay asked, and Harlee nodded. "Sounds interesting. You want a good start-up, you ought to buy the *Nugget Tribune*."

"I didn't realize it was for sale." And it wasn't exactly a start-up. The banner on the paper said it had been around since 1848. Harlee had bought a subscription when she first moved to Nugget to keep abreast of area news.

Unfortunately, the little rag was more of a shopper than a newspaper. Bake sale notices, a pet of the week column, and a small police blotter passed as journalism. The only section Harlee even looked at was the op-ed page. People in Nugget had a lot of opinions and a lot of free time to rant about them. Some of the pieces cracked her up, like the latest controversy over whether Griffin should keep the Gas and Go open twenty-four seven. One faction argued that big rigs would use the town as a detour to and from the interstate at all hours of the night, making noise and wreaking havoc on air quality. While others countered that it would be nice to have the extra business, not to mention the convenience of an all-night gas station.

"Yup," Clay said. "Lila Stone bought it twenty years ago when she moved here from Marin County. Back then it was a nice little paper. High school sports scores, little features about the shop owners, a fish report, and even a ranching column. But she's older now and I suspect tired of writing all the articles and selling all the ads. I'm guessing it's probably not as profitable as it used to be."

No newspaper was anymore, Harlee thought sadly. And as far as the *Nugget Tribune*, you could get more hard-hitting news off of Twitter and Facebook.

"I think the Addisons put in an offer," Clay continued, and shook his head.

"Those people who own the Beary Quaint? What, you don't like them?"

"They're petty and vindictive. I'd hate to see them use the paper to even up scores. I thought about buying it and hiring someone else to run it. But I don't know if I could trust myself not to use the paper to push my own agenda. It's heady stuff owning a media outlet. You have a duty to be balanced and objective, otherwise you're just a propaganda machine, giving people skewed facts to make them buy into your own beliefs."

Harlee was impressed. Clay McCreedy was a smart and honorable man.

"It's too small-town for Harlee," Colin piped in. "She needs a big-city newspaper."

Harlee was taken aback by his adamancy. She had no intention of buying, or for that matter working, at the crappy little *Nugget Tribune*, but it was as if Colin wanted to make it crystal clear that this thing they had together was only temporary, which of course it was. It shouldn't have hurt her feelings, because it was absolutely true. Harlee wasn't ready to give up working at a metropolitan paper. It was who and what she was.

But it had.

She turned to Emily. "This was delicious."

"It's the McCreedy beef," Emily said, and looked at Clay with such love in her eyes that Harlee could feel the staggering weight of it from across the table.

"I need to get back to work," Colin said. He stood up and started to clear the dishes. "Uh, no sink."

Emily laughed. "I'll take everything over to the barn."

"I'll help," Harlee said, wanting to see more of the place.

"Great." Emily found a box and loaded up the dirty plates. "I'll give you the nickel tour on the way over."

Emily led Harlee down a flagstone trail, casually indicating points of interest. Things like: Down there are the stables. Over that mountain is a gorgeous little lake where Clay takes the boys canoeing. Here is the Hot Spot, the beach where we spend our summers, lounging next to the Feather River.

Nowhere in Emily's voice did Harlee detect boastfulness. The woman wasn't trying to show off. Everything was said with a degree of pride, like this is my husband-to-be's history, look how well he and his family have preserved it. From what Harlee had heard, the McCreedys were generous benefactors who often hosted fund-raisers and gatherings at the ranch.

When they came upon the so-called barn, Harlee let out a sigh. The picture in Della's book didn't do it justice. It was red with white trim, had a Dutch front door, dormer windows, old-timey lantern light fixtures, and a rooster weather vane. It was singularly the most charming building Harlee had ever seen.

"Wow, Emily."

"Isn't it, though? Wait until you see the inside."

She opened the door and Harlee caught her breath. The place was all open beams, wide-plank floors and spectacular picture-window views of the river and mountains.

"This is spectacular." Harlee gaped.

"Jennifer had good taste. That was Clay's late wife."

Harlee figured there was a story there, but didn't know Emily well enough to ask. Although it took great restraint.

"So you and Colin are seeing each other, huh?" No such restraint from Emily. But to be fair, Harlee had brought him lunch. That was a pretty girlfriend-like thing to do.

"Yeah," she said. "It's pretty casual, but . . . well, you know."

Emily smiled and carted the box into the kitchen. "Yes, I definitely know. Although I have to say I wouldn't have put you two together."

"No? Why's that?"

"You're so outgoing and Colin is . . . uh . . . reserved. But you know what they say, opposites attract."

Harlee nodded in agreement, but she didn't really think she and

Colin were so very different. He wasn't all that reserved around her. Especially in bed. But she supposed people saw Colin as eccentric. She thought part of that was his demophobia. He hid it well and as a result people just assumed he was antisocial. But she'd seen him one-on-one with Darla, Griffin, Maddy, Sophie, and Mariah, and his interactions with them were quite natural. Charming, really. He was a great listener and very caring. And humble, although an incredibly gifted carpenter with a real knack for business. He'd given her good money advice, yet didn't seem to judge the fact that she was a financial train wreck.

At least she was working on that. Since moving to Nugget, she hadn't gone on any huge shopping sprees, mostly cooked at home, and other than a few bowling expeditions, spent very little money on entertainment. If she kept it up, Harlee might be caught up in, oh, say, twenty years. How depressing.

"So you and Clay are tying the knot in June, huh?"

"We are." Emily beamed so bright the barn practically lit up. "You and Colin absolutely have to come."

"We'd love to." At least Harlee would—if she was still here. "You're holding the ceremony and reception on the ranch?" Harlee remembered Emily talking about the wedding at yoga. Something about using big white tents.

"On the front lawn."

"That'll be beautiful," Harlee said. The property, at least the small part she'd seen, was breathtaking. "You're not doing the food yourself, are you?"

"No," Emily said. "I'm still working on that, but we'd like to keep it simple. Maybe a big tri-tip grill with all the fixings."

"That sounds perfect." Very California. Very country. And Harlee presumed they'd use McCreedy beef. Nice! She almost hoped she'd still be here for the big event. If Colin wouldn't come with her, she'd take Darla as her date.

"I hear your mom has been selling quite a bit of Colin's furniture." Emily started rinsing their lunch plates in the big farm sink and loading them into the dishwasher.

"Her customers love his stuff," Harlee said with pride. "Unfortunately, she can only stock so much, because her shop is pretty small. She mostly sells housewares, linens, soaps, and tchotchkes.

But over the holidays she managed to cram one of Colin's four-poster beds in the store and it went in a matter of days."

"That's great." Emily closed the dishwasher and turned it on. "His work is amazing and I like that it's getting out there."

Harlee knew that he could stock his pieces in a lot more stores if he participated in the big furniture convention shows. That's where retailers went to find new lines. Harlee had been to one once at the Moscone Center with her mother. It had been jam-packed with every kind of accessory and furniture imaginable—modern, contemporary, traditional, vintage, antique reproductions, even repurposed garbage. She and her mother had spent eight hours taking in the showrooms and hadn't even seen half of them. But the swarms of people would send Colin over the edge.

"I hope he doesn't mind," Emily said, "but I told that new woman, Samantha, about his furniture. She's moving into one of the Sierra Heights homes for the winter and needs to set up house."

"Griffin told me that she was thinking of renting one of the homes. Why doesn't she just live in the innkeeper's quarters at the Lumber Baron, since she'll be working there?"

Emily lifted her shoulders. "I don't know that Maddy offered it. I think no one is really sure that Sam is all that serious about staying here. She seems a little flighty. But she did pay Griff first and last months' rent and a substantial deposit, so we'll see. In the meantime, Colin shouldn't be surprised if she calls him."

"That was nice of you to pass his name along. I know he'll appreciate it."

"If you don't mind me saying, he seems different these days."

Harlee tilted her head. "What do you mean?"

Emily grew slightly uncomfortable, like maybe she had overstepped her bounds. "I don't know." She fidgeted with an egg timer on the kitchen counter. "He just always seemed sad before. I never wanted to pry, but having had my own tragedy, I suspected that there might've been something difficult in his past. Anyway, since you moved in next door to him, I've noticed a change. He seems, well, happy."

Harlee didn't know what to say. From their first meeting, Harlee had concluded that there was something different about Colin. But the difference is what made him interesting—and attractive. Some might see his phobias as tragic, but she didn't. Unfortunate, for sure. But they were just part of him, the same way some people had nervous ticks or allergies. Instead of dwelling on the issues, you just learned to work around them, like going gluten free or whatever.

"He's just shy." Harlee tried for nonchalance. "Being around me has probably made him less so. That's all."

"Maybe that's it." But Harlee knew Emily wasn't buying it.

"I need to get going." She had a new client who wanted her to run a check on two different love interests. The woman thought a background check might help her eliminate one of them. "Thanks for the wonderful lunch and for showing me around. In the interest of full disclosure, I was super curious about the place."

"You're welcome anytime, Harlee." Emily smiled.

When they got back to the main house, Harlee went inside to say goodbye to Colin, who was ripping out the rest of the tiled countertops with a crowbar. He walked her out to her truck and pinned her against the driver's door.

"You get a good look around?" He winked.

"What? I came to bring you lunch, which by the way I left inside if you get hungry and want a snack."

He chuckled, low, deep in his throat. "Sure you did."

"Hey," she said back, "I secured us an invite to the big wedding."

"I don't do weddings."

Harlee got the strong impression that those four words carried a double meaning. And for some inexplicable reason that bothered her. A lot. "Well, if I'm still here, which I pray to God I'm not, I'll be going to that wedding."

Colin frowned, his eyes fixed on hers. They seemed to say, "What are we getting ourselves into, you and me?" Then he kissed her, his body firmly pressed against her until she felt heat pool way down in her midsection.

"Go," he said against her lips. "Otherwise I can't be responsible for my actions."

She left with the taste of him still on her lips and the niggling fear that things had just gotten unexpectedly complicated.

"Can you put this on the list too?" Samantha Dunsbury, Nugget's mystery resident, ran her hand down the pine log of a canopy bed.

Colin looked at Harlee, who gave a little half shrug, grinned, and added the bed to the list. For about an hour Sam had been walking through his cluttered wood shop, picking out pieces of furniture with the same casualness as a shopper buying groceries.

True to Emily's words, Sam had called, saying that she needed a couple of pieces for her new rental. Sam's idea of a couple of pieces had turned into four rocking chairs, a coffee table, a hall tree, a dining room set, and the bed.

"So you don't do couches, huh?" Sam asked as she bounced between a nightstand and dresser.

"Nothing upholstered," Colin replied, and glanced out the window to see that the heavy downpour of rain that had cut his day short on Sophie and Mariah's job had turned into a light dusting of snow.

"I think leather would look great with this stuff, don't you?"

Colin hadn't given it much thought, but muttered, "Sure," just to be agreeable. "Hey, Sam, this stuff ain't cheap." She hadn't once asked the price of any of his pieces.

"I wouldn't imagine it would be." She looked up from the chest of drawers she'd been examining and smiled. "You're an artist, Colin Burke. I'll take this, as well as the nightstand. Is there a delivery service around here I can hire?"

"I'll deliver it," Colin said. He'd never had a single sale this large. The least he could do was throw in free delivery. Hell, he'd even set up the bed for her.

"Awesome," she said. "I guess I'll order the sofas on the Internet. I'm seeing a lot of neutral colors, cozy rugs, maybe some Western art."

"It sounds like you're planning to stay a while," Harlee said.

"We'll see." Sam stared out the window at the surrounding mountain range. "I've never lived in California before. It's different. Freer."

Freer than what? Colin wondered. To him, any place was freer than the six-by-eight-foot cage he'd lived in. Then again there were all kinds of prisons, he reckoned. Even gilded ones that looked like palaces.

"When would you like me to deliver everything?" Colin had totaled up a number and scrawled it on the list.

"I'm planning to paint first, so next weekend would be good."

"The weekends I put in long hours on the McCreedy's kitchen redo. I could probably bring the furniture over late Monday afternoon." After he punched out on Sophie and Mariah's house. "This price work for you?" Colin showed her the amount he'd tallied.

"That'll work just fine," Sam said.

"It sounds like you're putting a lot of personal touches on the house." Harlee glanced at the piece of paper Colin had just shown Sam and imperceptibly lifted her brows.

"I think it'll be fun to decorate it. I took a few courses in New York."

Harlee smiled and Colin knew that she thought Sam was on the dizzy side. But not in an unkind way. Harlee didn't roll bitchy, mean, or intolerant. "So I hear that you plan on working at the Lumber Baron?"

"Yes. I'll relieve Maddy when she goes on maternity leave. I'm also hoping to develop the inn's event planning program. It's such a charming place—they could be doing so much more than weddings."

"Did you used to do event planning when you lived in Connecticut?" Harlee asked. Colin's Brenda Starr was on the trail of a hot story.

"Not professionally, but I planned a fair amount of parties and events."

"I'm sure Maddy will love having you there," Harlee said.

"I hope so." Sam rummaged through her purse and handed Colin a credit card. "You take plastic, right?"

"Yep. I've got to run it inside. Would you like to come in and have a cup of tea or something?"

Harlee looked at him like he was an alien.

"I'm fine," Sam said, and continued to wander around the shop. "Don't worry about me."

Colin left the two women alone, went inside his office and ran Sam's credit card. When he returned, Sam said her goodbyes and they finalized plans for the delivery.

"You'll be okay driving in the snow?" Colin asked, eyeing her Mercedes hardtop convertible.

"I'm from the East Coast," she said, and flashed a smile. "See you next Monday."

He and Harlee stood there, watching until the glow of her tail-lights disappeared.

"Good sale," Harlee said.

"Damn right." He wiped snowflakes from her hair. "Let's go inside."

In the living room, Max lifted his head from the fleece doggie bed where he slept. Those mixed eyes looked at them curiously, then he plopped his snout onto his paws and resumed napping. Colin got to work building a fire.

"You have anything to make for dinner?" Harlee asked.

"I'm sure we can scrounge something up." He waited to make sure his kindling caught, threw on a log, and followed Harlee into the kitchen.

He searched his refrigerator, then the freezer. "Chicken." In the cabinet he pulled out a bag of rice. "I've also got one of those salads in a bag."

"I can work with that," she said, and ran hot water over of the packages of boneless, skinless breasts. Scouting through the cupboards, she found a package of spaghetti and a jar of pasta sauce and put the rice back. "Chicken parmigiana."

"Sounds good." Before Harlee, he would've been satisfied with canned soup or chili. She'd sort of ruined his hobo palate.

"So what did you think?"

"Of what?" He started to set the table.

"Of Sam." Harlee gave him a long, slanted look.

"She's got good taste in furniture and deep pockets."

"Yes, she does." Harlee turned off the water and felt the breasts to make sure they were defrosted. She found two plastic sandwich bags in one of the drawers and a cooking mallet in the other, and pounded the crap out of the chicken.

"You making sure they're dead?"

"Here." She handed him the mallet. "Take over for me. Get them about this thin." Harlee demonstrated a half inch with her fingers.

She grabbed a couple of bowls and found a bag of flour. "You have panko?" When he looked at her in question, she shook her head. "Bread crumbs?"

"Nope."

Harlee went rummaging through his pantry and came out with a box of cornflakes. "This will have to do," she said, and grabbed a couple of eggs from the fridge.

She poured the cornflakes into another baggie, took back the mallet and decimated them. She filled one bowl with the flour, the other with the cornflake crumbs, and a third with beaten egg and began dredging the chicken breasts. "Would you prepare a sauté pan with a little olive oil?"

"Sure." He liked working with her in the kitchen this way. Oddly, the domesticity of it, especially Harlee in an apron, got him off.

She filled a pot with water and put a flame under it to boil. "Did you think she was pretty?"

He'd sort of lost the train of their Samantha conversation, but he was smart enough to know that this right here was dangerous territory. "I don't know. Do you?"

She fixed him with an *Are you an idiot?* look. "Either you thought she was pretty or you didn't, because you seemed extremely attentive. Like more attentive with her than I've seen you with any other woman."

"Hell yeah, I was attentive. I get that way when people are writing me really big checks."

"You invite them in for tea? Because last time I looked, you didn't even own a tea bag until I brought a box over."

"I was just trying to be polite, Harlee. The woman pretty much made my fiscal year."

"I know that, Colin. But just tell me, did you find her attractive?"

"Why does it matter?"

"I've just never seen you that way. *Will you be okay to drive in the snow?*" she mimicked.

"Are you for real?" Colin couldn't remember having a more moronic conversation. Not even with the brain-dead inmates in his cell block. "All right, if you want to know so badly, yeah, I thought she was pretty. The red hair. The green eyes. She reminded me of my sister, Fiona."

Harlee browned the chicken in the sizzling oil. "I knew you were attracted." He watched her flip the breasts, all the while making a real effort not to look at him. "Can you please get me a baking pan?" She turned on the oven.

"Like this?" He pulled a rectangular one out of a lower cabinet and waited for her to turn her attention on him.

"Mm-hmm," she said, but still no eye contact.

He put the pan on the counter next to her. She laid the browned breasts inside and popped the pan in the oven. The water had come to a boil and Harlee dropped in the pasta, stirring it occasionally. She found a big bowl and got to work on the salad.

"Harlee, you can't really be angry that Sam reminded me of my sister?"

"I'm not angry." She made a big show of tossing the salad.

"Well, you're acting like a jealous baby, when you have nothing to be jealous about."

"I guess I'm feeling a little insecure." Harlee put the salad bowl on the table and waited for the chicken and spaghetti to finish cooking while she heated the sauce. "It's not like we're a serious couple or anything, but I don't want to sleep with you if you're planning to sleep with other people."

Colin took her by the arms as gently as he knew how, because he was losing his patience. "Can I ask how we got from Sam being attractive to me sleeping with other women? Maybe I'm slow, but I'm having trouble tracking this conversation."

"I need to get the chicken out of the oven." She pulled away from him, made up their plates and put them on the table. "Let's just have a nice dinner, okay?"

"Not until we clear this up."

Harlee let out an audible sigh. "I'd prefer we just forget about it. I'm embarrassed that I even brought it up since you're perfectly entitled to find another woman attractive. There are a lot of men in this town who I find handsome, and it doesn't mean anything. It's just that you caught me off guard; you're usually so reserved. That's all."

"Like who?" Colin wanted to know. "Griffin?"

"Sure. Griffin, Nate, Rico, Clay McCreedy, the police chief, even Wyatt to some extent. The point is, I'm not contemplating sleeping with any of them—only you. Look, this is stupid. It's not like you were fawning over Sam or making a pass at her. You didn't do anything wrong. She's a beautiful woman and I could tell that you appreciated that and it bothered me because you're typically not attuned to things like that. Let's eat now and forget about it, please."

"Come here." He held his arms wide. When she wouldn't come, he crooked his finger until Harlee came close enough so that he could pull her into his arms. "Sam is pretty, no doubt about it. But you are the most beautiful woman I've ever laid eyes on. From the first time I saw you hanging off the edge of the road in that ridiculous Mini Cooper, I thought you were a freaking mirage. That's how impossibly beautiful you are. But I'm not so shallow as to be taken in by a woman's looks. It's what's in here that counts." He pressed his hand against her heart. "And Harlee, no one has you beat there either."

She rested her forehead against his chest. "Are you feeding me a line, Colin Burke? Remember, I investigate smooth talkers like you for a living."

"Harlee"—he lifted her chin—"I may be a lot of things, but a smooth talker isn't one of them." He covered her mouth with his and took what he wanted. All of it.

And hours later, with their dinners cold on the table, they fell asleep together in Colin's big log bed.

Chapter 18

The following week, Harlee and Colin used their trucks to deliver Samantha's furniture. Griffin also offered to help, lending his Range Rover to the cause. So the three vehicles, packed to the rooftops, caravanned down Grizzly Peak to Sierra Heights, where Sam waited to begin moving in.

Harlee looked forward to seeing what Sam had done to the place. A lot of people in Nugget were talking about how she was investing too much time and money painting and decorating a mere rental. But Harlee suspected that neither time nor money meant much to Sam, since she had plenty of both.

Luckily, the weather was cooperating. And with four sets of hands, Harlee hoped they could get all of Colin's pieces inside the house and assembled before nightfall. Colin had been putting in long hours at Sophie and Mariah's job site, but had managed to sneak away early enough to make good on his promise to deliver her purchases.

When they got there, the house had already been half furnished with comfy sofas, overstuffed leather chairs, a flat-screen TV, and lots of rugs and pictures on the walls. Sam had even managed to hang window treatments in the master bedroom, which looked custom-made.

"Wow." Harlee turned in circles. "The place is gorgeous."

"I love it," Sam said, her mouth spreading into a wide smile. "I bought a mattress, so if we get the bed set up tonight this will be my first time sleeping here."

"You've been staying at the inn all this time?" Jeez, the woman's pockets went even deeper than Harlee thought.

"Maddy gave me a discount, of course—now that I'm working there."

Colin and Griffin carried pieces of the canopy part of the bed inside and went back out to get the rest. The women joined them, toting in dresser drawers and dining room chairs. Within an hour they had everything unloaded and Colin worked in the master suite, putting the new bed together, while Sam gave Harlee the rest of the tour. The large home, with its soaring cathedral ceilings and walls of glass, had magnificent views of the golf course and the surrounding mountains. It was a prime piece of property for Griff to tie up. But Harlee supposed renting it out served a better purpose financially than letting the house collect cobwebs.

She wondered if Griff might be interested in Sam, given that he was at loose ends with Lina. They seemed to get along great, but Griff had a knack for making friends and making everyone around him feel included.

She had definitely noticed that Colin had refrained from being too friendly to Sam, obviously taking Harlee's feelings into consideration, which showed what a wonderful man he was. If Harlee wasn't careful, she'd let herself fall in love with him. She was already more than halfway there.

While the three of them stood in the loft, where Griffin tried to talk Sam into putting a pool table, a knock sounded at the door.

"Can't imagine who that could be," Sam said, racing down the stairs. She and Griffin followed. Harlee wanted to check on Colin's progress and see if he needed any help.

Nate stood at the threshold, looking mildly put out. "I couldn't find the keys," he said to Griffin.

"Damn, I forgot. They're in the Range Rover. Hang on a sec." Griffin jogged out the door.

Nate stood there, his hands shoved inside his pants pockets, craning his neck to get a look inside. "You painted?"

"Yes," Sam said. "Would you care to come in?"

"Just for a few minutes," he said, but Harlee could tell he was curious.

"Where's your house, Nate?" she asked.

He lifted his chin and pointed to the house next door, annoyed. "I guess everyone wants on the golf course."

"Why does Griffin have your keys?" Harlee asked, knowing that Nate's house closed weeks ago.

"There was some work that still needed to be done as part of the sales agreement." Nate wandered around the front rooms, taking in Sam's touches. "That Colin's table and chairs?"

Harlee nodded. "Colin's in the master, assembling one of his beds."

Nate seemed to know the floor plan, because he headed to the back of the house to the bedroom and popped his head in the door. "Hey, Colin."

Colin looked up from what he was doing and grunted a hello. "Help me with the mattress, would you?"

Nate slipped in and started taking the plastic off the mattress while Colin piled his tools in the corner. Together, they hefted the bed onto the frame and stood back to look at it.

Harlee popped her head inside and said, "It's fantastic." Initially, she'd feared that the large bed might dwarf the room, but it fit beautifully. Sam had already put the dresser kitty-corner to the bathroom, and Colin got the nightstand out of the walk-in closet and placed it next to the bed.

"You have any of these without the canopies?" Nate gave the bed frame a shake to test its sturdiness. "I'm sleeping on an air mattress."

"I've got a four-poster with your name on it," Colin said. "You up from San Francisco for the week?"

"Yep. I thought I'd break in the new pad and spend some time with Lilly."

"She's a pretty girl," Colin said. "Your place look like this?"

"Similar floor plan, but my furniture consists of a lawn chair, a card table, and a bed that leaks air. Will you deliver and set mine up too?"

"Yep," Colin said. "But you've got to get your own mattress."

"It's a deal. Come by the inn and I'll write you a check."

Sam wedged her way into the room and Harlee feared that Colin might be feeling a little hemmed in. She caught his eye and he must've read her concern, because he nodded a silent signal that he was okay.

"It's fabulous," Sam squealed.

She scurried into the walk-in closet and came out with bags of bedding and matching throw pillows. This time Nate did roll his eyes.

"I've got to get going," he said.

"Griffin left your keys on the new hall tree," Sam said. "He had to get to the Gas and Go for an appointment."

"All right." Before Nate left, he said, "Maddy is taking the day off tomorrow for a doctor's appointment. Make sure you're on time."

Sam straightened from putting the mattress cover on the bed. "I'm always on time."

"Good. Then there shouldn't be a problem." Nate avoided her glare and turned to Colin and Harlee. "See you guys."

Sam waited until she was sure Nate had left and said, "I don't know what I did to that man, but he sure doesn't like me."

Harlee had to wonder herself. Nate didn't seem rude by nature, but humiliating Sam like that . . .

"I wouldn't worry about it," Colin said, clearly trying to downplay Nate's behavior. "Nate's a good guy, but sometimes he comes off a little strong. It probably comes from running so many hotels. But Maddy is the one in charge of the inn and she's good people."

Colin wrapped his arm around Harlee. "I hope you enjoy your new furniture. The place looks great. But I've got to get my girl home now and make her dinner."

If Harlee was more than halfway to loving him before, she was all the way now.

Wyatt wanted a haircut and Darla wanted to throw him out of her shop. But business was business. It wouldn't do her any good to refuse service to one of Nugget's finest. For that reason she plastered a smile on her face and led him to the shampoo bowl.

"Uh, I just washed my hair this morning," he said.

"I'm not a barber, Wyatt. I'm a stylist. We cut hair wet."

"All right then." He sat there, his body tight as a bowstring, as she rubbed shampoo into his scalp.

"Relax, Wyatt. Most people enjoy this."

"I'm enjoying it." And sure enough, in his lap was proof.

"You're disgusting, Wyatt."

"You told me to relax and enjoy it." He grinned, a mischievous gleam in his eyes.

"Does your little blond girlfriend know that you're popping boners all over town?"

"Not all over town. Only in your shop, Darla. And what little blond girlfriend? You're the last blond girlfriend I've had." He stared up at her pink hair. "Why do you do that?"

"What?" Oops. She accidentally sprayed his face with the hose. How unprofessional.

He grabbed a towel off the shampoo bar and wiped suds out of his eyes. "You've got the prettiest hair. Why do you need to dye it all those crazy colors?"

"Because I like to and that's reason enough for me. So who's the blonde you're always groping on the square?"

"I don't know what you're talking about, Darla."

She wrapped his head in a turban, made sure to knot it extra tight, and guided him back to her chair. "What do you want? A crew cut?"

He stared back at her in the mirror. "Just an inch off."

She had a good mind to shave him bald, but he really did have nice hair. Thick and shiny with a little bit of curl. She cleaned up his neckline, rounding out his tapered nape, and snipped around his ears, careful to keep his natural arch. Otherwise poor Wyatt would look like Dumbo.

"Tessa?"

"No, I'm Darla."

"I've been racking my brain over who you're talking about. Is Tessa who you saw me with?"

"I don't know her name, Wyatt." *I just know that she's skinny and drives a station wagon.* "Volvo."

Wyatt grinned. "Yeah, that's her. She's not my girlfriend and I definitely wasn't groping her."

"Well, it looked that way to me. You want it thinned out?"

"A little, yeah. Tessa's my best friend's wife."

Darla lowered the chair a smidge and busted out her thinning shears. "Uh-huh. There's like a million country-western songs about men doing their best friends' wives. Why should you be any different?"

"Ah, that's just low, Darla. When have you ever known me to be a cheat?"

"You've got me there," she said, snipping away. "When I knew you, you were a runner, not a cheater. When the going got rough, Wyatt Lambert got going."

The room went so quiet that Darla could almost hear wisps of Wyatt's hair hitting the floor.

"I screwed up, Darla. Not a day goes by when I don't regret it."

"Really? You ever think about picking up the phone and saying, 'Darla, I'm sorry I ran out on you during the lowest point of your life?' " She watched him in the mirror drop his eyes. "I guess not."

"I was eighteen years old, Darla."

"Did you pick up the phone when you were twenty? How about twenty-four? No, you waited until I came back to town, when you'd have to see me every day."

"It was wrong," he said. "But sometimes, when you don't know how to right a wrong, you don't do anything at all. It's not an excuse. It sucks. And I'd do anything to go back in time and do right by you. Anything."

She flipped on the blow dryer as much to tune him out as to dry his hair. After she finished, Darla blew warm air over his neck to get rid of the loose hairs and turned his chair around so he could see the back of his head with a hand mirror. "All done," she said.

"Yeah, that's the thing, Darla. I don't think we are. Not by a long shot." He slapped a couple of bills down on her workstation, grabbed his jacket, and left.

Pleased with the progress on Sophie and Mariah's house, Colin cut out early Friday, swung by McCreedy Ranch to check out the new appliances Emily had ordered, and stopped at the Nugget Market on his way home to pick up dog food and fixings for dinner. He sat in his truck, watching the entrance of the grocery store for about twenty minutes, waiting for a pack of customers to thin out before going inside. For the most part the market only got really busy in summer, when tourists flocked to the Sierra to take advantage of the great outdoors. But today it seemed to Colin that every person in Nugget had come to do their last-minute weekend shopping.

He hadn't returned to the acupuncturist since before Christmas, feeling that the whole ordeal had been a waste of time. Harlee had already begun looking into other possible cures for Colin's demophobia and wasn't likely to give up until he could handle a sold-out sports arena. The woman could be crazy determined when she got her mind stuck on something.

With the holidays behind them, she'd ramped up her job search and Colin knew it was only a matter of time before she'd leave Nugget to go off to a big metropolitan newspaper somewhere. Colin was good at compartmentalizing. He'd had to be to survive prison life. But now he wondered whether he'd be able to simply file Harlee away in the "short-lived winter romance" box. Then again, what choice did he have? He couldn't keep her from chasing her dream and he couldn't go with her.

Colin wheeled his cart down the dairy aisle when he almost collided with Griffin, who looked like he hadn't slept in days.

Griffin bobbed his head in greeting. "What up?"

"I got nothin'. You?"

"Nothing." Griffin shook his head.

Colin wanted to say, *"Then how come you look like shit?"* But it wasn't like they were pals or anything. Griffin was an okay guy. That is when he wasn't hanging around with Harlee. Even though Colin knew they were just friends, because Harlee befriended everyone she met, it rankled him to no end that they sometimes trucked together. At least Darla always seemed to be with them. The gruesome threesome.

"Want to get a beer?" Griffin asked.

That knocked Colin for a loop. He didn't think anyone in Nugget had asked him that before. Not because people here weren't sociable, but Colin had made sure to steer clear of those kinds of invitations. Everyone knew he was a loner. Besides, he didn't drink. He looked at Griffin again—assessed him the best he could without staring. Bloodshot eyes. Crazy hair. Wrinkled clothes that looked like he'd slept in them. Colin wondered if the guy had gone on a bender.

"My milk will go bad," he said, indicating the jug in his cart, which he hadn't even paid for yet. Griffin absently nodded his head, like he was lost, defeated, or both, making Colin feel guilty. "You want to come over to my place? I'll grab a six-pack."

"Sounds good." Griffin perked up, put his mozzarella sticks back in the case, and followed Colin to the refrigerated beer section of the store.

"You like any of these?" Colin didn't know what the hell the guy drank.

"Whatever. Any of 'em will work."

Colin grabbed some Sierra Nevada, stuck it in his cart, and headed to the checkout stand. "You want a ride or are you okay to drive?"

Griffin looked at him funny. "I'm fine to drive. I'll meet you there."

Twenty minutes later they sat in Colin's living room next to a raging fire with Max on his back, begging for belly scratches. Griffin popped the top off of one of the beers and stretched his legs until he was slumped down on the couch.

"You got any chips?" he asked.

Colin went into the kitchen, found a bag of pretzels Harlee had left behind in the cupboard, and tossed them to Griffin. "Best I can do." He grabbed a glass of water and sprawled out on a leather recliner.

"Where's Harlee?" Griffin asked.

"Working." She'd been hired to do a background check on an alpaca farmer in Redding. So far he'd come up clean. Colin expected she'd be over in a couple of hours. They'd make dinner together. It had become their thing. A nice thing. A thing he looked forward to like he did his next breath.

"Can you believe some of the dudes she runs?" Griffin laughed. "The crap these guys lie about, or worse, leave out. 'Hey, babe, forgot to mention that I'm married.' "

Or worse, Colin thought. *Hey, babe, forgot to mention that I'm an ex-con. I did time for murdering an entire family.* Yeah, time to change the subject. Griffin's next sentence saved him the trouble.

"Lina dumped me."

Ah, hence the dishevelment. "Sorry," Colin said, because what else do you say? She was a bitch anyway? Lina was actually a very sweet girl, *girl* being the operative word.

"She's dating some RA in her dorm."

Colin must've looked flummoxed, because Griff said, "Resident adviser. I had no idea either. Never lived in a dorm. Never even went to college. You?"

Yeah, he'd lived in a dorm, with sociopaths and crazies. "Nope."

"Really? You seem like an educated type."

"Self-taught," Colin said, which was true. Lots of time to read and study in the joint. "You okay with it? The breakup, I mean."

"Yeah. Sure. No big deal."

"So, you're pretty broken up about it is what you're trying to say."

Griffin coughed up something dry in his throat. "Yeah." He looked down at his feet. "I love her, but she's too young. This guy, this RA, he's age appropriate. And he's there and I'm here."

"There's that," Colin said. He felt totally ill equipped to have this conversation and wondered why Griff hadn't unloaded on the women—Harlee or Darla. They'd know exactly the right things to say. "Maybe this dude is just a temporary infatuation."

"Nah, I was the temporary infatuation. He's probably the real deal."

Colin found it interesting that a guy as wealthy as Griffin Parks could be insecure. Then again, Griff had only recently come into his money. His estranged father was Native American, entitling Griffin to a percentage of the tribe's earnings. It just so happened that the tribe owned the most lucrative casino/resort in California.

"She is really young," Colin said.

"Yep. I wanted us to wait a year before we were an official couple—give her time to grow up a little. She didn't want to wait anymore. Said she wanted to start her life, whatever that means."

"She's eighteen years old, Griff. You're what, twenty-five?"

"Twenty-six."

Colin cringed. "Even at nineteen, she'd be too young for you. Give her a few more years. If it's meant to be, it'll happen." When the hell had he become so philosophical?

"You're probably right," Griffin said, looking about as optimistic as a guy hoping for a stay of execution on his way to the gas chamber.

"I'll call Harlee and you can stay for dinner." Colin couldn't believe he was actually entertaining, but he felt sorry for the guy. And Griff had helped Colin when he'd gotten sick. He pretty much helped everyone. The least Colin could do was pay it forward. "You like veggie burgers?"

Griffin eyed Colin's glass of water. "Are you like a health-food nut?"

Colin guessed he sort of was. After living years on the "spread," layers of ramen mixed in with anything from the prison store — potato chips, jerky, canned meat—he'd become very conscientious about what he put into his body. "What, you don't like veggie burgers?"

"I like beef ones better," Griffin said. "But I'm down with it. I could use the company."

While Colin called Harlee, Griffin walked around the front room, taking in the view from the huge picture windows. The now empty pretzel bag sat on the coffee table. Colin scooped it up and threw it in the kitchen trash.

When he got off the phone, Griffin said, "I can't believe you built this place. It's effing genius, dude."

Given that Griffin lived in a log mansion in Sierra Heights, it was a nice compliment. "Thanks. Harlee will be over in about thirty. She's got a few things to tie up."

"You guys are pretty serious, huh?"

"We're together," Colin said, hoping to leave it at that.

"The two of you have a nice thing going. And at least Harlee's your age." He regarded Colin for a few seconds and smirked. "Well, close enough."

"I'm thirty-one and she's twenty-eight, a three-year difference. Not like you and Shirley Temple."

"Hey, Lina's mature for her age."

"Okay," Colin said. "If you say so."

Griffin got another beer from the kitchen. "What will you do when she finds another newspaper job?"

He'd let her go and give thanks for the best thing that ever happened to him. "We'll cross that bridge when we get there." How was that for a cliché?

"Sounds like that opening at *USA Today* could be promising," Griffin said, crouching down in front of the fire to rub Max's belly.

USA Today? This was the first Colin had heard of any job there. Wasn't that paper based in New York? Why didn't he know about this?

"Could be," he said.

"I guess it helps to have friends there," Griffin said. "It's not what you know; it's who you know, right?"

"Yep." Why the hell hadn't Harlee told him? That's what Colin wanted to know.

Chapter 19

"I still don't understand why you told Griffin about *USA Today*, but not me."

Ever since Griffin had left after dinner, Colin and Harlee had been going round in circles on the *USA Today* job. She didn't get why it was such a big deal.

"The position has already been filled, Colin. There was no reason to tell you, since it's not happening."

The truth was Harlee had gotten herself pretty excited about the job. A friend of a friend had been acting as her intermediary and seemed to think Harlee would be a slam dunk. Apparently that person didn't have enough juice in the organization to know that upper management already had their eye on someone else. It happened all the time. Usually in the newspaper industry when a position got posted it was already filled. Management was just following protocol. But it hadn't stopped Harlee from getting her hopes up and feeling like a loser when it didn't come to fruition.

"Why couldn't you just tell me that?" Colin's face was red. "Why the hell should I hear it from Griffin?"

"Griffin just happened to be around when Leah called. He overheard most of it. I didn't purposely keep you out of the loop, Colin. It was a lead that didn't pan out. Not worth talking about."

She also had her pride, and all the rejection stung. By now she surely thought she'd have her pick of jobs, and the humiliation of being constantly passed over wasn't something she wanted to share.

Colin let out a breath and gathered Harlee in his arms. "Do you feel bad that you didn't get it?"

"No . . . Yes." And just like that she started to cry. "I'm a really good reporter, Colin. I know you think I'm delusional because if I was so great, why wouldn't I have a job by now? But it's . . . it's just really hard out there."

Words of the famous crime reporter Edna Buchanan popped into her head, "Never let them see you cry," and Harlee wiped her nose with the back of her hand. "You probably think it's an excuse. But it really is hard out there."

"Give me a little more credit, Harlee. I may not be a journalist, but I know that newspapers have been hit hard by the economy and the Internet. And I know you're a great reporter." He lifted her chin with his finger. "I've Googled your stories."

She gave him a watery smile. "You did?"

"Of course I did." He kissed the tip of her nose and dabbed a tear away with the pad of his thumb. "You're a great writer."

Actually, her editor was the great writer. He'd definitely got his money's worth out of Columbia, because he still had a job and she didn't. But he couldn't find half the dirt she could dig up. The man didn't even know how to use Nexis. "Thanks," she said, and sniffled.

"Harlee, did you keep this job from me because you were embarrassed?" Colin asked gently.

"Colin, I didn't tell you because it's a nonissue. Can we not talk about it anymore?"

"I'll stop talking about it, but just for the record, you can tell me anything."

"Yeah," she said, "because you're such a sharer." Harlee was teasing, but Colin was looking at her strangely. "What? I just meant that you don't talk about yourself much."

His eyes dropped to his boots and Harlee could've sworn there was something he wanted to say. "Colin?"

"I told you about my phobias." Colin swallowed uncomfortably. "I haven't told anyone about that except for Fiona and Steve."

"I know," she said, and hurt for him, because having fears like that had to be emasculating for a guy as proud and alpha as Colin. "And

I'll never forget the fact that you overcame the demophobia to protect me. That's hot for a woman, you know?"

"Yeah?" He pressed her against the kitchen counter where they'd been doing dishes together and kissed her.

The man was incredibly affectionate. Always hugging, kissing, and touching her. It made her feel perfect. As his lips worked their way down her neck, she nearly blurted that she loved him. Recently, her feelings for him had been building with the velocity of a gale force. Now it swept her up like a tornado. Although plenty of men had looked, no one had ever looked at her the way Colin did. It was always right there in his face. To him, Harlee was the be-all and end-all, the most spectacular individual on God's green earth. The best part was that she saw Colin the exact same way. He was goodness personified, and she'd never met a man who matched him.

But she sensed that Colin would be skittish about her declaration of love. So she kept her newfound feelings to herself and let him continue with the nuzzling.

"Wanna take this into the bedroom?" Colin whispered in her ear as he scraped his teeth against her lobe.

"Uh-huh." She could barely stand. But then her cell phone started playing the Beach Boys' "Wendy," and the mood was shot.

Colin chuckled. "That's your ringtone?"

"Only for Wendy. She's one of my best friends at the *Call.*"

"Clever," he teased. The phone stopped ringing. "Looks like you missed it. You better call her back."

"You don't mind? We were sort of in the middle of something."

Colin's lips inched up into a lascivious grin. "We've got all night."

Harlee kissed him. "Okay, then I'll just call her back real quickly. She usually just texts or emails, so this might be important."

Colin gazed down at her chest where her nipples had hardened through her sweater. "Hurry."

She tapped Wendy's number, pressed her cell against her ear, and walked into the great room. "Hey, what's up?"

"Jerry quit."

"Get out," Harlee said. "I thought he was a lifer."

"He got a job at the *Seattle Times.* Executive editor."

"You're kidding me?" The *Times* had a slightly smaller circulation than the *Call,* but it was the paper of record for the state of Washington, and the executive editor was top dog. "San Francisco is Jerry's town—the Giants, the politics, the cioppino."

"The layoffs broke his heart," Wendy said. "There's a rumor that corporate has ordered another round. Jerry wants no part of it, says you can't run a great newspaper with so few reporters, so he's leaving."

"You guys know who will replace him?"

"Lots of rumors, but no one knows for sure. Probably some corporate toady who's cheap."

"I'm sorry, Wendy." Jerry was the kind of editor people walked through fire for. Not a lot of those around anymore, mostly drooling dullards who spouted the company line and only cared about how many clicks your stories got on the Internet. Those being photo galleries of celebrity offspring and the best boy bands, *ever*.

"The place won't be the same. But it hasn't been since you left, anyway."

"That's nice of you to say." Harlee couldn't help being touched.

"Look, this could be good for you," Wendy said. "Everyone knows you were Jerry's pet. Maybe he'll hire you in Seattle."

"Jerry's pet? The guy was constantly haranguing me about my spelling and grammar."

"That's the way he shows affection. You should call him."

"Okay," Harlee said. "I'll do that. Thanks for letting me know, Wendy." Seattle would be a good place to land. The paper was respected and at least she'd still be in the Pacific Northwest.

When Harlee got off the phone, Colin was waiting to get the skinny. They both sank into the leather sofa and Harlee sat sideways, draping her legs over Colin's thighs.

"My old managing editor quit to go to the *Seattle Times*," she told him. "Wendy thinks I should call him about getting a job."

Other than a slight twitch in his right eye, Colin's face remained impassive. "You think this guy would hire you?"

"Possibly. Wendy thinks he will. But who knows. The *Times* has plenty of good reporters."

"Would you want to work at that newspaper?"

"Absolutely. It's very well thought of."

"Then you should definitely call him," Colin said.

Harlee's stomach pitched in disappointment. It was ridiculous, since all Harlee had done since she'd gotten to Nugget was obsess over getting another newspaper job. But a small, impractical part of her wanted him to ask her to stay. To keep running DataDate, help him with his furniture business, get him past his phobias, and take her to Emily and Clay's wedding this summer. And to love him, which she already did.

But he didn't and he wasn't going to, because Colin Burke had made it perfectly clear that he was a solitary man.

"Darla, do you have time to give me a cut and highlights today?" Emily stood at the entrance of the barbershop, one foot out the door. "I have to tell Clay. Otherwise he's going to run me to Reno."

Darla looked around her empty shop. "Uh, yeah. You want to do it now?"

"That would be great. Let me just tell Clay. He's waiting in the truck."

Darla nodded and waited for Emily to return, thrilled that she'd soon have one of the town's revered citizens in her chair. Emily was the kind of client who could turn business around for Darla.

"I'm back." Emily tugged off her ski jacket and hung it on the coatrack.

Darla sent her into the bathroom to take off her wool sweater and put on a cape; she didn't want to get color on Emily's nice clothes.

"I thought you used Donna's stylist," Darla said to Emily when she came out, tying the belt of her cover-up.

"I do, but it's such an ordeal going to Reno, especially when the weather's bad. I've only been going to her for a few months. I don't have the same loyalty as Donna, who's been going for years. And I love what you did with Sam's hair. I didn't see it before you fixed it, but from what I've heard . . ." Emily made a face.

"It was bad," Darla said, playing with Emily's hair. She had a nice cut, but the layers were a little heavy for Emily's bone structure. She was a small woman. "I think we should thin it out a little and do some lowlights. What you have now is a little brassy. You okay with that?"

"You're the boss," Emily said, which gave Darla a boost of confidence. "Clay and I just had breakfast at the Ponderosa and Sophie was there with Lilly. She's getting so big."

Darla wondered if it was difficult for Emily, having lost her daughter. "She's a cutie-pie."

"She sure is. How's business been?"

"Still slow," Darla said. "Although my dad still has his regulars."

"I hear the fellows are hanging out over at the Gas and Go these days."

Darla snorted as she mixed Emily's color. "Thank God. They aren't exactly good for business, at least not at an upscale salon." The place might not look like one yet, but Darla was working on it.

"How's Griffin?" Emily asked, and they both knew what she was talking about.

"Holding up." Darla wanted to kill Lina for breaking Griff's heart. The man was a hunk of burning love. Who gave that up for some college dweeb?

"That's good. He'll find a nice girl." Emily suddenly turned in her chair to look at Darla. "How about you?"

Weird as it was, Darla felt nothing for Griffin other than friendship. He was the best-looking single man in Nugget, richer than an Arab sheik, and sweeter than apple pie. But if she wanted to be honest with herself the only man who did it for her these days was Wyatt Jerk Lambert, because Darla was a glutton for punishment.

She handed Emily a stack of square foils, told her to hand them to her one at a time, and swiveled the chair so it faced the mirror again. "He's a good friend. That's all."

"You never know, things could change," Emily said.

"You never know," Darla agreed, but knew they wouldn't.

Through the mirror, she watched as Wyatt slid into his police rig. This week he worked the night shift. She didn't need people to know how she knew. It's not like she was proud of her methods. But Harlee wasn't the only one who knew how to get pertinent information. Darla finished wrapping strands of Emily's hair in the foils and had her sit under a hair dryer with a magazine.

When the timer went off, Darla spent a good hour trimming and reshaping Emily's hair. The results were subtle, but Darla saw a marked difference in how the now thinned layers highlighted Emily's delicate face.

"It's a gorgeous cut, Darla." Emily stared at herself in the mirror. "I hate to say this, but you're way too good for Nugget. My goodness, woman, you could be cutting hair for the stars in Hollywood."

The praise pleased Darla to no end. "Do me a favor, Emily. Spread the word, please." *I'm dying here.*

"Of course I will. In fact I'm going to march on over to the Lumber Baron right now and show Maddy. She goes to Donna's woman too. However, I happen to know for a fact that she's sick of the schlep, especially as pregnant as she is."

"I appreciate it," Darla said.

"Before I go, tell me which products I should buy."

Darla picked out a shampoo and conditioner that she knew would be color safe for Emily's lowlights, rung her up, and waved goodbye. With her confidence riding high, she walked to the back of the shop and sent Wyatt a text.

"DROP BY DURING YOUR DINNER BREAK. WE NEED TO TALK."

February rolled in and the weather got colder. The Nugget Unified School District had already called two snow days in a row and Harlee had yet to call Jerry. She supposed a part of her was afraid of more rejection. And maybe another part of her didn't want to leave Nugget, and most of all Colin. The two of them had settled into a cozy routine: meeting at each other's homes after work, cooking meals together, and spending the nights making love. Sometimes in the evenings, Harlee would join Colin in his wood shop, huddle next to the potbelly stove, and watch him build his beautiful furniture.

While they had never discussed the depth of their feelings—Harlee's went as deep as the Mariana Trench—she sensed that she was important to Colin. He'd made a place for her in his life, which she suspected he'd never done for any other woman before. But that elusive connection was all he seemed capable of giving. There had never been a firm commitment or even the words Harlee longed to hear. And he'd never once asked her to stay. The independent Harlee told herself she should go. Ask Jerry for a job and take DataDate, which had finally started to generate a living wage, with her. But the wimpy Harlee couldn't seem to pull the trigger.

She stared out the window, watched the snow fall, and wondered if Colin would come home early on account of the weather. Most of the work left on Sophie and Mariah's house was on the interior, so it was highly unlikely. And even if the crew decided to quit for the day, Colin would head over to McCreedy Ranch to finish Emily and Clay's kitchen. The man had an amazing work ethic. To think that he ran a construction site by day, picking up side jobs along the way, and operated his furniture business at night and on weekends, boggled the mind. In her newspaper days, Harlee had pulled many long, exhausting hours, but it was far from physical labor.

Harlee went back to her computer, signed off, and went downstairs to rummage through the refrigerator. Not so much hungry as she was bored, she closed the fridge door and decided to brave the snow and go into town, check her post office box, and stop off at the barbershop to visit Darla.

Bad idea.

Halfway there she had zero visibility, and despite her studded tires she was sliding all over the road. She wanted to turn around and go back, but she couldn't distinguish where to pull off to hang a U-turn. The inability to see anything but white was terrifying, like walking a tightrope blind. She'd had a similar sensation once, driving over the Bay Bridge in the fog. It had felt as if she would suffocate in the thick shroud of vapor that hovered over the upper deck like a smoke bomb. At least then she'd had other motorists' lights to guide her to the other side.

Here, her equilibrium was off. She couldn't tell east from west or north from south. Riding her brake, squinting into the snowy downpour, she tried to make out a safe place to pull off. Up ahead, she spied what she thought might be a driveway where she could wait out the storm. She'd lost track of where she was, and without any discernible landmarks couldn't tell what the empty stretch of land was. Harlee carefully veered off the road, nosed slowly into the alcove, and *bang*, she hit something hard.

The last thing she remembered was her airbags going off. When she came to, a man in a green uniform had the door open and was leaning over her.

"Is that you, Wyatt?" she asked in a weak voice she barely recognized.

"I've been following you for the last two miles. You okay?"

"I think so. Can you get this thing off of me?"

"Yeah. You're bleeding, Harlee." Wyatt went back to his SUV and returned with a first aid kit, using a towel to stanch the bleeding on her forehead.

"I'm not sure if I got the wind knocked out of me or if I blacked out. What did I hit?" Oh God, what if she'd plowed into another car or a person.

"A tree," Wyatt said. "You feel nauseous, dizzy, blurry?"

"I don't think so. Is my Pathfinder okay?"

"Never mind that. How many fingers am I holding up?" He held up four.

"Twelve," Harlee said. Wyatt was not amused.

"I want to get you over to the hospital just in case you have a concussion. How's your neck?"

She leaned forward as Wyatt managed to clear the airbag, and twisted her neck from left to right. "It's fine. It's mostly my stomach and ribcage that hurt."

"You think you're okay to ride in my rig?"

"I think so." She started to get out of the truck, but Wyatt lifted and carried her to his passenger seat. He seemed pretty used to walking in the snow.

He buckled her in and made sure the strap wasn't too tight. "This okay?"

"I'm good," she said. "I didn't see you behind me."

"I kept flashing my lights, but in this"—he motioned at the snow pounding his windshield—"you can't see dick, especially in daylight."

"You think we should wait it out before going to the hospital?"

"I'll call it in, but I don't want to wait too long in case you have a head injury or a couple of broken ribs from that airbag."

Wyatt got on his radio and Harlee could hear Connie responding on the other end. There was something comforting about living in such a small town where even the emergency dispatcher was a friend.

Rhys got on the radio and told Wyatt to stay put until he came to escort them in his own rig, although Harlee didn't know what good that would do. They sat there listening to the wind make whistling noises through the trees, the sound eerie, like a howling train gone amok.

Harlee began to shiver. Wyatt turned on the engine and flipped on the heat, letting out a blast of warm air that filled the cab of his police SUV.

"Better?" he asked.

"Yes." She sniffled, the start of a cold coming on.

He took off his jacket and wrapped it around her. "You think you're going into shock?"

"No." Other than feeling sore all over and a bit jolted, Harlee didn't think she'd suffered anything too serious. Although her ribs ached something fierce.

"Rhys is here." They both heard his truck pull up.

The police chief walked up to the driver's side and tapped on the window until Wyatt rolled it down. "You okay, Harlee?"

"Yeah," she said, shuddering from the gust of cold that blew in.

Rhys came over to her side and opened the door, giving her a thorough perusal. First her eyes. She supposed he was checking for broken blood vessels or whatever you look for to determine whether someone has a concussion. Then he removed one of his gloves with his teeth and took her pulse.

"Okay," he said, seeming satisfied that she wasn't going to drop dead anytime soon. "We'll take it real slow, with me leading. Wyatt, if Harlee starts feeling bad, you radio me, you hear?"

"Yes, sir."

It took them nearly two hours to make the forty-minute drive to Plumas General, the same hospital where Colin had spent the night with the flu. Wyatt pulled up right in front of the emergency room and against Harlee's protests carried her inside. Rhys held back, letting Wyatt tend to the details.

Despite a fairly full waiting room, they took Harlee instantly, ushering Wyatt to an empty bed, where he left her, told her he'd be waiting outside until the doc checked her over, and shut the curtain. Harlee lay back, staring up at the ceiling, listening to the man in the bed next door moan in pain.

During her reporter days, Harlee had been no stranger to emergency rooms. Like the time when a six-year-old girl had been struck in the neck by the stray bullet of a gang member while playing in her front yard. The girl's parents had taken a shine to Harlee, and she'd been the only reporter allowed to hold vigil with them while the child clung to life. Four hours later, she came through the surgery, but would never walk or use her arms again. Stories like that had been difficult to cover, but there were others that made up for it.

For instance, the time a fourteen-year-old girl had been abducted by a registered sex offender and handcuffed to the seat of his car, yet managed to steal the key from his glove box, free herself, and flag down a passing truck driver, who drove her to the nearest police station. Harlee had gotten the tip, hauled ass to the station with a photographer, and been the only reporter there to document the girl being reunited with her parents. The scene had moved her to tears and she'd hidden her face behind the broad back of the photographer, surreptitiously wiping her eyes with the back of her sleeve.

The doctor, the same one who had treated Colin when he'd had the flu, came in. "I heard you tangled with a tree."

His examination mirrored Rhys's, except the doctor used a penlight to scan her pupils. "How's your husband?"

Harlee sat up, baffled. Then remembered her fib. "He's good," she said a little guiltily. "I can't believe you remember me." The man must see more than a dozen patients a day.

"I remember all the pretty ones." He gave her a fatherly wink, and she smiled.

"Am I going to live?" she asked when he'd moved on to her ribs.

"Yep. But those airbags, while saving lives, can do a lot of damage. Breathe in and out for me, would you?"

He listened to her lungs with his stethoscope and pushed on her chest. "I don't think you fractured any ribs. You tender?" Before she could answer he lifted her top, where she saw the beginning of two nasty bruises.

"Ah, Jesus."

She and the doctor lifted their heads at the intrusion. Colin had come through the curtain without knocking and was staring at the contusions on her chest and stomach.

The doctor nodded a greeting as he continued his checkup. Colin moved closer to the bed and took Harlee's hand.

"How'd you know I was here?" she asked him.

"Rhys called me."

"I can't believe you drove in this."

"Guess I could say the same." Colin turned his attention on the doctor. "Is she badly hurt?"

"Nope," he said, wheeling his stool backwards, swiveling around and making a few notes in a file—Harlee's file. "I'm writing you a script for eight-hundred-milligram ibuprofen. You'll likely feel sore for a while, so it'll help alleviate the pain and keep down the swelling. And then I'm cutting you loose."

"Sounds good," Harlee said, and looked over at Colin to find him scowling.

The doctor handed Colin the prescription. When he left, Colin helped Harlee off the bed and pulled her into his arms. "You sure you're okay? Jeez, Harlee, Rhys's call took ten years off my life."

"I'm sorry," she said. "I'm fine. Really I am. You shouldn't have driven here in this weather. Wyatt waited to take me home."

"I sent him and Rhys on their way. We'll get a room and stay in Quincy tonight. I want you near a hospital—just in case."

She would've preferred sleeping in her own bed—or Colin's bed. But given the dangerous road conditions, she didn't intend to argue. "Okay. You have a place in mind?"

"There's a small bed and breakfast down the road. Hopefully they'll have a room."

Harlee had only driven through Quincy a few times and didn't know much about the town, which served as Plumas County's principal city, housing the courthouse, the sheriff's department, and a number of government buildings.

When they got outside, the snow had let up, but it had gotten dark and the temperature was still as frigid as Alaska. Colin wrapped his arm around her and walked her to the truck. When they got inside, he hiked up the heat and kissed her. As Harlee melted into the embrace she felt Colin tremble.

"You okay?" she asked him.

"No. You scared the shit out of me."

It wasn't a declaration of love, but it was something. "Thank you for coming."

"You think I wouldn't have come?" He sounded gruff, almost angry. "If you're in trouble, I'm there. That's the way it is, Harlee."

The B & B was lovely. It didn't have as much character as the Lumber Baron, but it was cozy and sweet. Every room had its own gas fireplace and Harlee used the remote control to flick on the fake logs as soon as they shut the door. She'd tried to give the desk clerk her credit card when they'd checked in, but Colin had gotten huffy and paid. They were in the center of town, near a few cafés and restaurants, and a drug store where Harlee planned to walk later to buy them toiletries and clean underwear.

"You hungry?" Colin asked, running his hand down her back.

"I could eat. But I'm worried about my truck. I don't even know how badly it was damaged."

"I called Griffin on my way to the hospital." Colin tugged her down onto the bed with him. "As soon as the weather allows, he'll tow the Pathfinder back to his shop. He said he'd call as soon as he has a look."

She shut her eyes. "I had to have hit that tree pretty hard to deploy the airbag, don't you think?" If the truck was totaled, she didn't know how she'd buy another one. She still owed her parents a substantial amount on the loan they'd made her.

"Harlee"—he cupped her chin in his large callused hand—"I'll help you with this. We'll work it out."

A tear leaked its way down her cheek before he wiped it away with his lips. "You don't have to. I'll figure it out."

He pulled up her top to look at her bruises again. They'd become deep red, on their way to turning purple. Gently touching each one with his lips, Colin bathed her in kisses.

"We'll get dinner later," he said, and proceeded to make love to her with his hands and his mouth, as if every electrifying touch was meant to convey all the words he couldn't say.

Chapter 20

Harlee's truck needed a thousand dollars' worth of repairs. Colin doubted that the Kelley Blue Book value on the Pathfinder warranted the cost. But he told Griffin to fix it and he'd pay. Harlee would be angry, but she couldn't afford the hit. And he could. Financially, the last year had been good to him. His furniture business had grown and he'd earned a solid reputation in the county as a reliable carpenter. Jobs kept coming his way.

DataDate had just started paying the minimum payments on Harlee's bills. The woman had more clothes and shoes than a department store and thanks to him nowhere to wear them. He'd like to fix that. Nothing would make him happier than to take her out on the town—a nice restaurant in Reno or a show at one of the casinos.

Initially, when he'd first gotten out of Donovan, crowds hadn't fazed him. In fact, he'd enjoyed eating in restaurants with Fiona, Steve, and his nephews, having the freedom to order off a menu filled with so many choices his eyes glazed over, drink from a real glass instead of a state-issued plastic cup, and eat with some assurance that he wouldn't be shivved in the back. Often, while delivering furniture for Steve, Colin would pull off the interstate, find a truck stop or a nice bar, order an iced tea, and watch people interact. He'd reveled in the normality of it and sometimes he'd even gotten lucky with a pretty woman.

Then one night he'd sat in a honky-tonk just outside of Modesto, gazing into a flashing neon beer sign while he nursed a nonalcoholic beverage. It wasn't a rough place, mostly just a hangout for locals and farmers looking to take a load off after a hard day's work. He'd ordered a cheeseburger—in the beginning he'd binged on junk food, appeasing the seventeen-year-old he'd been before incarceration— from a sultry redhead. She'd flirted with him and everything had been good. Better than good.

Then two men had gotten into a shouting match over by the pool tables. Colin hadn't paid attention to what they were fighting about. A woman? Money? Not his business. But in that moment, the din of the bar had risen to ear-splitting decibels, the walls had begun to fold in on him, his vision had gone fuzzy, and he'd had the petrifying sensation that if he tried to leave, the crowd would stomp him to death. So he'd sat there clutching his bar stool, gulping breaths of air to keep from suffocating, feverish and sweating.

He must've looked bad, even near death, because the redhead pulled him through the kitchen and got him outside, where he summarily threw his guts up. From that day on, more than ten people in a room and visions of violent stampedes filled Colin's head. The demophobia soon expanded to a terror of small spaces to the point where Colin had feared that he'd never leave the safety of Fiona and Steve's home, and focused on learning everything he could from Steve about mastering carpentry. The therapist had said his phobias were a combination of post-traumatic stress disorder and trouble assimilating to the outside world. After he'd learned about the breathing exercises and a few relaxation techniques, he'd taken to the road again, delivering Steve's furniture. But he avoided public places like he avoided everything else that was bad for him, including alcohol and junk food.

Then he'd found Nugget. The magnificent countryside, with its regal mountains, awe-inspiring forests, and starlit skies, let him breathe again. And despite living mostly like a hermit, he'd learned to be social, even friendly when the situation called for it.

Still, it was beyond a miracle that a beautiful, well-adapted woman like Harlee didn't find him a freak. He knew from her credit card bills just how much the woman liked to go out. In San Francisco, her social life had been filled with gourmet restaurants, expensive bars, and trendy nightclubs. And shopping. The woman was a fiend when it came to department stores.

"Hey, Colin, how's that girl of yours?" Pat pulled him from his thoughts as the whir of a circular saw had Colin scrambling down a ladder to hear his boss. "Heard about her car accident."

"She's fine. Her SUV, not so much."

"Well, I'm glad she's okay. That was a bad storm we had."

Colin nodded his head. "The inspector show up?"

"Not yet." Pat sighed and looked around the kitchen, where Colin attached the last of the trim work. "In a couple of months we'll stick a fork in this baby. Sophie and Mariah are anxious to move in."

That, Colin knew, was a fact. Living above a bowling alley and restaurant with a newborn had started to wear on them.

"I just bid another job in Graeagle," Pat said. "Plans for a big A-frame, perched above the Feather River. Beautiful spread. If I get it, you interested?"

"Sign me up." Colin grinned. He'd have to work double time to build up his furniture inventory. Already, Harlee's mom wanted more pieces. A friend of hers, who owned a shop in Carmel, wanted three rockers.

In the background, Colin could hear the crew packing it in for the day. He planned to swing by Griffin's to leave a check before Harlee tried to pay for repairs on the Pathfinder herself. After that, he and Harlee would make dinner together and take Max for a walk if it wasn't too cold.

They had a pretty awesome routine going. Colin couldn't believe how happy he was. But always at the back of his mind he knew it would eventually come crashing down around him.

When he got to Griff's, the Nugget Mafia sat around a space heater in the garage, playing pinochle. Colin eluded the group by sticking to the convenience store, where he paid Griffin and shot the breeze. The place was really shaping up. Griffin and his friend Rico had done the work themselves, and Colin thought it looked pretty professional. Griff showed him the area where he planned to sell hot dogs, soft drinks, coffee, and other assorted gas station food.

"I'm thinking of putting a few of your rocking chairs on the porch." Griffin had torn out the dry-rotted small deck at the front of the store and replaced it with a new one. "It'll give it a country look, don't you think?"

"Yeah," Colin said. "But I'd wait until spring." No one in his right mind would sit out in these freezing temperatures.

"I plan to put one of those old-fashioned coolers out here with soft drinks and ice cream."

"Nice. How you doing otherwise?" The question specifically pertained to Lina, but Colin didn't want to come right out and say *You over the girl yet?*

Griffin lifted his shoulders. "I'm getting there. How's Harlee doing?"

"She's good. Sore as hell, though."

"Good thing she was in the Pathfinder and not the Mini Cooper."

Colin didn't want to think about that. "How soon you think you can get the truck up and running?"

"A week and she'll be like new. Harlee have something to drive in the meantime?"

"When I can, I'll lend her my truck and take the bike."

Griffin gazed out at the mounds of snow that had been plowed to the edges of Main Street. Not exactly motorcycle weather. "The Harley?"

Colin knew Griff drove a Ducati, although he made custom bikes that sold in the high five figures. "Yeah, you ought to get yourself one."

Griffin snorted as if he wouldn't be caught dead riding something so lowbrow. "If she's in a bind I can probably scrounge up a junker for her to use until the Pathfinder is ready."

"We've got it covered." He'd prefer Harlee didn't drive for a while. Give him a little peace of mind. "Thanks for the tow. I guess I'll see you in a week."

Colin headed up Grizzly Peak, planning to pick Harlee up at the cabin and bring her back to his place. Once again he gave praise for the woman. Colin wasn't a religious man, but someone, at least in the last few months, had been looking out for him.

But when he drove down Harlee's driveway he no longer felt so fortunate. A Ford Explorer with an Oakland PD bumper sticker sat in the Pathfinder's usual spot. It was too late to leave; Harlee must've heard his truck wheels crunching down her gravel road.

No, he'd have to go in and face her brother, the cop.

Brad Roberts stuck out his hand and shook Colin's, giving him the once-over as he came in the door. "Heard a lot about you," Brad said, his voice neutral but not particularly friendly.

The guy had the same blue eyes and dark hair as Harlee. No one would miss that they were siblings. And no one would miss that Brad was sizing Colin up like a boxing opponent and deciding whether he was worthy of his little sister. Colin didn't know what Harlee had told her brother about their relationship, but clearly Brad knew that they were more than neighbors.

Harlee waved from the kitchen. "Hey. How was your day?"

"Good." He waved back. "What about yours? You rest?"

"I slept until Brad got here about three hours ago." She shut the refrigerator door with her foot. "My parents made him come to check up on me. I'll be right in."

Brad and Colin moved to the couch, taking seats on opposite ends. "Harlee says you make furniture."

"Mom's been selling his pieces like crazy," Harlee interjected, bringing a plate of cheese and crackers from the kitchen and setting it down on the coffee table.

"You can make a living like that?" Brad asked, sounding doubtful.

Colin nodded. "I also do construction, mostly carpentry."

If the man wanted to give him the third degree . . . bring it! It couldn't be worse than the alternative, Brad running Colin's name through the police database. Or maybe he'd do that too. Time would tell.

"You should see his house, Brad. He built it himself and it's gorgeous."

"I had help from my brother-in-law." Colin winked at Harlee, thinking she was trying a little too hard on his behalf, but was warmed by her loyalty.

"How long have you lived here?" Brad asked.

"About three years." Colin decided to fill him up on information so he wouldn't ask too many questions. "I inherited my mother's Hollywood Hills house when she died, sold it and bought my property here. The place had been in foreclosure, so I got a good deal. Bought one of those log-cabin kit plans and modified it."

"Young, single guy," Brad said. "You wanted to live way out here?"

Colin wasn't sure whether Brad was curious or suspicious. "Yeah, I love it. And when I crave city life"—*like never*—"I visit my sister and her family in Los Angeles." He could've told Harlee's brother about the demophobia, but it was none of his damn business.

"Nice life if you can get it," Brad said, stacking a piece of cheese on a cracker and shoving it in his mouth. "I'd move out here if I had a way of supporting my family. It's a good place to bring up kids. No crime. Good schools."

"You and Leslie ought to check out the places at Sierra Heights," Harlee said. "They're seriously gorgeous. You guys could buy one for a vacation home and move up when you're ready to retire."

"Sure. I'll get right on that with all my extra cash." Brad chuckled and turned his attention back to Colin. "You hunt?"

"Not my thing," Colin said. According to his parole conditions, he wasn't even allowed to own a gun, which suited him just fine. "But I fish from time to time."

"The fishing up here is spectacular. Before Harlee took over the cabin, a few buddies and I used to come up for salmon and steelhead runs. You ought to fish with us one of these times."

Colin figured Colin's buddies were cops . . . and wouldn't that be awkward. But he resisted the urge to say *"No way in hell,"* because Harlee's face lit up like she knew Colin had just passed muster with the big brother.

She tried to curl up in one of the recliners, cringing as she favored her right side.

"You okay, Harveyleigh?" Brad got up and tossed her a crocheted lap blanket.

Colin's lips quirked at the nickname. Harveyleigh? That's right, she'd told him that her name was a combination of her father's and mother's.

"That's where the airbag got her," he told Brad, then asked Harlee, "When was the last time you took your painkillers?" He went into the kitchen, filled a glass with water, and snagged the bottle of ibuprofen on the counter.

"Not since this morning," Harlee said, and waited for Colin to shake out two pills and hand them to her, before she swallowed them in one gulp.

Brad stoked the fire and sat back down. "Harlee says you were there with her at the hospital." When Colin nodded, Brad continued, "You think the docs there know what they're doing?"

"No, Brad. They all got their medical licenses online," Harlee said. "I'm fine, just a little sore. Dad had my chart faxed to him, and he agrees with everything Dr. Morgan did. So stop it."

They were a good family, the Robertses. They looked out for each other, like Fiona did for Colin.

"She's okay," Colin told Brad. "I've been paying attention."

"What about her truck?" Brad asked. "I thought I could take care of that while I'm here."

"Hello," Harlee trilled. "I'm right here."

Colin put his hand on her shoulder. "I've got it covered."

Harlee tried to bound out of the chair, letting out a bark of pain in the process. "What do you mean, you have it covered?"

"We'll talk about it later, Harlee." Colin pinned her with a look and then focused on Brad. "We've got a great mechanic in town who happens to be a friend."

"Sounds like you have it all worked out." Brad looked from Harlee to Colin and flashed a wise-ass grin. "She's all yours, Colin."

Damn straight.

At the barbershop, Darla was finally getting that meeting with Wyatt. A slew of weather-related accidents, including Harlee's, had kept him from stopping by on the evening she'd texted him. But he was here now, making Darla chew her bottom lip with nerves.

"You want to grab a bite?" Wyatt offered.

"No. What I have to say should be done in private."

"Okay." He leaned against the front counter, shoving his hands in his Wranglers. Off duty, he'd resorted to the clothing most men in Nugget wore—jeans, Western shirt, and cowboy boots.

"First, I want to say thanks for helping Harlee the way you did. She told me you were a rock."

"I'm a cop, Darla. That's what I do." But Darla noticed that he thrust his chest out at the praise.

On someone else, Darla might've thought his preening was comical, but she loved him, pure and simple, and was pleased that the townsfolk saw him as a man to depend on. But could she depend on him? That was the million-dollar question.

"Well, I know that Harlee was appreciative of all that you did."

"She feeling better?" Wyatt wanted to know.

"She is. Her brother's here—drove up from the Bay Area this morning."

Darla hung the "Closed" sign on the door, rolled down the blinds, and sat in her father's old barber chair, crossing her arms over her chest. Wyatt grabbed one of the plastic waiting chairs, turned it backward and straddled it. "We gonna talk about this now?"

"I think it's time, don't you?" She swallowed hard and tried to organize her thoughts. She'd had nearly a decade to formulate a lot of angry rebukes, but all she could seem to summon was, "Why? Why did you leave me like you did?"

Wyatt let out an audible breath and lifted his chin until his eyes were level with hers. "Because I was scared witless, Darla. We'd lost our baby, you were falling apart, and I didn't have the first clue how to make it better. I was so freaked out that I did the chicken-shit thing and ran. Then I couldn't face that I'd run, so I never contacted you.

"But I kept tabs on you," he continued. "I'd write letters home and ask about you. My mother wasn't proud of what I'd done and she made sure to let me know it, sending me regular updates on just how fine you were getting along without me. By the time I came back, you'd enrolled in beauty school over where your mother lives, and Owen let me know that you had no shortage of men after you."

Darla had to laugh at that one. Sure, she'd dated a few men, but it wasn't like they'd been lining up. Not everyone went in for her colorful hair accessories and lively style. Only confident men, in for the long haul.

"You made me think that you didn't really love me. That you'd only said you did because you wanted to do the right thing." She met his eyes, ready to get this out on the table for once and for all. "Did you really love me, Wyatt? I deserve the truth."

"I think I did." He turned his gaze from her. "But to be fair, Darla, I was eighteen years old. What the hell did I know about love? Obviously not enough to stick by you."

She'd been right. He'd bailed because he didn't love her. Still, to hear him all but admit it, felt like a pickax through her heart. For days after she'd gotten his Dear John letter she'd waited for him to call and tell her that he'd made a horrible mistake. It had taken her nearly a year to stop jumping every time the phone rang.

"What I know now is that I'd stick, Darla. I don't want to go another nine years—hell, I don't want to go a day—without having you in my life."

Pretty words. "What am I supposed to do with that, Wyatt? How am I supposed to trust you?"

"By giving me a chance to prove myself."

And put her heart on the line only to have it bludgeoned if Wyatt decided this sticking business was too difficult? She'd already taken a gamble by starting a salon in a town where the residents only wanted a barber. How much more could she risk?

"We could go slow, one day at a time," Wyatt said, clearly seeing the ambivalence in her face. "A lunch here and a dinner there. Bowling. A ride to the coast. We could get to know each other again."

"I already know you." Her tone was terser than she'd meant it to be.

"No, you don't, Darla. I'm a man now, not a boy. And I want to court you."

Who said "court" anymore? Maybe Darla's dad. Certainly not a twenty-seven-year-old, living in the twenty-first century. But Darla kind of liked the old-fashioned term. To her it conjured images of ice-skating parties, lemonades on the front porch, and stolen kisses under the oak tree.

"How do I know you won't cut out the first time anything goes wrong?" She got to her feet and peered through the slats in the blinds for the sake of having something to do. The way Wyatt looked at her, like she held the key to their future, made her nervous.

He came up behind her and wrapped his arms around her waist. "You'll just have to give me a chance and find out."

She glanced over her shoulder and speared him with a look. "Who says you can touch me?"

He immediately took his hands away, but grinned like a fool. "Sorry."

"I thought you were courting me." She put air quotes around "courting."

"We could start right now." He looked so hopeful that a little shiver of happiness went up Darla's spine. "I'll take you over to the Ponderosa for a steak."

"I don't eat steak." She said it just to be contrary.

"Then a salad, or whatever you want."

"I need to be home by seven," she said.

"Okay." Wyatt looked at his watch. "No problem, but why?"

She fluffed her curls in the mirror. Today she'd gone cinnamon with honey highlights. "I have to wash my hair." With that she grabbed her purse, put on her coat, locked the barbershop door, and let Wyatt take her to dinner.

Chapter 21

"So you're getting back with him?" Harlee twirled one of her newly curled locks around her finger.

"Stop doing that," Darla said as she wrapped another strand of Harlee's hair in her hot iron. "You're taking out all the curl."

"You didn't answer my question." Harlee watched her friend in the mirror pretending to be wholly focused on styling Harlee's hair. The hairdo was just for fun, since Harlee didn't have anywhere to go. A week after the accident and she could still barely bend over to tie her shoes. At least she had her Pathfinder back. Griffin had made it as good as new.

"I'm giving him a chance." Darla put the curling iron down to run for the ringing phone. "That's all."

Harlee could hear her making an appointment, and when Darla hung up, her eyes glittered with excitement. "That was Maddy Shepard. She wants me to cut her hair."

The two women high-fived.

"Oh my God, Darla, it's happening. I told you it would."

"And I sold three hundred dollars' worth of product yesterday."

"Get out." Granted, Darla's shampoos were pricey, but that was still a lot of product to move, especially in a small town like Nugget.

"One of the guests at the inn forgot her toiletry bag and couldn't lower herself to use hotel shampoos. Maddy, bless her heart, sent her over here. And Ethel over at the Nugget Market needed an emergency remedy for itchy scalp. This dry, cold weather is murder. And Donna has become a regular—for product, anyway."

"That's fantastic, Darla."

"How 'bout you? How's the job hunt going?" Darla swiveled Harlee's chair around and handed her a mirror so she could see the half-dozen bouncy curls that now skimmed her upper back.

"Very pretty," Harlee said, and let out a sigh. "I haven't been looking too hard."

"No?" Darla beamed. "Okay, I'm just gonna put it out there. I'll die if you leave."

"You won't die. And without my negative influence, you'll actually go to yoga instead of ditching to get breakfast at the Bun Boy with me."

"But DataDate's taking off, right? And you've got Colin. And Griffin needs us to get him through his breakup with Lina. And what about Clay and Emily's wedding? And Maddy's baby? You'll miss it all."

"Uh, no pressure or anything." Harlee laughed. The truth was, life would go on in Nugget without her. But leaving this place would hurt. Badly. "I don't think Colin can give much more than he's giving, Darla. And if I stayed that would become an issue."

"Because you're in love with him?"

"I'm pretty sure I am." Harlee gave a wan smile. "And I'm also pretty sure that if he knew, it would send him off the ledge."

"There's no way he can't know," Darla said. "It's all over your face, Harlee."

"Colin isn't like a regular guy, Darla. He's sort of dense about that kind of stuff."

And he's different, Harlee wanted to say. It was as if Colin had survived a trauma that he never completely got over and never talked about. Hence the phobias and the aloofness. But he cared for her. That much she knew.

"You need to talk to him, Harlee. Tell him how you feel. What if you leave and he feels the same way as you do? That's a missed opportunity, and believe you me, I know about missed opportunities."

Harlee got to her feet, walked to the window, and gazed out over the square. "My old editor at the *Call* is going to the *Seattle Times*. I've been thinking of calling him . . . see if he'll hire me. Colin knows. He hasn't asked me not to."

"Have the conversation anyway, Harlee. Maybe Colin just doesn't want to hold you back. You ever think of that?"

"Maybe." Harlee gave a halfhearted shrug. "Now tell me about you and Wyatt."

Darla plopped into the barber chair. "He wants us to date, go slow, but try to win back the feelings we once had for each other."

"Can you forgive him, Darla?"

"I don't know. Do you think I should?" The phone rang. "Hold that thought."

Darla dashed over to the cash register, picked up, and chatted away while she scribbled in her appointment book. After the call, she told Harlee that it was Grace from the feed store. "She wants a haircut."

"Okay, that's two in an hour," Harlee said. "We're celebrating with lunch at the Ponderosa. My treat."

"Whoot!" Darla started to grab her coat and hat, but stopped. "Should I forgive him, Harlee?"

Harlee pulled on her jacket, ready to brave the cold. "That's something only you can decide, Darla. But I like Wyatt and I'm rooting for you guys."

When they got to the Ponderosa, Sophie had hostess duties. Lilly lay tucked into her baby carrier next to Mariah, who waved from the bar. Sophie started to take them to their usual corner booth, but Harlee and Darla took a detour to say hi to Lilly.

"Don't you dare wake her up," Sophie said. "The little stinker kept us up all night."

You'd never know it. To Harlee, Sophie looked as fresh as the marketing executive she used to be.

"Colin says the house is almost done," Harlee whispered, not wanting to stir the baby.

"Hallelujah!" Mariah chimed in. "It'll be nice to finally live separately from where we work."

"When she wakes up, let us play with her," Darla said, staring down at Lilly like she wanted to eat her up.

"I'll bring her over," Mariah said, and Sophie got them seated.

"They should put that baby in commercials," Darla said when Sophie went off to seat the Addisons, who had just walked into the restaurant.

As usual, the couple wore their bear gear. Harlee understood their desire to brand themselves as the owners of the Beary Quaint, but adults decked out in 3-D animal wear was a little creepy. Sandy Addison actually had the gall to stare at Darla's hair du jour. A purple bob with fringe bangs—a wig, of course.

"Don't pay any attention to them," Darla said. "They're trolls."

Harlee reached over the table and whispered, "Clay said they're buying the *Nugget Tribune*."

"There goes the First Amendment." Darla pretended to shudder and scanned the menu. "What are you getting?"

Harlee opened hers as well, but it wasn't like she didn't know every entrée and appetizer by heart. "I don't know yet. But let's go balls out and get something totally decadent, to celebrate."

"You think we're jinxing it?"

"Hell no," Harlee said. "You're a freaking great stylist, Darla. You should move with me to Seattle and open a salon there. We could be roomies."

"Yeah, because they don't have enough hair salons in Seattle." Darla laughed, then grew serious. "I think I want this thing with me and Wyatt to work."

Harlee stopped perusing the sandwich selections and met Darla's eyes. "I think he might be a really good man, Darla. I think when he was eighteen years old he made a terrible decision, but he's grown up since then."

"I hope you're right." Darla closed her menu. "Because if he turns out to be a loser, I'm gonna be devastated. I'm ordering a lemon drop, by the way."

"Ooh, that sounds good. I'll get one too. Let's run him, Darla."

"What?"

"Let's do a background check on Wyatt. He's a cop, so he'll come up clean. But we can at least see how much he paid for his house."

"I don't know," Darla said. "It seems like an invasion of his privacy."

"Yeah, so what's your point?"

A server came to take their order. When she finished, Harlee said, "I won't do it if you don't want me to."

"Can you find out if he's been married before?"

"Yes. But if Wyatt had been married, you'd know. The whole freaking town would know. This is Nugget, Darla."

The server came back with their cocktails and both women took healthy sips.

"This is the kind of town where even huge secrets come out," Harlee continued. "If Wyatt was a cross-dresser, Donna Thurston would be singing it from the rooftop of the Bun Boy."

"Then what's the point of doing it?" Darla took another gulp of her lemon drop.

"Just for fun," Harlee said. "It'll keep my investigative skills sharp. And who knows, maybe we'll find out that he inherited half of Nugget."

Darla laughed. "That wouldn't be all that impressive."

The waitress put down their burger plates and a heaping basket of tempura. From across the dining room, Harlee could see Sandy Addison watching them. The woman really was a troll.

"All right." Darla speared one of the fried zucchinis with her fork and dipped it in catsup. "Go for it. But don't tell me if anything really bad turns up about him." She took a big bite of the burger and with her mouth half full said, "On second thought, tell me everything."

Wyatt Lambert's background check was cleaner than an operating table. As far as Harlee could tell, he'd never so much as had a ticket. His military record may not have been the stuff of best-selling memoirs, but there had been nothing out of the ordinary during his tour of duty.

He owned a house that he'd paid 220,000 dollars for with a 20 percent down payment. It sat on five acres on the other side of town, about two miles from his parents' house. He and his neighbor shared a legal easement on the driveway.

Darla would be pleased to note that he'd never been married. She might not be so pleased about the fact that he was a registered Republican. But they could work out the politics later. Bigger obstacles than party affiliation had been overcome.

On paper, Wyatt looked perfect.

Harlee was just about to shut down for the day when an email popped up in her in-box. The subject line said Dearling Bros. She thought it might be a new background-check assignment, clicked on the missive, and read.

DEAR MISS ROBERTS,
MY SISTER HAS USED YOUR DATADATE SERVICE AND I MUST SAY
I WAS VERY IMPRESSED. I'M THE CO-OWNER OF DEARLING

Bros., a private investigation firm with offices in Dallas,
New York, Miami, and Chicago. Later this year, we plan
to open in the Los Angeles area.
I'd be interested in talking to you about a business pro-
posal. If you're interested, let me know and we'll set up
a meeting.
Signed,
Bix Dearling

Probably a nut job. But Harlee looked up Dearling Bros. just for
kicks. Her first search netted pages of information about the private
investigation firm and the pair of Texas brothers who owned it. Bix
Dearling was no joke. He'd been a Dallas police detective, who'd
gone out on his own with the help of his brother, a former Navy
SEAL. Together they'd built a private investigations empire, contract-
ing with large law firms as well as doing major consulting work for
law enforcement agencies. Why in the world would he be interested
in her little one-woman start-up?

May as well hear what he had to say, Harlee thought as she quickly
replied to his email. Then she picked up the phone and hit speed dial.
"Hey, Connie, it's Harlee. Is the chief available?"

Connie transferred Harlee to Rhys, who picked up on the third
ring. "What's up?"

"You used to be a Texas cop, right?"

"Houston PD. Why?"

"Do you know Bix Dearling?"

"He's from Dallas, and no, not personally, only by reputation.
What's going on with Bix?"

"I don't completely know," Harlee said. "He sent me an email that
he might be interested in doing business—something to do with
DataDate. What's his reputation?"

"Great cop. Entrepreneur extraordinaire. Womanizer. Not necessarily in that order."

"But he's on the level?" Harlee asked. In the background she
could hear Rhys clicking on his computer.

"He's definitely on the level. He did some consulting for Houston
PD—wowed everyone. You interested in whatever he's peddling?"

"I don't know yet." If it was big money she definitely was interested. "Maybe."

"Then hear him out. I've gotta go, but let me know what happens."

"Will do," she said and signed off.

Hmm, Harlee thought. What an interesting turn of events. It would probably wind up being nothing, but it was fun pondering the possibilities. She started to power off and planned to head over to Colin's place to start dinner, when Bix pinged her back, wanting to set up a meeting. She sent him her phone number, but he insisted that they talk in person. When she explained that she lived in a rural town, four hours from San Francisco, he asked about airports close to Nugget where he could land his corporate jet.

Harlee had no idea about landing strips. But she knew Clay owned a couple of planes and told Bix she'd find out what airport he used. Surreal. Her fledgling business brought in just enough money to carry Harlee, who lived rent-free. It wasn't exactly Microsoft. Then again, with the resources of a company like Dearling Bros., it could be quite profitable.

She left a message for Emily, asking about local airports, and hiked up the hill to Colin's house. Max sprung out of his dog door in greeting, jogging in circles around Harlee as if he hadn't seen her in months.

"Here, boy," she called, trying to get him to heel before his exuberance caused her to trip over him. "Where's Colin, Max?"

The dog cocked his head to one side and let out a whimper.

"Hey." Colin stood at the entryway, one shoulder propped against the doorjamb, his hair wet from a recent shower. Just the sight of him made her insides slam.

"I've got some interesting news," she said, and climbed the porch stairs.

"Tell me in front of the fire. It's damned cold." He waited for Max to do his business and whistled for the dog to come inside the house.

"Did you just get home?" She kissed him, inching her hands under his shirt to feel his damp skin.

"About forty minutes ago. I thought we'd do something different tonight," Colin said.

"What's that?" They'd already had sex in every room in the house, including the wood shop.

"You go first." He patted a place next to him on the couch.

She told him about the email she'd gotten from Bix Dearling, how he owned a national private investigation agency and that he wanted to discuss a possible business deal regarding DataDate, in person.

"You think the guy is serious?" Colin asked.

Harlee lifted her hands up. "He wants to fly here all the way from Dallas. What I don't get is why he doesn't just steal my idea, do it bigger and better. I presume his company already does background checks. What I do is essentially the same thing, except I'm probably way cheaper."

"I agree that it sounds a little odd." He got up, went to the hearth, and pushed a few logs around with a poker, trying to extinguish the flames. "But there's only one way to find out—listen to what the guy has to say. I can come with you to meet with him if you want."

"Don't you think that would look lame, like I'm not leaning in?"

"Leaning in?" Colin looked at her like she was speaking a foreign language.

"You know, the book by Sheryl Sandberg, the chief operating officer of Facebook. It says women need to be more aggressive—become leaders and not let men take all the credit."

"Whatever." Colin all but rolled his eyes. "I just don't like the idea of you meeting some strange dude by yourself. If I go with you, I could, you know, recline. Hell, I could just lie on my back; that way he wouldn't think I was trying to out lean you."

Harlee tried to hide her amusement. "I'll have Bix meet me in a public place."

"Just don't give him too much information in case the guy is on a fact-finding mission."

"Duh," Harlee said, and kissed him.

"You want to go out to dinner?" He reached around her waist and slid his hands down to cup her butt.

She stopped kissing him and stared. "Like . . . to a restaurant?"

"Today, while installing bathroom fixtures, this plumber told me about this new Italian place in Blairsden. It's mostly takeout, but has about six tables. I called and made a reservation, thinking we could try. Worse comes to worse, we'll take the food to go. What do you think?"

"I think this is good. Wow, Colin, you sure you want to do this?"

"What I think, Harlee Roberts, is that you deserve a real date."

"Colin, we have good dates at home. I have never felt deprived."

"We should have a real date," he said softly. "At least once before you leave."

Before you leave.

He just threw those words around like they were nothing. Like they weren't even worth a conversation. It shouldn't hurt like it did, because she had made it crystal clear from the get-go that Nugget was a temporary stopping place until she found another newspaper job. But now her feelings had changed. Couldn't he see that, or did he just not care?

The restaurant was even smaller than Colin had expected. There were only two other couples in the place. Still, he asked if they could be seated close to the door in case the walls started moving in on him and he had to make a run for it.

Despite its hole-in-the-wall appearance from the outside, inside the place had white linen tablecloths, little candles on every table, and a small stone fireplace in the corner. Classy.

Harlee's face lit with delight, which made him even more determined to endure the fear that had gripped him ever since he walked in the door. She'd even changed into a dress and high-heeled boots for the outing.

"Colin, this place is perfect." She took off her coat while he pulled out her chair.

"Yeah, not bad." He focused on his breathing, slowly inhaling through his nose and exhaling through his mouth.

Harlee flipped through the menu. "What are you getting?"

"What looks good to you?" Too busy watching a family of four come through the door, Colin hadn't so much as glanced at the long list of entrées.

"Want to share the grilled polenta for the antipasto?"

"Sure," Colin said, trying to regulate his heartbeat while the little restaurant continued to fill up.

"Then I'm going with a salad and the scaloppini."

"Yeah. I'll do the same." Colin undid the top button of his shirt and pulled his sleeves up.

"Wouldn't you rather have the chicken?" Harlee reached across the table and grabbed his hand, fixing on his tattoo for a second. Sometimes, during sex, she'd trace it with her finger. "We could take it to go, Colin. You don't have to prove anything."

"I'm good," he said, trying to smile as a trickle of sweat ran down his back. "It's just hot in here."

She pinned him with a look. "You seem on the verge of a panic attack."

Before he could say anything, a waitress came and took their order. Colin got a bottle of Chianti, deciding that a little alcohol might calm his nerves. Plus, he knew Harlee would like it. Their server returned quickly with the wine, poured, and moved on, much to Colin's relief. Having her hover wasn't helping the situation.

He clinked his glass to Harlee's and took a sip. "Good."

"Ah, Colin. I don't want you to do this if you're uncomfortable."

"Just talk to me and I'll be fine. Promise." Two men came in and were seated next to the fireplace. That made ten people, not counting him and Harlee or the staff.

"Okay," Harlee said. "Tell me about the tattoo on your arm. I've never seen anything like it. What's its significance?"

Colin glanced down at the black dots that peeked out under his rolled-up cuff. That was the last thing he wanted to talk about. "It was a youthful indiscretion."

"But it must mean something. Why else would you have chosen it?"

Their polenta came, and Colin was thankful for the reprieve. "It looks great," he told the waitress. He served Harlee a portion, then tried to swallow a bite, but it felt like sawdust in his mouth.

"This is really good," Harlee said. "As good as anything in San Francisco. So tell me about the tattoo."

Colin made the mistake of glancing around the room. Nearly every table was full. "I don't want to talk about this right now, Harlee." From the look on her face, he knew he'd said it too sharply. "Ah jeez, I'm sorry."

"It's okay," she said, probably noticing the way he used his linen napkin to blot the sheen of sweat that covered his face. "Would you like to go outside and get some air?"

If he went outside, he'd never come back in. "No. I can do this."

He could tell Harlee wanted to argue, but she bit her tongue. "Have another sip of your wine."

Colin felt his hand tremble as he lifted the glass to his lips. "If I didn't tell you before, you look really fantastic tonight. The dress is...just wow." It was blue to match her eyes and mouthwateringly clingy.

"Thank you." She smiled, but her eyes remained worried.

The salads came and Colin did his best to get a few pieces of lettuce down. One of the original couples got up to leave, taking so long to put on their coats that Colin thought he'd suffocate from having them linger so close.

"The dressing on this salad is fantastic," Harlee said, clearly trying to make small talk while Colin broke out in a sweat.

Finally the couple left and Colin tried to take solace in the fact that the restaurant now had two fewer people. But then another family—husband, wife, and two little kids—came in and Colin thought he'd hyperventilate. He saw Harlee's lips moving but couldn't hear a word she said. Just white noise.

The waitress came to take their salad plates away and the motion of her clearing the table made him nauseous, like he was in the cabin of a rocking boat and couldn't see the horizon. By the time their entrées came, his chest felt so constricted that he thought he'd pass out from lack of air.

"I can't do this." He fished his wallet from his pocket, put it down on the table, and staggered outside.

When Harlee found him fifteen minutes later, he was crouched next to his truck, his head between his knees. "I'm sorry."

She touched his back and he flinched. "Should I take you somewhere?"

Colin knew she meant the hospital. Hell, probably the psychiatric ward. "No. It'll be okay in a few minutes. Wait in the truck, it's cold."

But she sat in the dirt in her pretty blue dress, looking so achingly beautiful that he wanted to grab on to her and never let her go.

"Colin, it was too much, too soon. Next time we'll start small, like—"

"Not now, Harlee." He hadn't meant to bark at her, but the humiliation was more than a man could take. Thrusting his keys at her, he told her to get inside the cab and turn on the heat.

When he finally pulled himself together, he found her behind the wheel with the seat pulled up enough for her to reach the pedals.

"I'll drive," she told him.

"The hell you will." He motioned for her to climb into the passenger seat, and to her credit she didn't argue.

They drove in silence with only the sound of the heater humming. Colin would have preferred to open his window and let the frigid air blast his face, but he didn't want Harlee to catch a chill. A full moon illuminated the winding road; miles of freshly plowed snow berms shimmered white in the light. A big buck danced across the lane, stopping to stare into Colin's headlights. Good thing he'd been driving slow. He and Harlee watched the animal lift its antlers and leap off into the distance.

Although the food Harlee had carted away from the restaurant in to-go bags filled the front of the truck with tantalizing smells, Colin had no appetite. The meal would likely taste as bitter as his mood. The night had been an absolute disaster and he'd behaved like a god-damned pussy.

A woman like Harlee deserved better than that. She deserved better than him.

He took the turn to Nugget and climbed the steep grade up Grizzly Peak, careful to keep a watch out for more deer, or even bear. The lumbering creatures weren't hibernating as long as they used to and often roamed the road, looking for food.

At the bottom of Harlee's driveway, he parked and walked her to the cabin. She unlocked her door and he handed her the to-go sacks.

"Aren't you coming in?" she asked.

"Not tonight."

"Colin," she called to him as he started to walk away. "Why are you doing this? Why are you being so ridiculously hard on yourself? Come in. Please."

"I'll talk to you tomorrow, Harlee." He made a beeline for his truck, but she came after him.

"You should be proud that you tried. That you made it as far as you did."

Made it as far as he did? From the second they'd arrived at the restaurant he'd been tied up in knots.

"Leave it alone, Harlee. All I'm asking for is a little distance here. Can you just give me that much, please."

"No!" she yelled. "I can't."

"Why the hell not?"

She grabbed him by his down jacket. "Because I love you. Can't you see how much I love you?"

God, he didn't want her pronouncement of love. He wasn't the least bit worthy of it.

Anyway, what she thought she felt for him had nothing to do with love. What she felt was pity. And he needed her pity like he needed a hole in the head.

"I'm going," he said, and turned away, peeling off in his truck.

Chapter 22

Harlee knew it probably hadn't been the best time to drop the L-word.

For a proud man like Colin, dinner had to have been mortifying. Harlee got that. But she couldn't help how she felt, and watching him suffer had undone her.

After shoving their leftovers in the refrigerator, she grabbed the phone and plopped down on the couch. Maybe, once he got inside his lonely house, he would change his mind and come back to the cabin.

Ha, who was she kidding? Colin liked lonely. He goddamned loved it. Did he ever think that maybe he was demophobic because it gave him an excuse to avoid civilization?

She halfheartedly sorted through the mail on the coffee table, thinking that she'd spent a lot of time on this sofa giving Colin "space" and "distance." They'd also made love on the plaid foldout a time or two. She tried to focus on the good times, because for all his faults he was the best man—the best person—she'd ever met. Honest and hardworking. Still, she wondered whether it was finally time to hit up Jerry and move on.

The phone rang, startling her out of her thoughts. She looked at caller ID and picked up with a slight smile in her voice. "Hello."

"I'm sorry," Colin blurted. Besides remorseful, he sounded sad and embarrassed.

"It was a milestone, Colin. What you did took guts."

"Yeah, I'm not really into talking about it, but I feel shitty about how we left things."

You mean when I told you that I loved you, and you said . . . uh, nothing?

"You were disappointed," Harlee told him, knowing disappointment was a mild way to describe it. "Look, I know you think you had a climbing-the-walls freak-out. But the strides you made tonight were huge, Colin. I'm serious, you're on your way to kicking—"

"Not tonight, Harlee. Okay?"

"Okay," she reluctantly agreed.

"Thank you," he said. "And Harlee?" Long pause. Then his voice went low and raspy. "I'm really sorry I ruined our first real date."

"We've had lots of real dates, Colin. We don't need restaurants to make them real. You do get that, right?"

"We'll talk about it tomorrow," he said, avoidance being his middle name. "I've got to get up early, so I'm turning in. Goodnight, Harlee. I . . . I . . . look forward to seeing you tomorrow."

"'Night, Colin." She thought that maybe he'd been about to say those three little words and felt a little more optimistic than she had an hour ago. She stuck the phone on its charger stand and got ready for bed.

The next morning, she noodled around on the Internet, first sending Bix information about Nervino Airport, a small runway just a few miles from Nugget. Then she ran a partial background check she'd been hired to do.

She was about to make herself some lunch when she decided to research Colin's tattoo. The five-dot geometric symbol intrigued her, mostly because Colin had been so resistant to talking about it. Maybe the quincunx represented a lost lover he didn't want her to know about. Or maybe it stood for a religion that he no longer believed in.

She punched in a few search terms and pages upon pages came up. According to the World Wide Web, the ancient pattern represented everything from fertility to close friendship. Crazy enough, even Thomas Edison had had one tattooed on his forearm.

But what made the hairs on the back of Harlee's neck stand up was that lots of inmates wore the tattoo to represent time in prison.

The outer four dots denoted the prison walls and the inner dot symbolized the prisoner. Years of honing a sixth sense as a reporter told Harlee that she was on to something.

And then suddenly she knew.

As fast as her fingers could move she began scrolling through databases, starting with Los Angeles County Superior Court criminal records. Colin Burke was a fairly common name, but from her time working on his furniture books while he'd been sick, she'd memorized his social security number. Pages and pages of court transcripts came up. By the time Harlee finished reading them all, she'd gone through an entire box of tissues. Nearly a third of his life had been spent in prison for a liquor store robbery in which three people were killed.

Colin, how could you have kept this from me?

When she finished with the court records, she Googled every newspaper article she could get her hands on. And there were plenty. Although Colin had been a minor during the shootings, he'd been tried as an adult. And the media had had a field day.

Reading the articles gave her perspective, but in no way allowed her to understand how he could've deceived her.

She grabbed her jacket, purse, and keys and headed for the only person who could help her make sense of this horrible revelation.

By the time she sat in Rhys Shepard's office, Harlee was pretty sure she'd gone into shock. She couldn't even remember making the drive, her head too filled with the stories she'd read about Colin.

"You talk to Bix? What did he have to say?" Rhys asked, his feet propped up on the big oak desk.

"You knew, didn't you?"

"Harlee?" Rhys sat up straight and assessed her. "You're not talking about Bix, are you?"

"No, I'm not. I just got done reading the transcripts from Colin's triple-murder trial."

Rhys sat quiet, contemplating. "This is something you ought to talk to Colin about, Harlee. Not me."

"I would've, if he'd told me. But he didn't. Not one word. But you knew. Police chiefs know their resident parolees, don't they?" It was a rhetorical question. Of course he'd known.

Rhys let out a breath. "Talk to Colin, Harlee."

"Do you believe his defense . . . that he didn't know? That he was merely the unwitting driver?"

"You know him better than I do, Harlee. What do you think?"

"I don't know what to think. Three people . . . dead . . . a baby, for God's sake . . . all because two rich boys wanted beer without having to pay for it. Three, if you count Colin."

"Are you counting Colin?" Rhys cocked his head to the side.

"A jury did."

"Juries are sometimes wrong—unless you believe O. J. Simpson was innocent," Rhys challenged. "No one ever accused Colin of being inside that liquor store or pulling the trigger on that poor family. But under California's felony murder law he was held accountable for driving the car."

"Because the prosecution said Colin was part of the plot to hold up the store," she said, trying to keep from getting hysterical.

"Harlee?" Rhys said. "I'm asking you again. Knowing what you know about Colin, do you think he was in on the robbery or that he conspired to kill the bodega owner and his family?"

"No," she said softly, embarrassed that tears had started trickling down her face, but powerless to stop them. "I think he was the awful casualty of politics. A drunken boy, hoodwinked by his so-called friends into believing that he was going on an ordinary beer run, only to be caught up in what was to become a major murder case. Jeez, the case had as many racial overtones as Rodney King's."

Harlee had read how the owner of the liquor store was a revered leader in the black community. The killers, spoiled Hollywood brats.

"What I think," Rhys said, "is that the justice system needed to make examples of these kids and that Colin was doomed before he ever walked into the courtroom."

Harlee agreed. It was a travesty for Colin, for his family, and for the family that had died. At least the two boys, the shooters, had gotten life in prison without the possibility of parole. But how could Colin have lied to her? She was angry with him, but even angrier with herself. She'd let herself believe that he was honorable, so much better than the cheaters and deceivers that she investigated every day.

"Harlee," Rhys said, reading her face as easily as a newspaper, "give Colin a chance to explain."

"Do other people know?" Translation: Was she the last one in Nugget to know that Colin was an ex-con?

"I don't know what other people know."

"Does Maddy know?" Harlee asked a little more forcefully than she had meant to, but he was purposely being elusive.

"No. I don't think she does." Which more than likely meant that it wasn't common knowledge. But this was Nugget, where everyone knew everyone else's business. "What I do know is that people here admire and trust Colin. I don't think this would change their opinion. But clearly"—he looked at her pointedly—"this is very private to him."

What, did he think she'd sell the story to the *Nugget Tribune*? She loved the man. "It shouldn't have been private to me."

"That's between you two," he said, but not unkindly. "All I'm saying, Harlee, is you can see why something like this would be a man's deepest and darkest secret."

Well, she uncovered secrets for a living. Apparently, she wasn't as good at it as she had thought. "Thank you, Chief, for taking the time."

He stood up, walked around the desk, and gave her an awkward pat.

Three hours later, she found Colin in his wood shop. Harlee found it appropriate that he had Lucinda Williams's "Ugly Truth" playing on his iPod. He turned it off when he saw her come in.

"Hey, I've been looking for you." He regarded her tearstained face, puffy from crying. "What's wrong?"

"I know, Colin."

He stood there for a few seconds, weighing what she'd just said, then closed his eyes, resigned. "A dozen times I wanted to tell you."

"And a dozen times you didn't."

"No," he said in a voice so low Harlee could barely hear him. "I should have, but I knew I'd lose you. And I wanted you more than anything I've ever wanted in my life. More than freedom from that goddamned cage I lived in. More than—"

"Stop!" She held up her hand. "Just stop. You lied, Colin. I trusted you and you lied."

He staggered back a little. "I kept it from you, Harlee. But I didn't lie."

"And you think there's a difference?" she shouted. "Do you know how stupid I feel? You were convicted of murdering three people, Colin. Don't you think I deserved to know that before you let me fall in love with you?"

"God, Harlee. . . . Oh Jesus." He leaned against the wall like he needed it to hold him up. "I didn't know. I swear to you, if I had known what they had planned . . . It wasn't until they got back in the car, their clothes covered in blood. You've got to believe me, Harlee . . . I didn't know."

"I believe you." She started to cry, for him, for her, for a situation that was more tragic than any story she'd ever written. "I read the transcripts and the news accounts, Colin."

He slid down the wall and sat on the cold concrete floor. "The kid was only two," Colin said, wiping his eyes with the back of his hand. "Skip shot him because he was crying. That's what Ari told the police, trying to get himself a deal. Who knows what really happened. But the bullet matched the gun with Skip's fingerprints, at least that's what my lawyer told me."

"Your lawyer sucked," Harlee scoffed. As far as she was concerned, someone better, a big name like Thomas Mesereau, would've proven Colin's innocence.

"Harlee, Perry Mason couldn't have helped me. You weren't there, you don't know what it was like. Threats of riots and TV commentators calling for our heads. Sure I didn't have a family with the kind of money that Skip and Ari's did. I got a public defender, but she was good, Harlee. Despite the lynch-mob atmosphere, she managed to get me fifteen years to life. I got out in ten with good-time credits."

She sank into one of Colin's newly finished chairs, the thought of him in prison making her physically ill. "It must have been horrific."

His eyes downcast, Colin said, "It wasn't the death sentence that the Weaver family got."

No. But Colin's only offense had been partying with the wrong people. Sitting behind the wheel, thinking that his friends had gone inside the store to buy liquor.

And lying. To her.

"Did you have the demophobia in prison?" The notion of how difficult that would've been made her sick to her stomach.

"Not until I got out," he said.

Thank God. "But it's related, isn't it?"

He simply shrugged. "Come here, Harlee." Colin motioned for her to join him on the floor.

"Why?" She stayed put.

"You can't, can you, Harlee? Not now that you know what I am. Do you see why I didn't tell you?"

"Precisely the reason you should've told me." Her voice hitched. "You spent a third of your life in prison . . . It's the reason why you're afraid of crowds and small spaces. My God, Colin, don't you think it would've been helpful for me to understand the hell you've lived through?"

She held up her hands to keep him from interrupting. "I know you had nothing to do with killing those poor people and never would have." Harlee swiped at the tears stinging her eyes, trying hard to keep it together. But she felt eviscerated, like her insides were ravaged and raw. "But I can't get beyond the fact that you took my heart without giving me your trust. You should've believed in me, Colin. God knows I believed in you."

A sob bubbled out of her like a hiccup and Colin quickly got to his feet. She expected him to come to her. To hold her. But he walked to the other side of the room and stared out the window.

She wanted comfort and a guarantee that from here on in he would trust her. Confide his secrets to her, like he'd done with the demophobia. But neither came. Instead, he'd emotionally pulled away, leaving her aching, confused, and wondering how she'd ever been so blind, trusting, and stupid in the first place.

Colin wanted to touch her. But he fought the impulse with every ounce of willpower he had. He'd become so complacent in their relationship that he'd stopped planning for this day. But here it was, in all its Technicolor horror. One look at Harlee's face and he could see her disgust. How could he blame her? He was an ex-con on parole, only four years out of prison. The kind of guy she would only write about—not sleep with, let alone give her heart to.

So instead of reaching out to her, he stood there, feeling lower than dirt, and watched her cry, knowing that the best thing for both of them was for him to end it. Now, before the pain became too excruciating.

"It was a selfish thing to do . . . not telling you," he said, resting his elbows on the window sill so he could stare outside at anything besides Harlee, because her repugnance was palpable. "But I knew you'd run for the hills once you found out. Who could blame you?"

"I thought you understood me," she said, her voice sounding small but angry. "Yet you completely underestimated me. How can you think I'm that shallow?"

"Shallow?" He let out a harsh laugh at the feebleness of the word. "How about realistic? For God's sake, Harlee, do you know how hard life is with an ex-con? If this town knew about the murders . . . they'd . . . they'd shun me. And your mother? You think she'd be proud to know that her daughter is seeing a felon, a man who spent much of his adult life in a six-by-eight cell? How 'bout your dad the doctor, or your brother the cop? You think you could just tote me along to family outings? 'Here's my boyfriend, a convicted murderer.' How do you think that would play with your nice, affluent, well-educated family?"

"I don't care," she said. Colin turned around to find her holding her chin stubbornly, while her lips quivered. "I know who you are."

"Of course you care," he said. "You love them. And they love and want what's best for you. Shit, Harlee, if I were your brother, I wouldn't let you date a man like me. Ever."

"It's not my family's choice. It's my choice. So the way you handle it is to keep me in the dark? Ignorance is bliss?"

That's right. Because now, not only did she know that he was a filthy ex-con, but a liar too; just like all those other men she ran background checks on. Only worse. They at least hadn't been convicted of murdering three innocent people.

"Colin, answer me."

He closed his eyes and pinched the bridge of his nose, saying nothing. Colin would move the Sierra mountains to regain her trust, but what was the point? There was no hope for them and there never had been. The whole time he'd been deluding himself and pretending to be something he wasn't. A regular guy with a clean past.

Harlee got out of her chair and moved closer to the iron stove. "We need to work through this, Colin."

"There's nothing to work through, Harlee," he said, forcing himself to stand firm, because when it came to her he was weak. "I'm not the right man for you."

"What are you saying?"

"That you and I were never meant to be."

She didn't respond. She didn't need to. Her response—and her pride—shone in her eyes.

With anguish far worse than anything he'd ever seen, even inside his bleak prison walls, she walked out of his wood shop, closing the door on him and on any life they could have had together.

Chapter 23

Bix Dearling didn't mess around. In just the five days since Harlee had emailed him about the airport in Beckwourth, he'd managed to file a flight plan, book a room at the Lumber Baron, and come to Nugget.

In those same five days, Harlee had barely gotten out of bed. Just to use the bathroom and eat an occasional meal when Darla pounded on her door, holding a Bun Boy bag, and insisted. Harlee couldn't bring herself to tell Darla the truth. It was Colin's secret to tell, not hers.

The bastard hadn't called once. Not that she had wanted him to. He'd made it clear that he was through—that she wasn't worth the work it would take to resolve their trust issues. A clean break was exactly what she needed. If he called, she'd go back to square one, the part of the program where she played Bonnie Raitt's "I Can't Make You Love Me" over and over again, buried herself under the blankets, and cried until her well ran dry.

Today she'd actually showered. But that was only because of her meeting with Bix. It wouldn't look professional to show up with her hair going in twenty different directions, stinking like a wine press. She searched through her closet for something presentable. Not a suit, because, uh, this was Nugget. But not jeans either—too casual. Finally, Harlee settled on a pair of black pencil trousers, a white blouse, and a tailored camel jacket. She finished it off with a pair of nude wedge pumps.

To accessorize, she flipped open Colin's handmade jewelry box, which set her off on a fifteen-minute crying jag. Luckily, she hadn't put on her makeup yet. Harlee dabbed her eyes dry and tried to cover up the dark circles with concealer stick. After she'd applied some shadow, put on mascara, and glossed her lips, she headed out the door.

"Here goes nothing," she muttered under her breath, doubting that the meeting would turn into anything significant. If she had to guess, Bix was on a fact-finding mission to start his own version of Data-Date and wanted to pick her brain.

Since it was the only way she currently had of supporting herself, she had no intention of giving away any proprietary information. Although she really didn't have any. Her clients found her through word of mouth, all originating from that one article she'd written for the *Call*. It's not like she had developed a "brand." God, she hated that word, one of the most overused in the English language.

She parked and reached for her purse on the front seat, when her heart lurched. Across the square a man in faded jeans and a green down jacket—just like Colin's—walked toward her. But when he got closer, she realized it wasn't Colin. Now that she got a better look, he didn't even resemble him. Too short. Too old. And not nearly as good-looking. Anyway, it was highly unlikely that Colin would be hanging out in downtown Nugget.

Since their breakup she'd lie in bed and listen really hard for his truck to drive down Grizzly Peak on his way to work in the morning. When the wind wasn't blowing, she could hear the sound of his engine. But it only lasted for a few seconds and then he was gone.

A blast of cold air hit her as she stepped down from her SUV. If she wasn't mistaken another snowstorm was on its way. She hoped for Bix's sake that it waited until he left town.

Samantha stopped shaking out an area rug over the Lumber Baron's front porch railing and waved. Harlee checked her watch and strolled across the green to say a quick hello. Although she wasn't feeling too social, it was better than sitting nervously in the Ponderosa waiting for Bix, since she'd come early. Normally, not much made her nervous, but she felt like her mojo had deserted her in the last few days.

"Hiya," she said. "Haven't seen you around in a while. How's everything going?"

"Great." Sam beamed. "The guy you're meeting just called to make sure we had his room ready. Apparently he just landed."

Jeez, did the whole town know? Of course they did, Harlee thought to herself. And she'd be willing to bet that they knew that she and Colin had broken up, too. Crazy how they had missed the biggest secret of all. But then Harlee had also been deceived, and she was a professional investigator.

"I guess I better get over there then," she told Sam, and on impulse asked, "Any advice?"

"Colin's a great guy, Harlee. Damn, I gotta run, the phone's ringing and I'm the only one here." She dashed inside the inn, taking the rug with her.

Yep, everyone knew. Worse, Harlee started visualizing Colin and Sam as a couple. He himself had said that he found her attractive. God help her, she had to stop doing this to herself. Whatever hope she had of finding true love in Colin Burke died the moment she found out the truth. Not because she believed for one millisecond that he was a killer or a getaway driver or a thug. Colin was the kindest man she knew. A man who fate had dealt an unimaginably horrible hand. It was the fact that he'd blindsided her. She could not build a foundation with someone who would withhold such a crucial part of his background. It would never work, she told herself. He knew that, so why was she having such a difficult time accepting it?

Harlee headed back across the square and let Mariah escort her to the back corner booth, away from the entrance to the bowling alley.

"So today's the big meeting, huh?"

"Yep." Harlee sighed. "My guess is that it won't last long."

Mariah leaned her hip against the banquette facing Harlee. "You've probably got this covered, but Sophie made me promise to tell you that you should let him do all the talking—don't give anything away."

Harlee smiled. It was nice to live in a town where the people had your back. "That's the plan."

"And, Harlee," Mariah said as she started to walk away, "we're all really sorry about you and Colin. You guys seemed so good together, and honestly I'd never seen him so happy. I'm keeping my fingers crossed for a reconciliation."

There wouldn't be one, but Harlee nodded to be polite. "Thanks."

"Break a leg, girl."

Harlee played with her menu to kill time until a hulk of a man in a cowboy hat, Western suit jacket, and a silver belt buckle the size of an appetizer plate came into the restaurant. That had to be Bix Dearling, although a lot of men wore Western attire in the Sierra. What gave it away was the way he carried himself—part gunslinger, part *I've got the whole world in my hands*. Mariah led him to Harlee's table and as he got closer she noticed that he'd removed his hat and his hair was coal black and his cowboy boots were monogrammed. A big "BD," like a ranch brand, on each foot. She scooted out of the booth and stood up to shake his hand, and the man actually had the audacity to let his gaze leisurely wander over her.

"Nice to meet you." He waited for her to sit back down, and took the opposite bench.

Mariah handed him a menu and before she could leave, he said, "What's good here, darlin'?" which made Harlee cringe to the roots of her hair.

Then Mariah amazed the hell out of her by planting her butt next to Bix's, opening the menu, and pointing to the filet mignon from McCreedy Ranch. It also happened to be the most expensive item at the Ponderosa. Score one for Mariah. "This is from one of our local ranchers," she proceeded to explain. "Best beef in the state. And if you're not driving, I strongly recommend one of our artisan cocktails. We make everything with fresh seasonal ingredients and whenever possible we use spirits from local distillers. Or, if you'd prefer, we have a number of lovely craft beers from Plumas County on tap."

"So I guess if I just wanted a Jack and Coke that would be too common for y'all?" He slid his arm on top of the back of the booth.

"We can certainly do that for you," Mariah said. "Although why ruin perfectly good whiskey?"

To Harlee's surprise he let out a bark of laugher.

"Bring me whichever drink is your favorite, nothing too sweet," he said. "And whatever the lady here wants."

"Just coffee for me, please." Harlee was smart enough to know she'd be no match for Bix in the drinking department. She'd known reporters who liked to ply their sources with liquor for a good story. But those journalists were all part of a bygone era now.

"All righty," Mariah said. "I'll give you time to look over the menu."

When she left, Bix turned up his smile. "Well, Miss Roberts, I've got to tell you, you're even prettier than your picture on the website."

"Call me Harlee," she said, hoping she'd make it through the meeting without smacking the guy. "And I'll just call you Bix."

"Sounds good to me." He gave her a slight nod. "I'm getting the steak. How 'bout you?"

Harlee just wanted a salad, but suspected that in order to be taken seriously by Tex, she'd have to get a slab of beef too. "Steak for me as well."

He shut his menu and motioned Mariah back over.

She brought Bix's drink and Harlee's coffee. "That was quick. What'll you have?"

"Two filet mignons."

"How do you want those cooked?"

Harlee asked for medium rare and Bix wanted "bloody."

"Coming right up," Mariah said.

"I didn't have too much of a chance to look around," Bix told Harlee. "But it seems like a nice town. Beautiful drive from the airport."

"I hope you brought a coat." Harlee noticed he hadn't been wearing one when he walked in. "It looks like it might snow."

"Yeah, I saw that on the weather. Got one in the car. So this is downtown, huh?"

"This and Main Street, where there's a supermarket, gas station, post office, and a real estate business. But what you see is pretty much what you get."

"I grew up in a small town, so I get it. The folks over at the airport said this is one of the original gold rush tent cities."

"Mm-hmm," Harlee said. "But it's also the place where the Donner Party got stranded." In 1846, snowbound pioneers got trapped in the snow and turned to cannibalism to survive—the event had been etched into California history.

"No shi. . . . Well, I'll be," he said. "Right here?"

"Not right in this spot, but down the road at Donner Lake."

"Now isn't that something." He scrubbed his hand through that jet-black hair of his.

"The Lumber Baron has a lot of information about it if you're interested."

"Hot damn," he said, taking a sip of his cocktail and holding it up to the light to admire the flamed orange twist garnish. "Not bad. How long have you lived here?"

"My family has owned a cabin here for forever and we've been coming up on vacations for years, but I only started living here full-time since November."

"To run DataDate?" he asked, and checked her ring finger. The man really thought highly of himself.

Mariah brought their salads. "We need any refills?" She eyed his nearly empty drink.

"I'm good," he said, and Harlee indicated that she was fine as well.

"I like what you've done with the company," he told Harlee after Mariah left. "My sister certainly sings your praises. Before you, the last jackass she dated cost me a bundle."

Harlee didn't ask why, even though she burned with curiosity. "Thank you."

"You bring your P&L statement?"

She did a double take. "I'm not opening my books to you."

Now it was his turn to look surprised. "Darlin', you ever sell a business before?"

"Oh . . . uh . . . I wasn't aware that's what you had in mind. I figured this was just an informational meeting."

"I want information, I use the phone," he said, looking partly annoyed and partly amused. "I'll need to see your financials, balance sheets, and tax returns before I make an offer, but I'll give you a letter of intent to buy, if it'll make you feel better."

Whoa, this was moving way faster than Harlee had ever anticipated and she felt extremely ill prepared. She'd only started the business a few months ago and didn't have an accountant, let alone balance sheets.

"Can I ask you something, Bix?"

"Shoot."

"Why are you even interested in my business? You run one of the largest private security firms in the country. You can replicate what DataDate does in a heartbeat, but why would you want to when the big money is in investigating corporate espionage, class action lawsuits, and a dozen other things I can think of off the top of my head?" She hadn't divulged anything that Bix Dearling didn't already know.

And just to prove it, he grinned. Big. "You're right. My guess is you barely clear fifty thousand a year."

If Harlee grossed thirty thousand this year, she'd be dancing in the streets.

"But you've got this trust thing going on," he continued. "Women take one look at my brother and me and we're exactly the guys they should avoid like a bad case of the clap. No way are they coming to us to filter out the players, because we are the players. On the other hand, they take one look at you and those big baby blues, and they see their savior."

"So basically you need a face?"

"Basically we need a face." He nodded.

"I still don't see why you'd even bother with this kind of penny-ante business."

Mariah appeared with their steaks and they both stopped talking. "We all good here?"

"We're definitely good," he said. "But what would make me great, darlin', is another one of those cocktails. How about you, Harlee?"

"No, thanks," she said.

Mariah gave her an approving nod and said, "I'll be back in a jiff."

Bix cut into his meat, seemed satisfied that it oozed red, and said, "Back to your question. We're not planning to run individual back-ground checks. That's just nuts. You and DataDate are about to be-come an app. With one tap of a finger, a gal can run a guy through all the databases you check by hand. Of course there will be a monthly subscription fee for the privilege."

Harlee sat back against the red pleather upholstered seat. Genius. The idea was freakin' genius. "Why are you telling me this? I could do it myself."

"Yeah? You got the start-up cash for the software this is gonna take? For the marketing and the distribution?" Clearly a rhetorical question.

"I know people," Harlee said, and shrugged, trying to play it cool.

"Yeah, darlin', you know me."

His second cocktail magically appeared on the table. Mariah, ob-viously sensing that the deal was going down, made herself scarce. Chief Shepard, not so much.

"That the law over there?" Bix nudged his chin at a stool where

Rhys sat, watching them in the back-bar mirror. "He your boyfriend or something?"

"No. He's the husband of the owner of the Lumber Baron. So I wouldn't make any moves on her if I were you." The comment prompted a chortle. "How did you know Chief Shepard's the law?" Rhys always wore plain clothes.

"We all look the same," he said. "Why does he keep glancing over here like he's worried I'll eat you up?"

He's looking after me, because that's what people do in this town. "I don't know. He probably wants to meet you." She figured the lie would appeal to Bix's Texas-sized ego. "He's a former Houston narcotics detective, so he knows about your work in Dallas."

"Well, call him over."

Harlee walked to the bar, pretty sure that Bix was checking out her ass. At least Bix knew he was a dog. She kind of liked that about him. When she brought Rhys back to the table, Bix stood up, shook the chief's hand, and the two spent a few seconds sizing each other up the way men do.

"Nice town you've got here," Bix said.

"We like it."

They talked a little while about Texas, law enforcement, and other assorted topics they had in common. Rhys made sure to tell Bix that the pregnant woman running the Lumber Baron was his wife. Then Rhys patted Harlee's shoulder and said, "I'll leave y'all to your business."

As soon as Rhys left, Bix said, "So, you and I gonna make a deal?"

"I want to be straight with you," she said. "I'm a journalist between jobs right now. DataDate is how I make my living. To someone like you, it's a modest living. But I can't afford to give the company away. And the truth is, Bix, I only started this business in earnest a few months ago. I don't have all the financial statements you want. I haven't even filed my quarterly taxes yet and have sort've been running things by the seat of my pants. But I can certainly show you what I have."

"Fair enough. You want to drop the paperwork off at the Lumber Baron? I could look it over and we can talk money before I leave."

"Sounds good," she said.

"Say we do work something out. How would you feel about moving to Dallas to work in the firm and help us get this app off the ground?"

Harlee was flabbergasted. She hadn't been expecting a job offer. To be honest, she hadn't been expecting any offer. It was a lot to contemplate. But it would solve a plethora of problems, including the big one of staying employed. It would also get her out of Nugget and away from Colin, giving Harlee that clean break she wanted. At the same time, however, it would be putting her newspaper dreams on hold.

"We could talk about it," she said. "In the meantime, I'll bring over what I have."

"Sounds like a plan." Bix polished off the rest of his cocktail. "I'm thinking I'd like to mosey around this square a bit and maybe drive to that Donner Lake you talked about. But I should be back at the hotel in a couple of hours. I was thinking of going to Reno for a late dinner. Any chance you'd be interested in mixing a little pleasure with business?" He lifted his brows and stopped short of actually waggling them.

The man was a complete hound, but he was a charming one. A cross between a wolf and a Labrador retriever. "Nope," Harlee said.

"I didn't think so." Rather than act snubbed, he seemed amused. "Then we'll be in touch."

"Yes, we will," she said. But first she had to make the call she'd been putting off. The call that would determine her future.

Chapter 24

Colin sat outside the barbershop, watching Harlee leave the Ponderosa. He didn't want her to see him, so he crouched down in his truck, hiding. The simple reason: He was ashamed. Ashamed of keeping the truth from her, which in his view was the same as lying. And ashamed of not being good enough for her.

He'd never intended to rob that liquor store. He had nothing to do with killing those innocent people. And Colin hadn't known the two teens he'd been drinking with that night were even capable of such violence. Still, he'd spent the formative years of his life behind bars, mixing with lowlifes. He had no bachelor's, or even an associate's degree, just a junky GED from prison. And he couldn't even take Harlee to a restaurant without losing his shit.

Colin knew she was better off without him, but just seeing Harlee made him double over in pain with yearning for her. God, he loved her so much he could feel it in every pore of his skin. And that's why he had to let her go. She deserved everything good, especially a man she could be proud of.

He watched her drive off in her Pathfinder, wondering how the meeting went. Soon enough he'd find out, because everyone in Nugget would be spreading the details. That's the way the townsfolk here rolled. And yet he didn't believe for one second Harlee had told anyone, not even Darla, about his past. She might be a reporter, but she wouldn't do him that way.

He got out of his truck and went inside the barbershop, catching Darla and Wyatt in a lip lock. They pulled apart and Darla's eyes grew round with surprise.

"You look awful," she said.

"Thanks. Got time to give me a trim?"

"Honey, you need more than a trim. What happened to your eyes? They're all swollen."

"Allergies," he muttered, and wished she'd shut the hell up. At least his hair wasn't fuchsia.

Wyatt tried to run interference by asking questions about Sophie and Mariah's house. When would it be finished? Hadn't they lucked out on the weather? Blah, blah, blah. Couldn't a man get an effing haircut without all the damn chitchat?

Darla snapped a cape around his neck and practically pushed him to the shampoo bowl. Wyatt said something about being late for duty, gave Darla a peck on the cheek, and headed out.

"You together now?" At least if he turned the conversation to her, she wouldn't ask a lot of nosy questions.

"We're working on it," she said, lathering up his hair while his head rested against the cool porcelain bowl. "Are you okay, Colin?"

"How did her meeting go?" was all he said.

"Good. She just texted me. He wants all kinds of financial information, which Harlee rushed home to try to throw together. She doesn't have a lot of it. But he says he wants to buy DataDate and turn it into a phone app."

Colin lifted his soapy head. "Seriously?"

"I know, right?" She pushed his head back down for rinsing. "He even wants her to move to Dallas and consult on getting the program up and running. You can't let her go, Colin."

For her sake, how could he possibly ask her to stay? "It sounds like a good job . . . you know, until she can get a newspaper gig."

"Okay, you're going to think this sounds totally self-serving, but I swear it's not. She belongs here, Colin. With you. I know she loves you and she loves this town. All that's missing is a job. She hasn't even applied at the Reno paper or tried freelancing."

"It would never work, Darla. Trust me on that."

"Why not?" Darla put her hands on her hips. "Why can't it work? I can't get a straight answer out of her. All I know is one day you two are happy as clams, the next you're broken up. What don't I know here?"

Screw it, Colin thought. "I have a past, Darla. An ugly one."

Darla shut off the water and stared down at him. "She did one of those background checks on you, didn't she? She did one on Wyatt too."

Colin didn't say anything. He just wanted Darla to move his haircut along.

Darla didn't seem much in a hurry, though. "What did she find out?" When he didn't answer, she pressed. "Come on, it can't be *that* ugly. You may be a little strange, but you're a good person, Colin."

"I went to prison when I was seventeen for driving the getaway car during a liquor store holdup in which three people were murdered." He waited for that to sink in and said, "I thought I was driving us to get beer. Apparently the kids I was with had different plans. I didn't even know they had guns."

"My God, Colin." Darla kept watching him, not quite sure what to make of his admission. "Didn't your lawyer tell the police that you didn't know?"

"She did, but no one believed me. So you can see why I wouldn't be the right kind of guy for Harlee."

Darla moved him to her barber chair and quietly started trimming his hair. Colin could see her digesting the information he'd sprung on her. Measuring it in her head. Maybe now that Darla knew, she didn't feel safe with him.

But then she did the damnedest thing. Darla spun his chair around and gave him a big hug. "Don't you say that, Colin Burke. You're a good man. And I believe you. Every word. Does Harlee realize that you weren't involved—that you were railroaded?"

"She believes me. That's not what's at issue."

Darla weighed that too. "You should've told her," she finally said. "She deserved to know. But why can't you just talk it out?"

"It's more complicated than that. And Darla, I would appreciate it if you didn't blab what I told you all over town." He still had to live here.

"I won't," she said. "So if this Bix guy buys DataDate, you'll just let her go? Let her walk away forever?"

"I'm no good for her, Darla."

Harlee might have every reason to despise Colin for keeping his past from her. Eventually, though, Colin knew she'd forgive him. But she'd never get over having a man with a sheet. Despite having paid his debt to society, he'd always be viewed with mistrust. And so would the company he kept. It was enough that he'd ruined his own life; he wasn't about to ruin hers too.

After his haircut, Colin made his way back to Grizzly Peak, passing Griffin on Main Street. Both backed up so they were side by side and rolled down their windows.

"You doing okay, man?" Griffin asked, leaning his head out into the cold.

"Yep." Apparently Colin and Harlee's breakup was front page news.

"You want to come over for a beer? Commiserate?"

Colin guessed that Griff and Lina were still on the outs. "I'll take a rain check, if you don't mind."

"Sure thing," Griffin said. "Hey, it gets better with time."

"Has it for you?"

"Nah. But I keep hoping it will."

Colin didn't think it ever would for him. That's why he changed the subject. "How's business?"

"I'm almost ready to open the Gas and Go, got a couple custom bikes in the works, and have two more houses in Sierra Heights in escrow. That Sam may seem a little flaky, but she's great at spreading the word. Any Lumber Baron guest with deep pockets, she sends my way. Two of them were looking for vacation homes."

It was just a dent, considering that Griffin still had something like seventy vacant houses left to sell. But Colin figured that as rich as Griffin was, he could probably afford to sit on them. Although you'd never know the guy was wealthy; he acted like the rest of Nugget's mostly blue-collar residents. That's what Colin had come to like about him so much.

"Nice," he said. "It'll be good when the Gas and Go reopens— save everyone a trip to Graeagle."

"Yup." Griff split a grin. "That's what everyone says."

"I'll catch you later." Colin continued up the hill, passing Harlee's cabin on the way home.

He saw her Pathfinder parked in the driveway and assumed she was inside, busy preparing a financial prospectus. He could've helped with that, having done it for his furniture company and carpentry business.

Instead he kept going, pulling into his driveway only to find Al's Crown Vic taking up space next to the garage. The parole officer leaned against his car, seemingly immune to the cold, playing fetch with Max. Colin knew the dog made regular visits to Harlee's house when he wasn't home. Sometimes he could even smell her perfume on the shepherd.

He pulled up alongside Al's cruiser and opened his door. "Hey."

Al didn't say anything, just motioned that they should go inside.

Colin led the way. So much for the old expression that lightning never strikes twice . . .

A week after Bix returned to Texas, Harlee accepted his deal. He'd offered a good price for DataDate, not enough to make her independently wealthy, but a sufficient amount to pay off her debt and keep her going for a while. Everyone, including Brad, thought she'd be a fool not to take it. Bix's proposal that she work for the company was still on the table, but that decision would be determined by one person. And today was the day.

All morning she'd been unable to concentrate on anything other than listening for the sharp tone of her cell phone. That, and listening for Colin's truck. According to her count, he'd made the trip on Grizzly Peak three times—once to leave and then return and then to leave again. Each time she heard the crunch of gravel underneath his steel-studded tires, her longing for him grew more unbearable. Over the last couple of days, she'd considered going to him. To say what, she wasn't completely sure. In the end, though, she'd determined that there was no hope for them.

Colin had never asked her to be a permanent part of his life. A man who kept secrets wasn't a man who could commit. If he was, he would've tried harder to work this out with her.

Darla had relentlessly begged Harlee to forgive him. But just because she and Wyatt were able to patch up their differences, didn't mean the same could be said for Harlee and Colin. Too much deceit. His deceit.

She was still reeling from the fact that Colin had divulged the situation to Darla. The shootings. The prison sentence. All of it.

If only he had done that with Harlee months ago.

She stuck her head in the refrigerator, not really hungry but needing something to do to pass the time. It struck Harlee that she'd spent a great deal of her career waiting for the phone to ring. Waiting for the mayor to call with a quote, or a police spokesman with pertinent information, or a witness who could give crucial details to flesh out her story. And here she was, waiting again.

She shut the refrigerator door and flipped on the TV. Nothing but daytime soaps and talk shows, so she turned the set back off. She supposed she could start packing, because no matter what today's outcome brought, she'd be leaving. Either for Seattle or Dallas.

Out the window, she gazed up at the snow-covered Sierra mountain range. The view always managed to take her breath away. And the dense thicket of pines, dusted in white, reminded her of fairy-tale Christmases. God, she would miss this place. After she'd lost her job, Nugget had been her salvation. Not just the scenery and the fresh smells of frost and sap and clean air, but the people. Especially Griffin and Darla. What would she do without Darla?

She'd miss Emily and Clay's wedding and Maddy and Rhys's baby, which would break her heart.

There was always email, she supposed, and Skype and the good old telephone. And on holidays and vacations she'd come back to visit. Perhaps her friends would come to see her too. Both Seattle and Dallas were easily accessible. The move was the best possible solution, she told herself. Nugget, after all, had always been intended as a temporary stopping place to regroup. She now had the money to pay off her bills and start over. And she fervently prayed that it would be in journalism. But beggars couldn't be choosers and Bix paid well. At least while she worked for him getting the DataDate app off the ground, she could apply at the area's two big newspapers. She would be right there to make a pest of herself.

At the kitchen table she pulled up a chair, silently implored the phone to ring, and sifted through a stack of *Nugget Tribune*s that had been sitting there for days. As usual the paper was thin on news, but chock-full of ads. No wonder those jerk-off Addisons wanted to buy it. With a few tweaks, like cutting out print, paper, and distribution costs by making the paper a digital-only product, the *Trib* could be a potential goldmine. Of course it would depend on whether local advertisers and readers were ready for an online newspaper. But Harlee had seen plenty of townsfolk reading on their tablets, smartphones, and laptops. Nugget might not be the Athens of the West, but it seemed to have embraced technology just fine.

The paper would probably attract more readers online, especially people from out of the area who had vacation homes here or just wanted to know what was going on in their neighboring town. And if there were actual stories in the paper, like updates on what city hall, the school board, and the county board of supervisors were up to, more people might actually read the *Trib*. She wondered if the Addisons, who last she'd heard were in escrow to buy the newspaper, had made similar observations.

The phone rang, startling Harlee out of her reverie, and she grabbed it, taking in a breath before she answered.

"Hello."

"Harlee, it's Jerry. If you want the job, it's yours."

When she'd called a week earlier, right after she'd met with Bix, Jerry had told her there was a chance of an opening. A *Seattle Times* reporter had been offered a higher-paying position as chief of communications at a local agency. Management at the *Times* had been in negotiations with the reporter, but apparently she'd taken the other job.

"I don't need to come in for an interview, take a drug test or anything?" Harlee couldn't believe it could be this easy.

"You can take the drug test in California. HR will send you a list of clinics we use and a bunch of other crap paperwork you need to fill out. As for the interview, you'll be getting a call from the metro editor in a few hours. Don't worry about his call. It's pretty much meaningless, since I'm firing his ass in a few days. I think the guy's retarded."

Harlee didn't have the guts to tell him that the correct term was "developmentally disabled," which described most newspaper management, except, of course, Jerry.

"And, Legs, bring an umbrella. It rains about 150 days out of the year here."

"Okay," she said, baffled. "Am I just supposed to show up? This is it? I don't even know what my salary will be."

"I'll pay you a hundred bucks over scale. That's the best I can do. HR will work out the rest, including your start time. Someone will call you to set up your move and an advance flight to find a place to live. That work?"

"What is top scale there?" Not like it mattered, since it was the only journalism job being offered to her.

"Same as the *Call*'s," he said. Not bad, since Seattle's cost of living had to be way less than San Francisco's. "Four weeks of vacation a year. General assignment reporters are required to work some nights and some weekends. But you don't give a crap about that."

No, she didn't. She'd be single in Seattle. No friends. Nowhere to go.

"Thank you, Jerry. I really appreciate you believing—"

Before she could finish, Jerry said, "Gotta go. See you in a few weeks," and hung up.

And just like that Harlee was back in the game. She'd done it. She'd gotten a great job at a great newspaper, working for a great editor in a great city. More than she could ever have hoped for. So why did she feel like something was gnawing at the pit of her stomach? And even sadder than when she'd been fired from the *Call*.

It was just nerves, she told herself, and tried to psych herself up for the move.

Seattle!

Job!

Yay!

But it still wasn't working.

Chapter 25

One week later, Harlee maneuvered her rolling carry-on through Reno-Tahoe International. She needed to find an apartment in Seattle, stat. Jerry wanted her to start as soon as possible. The moving company was coming in six days and she still hadn't packed.

The move was happening so fast—maybe too fast—that Harlee could barely catch her breath. The whole thing felt a little like déjà vu. Only five months earlier, she'd impulsively hitched a U-Haul to the back of her Mini Cooper and made the trek to Nugget. Now she was doing it all over again. At least this time, the *Seattle Times* was footing the bill.

Shortly after Jerry had offered her the job, she'd hit the Seattle classifieds online and set up a bunch of appointments to see apartments in Queen Anne, a neighborhood of mostly young singles. Today, if all went well, she planned to plunk down a deposit on something, stop in at the newsroom to shake a few hands and meet a few people, and fly home to ready for the move.

Harvey and Leigh had promised to deliver the furniture she'd stowed in their garage and stay in Nugget a few days to help box up her belongings. People had already started a slow trickle through her cabin to wish her well. And Darla planned a big send-off bash at the Ponderosa.

But there hadn't been a sound out of Colin. The fact that everyone in town knew she was leaving and he hadn't said so much as congratulations, solidified her belief that a serious relationship between them had never been in his plans. Just a winter fling. Still, the possibility of never seeing him again, never feeling his arms around her, made her ache so desperately that she'd had to stop herself a dozen times from going to him.

Seattle was the right thing to do. At least that's what she told herself. She intended to bury herself in the job, break big stories, and make the *Call* sorry for sacking her. And in no time at all she'd forget Colin Burke. Except for she knew she wouldn't. She'd never forget him.

Ever.

Sometimes she woke up in the middle of the night, regretting that she'd looked up his damned tattoo or his prison record. It made her wonder how many other women's lives she'd ruined the same way. She used to think that information was power; now she wasn't so sure. Maybe if Harlee had minded her own business, she and Colin would still be together. Well, hindsight was twenty-twenty.

She found a Starbucks and waited in the long line, thinking that at least in Seattle there would be good coffee. After getting her latte, she wended her way to the gate, grabbed a seat, and tried to distract herself with the sights and sounds of the airport. It seemed like the whole world planned to travel today. Families and business people, tugging their suitcases and overnight bags, clogged the terminal.

Harlee watched as one irritated traveler looked ready to throw a temper tantrum because she didn't like her seat assignment. Even from the sidelines, Harlee could tell the woman was higher maintenance than a toy poodle, and prayed she wouldn't have to sit next to her.

The call came for first-class passengers to board the plane. Harlee got her ticket out of her purse and joined the economy-class hordes elbowing for priority. As everyone else did, she worried that all the overhead space would be taken before she could claim a seat.

In the distance, a man jogged toward the gate. He looked so much like Colin, Harlee did a double take. Like the time in the square, she was still seeing visions of him everywhere. At the Nugget Market. The Bun Boy. Main Street. Sometimes she conjured him out of thin air.

Ridiculous, because the one thing Harlee could be sure of was that Colin wouldn't step foot in a packed airport. Not with his demophobia.

She turned away, trying desperately to block Colin from her cranium, and waited for her section to be called. People rudely tried to cut in before their turns. This is why she hated airports and flying. The couple next to her stuffed airport sandwiches into their knapsacks, making her kick herself for not doing the same. Maybe, if she was lucky, there would be pretzels or peanuts on the flight.

A jostling from the tide of people made her lose balance, and in her haste to keep from falling she clutched the person next to her. When she looked up, it was him.

Colin.

Suspended in time, they stood stock-still, staring at each other. All around them babies cried, people pushed luggage, and muffled voices came over the loudspeaker. But for her, there was only him.

"What are you doing here?" she asked, finally breaking the spell.

"I bought a ticket," he said, out of breath, like he'd run the whole way. It explained how he'd managed to get through security.

He pulled her out of line and near one of the big windows that looked out onto the runway. That's when she noticed that his face was covered in sweat. "God, Colin, you okay?"

"I screwed up," he uttered. His eyes, pleading and flooded with emotion, met hers. "I love you. I always have. Don't go. But if you have to go, let me come with you."

Through her peripheral vision, she could see her group boarding. "What are you saying? You'll come with me to Seattle?"

"I'll go with you to the moon, if you'll take me back. Give me a second chance." He looked about ready to pass out.

She glanced around the terminal. It seemed as if the number of people had swelled in the last forty minutes. "I'll miss my flight, but do you want to go outside?"

"Say you'll take me back, first. The last week has been freakin' miserable, Harlee." Colin rested his forehead against the glass. "Do you still love me? Darla says you do."

She nodded, becoming teary eyed. "I do." Despite his deceit, she'd never stopped. "But—"

"My history's a deal breaker, right?" he said, staring out past the airplanes, past the runway, into the Nevada desert, looking beaten. "Goddamn Al."

"Your history was never an issue."

"Then come back to me," he said.

She looked away, afraid to meet his eyes. "You're the one who sent me away, Colin. The whole time we were together you never seemed all in. Right off the bat you tried to sabotage us by keeping the truth from me." He'd made her doubt her judgment and worst of all, he'd lost her trust.

"Not intentionally, Harlee. I was scared. I didn't feel worthy. But I'm all in now. One hundred percent. No more secrets. Not ever again. Please, give me a second chance."

"Why?" Harlee demanded, absently finding a tissue in her purse and blotting Colin's face with it. From the start, all she'd ever wanted him to do was put this right and rebuild her faith in him. Make her believe again. "Why now?"

"Because you make me feel worthy. For the first time since I got out of Donovan, you made me the man I want to be . . . the man who, given even half a chance, will love you forever. I should've told you the truth from the beginning, Harlee. But I was so damned ashamed."

"Colin, you have nothing to be ashamed of. And you have always been worthy."

"I know it's selfish," he said. "I know that living down my past and my phobias will be a struggle—for both of us. But I've had time to think about it and I know, if you let me, I can make you happy, Harlee. Really, really happy."

"You did make me happy." The happiest she'd ever been.

He regarded her with such hope that it made Harlee long for the life they could have together. "Does that mean we're gonna do this? You and me?"

She didn't answer, just walked into his arms and held him tight. "I love you."

And there, in the middle of Reno-Tahoe International, standing amid the crowds, as groups of travelers zigzagged around them, stopping to check flight statuses, find gates, or readjust luggage straps, as the constant cacophonous buzz of conversation permeated the terminal like a symphony of bees, he kissed her. And kissed her and kissed her and kissed her, stopping just long enough to say, "Let's get out of here . . . figure out a game plan."

The only game plan Harlee cared about was spending her life with Colin. He grabbed her hand, and with single-minded determination, followed the overhead signs to the exit.

"Colin?" She raced to keep up with his long-legged strides. "Who's Al?"

"Who?" He looked at her, confused.

"Al. You said something about goddamn Al."

"Oh, that Al. He's my parole officer." He continued to maneuver them through the throngs of people.

But she forced him to stop and cocked her head in surprise. "You told your parole officer about us?"

"Of course I did," he said. "You're the most important person in my life."

"What did he say?"

"To man up and stop acting like a wuss."

"He actually said that?" Harlee asked.

"Yeah." Colin chuckled. "He's kind of a dick."

"He sounds smart to me."

Colin shrugged. "He's a pain in my ass, but at least he made me realize that I was trying too hard to protect you. That you're a tough woman, capable of making your own decisions."

"I'm pretty sure I told you that myself," Harlee said, trying not to roll her eyes.

"I guess I needed to hear it from a third party."

She looked around the crowded terminal. Although perspiration still beaded Colin's forehead and his breathing seemed erratic and his color looked paler than usual, he wasn't the chalk white he'd been at the restaurant. She pointed to the masses surrounding them. "You okay with this?"

His lips quirked up into a giant grin that made his whole face glow. "Now that I have you, I am, but I wouldn't mind getting out of here. Like soon."

By the time they made it home, Harlee knew exactly what she planned to do. One look at the town's welcome sign, proclaiming Nugget The "Pride of the West," and she teared up. At the sight of the square, where she'd made so many memories, Harlee melted. But it was Colin's house, with its thick log walls that he'd stacked by hand, that made the decision final.

"We're not going to Seattle," Harlee told Colin.

"We're not?" He seemed surprised. "What about Jerry and the newspaper?"

"I love being a reporter. But I love you and this town more."

He gathered her up in his arms and once again kissed her breathless. Max, who'd been lying by the hearth, sensed something monumental and joined their huddle, dancing around them, swinging his tail like a maniac.

"There's always the *Nugget Tribune*," Colin joked, and folded her against the back of the couch.

"I thought the Addisons bought it."

"Nope," he said. "Lila Stone won't sell it to them. Word is they'd planned to turn it into some kind of circular and that pissed her off."

"Good for her." Harlee started for his office.

"Where you going?" Colin called after her.

"First to call Lila, then Jerry."

"Come here." He pulled her gently by the arm and cleared his throat. "Harlee, you think you'd want to marry me?"

She froze. "Seriously?"

"You don't have to answer right now. Just think about it."

"I don't have to think about it. Yes! Yes!" She threw her arms around his neck and held him as tight as she could, because she was never letting him go.

"Colin," she said. "Uh, that parole officer . . . Al. You know we're inviting him to the wedding, right?"

"Unfortunately," he murmured, and began kissing her all over again. "Nothing can keep him away."

Epilogue

"We've gotta tear up the front page," Harlee told her new webmaster. "Ten minutes ago, Maddy Shepard gave birth to a baby girl. We're putting the story above the fold."

There was no fold.

Since taking ownership of the *Nugget Tribune*, Harlee had gone completely digital. But old newspaper lingo had been burned, like hot lead type, into her lexicon. The town had overwhelmingly endorsed the idea of an online newspaper, and as a promotion to celebrate the new format Harlee had given away e-readers to the first twenty subscribers. At only ten bucks a year, she'd had no trouble selling subscriptions. So far, advertisers had also embraced the online format. She'd already increased revenue 15 percent from Lila's previous year.

Clay had offered to do a monthly ranching column, which appealed to the local cattlemen. And Portia Cane, who owned a Nugget adventure-tour company, wrote the fish and game report. Harlee had even found a former world champion bronc rider to cover rodeo season, a big pastime in Plumas County. In early summer, Virgil Ross, the hometown historian, was going to do a five-part series on the Donner Party, which would coincide with a new documentary about the tragedy, debuting in Nugget. And next week, Emily planned to run a few recipes from her upcoming Sierra cookbook.

Harlee was still trying to persuade Colin to tell his story, but so far he wanted to keep it private. She suspected that besides Rhys and Darla, there were some in town who already knew but were keeping it on the QT.

Jerry blew a gasket when he found out she wasn't coming to Seattle. "Legs, I went to the mat for you."

After he'd had a while to calm down, he gave his blessing to Harlee's buying the *Trib*. "Hold me a job there," he'd said. "No telling what'll happen here the way the industry is going. They'll probably hire someone from the state mental hospital to run this place."

"Hey, you hear about Maddy?" Darla waltzed into Harlee's store-front newsroom, sporting a lime-green wig. While Wyatt still grappled with the many shades of Darla's hair, the couple had come to terms with what happened all those years ago and were going hot and heavy.

"Six pounds, seven ounces," Harlee called, as she wrote a headline to plunk on top of the baby story.

"Awesome, right! You guys book the Lumber Baron for the wedding yet?"

"August," Harlee said. In the meantime, Emily and Clay's big day was just two months away. "Sam's my wedding consultant and Sophie and Mariah are hosting us a shower at their new house."

"Okay, but I'm doing your hair." Darla looked up at the clock on the wall. "Shoot, I've got a hair straightening in five minutes and two cuts after that. Happy hour?"

"As long as no news breaks, I'm good to go. Let's invite Griff."

"He might be busy. He won't say, but I think he's seeing someone."

"No kidding?" Harlee looked up from her computer. "That's great."

"Anything that will help him get over Lina." Darla raised her head to the heavens in mock prayer. "I better get back to the barbershop. See you later."

As Darla walked out, Colin walked in.

"You hear about Maddy?" Harlee hopped up and kissed him.

"Yep. Just saw Donna." He looked over her shoulder at the article on the screen. "You better get that up before the mouth of the Sierra scoops you on the story."

"Spoken like the true fiancé of a newswoman." She clicked a few buttons and within seconds the Maddy article led the *Nugget Tribune*'s homepage.

"Bix called," Colin said. "He still wants you to consult on Data-

Date. He says he'll be here in a couple of weeks for a fishing trip and wants to take us to dinner. He also wants three of my rockers."

She looked up to fill her eyes with the hunk of man who would soon be her husband. God, she loved every inch of him. "I guess he really fell for the place. But then who can resist? Any chance you'd be up for happy hour at the Ponderosa with Darla and me?"

"I could be persuaded."

They'd been working on getting Colin to overcome his fear of crowds. He'd begun seeing a therapist in Sacramento who specialized in demophobia and had helped Colin make significant strides. The panic attacks were less extreme and fewer and far between. They hoped that by their wedding, he'd be ready to stand in the receiving line.

She'd already moved into his place so her family could use the cabin again. Every day seemed like a dream—waking up to Colin. As much as she loved the Sierra and all the wonderful friends she'd made here, he was the best part of her life. Solid and true. And to think that she had almost lost him.

All she could say was thank goodness for second chances.

Please turn the page for an exciting sneak peek of

Stacy Finz's newest Nugget romance,

STARTING OVER

now on sale!

Chapter 1

Nate shielded his eyes against the flashing red lights and followed the ambulance into the Lumber Baron parking lot and up to the front door. At least the driver had the good sense to kill the siren. No need waking the entire inn. Not at this hour, when they had a houseful of paying guests.

He wondered if Samantha had already arrived and kind of hoped she hadn't. His sister Maddy, while still on maternity leave, had been the one to hire the inept socialite to handle the everyday running of the Lumber Baron. Why, he had no idea. Samantha Dunsbury had more money than brain cells and wasn't exactly reliable. Just four months ago she'd left her fiancé at the altar without so much as a goodbye text, got in her car and drove west from New York City. Given that the Dunsburys were Old Greenwich, Connecticut, money and there had been bogus reports that Samantha had been kidnapped for ransom, the fiasco wedding made national headlines. Folks in Nugget couldn't stop talking about it. Of course, it didn't take a whole lot to get the residents running their mouths. Pretty much any-thing remotely titillating got broadcast through the California town's expansive grapevine like political fodder on the cable news networks.

Here, Samantha Dunsbury may as well have been Paris Hilton. And the mystery of why she'd dumped her groom-to-be, a Wall Street tycoon, in the eleventh hour only added to the woman's mystique.

Nate didn't care what reason she had for leaving her intended standing in a Manhattan church looking like the world's biggest chump. His only concern was making sure she didn't treat the Lumber Baron with the same indifference. He suspected that the spoiled heiress would have no qualms about leaving him in the lurch when she got bored with playing innkeeper.

Nate glanced at his watch, let out a frustrated breath, and hopped out of his car. By the time he got inside the inn, the paramedics were rushing up the staircase to room 206. He trailed behind them, not wanting to get in the way, only to find that Samantha had indeed beaten him to the scene.

"Take deep breaths, Mrs. Abernathy." Sam held the guest's hand. Nate didn't know why Sam wanted the woman to focus on her breathing. According to Maddy, Mrs. Abernathy was having stomach problems, not a baby. "Maybe it's just one of those twenty-four-hour flus."

"Sam, dear, I'm an emergency-room nurse," Mrs. Abernathy said, her face mottled in pain. "It's appendicitis and I want the damn thing out."

Sam looked up from Mrs. Abernathy and made eye contact with Nate. "What are you doing here?"

The woman clearly thought she was the lady of the manor, and Nate wanted very much to set her straight. Not the time, nor the place, he told himself. "Maddy called me."

"Oh," was all she said as one of the medics jostled her aside.

"You need help, Mr. Abernathy?" Samantha called to a man Nate presumed was Mrs. Abernathy's husband. He'd been hurrying around the room, gathering up assorted personal items and stuffing them into a suitcase.

"I think I got everything," he said, his brows knitted as he watched the paramedics check Mrs. Abernathy's vital signs and move her onto a gurney. "How you doing, Alice?"

"I've been better," she responded, and Mr. Abernathy stopped packing to gently squeeze her foot, the only part of her he could get to while the medics worked.

"If you leave anything, don't worry," Samantha assured him. "I'll mail it to you. Let me take you to the hospital, Mr. Abernathy. I hate for you to drive when you're stressed out like this. I could drive your car and Nate could follow. Or maybe you would prefer to go in the ambulance?"

"You've gone to enough trouble," Mr. Abernathy said, patting Sam on the back. "We appreciate everything you've done and hope we didn't wake the entire inn."

"Don't be silly. I'm just sorry Mrs. Abernathy is sick and that you'll miss your bird-watching tour. I know how much the both of you were looking forward to it."

Nate had to keep from rolling his eyes. Sam poured it on a little thick. He moved out of the doorway so the paramedics could get through with the stretcher. As they lifted Mrs. Abernathy out of the room and down the staircase, her husband reached for the suitcase. Before Sam could help him with it, Nate grabbed the handle out of her hand and joined the procession to the main floor.

"You sure you don't want me to take you?" Sam asked the husband again.

"I'm fine, dear." Mr. Abernathy pulled a set of keys from his pocket. "Alice is one tough cookie. Aren't you, Alice?" He winked at his wife, who responded with a faint nod.

"I'll live," she said, and reached for her husband's hand.

Mr. Abernathy turned to Sam. "You have my credit card number, so we're square, right?"

"No charge, Mr. Abernathy," Samantha said, and Nate stiffened. "You just come back and see us when Mrs. Abernathy is better."

"We will certainly do that. And thank you, Sam. For everything." Mr. Abernathy quickly headed to the back of the ambulance, told his wife he'd be right behind her, and kissed her on the forehead before the paramedics closed the door.

Afterward, Nate helped him load the luggage into the couple's Honda Accord and went back inside to find Samantha behind the check-in desk at the computer. She was probably voiding the couple's credit card transaction.

"Hey, little Miss Sunshine, next time you decide to give away three nights in one of our best rooms, check with me first," he told her. "We have a forty-eight-hour cancelation policy."

"I'm sure Mrs. Abernathy didn't know two days ago that she'd be coming down with appendicitis or she would have canceled," Samantha said, her blue eyes narrowing.

Nate didn't appreciate the attitude. "Those are the rules," he said. "I'm sorry she got sick. I really am. But while this may be a hobby to you, it's a for-profit business for the rest of us."

"Why do you always talk to me like that?" She raised her chin above the computer and stared him straight in the face. Still, he detected a slight tremble in her voice.

Here come the tears. It was nearly two in the morning and he didn't have the patience for any more drama. He wanted to go home and back to bed.

"You ever think that doing the right thing is good for business?" she asked. No tears. Just a bucketload of indignation.

Great, now she wanted to tell him how to run a hotel. Well, he had news for her: He'd been working in the hospitality industry before she was old enough to teethe on her silver spoon. His parents ran one of the most successful boutique hotel operations in the Midwest and he'd learned how to take a reservation before he could ride a bicycle without training wheels.

"Samantha, just check with me before you start comping the guests. Where's Andy?"

She looked down at her shoes, designer ones if Nate had to guess. "I told him he could go in the break room. There was no reason for the both of us to—"

"He's in there working on his music, isn't he?" Nate wanted to put finger quotes around music, because the emo crap Andy wrote sounded more like the caterwauling of a feline in heat. Nate shook his head and wondered when he'd begun running a charity for slackers and dilettantes. At least the members of his staff in San Francisco were professionals. Every last one of them. "Well, get him back in here. Come on, I'll follow you home. At least you can catch a few hours of sleep before opening."

"I don't need you to follow me home," she said, and headed to the break room in the back. The staff lounge was isolated from the guest rooms so that employees could take breaks without fear of disturbing sleeping residents. Sam returned with a repentant-looking Andy and seemed to be stalling. But Nate would be damned if he let her walk to her car alone. Nugget was a safe country town—his brother-in-law, the police chief, kept it that way. But bad things could happen anywhere.

When Nate and Maddy had first bought the Lumber Baron, they'd had their own brush with crime. A meth head had set up shop in the then-decrepit Victorian and attacked Maddy when she'd been there alone. Then Rhys Shepard saved the day. He shot the bad guy, married Maddy, and the town had been relatively crime-free ever since.

Nate glowered at Andy and turned to Samantha, who was gathering up her purse and jacket. "You ready to go?"

Between clenched teeth, she said, "You go ahead. I'm fine on my own." She clearly disliked him as much as he did her, which was fine as long as she did her job.

"Oh, for Christ's sake, Samantha, we live next door to each other." Not by Nate's choice. He'd bought his house before Sam and her Mercedes convertible had slammed into Nugget. That had been right after Christmas, back when half the town thought the woman had escaped from a loony bin. But because Sierra Heights had the fanciest homes in town, Miss Richie Rich had to lease the place next to his. Right on the golf course.

"Whatever," she huffed, and turned for the door, giving him a spectacular view of her heart-shaped ass, not that he wanted to look. He knew all about beautiful spoiled princesses. Been there, done that, and had the returned engagement ring to prove it.

He followed her to the gated community where they both lived, watched her taillights disappear behind her garage door, and waited until he saw her silhouette through the living room window before pulling into his own driveway.

He walked into his empty house. Other than the log bed he'd bought from Colin Burke, Nugget's resident furniture builder, he hadn't had time to purchase couches or even a kitchen table. Anyway, he usually ate all his meals at the Ponderosa, Nugget's only sit-down restaurant, which seconded as a bowling alley. His best friends owned the joint and were the reason he and Maddy had chosen Nugget as the location for their hotel in the first place.

Hoping that if they built it, tourists would come, he and Maddy had bought the Lumber Baron eighteen months ago. At the time, the Victorian mansion was the most dilapidated building on the town's square. They'd sunk a ton of money into renovating, fought the city for a lodging permit, and opened their doors on a wing and a prayer.

Ever since, business had fluctuated. Sometimes, like now, it was better than Nate could've imagined. But during the months of December, January, and February, when Nugget got socked in with snow, the place had been emptier than a bar after last call. Ordinarily, spring would've been the perfect time to go full bore on promoting the fledgling bed-and-breakfast with extra ad campaigns and more Internet visibility, but Maddy had to go and get herself knocked up. Nate tried to do his best, but he had nine other hotels to operate in San Francisco, four hours away.

That's why he constantly traveled back and forth. But living out of a suitcase had started to wear on him, so he'd bought the Sierra Heights house, thinking it would be a good investment. Mostly, though, he liked having his own space, especially since lately he spent more time here than in the city. The house—a sprawling two-story log cabin with mammoth picture windows—also had plenty of space for Lilly, his daughter. He went to bed thinking how much he missed seeing her every day and experiencing parenthood the way a normal father would.

Just about the time he drifted off to sleep, the incessant beeping of his clock roused him awake. Nate shut off the alarm and lay there for a few minutes with his arm covering his eyes, then got up and took a shower. The huge tiled stall had multiple spray nozzles and a rain showerhead. The house had a lot of great features: tall ceilings, radiant floor heating, a state-of-the-art kitchen, and views that wouldn't quit. But he hadn't exactly made it a home. Between the birth of his daughter and running Breyer Hotels, there hadn't been time.

In San Francisco he lived in one of his hotel's penthouses. Small but fully furnished, the suite came with round-the-clock room service. Being the boss, he never had to wait long for anything. Despite the ease of living there, he found it impersonal, and all the pampering and sucking up made him feel soft.

No pampering here. He didn't even have a coffeemaker. He knew Samantha had one; a stainless-steel job that looked like it would also rotate your tires. The one and only time he'd been inside her place, he'd seen the machine, along with enough paintings and sculptures to fill the de Young. If you asked him, she'd decorated the place a little over the top for a town like Nugget, where chainsaw bears and mudflap girls amounted to high art.

He put on a pair of boxer shorts, went to his bedroom window, and separated a few of the blind slats with his fingers to peek at her window. She had her drapes drawn so he couldn't see anything. For all he knew, she'd already left for work.

One thing he'd say for Sam was that she was always on time. He presumed she'd read somewhere that being prompt was a big part of keeping a job. According to Maddy, other than volunteering, Sam had never actually worked a day in her adult life. Nate couldn't imagine being that idle, not to mention that his parents wouldn't have tolerated it. The Breyers might be relatively well-off, but they'd earned their fortune, not inherited it. And they'd worked damned hard and had raised their kids to do the same.

He finished getting dressed, made half-a-dozen phone calls to check on his San Francisco hotels, and jetted over to the Ponderosa. He'd barely been there long enough to get comfortable when Owen slid into his booth. The barber was the unofficial leader of the "Nugget Mafia," a group of the town's powerbrokers who also happened to be the biggest busybodies around.

"What's up, Owen?" Nate had helped himself to a cup of coffee and was waiting for a waitress to take his order. There was no sign of Sophie or Mariah, the Ponderosa's proprietors. But Nate seemed to remember something about them doing errands in Reno.

"How's the redhead?"

"Who? Samantha?"

"No. Howdy Doody. Who else would I be talking about?" Owen waved over a server. "Who does a guy have to sleep with around here to get some service?" He pointed to Nate. "This fellow wants to order."

Nate got his usual: two fried eggs, hash browns, bacon, and toast.

When the waitress left, Nate said, "She's doing fine, Owen."

True to form, Owen actually expected Nate to share personnel information with him. Not a lot of professional decorum—or boundaries of any kind—in this town.

"Why do you ask?" Nate asked, curious. Sometimes Owen's nosiness paid off. The man usually had the best intel in Nugget.

"Just curious. You gotta admit she's a hottie."

She was that. She was also a fickle, spoiled, trust-fund baby. Something Nate didn't plan to lose sight of.

"Why do ya think she left that fiancé of hers?" Owen continued.

"How would I know?"

Nate's food came and he prayed Owen would let him eat in peace. No such luck. Owen was a man born to loiter. "Don't you have hair to cut?"

"It's Darla's day," Owen said.

Darla was Owen's daughter, who'd taken over the barbershop so the old man could retire. Nate, however, doubted that would ever happen. Owen liked being at the center of it all, and the barbershop was practically town hall. That's why the old geezer held on to a few longtime customers, mostly members of the Nugget Mafia.

"You think he might've been one of those Bernie Madoff characters?"

"Who?" Nate asked, flagging over the waitress for more coffee.

"Sam's ex."

"I don't know, Owen. I don't know anything about the guy." Just that Nate felt an affinity for the dupe.

"Well, why else would she have left him? Unless he beat her. You think he beat her?"

Nate blew out a breath. "You watch too much daytime television, Owen. But if you're so curious, ask Darla. She probably knows."

"Beautician-client privilege," Owen said.

But Nate doubted that even Darla knew the truth. From what he'd heard, the runaway bride had kept the secret of her failed nuptials pretty close to her Versace vest.

All anyone knew about Samantha Dunsbury was that she'd shown up in Nugget with a head of hacked hair and 2,700 miles of road stuck to her tires. According to her story, she'd gone scissor happy on her hair the morning of her wedding, got in her car, and kept driving until she landed here, the middle of nowhere. Then she holed up at the Lumber Baron until Darla fixed her hair and Maddy gave her a job.

None of her story sounded very credible to Nate. But then again, how could he know the mind of an airhead? He figured she'd eventually get bored living in a small town, working at a country inn, and would hightail it home to Wall Street Boy and her rich family.

Vaya con Dios.

Except for when she walked into the Ponderosa five minutes later in a stretchy nude dress that clung to her body like a second skin, he wasn't thinking about God.

Chapter 2

"Thank goodness you're here." Sam rushed to Nate's table. "Your cell's not working."

"Yes, it is." Annoyed, he pulled it from his pocket, played with it for a second or two, then pulled a face. "I must've inadvertently shut it off. What's the crisis?" he asked, intimating that if she had her hand in it, it must be a catastrophe.

Why the man had to be so boorish, Sam didn't know. For some reason he'd taken an instant dislike to her.

"No crisis," she said, and noticed the barber sitting on the other side of Nate's banquette. "Hi, Owen."

"How you doing there, missy?" He flashed his dentures and started to squeeze out of the booth. "I best be getting over to the bowling alley. Me and the fellows have a standing game."

Once Owen was out of earshot, Sam said, "A businessman from San Francisco may want to book the entire inn for a family reunion in July, but two of the rooms have already been spoken for on the dates he wants."

"Get him to take another date," Nate said, and drained his coffee before calling the waitress over to pay his bill.

"That's the problem. He only wants that one week and made a big deal that I should Google him. Can you imagine the audacity? I had half a mind to tell him to go elsewhere."

"Who is he?"

"Some guy named Landon Lowery. Owns a company called Zergy. I never heard of it."

Nate's eyes grew wide. "It's only the largest video gaming company in the world. Tell me you didn't tell him to go elsewhere."

"Of course I didn't. I've been around high-handed rich and famous people my whole life. I know how to handle them."

"Yet you didn't know who Landon Lowery was." Nate, obviously tired of waiting for the server to return with his credit card, stomped over to the cash register to complete his transaction, grabbed his sports coat off the rack, and shrugged it on.

"I'll take care of it," he told Sam, dismissing her like she had a feather duster for a brain. It reminded her of all those years of living with her dictatorial father. Well, she didn't plan to put up with it anymore.

"What do you mean, you'll take care of it?" She practically chased him across the square. But with those long legs of his, she didn't stand a chance of catching up. "It's my account."

He stopped at the stairs of the Lumber Baron, turned and squinted his chocolaty-brown eyes at her. "It's my hotel."

"Mr. Lowery and I already have a rapport."

"You all but said he was an asshole. What kind of rapport is that?"

"Enough of a rapport that he's coming to check the place out next week and wants me to show him around."

"Great." He rolled his eyes. "You've been here all of four months. What do you know about the Sierra Nevada?"

"Nate, Maddy put me in charge of event planning," she said, intending to hold her ground. This was her first job and she desperately wanted to show that she could do it. "Mr. Lowery wants his family reunion to have activities—organized tours, a meal program, shopping excursions. Basically, he wants a week-long party. I may not have hotel experience, but I know how to throw a party." It was the only skillset she had, and Sam wanted to put it to use—as a vocation, not a hobby.

Nate turned his back on her, went inside the inn, and disappeared into his office, shutting the door behind him. Conversation over. The man was truly insufferable—a complete jackass. Why couldn't he at least be ugly? A troll with a hunchback. But no, even that was too much to ask. Physically speaking, Nathaniel Breyer was a Roman god sent down from the heavens. A full head of thick, brown hair that made you want to run your fingers through it. An angular face, too sharp to be pretty but breathtaking just the same. And a lean, hard body that would make a weaker woman quiver.

The only thing lacking in Nate's road to perfection was a personality.

Sam stood at his door, wondering whether she should burst in and demand that he let her do her job, or give him a little time to come to his senses. Settling on the latter, she went into Maddy's office, which she had commandeered as her own, and returned three calls—brides inquiring about using the inn for their weddings. Her own had been an unmitigated disaster. Or at least it would've been if she'd bothered to show up. The marriage, however, would've been even worse. The four months she'd lived in Nugget, Royce had only called twice—once to scream at her for "making me look like a goddamned fool," and the second time to demand his ring back. He'd insisted that one of his ancestors had brought it with her on the *Mayflower*, when Sam knew for a fact that he'd purchased it on West Forty-Seventh Street, Manhattan's Diamond District.

Well, she was here now, away from Royce, and never before had each day seemed so filled with possibility. Like yesterday afternoon. It had been her day off, before Mrs. Abernathy had gotten sick, and she'd driven across state lines to Nevada's Washoe Lake to see the wildflowers. She'd been told that April was still a little early, but even so, the land was awash in color—greens and purples and yellows. No stranger to travel—Sam had been all over the world, but mostly to plush resorts and big cities—she'd never seen anything like the desert, where a person could see forever. It was solitary, but not lonely; silent, but so alive. It seemed freer than any place on earth. Not just the land, but the people. They didn't seem to care who you were or what you did or where you came from, only that you were a decent person.

People here even talked differently than they did on the East Coast. Not just the accent, a barely detectable twang, but they used odd expressions, like "airin' the lungs" for cursing or someone with a "leaky mouth" gossiped too much. Just the other day she'd heard Owen describe Portia Cane, the lady who owned Nugget's tour-guide company, as a "Montgomery Ward woman." Sam had thought he'd meant that Portia shopped at the department store, but Owen corrected her. *It means she's U-G-L-Y.*

She supposed Westerners were all around more colorful people. Here, the fact that she'd run out on her wedding made her a minor celebrity. Not a day went by when Donna Thurston, proprietor of the Bun Boy burger shack, didn't shout across the square, "You go, girl."

Back in Connecticut it had made her a laughing stock. But leaving that day had been the best thing she'd ever done, even if Daddy was threatening to cut her off. The truth was he could shut down her Dunsbury bank accounts and she'd still be wealthier than anyone had a right to be. Her mother, an Astor, had left her a fortune when she died, and Daddy couldn't touch that money. Oddly enough, she did miss him, though. George Dunsbury IV might be domineering, demanding, and detached, but she loved him. And she knew that he loved her too, even if he'd tried to "wrangle" (local rancher Clay McCreedy's word for forcing cattle to do things they didn't want to do) her into a loveless marriage.

Unlike Royce, he called every day, pleading for her to come home. And when that didn't work, he threw out harsh ultimatums. But she wasn't going anywhere until she figured out her future, which included carving out a real profession for herself. Life as the hostess with the mostest had become terminally dull—and meaningless. Samantha would never find a cure for cancer or balance the economy or invent a talking smartphone, but at least she could make a difference in people's lives, even if it was only to plan them the perfect weekend getaway.

A tapping at the door shook Samantha from her reverie. "Come in."

Nate pushed open the door and stuck his head in. "I'm having Tracy Cohen from corporate take over with Landon Lowery. Send me his contact info and the dates he wants."

"You're kidding me." Sam stood up and folded her arms over her chest. "Tracy has never even been here. When we talk on the phone she acts like Nugget's in a foreign country."

"Sam, this is too important to let you play at being an event planner. Lowery could mean big business for Breyer Hotels—not only this reunion, but corporate events. The man's a legend in the tech world."

Sam glared at him and Nate said, "Let me boil it down for you: It would be like having a Kennedy show up at one of your fund-raisers."

"Kennedys regularly show up at my fund-raisers." She pointed her chin at him in challenge. "That's why I'm perfect for this job."

He looked up at the ceiling, his patience clearly wearing thin. "Look, if this were an old blueblood looking to book a family reunion at the inn, I'd probably give you a crack at it. But this is Silicon Valley. It's a different breed than New England old money. They're like rock stars, and Tracy knows how to handle these people. Hell, she and Marissa Mayer went to Stanford together."

"So that automatically makes her more capable than me?" Sam had gone to Vassar with lots of successful people. At least she didn't go around bragging about it. Not like Nate. *I'm so great, I went to Harvard.* Whoop-de-do.

"She's more capable because unlike you"—he jabbed his finger at her—"she actually does this for a living." And with that he started to walk away.

"What do I do about the other guests, the ones who already booked for that week?"

"If we get the Lowery gig, we cancel them and hopefully get them to book for another time slot."

"We can't do that," Sam said in disgust. "Some of them may have already bought plane tickets or at the very least gotten the time off of work."

"Yes, we can. Read the fine print. Any reservation can be canceled for a conference, event, or large group."

Sam was aghast. "That's an awful way of doing business."

"That's the only way to do business." Nate propped his shoulder against the doorjamb. He looked so arrogant that Sam wanted to smack him. "Again, let me remind you, we're a for-profit company. Emphasis on profit. If you don't believe me, ask your father. Doesn't he manage one of the largest hedge funds in the country?"

It was clearly a rhetorical question, since they both knew that George Dunsbury's financial prowess was legendary. Her father had once been short-listed to be chairman of the Federal Reserve Board, but declined and Ben Bernanke got the position.

Nate walked away before she could answer and shut his door a little louder than usual.

She had half a mind to barge into his office and quit. But if she wanted to launch this new life of hers, she needed the job. The only reason she'd gotten it in the first place was that Maddy believed in her. That, and Maddy had been desperate to find a replacement during her maternity leave. Otherwise, Sam wasn't the least bit employable. Not unless you counted her bulging résumé of lunching with the ladies and throwing charity galas as a prerequisite for a job. But in a way, it was the perfect experience for planning events at a small inn. She had the fortitude to deal with difficult people—nothing was more challenging than planning a charity auction or cotillion with a group of insanely rich, narcissistic women. Hello, Judith Forsyth, the biggest bitch in Connecticut, who wanted to take credit just for breathing. And there was Muffy Vandertilten, whose husband would threaten to sue the committee if the Muffmeister didn't get her way. But the biggest takeaway was that Samantha knew how to make every detail, from the color of the napkins to the party favors, blend seamlessly with the theme of every event.

And no one knew better how to fix a last-minute catastrophe than Samantha. And believe it or not, large-scale society events were rife with catastrophes. When Tony Bennett came down with pharyngitis six hours before performing a charity concert in New Canaan, Sam had managed to rope Billy Joel into doing the show. She went over to Long Island and drove him back to Connecticut herself. She had a contact list filled with florists, caterers, and celebrities who would come to her rescue at a moment's notice. Sure, having the Dunsbury name helped, but even without it, Sam had an aptitude for creating memorable parties.

People were still talking about her Snow Ball. She'd put the entire affair under a glass dome, used nothing but diamond white as her theme color, and created a winter wonderland complete with a machine that dropped fake flurries from the sky to make the event look like a giant snow globe.

She might not be a cutthroat business person like Nate or her father, but she knew that if given the chance she could increase sales tenfold at the Lumber Baron. For that reason, she gritted her teeth and got back to work. She'd just gotten off the phone with a linen vendor when she heard a fuss coming from the lobby and went out to investigate. Maddy had come in to show off baby Emma to the housekeeping staff.

"Look who's here." Sam gave Maddy a hug and kissed Emma on the forehead, getting a sweet whiff of baby smell. "You look fantastic, by the way." Sam had only known Maddy since the tail end of her second trimester, but now she looked slender and glowing.

"Thanks. You too. Love that dress."

"You here to put in a few hours, or just visiting?" Sam asked.

"Just visiting. I'm meeting Emily and Pam at the Ponderosa in a bit, but is there anything I can do?"

Yeah, tell your bother he's a colossal jerk. "I think we have everything under control."

"Nate told me about the Abernathys," Maddy said. "I've never had a guest with appendicitis before. But it sounds like you handled it perfectly."

"Thank you." Now why couldn't Nate throw a little praise around every once in a while? "I called the hospital earlier and she's doing much better."

"Good," Maddy said. "Poor thing. Anything else going on?"

"Landon Lowery's interested in the inn for a family reunion."

"The gaming guy? He wants to stay here?"

Why was it that everyone knew who Landon Lowery was except Sam? "He's thinking of booking the entire inn for a week in July."

They were still standing in the lobby, near the reservation desk, where Andy pretended not to be eavesdropping. Maddy motioned that they should move the conversation to someplace more private, parked the stroller in a corner, and carried Emma into her old office. "You're kidding. That would be huge, not just because it's a guaranteed full house for a week, but it's . . . uh . . . Landon Lowery. Wow!"

"He's coming next week to tour the grounds."

"Be sure to show him the millpond in Graeagle. And don't forget about the rodeo. You have that box, remember? Call Grace over at the Nugget Farm Supply to get the schedule. It might be something he'd be interested in." Maddy waved her hand in the air. "But you already know all this stuff."

"Nate's having Tracy from corporate handle it," Sam said, and tried not to sound peeved.

"What? She's never been to the inn. As far as I know she's never been to Plumas County."

Sam wondered if Nate was still next door and could hear every word they said. It wouldn't help their already tenuous relationship if he thought she was going around him. Although she got the sense that while Maddy was in charge of the Lumber Baron, Nate held ultimate veto power. Breyer Hotels was his, after all. The inn was the only property the siblings held together.

"She has a lot of experience and I'm pretty new at this," Sam said.

"Is that what Nate said? Because that's just bull." Sam tried to shush her, but Maddy wouldn't have it. "No. He's wrong. You love this place and that's what we want our guests to see. Tracy is an excellent event planner—for big luxury hotels, not small country inns. I'll talk to Nate."

"Don't get me in trouble, Maddy. He already doesn't like me." "Detest" was closer to the mark.

"Of course he likes you. Nate's just very brusque—and driven. When we were kids, my sister and I had to book appointments with his secretary, i.e., our housekeeper, when we wanted to talk to him." Maddy laughed. "But he's mostly bluster."

Sam must've looked doubtful, because Maddy said, "I don't know if you know this, but he bought this place to get me back on my feet after I went through a nasty divorce. And Sophie and Mariah... Well, look what he did for them. He's a good guy, Sam."

Everyone knew that Nate had fathered Lilly, Sophie and Mariah's child. Which even Sam had to admit was going above and beyond, even for a best friend. Truthfully, she never would've expected Nate to be so progressive. The man seemed more conservative than any person she'd met in California so far. And he was wound tighter than a spool of thread. Although, to be honest, he seemed fairly loose when he was around anyone besides her. For the life of her she didn't know what she had done to make him dislike her so much.

She was punctual, positive, and professional. But from day one he'd given her the cold shoulder.

The man's ears must've been burning, because he pushed the door open—he didn't even bother to knock—and stepped in.

"I heard a rumor you were here," he said to Maddy, and lifted Emma out of her arms and muttered something about her getting big.

"She's in the ninetieth percentile for length," Maddy said. "She must get it from her daddy."

Maddy's husband, Rhys, the police chief, was tall, even taller than Nate. In Sam's opinion, though, not as handsome.

"What brings you in?" Nate asked his sister. "I thought that husband of yours wanted you home, barefoot and pregnant."

Maddy took back Emma and punched him in the arm. "I'm meeting Emily and Pam, but wanted to drop in for a visit. I miss the place."

"Come back, then." Nate said.

"I don't miss it that much. Plus, you've got Sam. I heard she bagged you Landon Lowery."

Oh boy, here we go. "We haven't bagged him yet," he said. "But I'm confident Tracy'll reel him in." Clearly the comment had been for Sam's benefit.

"I don't think that's such a hot idea, Nate." Maddy swayed and bounced a fussing Emma.

"You want to come back to handle Lowery?" he asked.

"I think Sam should do it."

"Maddy"—Nate's voice dripped with annoyance—"you really want to do this now?" He looked at Sam pointedly.

"I was just leaving," Sam said, grabbing her pashmina off the chair and making a beeline for the porch.

She sat on one of Colin Burke's rocking chairs. The man had made half the furniture in her house. Before coming to Nugget, his rustic pine pieces never would've appealed to her. But now she wouldn't part with them for anything. She gazed out over the square and pondered the wisdom of getting a cup of coffee at the Bun Boy—her third one today and it wasn't even noon. She could see Donna's new employee, a local kid trying to earn college money, manning the window at the takeout stand, and waved. Carl Rudd had redone the windows of his sporting goods store with Tour de Manure bicycle jerseys. The race, a sixty-two-mile loop through the Sierra Valley's ranchlands and historic townships, brought cyclists from all over. The inn was already booked solid for the ride.

Yes, she thought, it was a nice town. No one here seemed to care about a person's net worth, portfolio, or bloodline. And while the townsfolk had been leery of her, as they seemed to be of any new-comer—she knew they called her the runaway bride behind her back—they'd accepted her into their fold. Especially Maddy.

She continued to survey her new home, thinking about how she'd chosen her own course for the first time in her life. And while she sat there reveling in that decision, her father sent her a text with his latest ultimatum.

And this time it was a doozy.

Stacy Finz is an award-winning former reporter for the *San Francisco Chronicle*. After twenty years-plus covering notorious serial killers, naked-tractor-driving farmers, fanatical foodies, aging rock stars, and weird Western towns, she figured she had enough material to write fiction. She is the 2013 winner of the Daphne du Maurier Award. Readers can visit her website at www.stacyfinz.com.

Printed in the United States
by Baker & Taylor Publisher Services